THE CANDLELIT COFFIN

Lady Fan Mysteries
Book Four

Elizabeth Bailey

THE CANDLELIT COFFIN

Published by Sapere Books.

20 Windermere Drive, Leeds, England, LS17 7UZ,
United Kingdom

saperebooks.com

ISBN: 978-1-912786-53-4

Chapter One

The boy, Perkin, hunkered well down behind his favoured gravestone, squinting through a chink under the angel's wing. The resurrection men were at it again. He had not heard them approach, but the familiar scrape and thud of their spades woke him.

Turning, he leaned against the stone, tugged the threadbare coat tighter about his thin chest, and debated the wisdom of flight. The dark, waited for in high summer so Perkin could slip through the railings and sneak in unseen, was by no means absolute. He knew the cemetery paths well and could zigzag a way out, but then so also did they. And that Truggery was a surly brute. Perkin did not relish a cuffing at his hands if he was caught. He was big, was Trug. Easier to outrun. The other, Stowe, was both younger and slighter. Not as mean, but fleeter of foot and he always did as his elder bade him. Best not to risk it. Perkin pulled his hat down over his ears and prepared for a long wait.

The rhythmic thunk, pause and slither of the dig blending with the familiar swish and pull of the nearby ocean lulled the boy into a doze. He was roused by the soft clop of hooves, the jingle of a harness and men's voices speaking low nearby.

"That him?"

"Who else this time o' night?"

A pause while the digging continued and the sound of wheels added to the approaching noise. Perkin struggled to a squat and put his eye to the convenient slit provided by the angel figure set on top of the large gravestone.

A moving shape was just visible on the road behind the iron fencing. Pallid light showed, intermittent between the trees. A coach then, with its lanterns to light the way. Intrigued, if a trifle nervous, Perkin brought his limited vision back to the men near at hand.

The robbers were down in the grave now, their moving arms and spades mere shadows, heads shifting out of sight and up again as they heaved earth from the deepening hole, the mound growing higher on one side. Their voices were muted but audible to one whose sharp hearing was part of his stock in trade.

"What's he want with a lot of ol' bones then?"

"Askin' me? Off his head belike. Who cares anywhen, long as he pays up?"

More digging and a clunk of spade hitting wood. A satisfied grunt came and a bitter complaint in Stowe's lighter voice.

"Deep in, this 'un. Should've told him to come later."

"Don't make no difference. He'll have ter wait. Dig the edge whiles I scrapes off the top."

The noises increased as the men set to with a will, despite Truggery's dictum that their customer must wait. Perkin returned his attention to the approaching coach, exercised by Stowe's question. What would a fellow rich enough to travel in luxury want with a skeleton? The resurrection men went after fresh bodies as a rule. He'd earned a couple of pennies now and then, reporting a new burial to these very men. Though they'd no notion the cemetery was home to him. Trug'd go mad if he knew his midnight raids were observed.

Perkin shrank his body closer to the gravestone as the bigger man climbed out of the grave. Leaning on his spade, Truggery wiped the back of his hand across his brow, looking towards the approaching coach.

It was slowing and must be nearing the gate, which was locked, though Stowe would have picked it open. Rumour had it he'd joined Truggery after a life of shop-breaking was brought to a summary end by a narrow escape from the law. However that was, he'd turned instead to breaking graves for bodies to sell over to the hospital up Dorchester way. But this client was no 'prentice surgeon to be wanting bones instead of flesh.

The coach had come to a standstill. A whiffle of horse breath and soft shifting of hooves whispered across the graves. There came the sound of feet hitting the ground, the click of a door latch and a curt voice speaking low.

Perkin could not make out the words, but he trained his gaze in that direction as the gate creaked and quick footsteps followed the path. In moments, a tall figure joined Truggery on the edge of the grave. It was swathed in a long cloak, its head mostly concealed by a three-cornered hat.

"You have one ready?"

The voice was cultured, with an odd edge to it that caused a shiver to rise up the boy's spine.

"Ready as it can be, though it won't be nothing but dust and bones, this 'un."

"It makes no matter. Bring the coffin out."

"Bring it out?" Truggery again, both surprised and aggrieved. "We don't never bring 'em out, mister. We brings out the bodies. Them coffins is half rotten."

The gentleman's tone sharpened, the dangerous edge pronounced. "I require the coffin. Bring it out."

Truggery grunted his dissatisfaction and dropped back into the grave. A low-voiced argument ensued, with Stowe evidently protesting. Perkin kept his eyes trained on the still figure above, a hawkish silhouette under the faint light of the moon. Shivering a little, Perkin dipped lower, unaccountably chilled.

An owl called. The man's head jerked up just as the clouds parted, throwing a stray moonbeam onto a dark patch where the upper part of his face should have been, giving him an even more sinister aspect. Perkin's pulse fluttered crazily and a fervent wish to be elsewhere attacked him.

The activity within the grave had grown noisy and fierce. Grunts and cursing from both men, accompanied by scrapes, bumps and heavy breathing. A long shape emerged, Truggery behind it. Had they upended the coffin? The big man shoved himself up from the hole and perched on the edge, grabbing hold of his end. The still figure shifted at last, moving out of the way as Truggery, with Stowe presumably shoving from beneath, manoeuvred the coffin out of the grave until the box lay along the path, the resurrection men panting beside it.

"Open it."

Truggery did not trouble to argue the matter this time. Perkin could tell he was angry by the way he got up, marched to the headstone and retrieved from behind it the cloth bag usually slung about his shoulder. Shoving a hand inside, he produced a short crowbar Perkin had seen before and handed it to Stowe, who fell to the task of prising off the coffin lid. Since this was usually done down in the hole, Perkin watched the procedure, intrigued.

Stowe's expertise made the job look easy as he slid the blade in, knocked it hard and moved along to do the same all around. Or, as this was an old one, perhaps the wood was rotting as Truggery said and easier to part. However it was, the lid came off without difficulty and the two men lifted it away, peering at the remains of the unfortunate within.

"Bones and rags, mister, like I said," Truggery told his client on a note of dour satisfaction.

"Empty it. Tip them into the grave."

Perkin almost gasped aloud. He clapped a hand to his mouth, unsurprised to see how both Truggery and Stowe turned to stare at the man.

"You don't want this here skeleton?"

"I want the coffin. I told you."

"The coffin?" A squeak from Stowe. "But yer could've got a coffin off the undertaker without no need of us going a-digging of it up out of the ground."

The gentleman did not trouble to respond to this, merely repeating his command in a sharper tone. "Empty it. I want it empty and set back there at the side of the grave."

Stowe's head turned back to his partner. Truggery shrugged and went to one end of the coffin.

"Take t'other end."

The two picked up the long box, carried it, with some effort, to the side unencumbered by the mound of freshly dug earth, and tipped it up sideways. The slither and clatter of the falling corpse made the boy feel quite sick. He dared not move a muscle, however, fearful of discovery while this man with his peculiar desire for an aged empty coffin was still present. Perkin's hope he would take his prize and go was disappointed.

"Thank you, that is all." The figure produced a fat purse and held it up. "Go now and tell none of this."

Truggery grabbed the purse and stowed it away in his coat pocket. "No fear o' that, mister. We won't say nothing to no one."

"See you don't, or it will be the worse for you. I know your trade of old. It's illegal and I am well acquainted with the colonel of militia here. And the justices in Dorchester, if it comes to that."

Knowing Truggery, Perkin was unsurprised when he turned belligerent, squaring up while Stowe slunk back.

"It won't come to nothing. Nor I don't hold with threats. We done what you asked and there's an end. And if it come to that, we knows summat of you and all."

"You can't speak of what you know of me without incriminating yourself," returned the other, in a tone that made Perkin feel as if ice was running down his back. One hand came out of the cloak and metal glinted in the moonlight. "Now go. Never let me see your faces again."

Stowe was already edging away. He twitched Truggery's sleeve.

"We'll be off then, eh, Trug?"

The other grunted, clearly unwilling to leave the field, despite the weapon in the gentleman's hand.

"We'll be off, and we'll keep mum. But we won't forget."

The figure said nothing, merely keeping the pistol trained upon Truggery's chest. A click said he'd cocked the gun. Stowe turned and made hastily for the gate. Truggery, somewhat to Perkin's admiration, held his ground, his head going up to confront the fellow face to face.

"You gone to a deal of trouble for a coffin, see. That give me to think, that does."

He nodded once, gave his habitual grunt, and walked off, presenting his back to the gun in a fashion Perkin considered foolhardy. Yet it seemed the client had no mind to use it. He slipped it back under his cloak, watching until the two men went through the gate and vanished into the shadows.

Chapter Two

Colonel George Tretower was at breakfast when his second-in-command brought the unwelcome tidings.

"Murder? You're certain?"

"Couldn't be more so, sir," said Lieutenant Sullivan on a note of distaste that caught George's attention.

"How so?"

"Whoever did it made no attempt to conceal as much. The reverse in fact." The lieutenant grimaced. "Pretty weird the whole thing, sir, I don't mind telling you."

"You'd best tell me all then." George waved him to a chair. "Sit down, man. Coffee? Ale?"

"I'll take a cup of coffee, sir, I thank you. Can do with it, to be frank."

"I wish you would be frank," said the colonel, signalling his batman, Marsh to bring a fresh cup from the dresser.

The neat dining parlour, with the sideboard, leafed table and wide windows overlooking the shoreline was one of the better features of the officer's accommodation at the barracks and George took full advantage of it. He eyed his junior as Sullivan dropped his slim and wiry form into a chair. A reliable lad, conscientious and efficient. He would not have brought the matter to his colonel without good cause.

"I trust you've secured the scene?"

"Of course, sir. Left Sergeant Puckeridge with a couple of our men to guard the coffin and the cemetery. But I've sent to Doctor Roffey and I'd best get back sharpish."

"Cemetery? A murder in a cemetery? Do you tell me the body was buried?"

"Not buried sir, but it is in the cemetery."

Marsh having produced a cup for the lieutenant, George poured coffee into it and then refreshed his own cup. Sullivan gulped the beverage with an eagerness that did not escape his colonel's watchful eye. He set down his cup with a sigh.

"That's better. Not easily unnerved, sir, as you know, but this—!"

"Yet I'm still in the dark."

"Beg pardon, sir. Thing is, the body's in an open coffin, an old one obviously taken from the grave because you can see the remains of a corpse thrown into the hole, and —"

"Hold a minute! Which corpse? I thought you said the body was in the coffin?"

"The murdered one is, sir, yes. I'm supposing the other is the original one and must belong to the grave."

"It's been thrown out?"

"That's right, sir."

"Good grief!"

"Yes, sir," returned Sullivan feelingly, "and that's not the worst of it."

George fortified himself with another sip of the hot, black coffee. "Go on."

Sullivan grimaced again. "Well, sir, it's bad enough the girl was stabbed —"

"Girl? The victim is a girl?"

"And a deucedly pretty one too. Even now she looks peacefully asleep, if you discount the blood all over, though the villagers who found her in the early hours say she looked quite lovely with the candlelight all around, and I can readily believe it."

Troubled by a niggling thought at the back of his mind, George struggled to make sense of this. "They took candles? Why not a lantern?"

"Not the villagers, sir. That's the weirdest part. The murderer set a raft of big candles around the coffin and left them alight."

"Weird indeed, Sullivan," said George, trying to picture the scene. "You'd suppose he wanted the body to be found."

"Yes, sir, but it wasn't. Not until near dawn and the candles were near burned down by then. There's not many dwellings in the vicinity of the cemetery and few pass that way in the night, I imagine."

"Except the murderer."

"Though I can't think he did the digging and got that coffin out all by himself."

"No, nor transported the body thither without some sort of conveyance." The notion triggered a question. "Here's a thought, Sullivan. Was the girl already dead when she was put into this coffin?"

"Or killed in situ, sir?" The lad looked even more disturbed. "Rather a vile thought if she was."

"Vile either way, my boy."

"True, sir. But setting the scene like that and then doing the deed? Strikes me as a tad macabre."

"Or theatrical." His lieutenant shot him a startled glance. The boy was jumpy, and no wonder. George downed the rest of his coffee and stood up. "We'd best get moving. I'll need to check over the scene before the body is taken. And Roffey will no doubt call in the coroner. I foresee a pleasing morning."

Sullivan was on his feet. He finished off his own cup and set it down. "Then we've to find out this murderer, sir."

"Yes, I had anticipated as much," George said on a gloomy note. "Wonderful. Do we have any notion who the victim is?"

"No, sir. Though Puckeridge thinks he's seen her before." An eager note sounded in Sullivan's voice as he cast a glance at George. "Odd you should have hit on the notion, sir. Puckeridge is convinced he's seen the girl on the stage, he says, here at the Theatre Royal."

The niggle at the back of George's mind flared into acute dismay. Not the little French girl he'd met the other week?

"Is she dark?"

"No, sir, she's fair. Golden hair and plenty of it. Like an angel. That's what makes it particularly distressing."

Not nearly as distressing as it might have been. But George kept that thought to himself, though the memory revived full force as he made ready and took to horse to visit the scene of the murder.

He had been called in to the only pawnbroker in Weymouth, who'd grown suspicious when a slip of a girl tried to dispose of a valuable necklace.

"She don't look as if she can rub two pence together, sir," Throcking confided in a low murmur, his gaze darting to the girl who was seated on a cane chair in a corner, looking both scared and indignant. "What's more, she's a Frenchie, and what with the threats of us going to war with the Frogs, I thought as I'd best bring you in, sir, for as there's no saying but there might be spies about, if she ain't stolen the thing in the first place."

Colonel Tretower gave the first of these notions no credence at all. A sometime soldier, he had offered the services of his own band of militia when the rumblings across the channel began to look serious, and had accepted this secondment to the coastal resort with alacrity. In the few months he had been in Weymouth, however, there had been no sign of any invading French and definitely no spies.

Throcking's second fear, that the necklace was stolen, might have carried more weight if the girl was English. George's immediate suspicion was borne out almost as soon as he began to question the girl, and in her own language which he spoke with reasonable fluency.

"I understand you wish to sell a necklace, *mademoiselle?*"

The girl looked up at him with resentful eyes. They were lustrous and dark, set in a delicate countenance just now pale and set, and surrounded under a straw bonnet with curling locks, black as midnight and flowing down her back. George was conscious of a tug of attraction.

"You will arrest me, no?"

Her voice was mellow and a trifle husky. Was she close to tears?

"Certainly not."

His smile had an instant effect. Her lips quivered and lashes fluttered over her eyes. She nodded towards the proprietor. "That man believes I am a thief."

"Or a French spy."

Her eyes widened. "How? That is what you think?"

"Not I, *mademoiselle*. If I may hazard a guess, I must rather suppose you to have escaped from the horrors in your country. Is that it? You are what we call here an *émigré?*"

She set her head on one side in an oddly endearing gesture. "*Émigré?* This word I like. Better, I think, than refugee." Her eyes clouded as she straightened again. "But this is indeed what I am, and all this pitiful collection of jewels is my fortune." Her fingers tightened on a reticule in her lap.

Beset with a stab of sympathy for the matter of fact way in which she spoke, George softened his tone. "Misfortune rather, *mademoiselle*. How do you come to be in Weymouth?"

"I am with the players, sir."

Was there a note of defiance? Did she think he would judge her? He kept his tone carefully neutral.

"Indeed, *mademoiselle*? How did that come about?"

She gave a little sigh. "They were performing in Chartres. It is not far from our home. My father was taken. My brothers also. My mother sought to save me at least. There was a negotiation."

"The players smuggled you into England?"

"That is so."

"And your mother?"

"She was too ill to venture. Also she was afraid to be recognised by the *canaille* of the town. Therefore I came alone."

The tale in the telling had no vestige of the tragic circumstances. The girl was stoic, but George could not but be exercised by the suffering that showed in her eyes. He proffered no words of pity, suspecting she would resent them.

"When was this? Not recently, I must suppose?"

"Since two years, or nearly."

"Yet you remained with the players?"

The dark eyes raked him. "Where else shall I go?"

Where indeed? But if she had this refuge, why did she need to sell her necklace? "Do they not pay you that you are in need of funds?"

Her chin came up, proud and defiant. "These funds I need for a reason into which I will not take you, sir."

George gave a slight bow. "Accept my apologies, *mademoiselle*. It was an impertinence."

She inclined her head with a poignant dignity George found touching.

"May I know your name?"

"I am Cecile Benoit, *monsieur*. And you?"

"George Tretower, entirely at your service." He held out an imperative hand. "Allow me to procure your release here. I can at least ensure you receive a fair price for your jewels."

"You are very kind, *monsieur*."

She took his hand and George assisted her to rise, guiding her back to Throcking and switching to English.

"This lady is neither spy nor thief, my friend. She is one of these unfortunates forced to escape the troubles in France. You will accommodate her needs, if you please."

He had waited while the proprietor counted out a quantity of coins and gave the girl a ticket of receipt so she could redeem the necklace. George had made a mental note to ensure Throcking did not sell the thing if the due date should have passed before Mademoiselle Benoit had means to retrieve her property.

He had bowed her out of the shop, and she accepted his escort as far as the street but not the door of the lodging house where the players were in residence. Intrigued and, if he was honest, inordinately attracted to the girl, George took care to attend the very next performance given by the company, a group under the auspices of a flamboyant actor manager proclaiming himself The Grand Ferdinando, much to George's amusement. The piece was indifferently performed, but Cecile Benoit, to his disappointment, made no appearance.

Although, was there not a golden-haired wench in one of the juvenile roles? The thought brought him back to the present moment and he discovered they had almost reached the cemetery. The doctor's gig was standing outside the gate, and George caught a glimpse of his redcoats at a little distance within the fence of iron railings that surrounded the tree-lined graveyard.

"Here we go, Sullivan. I can't say I'm looking forward to this."

"No, sir." His junior brought his horse to a standstill. "It promises to be a fair bit of a puzzle."

"Indeed." George bethought him of the one person who might be counted upon to unravel it. "I'm tempted to write to a friend of mine for assistance."

The lieutenant was swinging himself out of the saddle. He patted his horse's neck and looked up at his colonel. "Who would that be, sir?"

"Lord Francis Fanshawe."

"You think he might be able to help?"

"Not he, but his wife. This is precisely the sort of rigmarole to test Ottilia's ingenuity to the utmost."

Doctor Lister's grave expression was not encouraging and Lord Francis Fanshawe's frustrations rose to the fore. "Well, man? Have you anything to suggest?"

The surgeon cleared his throat. "There is nothing physically wrong with her ladyship, my lord, despite her weakness, which is to be expected."

This much Francis already knew. Ottilia had come through the disastrous ordeal alive, for which he was profoundly thankful, and her bodily hurts had mended over these fretful weeks. She was able to walk and perform ordinary tasks, as long as she took frequent rests. But her physical condition was not what was worrying him.

The doctor gave a delicate cough. "I regret to say, my lord, that her ladyship was extremely reluctant to allow me to make an examination."

Yes, he was aware of that too. "But you insisted?"

"I was obliged to state that it was upon your orders, my lord, before her ladyship capitulated."

Oh, Tillie. Playing the dutiful wife? It had become her practice and Francis loathed it. Like a ghastly game that had nothing to do with the woman he adored, who was almost a stranger to him now. He was desperate for a solution. Anything to bring her back to the mischievous, interested, loving, vital creature she was beneath the settled deadness of her current state.

He could wish Patrick had been able to remain. He trusted his skills far more than those of this man, competent though the fellow had proved to be. But he could hardly expect his brother-in-law to leave his own practice for such a length of time. Yet he must find a way.

"What can I do, Lister? Come, let us be frank. We both know the difficulty is in the mind. Have you nothing to suggest for her ladyship's relief?"

The doctor harrumphed. "Perhaps a change of scene, my lord? I do not recommend one of the watering places —"

"By no means!" Francis almost snorted. Tillie would fly out at the very suggestion. She was already beyond furious with him for suggesting she needed help. "My wife would not care for that notion, I fear."

"No, my lord, and I do not feel it would be conducive to her recovery to be racketing about such a place as Bath or Tunbridge Wells."

"Besides that, they are both at some distance. She is not well enough to travel far."

"True, my lord. However, we are not at a great mileage from the South Coast and sea air is always invigorating, and we have a warm August upon us. One of the smaller resorts might answer the purpose. Lyme Regis perhaps?"

Francis turned the notion over in his mind. It might answer. If he could get Ottilia to agree, that was the crux of the matter.

After the doctor had left, he moved to look out of the window, aware the view of the picturesque grounds of Flitteris Manor was the same as that Tillie saw in her little parlour in the room above this. Without being there, he knew she was seated on the daybed, unmoving and staring out, as she did whenever she was not required to participate in the day-to-day activity of the household. Whether she saw anything of the tiered terraces, the fountain or the little copses either side was doubtful. She seemed lost in her own dismal thoughts and the suspected tenor of them sat at the root of Francis's inability to reach her.

He might wait a little before raising the prospect of a sojourn elsewhere. Until perhaps he received a response to his frantic plea for help to the only person he dared trust. His mother would not fail him.

Once he had seen for himself the extraordinary scene created by this peculiar murderer, George could not but feel the more convinced that it smacked of theatricality. Moreover, the players who frequented Weymouth were his only lead to the possible identity of the corpse.

"I think my next move, Sullivan, is to track down The Grand Ferdinando."

His junior turned from watching the doctor's careful examination of the unfortunate female in the coffin.

"The what, sir?"

George grinned. "If it's the same players in town again, that's how their impresario styles himself." He bethought him of his sergeant. "Where's Puckeridge? Perhaps he knows if they're back."

His junior called across to where the men were still casting about for any other disturbance in the vicinity of the grave.

"Puckeridge! Over here!"

The stout, bewhiskered sergeant puffed over. "Sir?"

"The colonel wants to know about this theatre troupe."

Puckeridge saluted smartly, turning to look up to George's superior height. "Sir! They calls themselves The Company of The Grand Ferdinando, sir. He's the top man. One of them roaring actors he is, sir. Fancies himself a bit, if you know what I mean."

George knew exactly what he meant and concealed an inward groan at the prospect of dealing with the fellow. "Yes, I've seen him in action. You're sure you've seen this girl on the stage with him, are you?"

"Not to say with him, sir, but I'd stake a quarter's pay it's the same as what was in the piece I seen last time they was in the town. A month gone that would have been. Seems as they do one of them circuits, sir, going from one place to another round about the coast whiles the visitors are here for the summer."

"A big company, is it?"

Puckeridge frowned in concentration. "Not to say big, sir, no. A fair few players though. Enough for them comedies what I enjoy. *The Rivals* they was doing last time and this here girlie with the gold hair was in it, sir." A sigh escaped him. "'Tis a crying shame, if you ask me, sir, for her to come to grief in this horrid fashion."

"Indeed." George refrained from informing his sergeant that he had seen the same play but failed to notice the victim, if it was indeed her. "Do you know if they are here again at the moment?"

21

"They are that, sir. Just come back, they have. I seen the waybill and they was in the theatre last night and doing *The Country Wife* as I recall."

"Thank you, Puckeridge, that will be all."

The sergeant returned to his task and George set out for what was likely to prove his most unpleasant duty, leaving his junior in charge at the cemetery to document all they had found for the coroner, oversee the removal of the body to Dr Roffey's surgery and deal with the distress of the cleric, called in to perform the last rites in his own graveyard, and rebury the violated remains of the other unfortunate whose grave had been turned out.

It was perhaps an advantage that he had met Cecile Benoit earlier, even if it had caused him a momentary alarm when Sullivan told him the victim might be from the theatre company. At least he knew where the players could be lodging.

The door of the boarding house was opened to him by a weighty dame in a mob-cap and apron, who exhibited instant consternation at the sight of a military uniform.

"Gracious, sir! Is it the militia? What's happened? Have the French come?"

"Nothing of the kind, ma'am. I am Colonel Tretower and I believe you have a troupe of players staying here?"

The woman's alarm increased. "You've not come to arrest one of them, have you? I know there are those who consider theatricals thieves and vagabonds, but I've never had no trouble with them, sir."

George sighed. "My dear ma'am, I am not here to arrest anyone, but I must have a word with the impresario of the company. Mr Ferdinando?"

"Ferdinand it is, though he styles himself different. He's the dramatic sort, sir, if you know what I mean. Mrs Ferdinand now, she's different. More genteel-like."

Realising he might be kept on the doorstep for an age if he did not take a high hand, George cut in with his authoritative voice. "Yes, very well, ma'am, but I would be obliged if you will lead me to Mr Ferdinand without delay."

"Well, I'll go and see if he's up," said the landlady, turning into the narrow hallway and leaving the way clear for George to enter. "No early risers these theatricals, sir, that much I can swear to. If you'd wait in here, sir, I'll go up and tap on his door."

She ushered George into a musty downstairs parlour, evidently little used and kept for best. A couple of heavy old-fashioned sofas with scrolled legs graced the walls, their garish chintz upholstery echoed in the wallpaper which overpowered the two landscape paintings. Left to kick his heels, George discovered in himself a hope of again meeting the little French *émigré*, if indeed the victim proved to be who Puckeridge supposed.

He took up a stance before a fireplace with an elaborately gilded mirror atop a richly carved mantel, with a Chinese fire screen hiding the empty grate on this warm August day, and gave himself up to contemplation of the intricacies of the murder.

The one thing he pinned his hopes on was that there must have been at least one witness. If not to the killing itself, then by way of the digging of the grave. This was not the first instance of trouble in the cemetery. Indeed, Sullivan had supposed at the outset it was yet another theft perpetrated by the gang of grave robbers operating in the vicinity. He would have to report to the justices at Dorchester, who might have better information, not that the surgeons at the hospital there would admit to purchasing unlawfully acquired bodies for their anatomical studies.

Worse, the event having occurred in his jurisdiction, the justices would likely leave discovery to him. Lord knew he was no expert. As a soldier, he'd had plenty to do with death, but his only brush with murder to date had been the debacle when Lord Francis Fanshawe's sister-in-law was strangled. Ottilia, whom Francis had subsequently married, had been instrumental in sorting that one out. In this predicament, there was no one better qualified to help him.

His ruminations were interrupted by the sound of footsteps coming down the stairs. He looked towards the door as it opened and vaguely recognised the large gentleman of full habit who entered, at once throwing out his arms in a wild gesture and rolling his eyes.

"Heavens above, an officer of militia indeed! I hoped our good Annie had it wrong, but so it is. My dear, dear sir, I do trust and hope this does not bode ill? Tell me at once! What has he done this time?"

George introduced himself, eyeing the fellow in some amusement. Attired in an Indian banyan in a pattern of flowers of virulent hue, with an embroidered and tasselled soft cap crowning flowing grey locks, The Grand Ferdinando exhibited all of the drama of his trade, and more.

"But you have not answered me, Colonel," he protested in a voice rounded, mellow and as expressive as his gestures. "Is it young Jasper again? What was it? Gambling into the small hours and finishing up in a brawl? Have I to bail him out? I swear to high heaven, that boy will be the death of me!" He leaned towards George in a confidential manner. "If he was not the performer he is, I should have been rid of him long since, I assure you. But a regular Garrick, sir, I promise you. A Garrick in the making, there can be no doubt."

George seized his chance as Ferdinand paused to draw breath. "I have not come about your Jasper or any other young man as far as I know."

Sudden dismay clouded the impresario's grey eyes and he threw up a staying hand. "The French, is it? You mean to close the theatre!"

"Nothing of the kind, sir," George said with asperity. "Give me leave to speak without interruption and I will tell you my business. Which, I may add, is urgent."

The impresario waved hands as apologetic as his tone. "You must forgive me, Colonel. If you knew upon how many occasions it has been my misfortune to endure a visit from the local constabulary! But I must not anticipate. It is a fault of mine, sir, I confess it to be a fault."

Torn between exasperation and a desire to burst into laughter, George cut directly to the meat of the matter. "Can you tell me if one of your female players is a young beauty with golden hair?"

Consternation, question and rapid alarm showed one after the other in the fellow's mobile features. "Dulcibella! She is our juvenile. Why, what —? Is she in trouble? Not little Dulcie surely? Jasper, yes, but…"

George became brisk. "Have you seen her this morning? Is she in the house?"

Bewilderment and dismay were already gathering in Ferdinand's eyes. George began to dread his reaction if this Dulcibella of his proved to be the murdered girl.

"I must suppose so, sir, though I have not yet been into the common parlour. But why do you ask? Why our little Dulcie?"

25

Relieved that the impresario had abandoned the grand manner, George yet had no intention of speaking out before he knew whether the girl was here.

"Will you ascertain whether Miss Dulcie is in the house, if you please, Mr Ferdinand?" He bethought him of the havoc that might ensue if the fellow should speak of his question upstairs. "Should you object to it if I were to accompany you, sir?"

The impresario was at the door, but he turned, waving George forward in another expansive gesture. "By all means, Colonel. We have nothing to hide. Be so good as to follow me," he continued, as he started up the narrow stairs, George on his heels. "I have no doubt she will be found to be partaking of breakfast. I cannot think our little Dulcie could be mixed up in anything nefarious. Such an innocent as she is." He directed an enquiring look over his shoulder as he spoke, but George preserved his silence. The fellow appeared to be recovering his sangfroid, but if his little Dulcie proved to be absent, he was in for a rude shock.

The stair gave onto another meagre hallway leading into a corridor and then continued on up. Ferdinand took a turn and approached a door at the front of the house from which emanated a desultory murmur of voices. The impresario flung it open, leaving the door wide, and cast a glance about the room. He interrupted the conversations of the occupants without ceremony. "Has anyone seen Dulcie this morning? Is she yet up?"

No voice answered immediately. George, pausing on the threshold of a parlour that mirrored the one below but with a pleasanter atmosphere, found himself confronted by a battery of eyes.

Several persons, caught in the act of eating or drinking, were grouped around a large table near the window, which was set with dishes indicative of a substantial breakfast having been supplied, presumably by the landlady downstairs. By the mantel opposite, innocent of a fire in high summer, a good-looking young fellow stood, apparently checking his appearance in the mirror above. He had turned his head, however, his gaze riveted upon the military intruder. He was attired for the street, whereas an air of informality presided among the rest, most of whom seemed to be in a state of undress or casual half-dress.

In one of the chairs adjacent to the fireplace sat an elderly dame with commanding features, swathed in a large shawl as colourful as the impresario's banyan. It was she who first broke the silence of surprise, speaking in a pleasant cultured tone with none of the flourishes that characterised Ferdinand.

"Dulcie has not been in to breakfast yet. But why Dulcie, Arthur? Who is this? What has happened?"

Ferdinand swept forward. "My dear Jane, do not ask me! I am perfectly bewildered as yet as to his reason for being here, but my heart misgives me." He flung a pointing finger towards the table. "Cecile! Speak! You must know where Dulcie is, if anyone does."

A riffle disturbed George's pulse as he realised his little French *émigré* was at the table. He had not noticed her at first glance, seated as she was with her back to the window and thus a trifle shadowed by the streaming light of morning. Her troubled gaze was trained upon George and it struck him she knew something. But she was shaking her head as she spoke up, in accented English.

"I do not know, monsieur."

"You don't know? But you must know, curse it all!" Ferdinand's agitation sounded in his voice, which was turning peevish. "How can you not know? You sleep in the same bed, girl! Is Dulcie still asleep?"

"Arthur, don't snap at the child!" The older woman rose, moving towards George. "What is the matter, sir? Why are you asking after Dulcie? Who are you?"

"He's the colonel of the local militia, Jane, and I thought he had come for young Jasper here," said Ferdinand before George could answer. He bent a choleric eye upon the young man by the mantel. "Wretched boy! Just look at the state of you! I suppose you've been out carousing, have you?"

The fellow Jasper, who did indeed look a trifle dishevelled now George's attention was drawn to the matter, regarded his mentor with a curling lip.

"Well, he ain't come for me, old sobersides. P'raps Dulcie has been off carousing and you've to rescue her from the sponging house instead." He ended on a spurt of mocking laughter which caused the impresario to throw up exasperated hands.

"Impertinent boy! Jane, speak to him!"

"Do be quiet for a moment, Arthur." The woman Jane once more addressed George. "You have not answered me, sir."

"I've not been given the opportunity, ma'am," he returned on a trenchant note. He gave a curt bow. "Colonel Tretower, ma'am. Give me leave to ask Mademoiselle Benoit one further question."

She frowned, glancing from him to the girl Cecile and back again. "You know her, Colonel?"

George saw the instant consternation leap into the French girl's eyes. "I — er — ran into *mademoiselle* a while ago."

Without further explanation, he crossed to the table, noting how the others seated there shifted stance at his approach. There was a second youngish fellow, a man of middle years

28

and two other females: one also dark-haired and relatively youthful, the other, seated with her back to George, a round-faced dame with the thickened waistline of middle age.

"*Mademoiselle*," he said in French. "I regret to be obliged to press you, but this is important." She nodded but did not speak, looking if anything more concerned than before. "If you are sharing a room with Miss Dulcie, you will know if she slept here last night."

The girl looked perfectly dismayed at this, and a series of gasps told George that most of the assembled members of the company understood French.

"I do not know, *monsieur*," came the low-voiced answer.

George pursued her relentlessly, despite the attraction he'd felt at their previous meeting. "How is that? Come, *mademoiselle*. You sleep in the same bed. You cannot be ignorant of her presence or absence."

The girl's eyes took on the resentment she had exhibited before, but George held her gaze. He could almost feel her rising belligerence, at one with the suspenseful atmosphere building in the room.

At last the French girl's eyes sank. "Dulcie had not come to bed when I went to sleep."

"Had she gone out? Was there an assignation perhaps?"

The dark eyes rose again, apprehension in them. Had he hit the mark? If so, she did not buckle. "I do not know, *monsieur*."

"But you know she was still not in the bed when you woke this morning?"

"That is so." Spoken low and with a near vicious stab from the vivid eyes. Her lips tightened. She looked away, set rigid fingers to the cloth on the table. "I think perhaps she has slipped away early this morning. Perhaps to — to do the swim, or to walk upon the beach."

She was lying. George would swear she knew more than she was saying. But for the present, he had all he needed, which was sufficient to depress his spirits.

"I thank you, *mademoiselle*." He switched to English, turning back to the impresario. "May I have a word with you in private, Mr Ferdinand?"

The effect of this was powerful. The Grand Ferdinando's grey gaze showed both dismay and reluctance. Swift suspicion lit in George's breast. Guilt? Could he have been acting all this time? Did he know only too well what he was about to hear?

Before he could speak, the woman Jane broke in, her tone determined. "I will accompany you, Colonel. I am Mrs Ferdinand, you must know, and if there is anything to be said concerning one of our girls, I insist upon being present. Dulcie is more in my charge than my husband's, you understand."

George gave a small bow of acquiescence. "As you please, ma'am. If we may retire to another room?"

She crossed to the door, cast a glance about the company and spoke in a measured way to the rest. "Nobody move. If Wat or Aisling should come in, keep them here too. Come, Arthur."

The impresario, who appeared to be struck all of a heap, started and hastened to follow as his wife led the way out of the room. "Yes, yes I am with you, my dear. After you, Colonel."

Mrs Ferdinand spoke over her shoulder as she crossed the corridor, opening the way to a second parlour, set with sofas, chairs and occasional tables planted haphazardly or in groups. There was also a writing bureau in the window alcove, a full bookcase against one wall and a tall cabinet occupying most of another.

"This is our workroom, where we may hold readings or rehearse. None will disturb us here at this time of day."

"They are all accounted for, Janey, save Wat and Aisling. I dare swear they may have already gone to the theatre. There is that chair to mend, remember, and the proscenium flat must be painted. I can't think what Fitzgerald is about to allow it to become so disgracefully dilapidated."

"Yes, Arthur, but this is scarcely the moment to be thinking of such matters."

The impresario's mobile features, which had momentarily been overlaid with a look of discontent to match his complaining tone, here sank back into apprehension. He turned again to George, rocking back on his heels.

"Ah, yes, little Dulcie. I hope you mean to explain yourself, Colonel."

"Obviously I must do so, sir."

Mrs Ferdinand kept frowning brown eyes on him, question in her face. George drew a breath, casting a glance from one to the other and settling on the female.

"I regret to be obliged to inform you, ma'am, I have reason to suspect Miss Dulcie may be the victim in a particularly distressing murder."

Horror flared in the woman's eyes and her face drained of colour. The impresario, on the other hand, merely stared at George as if he had taken leave of his senses. Had he heard what was said? Or just not taken it in?

George returned his attention to Mrs Ferdinand. "Perhaps you should sit down, ma'am. I'm sorry to be the bearer of such black tidings."

She waved a dismissive hand, but did indeed sink into the nearest chair, covering her face with her fingers.

Ferdinand reached out to grasp George's arm. "What did you say? Murdered?"

"I'm afraid so, sir. I will require you to come with me, if you please, to make an identification."

He released his clutch on George's arm, his face grey, his voice for once devoid of drama. "It can't be Dulcibella. Not Dulcie. Murdered, you say? No, no, you must be mistaken!"

"It is possible I am mistaken, Mr Ferdinand, and for all your sakes I must hope it may prove to be so. Unfortunately my sergeant was certain he recognised the girl from a performance at the theatre here, which is why I sought you out."

The man looked every inch of his advanced years all at once. He staggered a little, and fell into a chair, gazing before him in something of a stupor. His wife dropped her hands and looked up at George, a determined look in her face.

"Tell me it all, if you please. Where and how did you find her?"

"You must excuse me, Mrs Ferdinand. Until I have ascertained whether the victim is indeed Miss Dulcie, I prefer to keep my own counsel."

"But is the word of this sergeant of yours all you have?"

"That, and the fact the girl is golden-haired and of great beauty. A description your husband at once attributed to this Dulcibella." Brisk, he addressed the impresario once more. "I must bid you rouse yourself and dress at once, sir. The doctor's house is not far and we may go there and settle the matter in short order."

The man remained where he was, apparently still stunned. His wife went up to him and shook his shoulder.

"Arthur, bestir yourself!"

He started. "What?"

"Go and dress!"

He rose, a trifle unsteadily, passing a hand across his brow. "Yes. Yes, I will do so at once. I will not keep you above a moment, sir."

But George had no notion of letting the fellow out of his sight. His demeanour, added to the undoubted theatricality of the murder, had put the most uncomfortable suspicions into the colonel's head.

"I will accompany you, sir."

The impresario gave him an odd glance, but made no objection. Mrs Ferdinand was more direct. She gave George a straight look.

"Why, sir?"

"Haste, ma'am, that is all." He added, prevaricating, "Mr Ferdinand is clearly disordered by what I have said." He forestalled any notion the woman might have of suggesting she did the chivvying instead. "I must request you to return to your company, ma'am, and see that no one leaves the house until my return. If the worst should prove true, I will need to question everyone concerned."

Without waiting for her response, he gave the still hovering impresario a push towards the door, ignoring the wife's expression of acute dismay.

Dread settled in Cecile's bosom, which was not helped by the excited speculation that broke out on the closing of the door, led by Hildegard Larkin.

"What in the world can the militia want with Dulcie? What has she been doing, I wonder?"

"We all wonder, Hilde," said Lewis Payne, so often her counterpart in parental roles when he was not playing the buffoon of the piece. He went on in his pinching way, turning to look at Cecile beside him, "Except for our Cecily here, who clearly knows more than she is saying."

All eyes turned on Cecile and she shrank for an instant, and then glared. "Only because we share the room?"

Hilde leaned across the table, patting her fingers still resting on the tablecloth with a pudgy hand. "Don't heed him, Cecily dear. Though I am bound to state it is an odd circumstance that you didn't notice Dulcie leaving the bed."

"She didn't leave the bed." Jasper lounged across from the mantel, his eyes fixed on Cecile in one of the mocking stares she loathed. "I'll wager she was never in it."

"Well, you were obviously not in yours, Jasper," retorted Kate, speaking up for the first time. She mimicked his sneering tone. "Perhaps you know where Dulcie was, if she was out all night too?"

A squabble immediately broke out between the two, rather to Cecile's relief since the others became involved in berating them or trying to keep the peace. Except Rob, she noted. Not for the first time, she wondered if the saturnine Robert Collins was to blame for Dulcie's distressing condition. He was darkly attractive, in a devilish kind of way, and Cecile had long suspected he cherished a secret passion for Dulcie, despite having a wife and two children tucked away in Dorchester. Although he had never been other than amiable, Cecile found it somehow fitting that Rob was often cast in villainous roles, if he was not playing a foil to Jasper's hero.

Anyone less heroic in life would be hard to find. Jasper was not in the least bit dashing, but Cecile knew that Dulcie liked him more than a little and had permitted him to take liberties with her on more than one occasion. Much to the scorn of Katharine Drummond who, Cecile suspected, was more fond of Jasper than anyone would suppose despite the way they carped at each other on every possible occasion.

Charged with having allowed him too much licence, however, Dulcie had denied Jasper's responsibility in her desperate problem. But Kate's accusation rankled. Could it be Jasper whom Dulcie went to meet last night? Yet if it was, why not return with him?

Despite Dulcie's vehement denial, Cecile could not but suspect one of the males in the company was guilty of seduction. Brought up in the strict fashion of the French aristocracy, she had been both shocked and awed by the casual lifestyle and irregular conduct of most of the players. Time had eroded her astonishment and the camaraderie had done much to assuage the loneliness, but nothing would serve to dissolve her adherence to the rectitude of her youth. Dulcie's fall from grace quite horrified her, but she was her friend and Cecile could neither revile her nor abandon her in a time of need.

But the entrance into the matter of this colonel of militia, after a night of worrying over Dulcie's absence, threw her into apprehensive suspense. She had good reason to know Colonel Tretower for a man of judgement. Also sympathy. Unwanted, but nevertheless kind in its intent. It had been a shock to see him enter the noisy parlour. For one horrible moment, Cecile thought he had come on her account, suspecting after all that the necklace was not hers to dispose of. But that he came instead for Dulcie was a terrible shock.

At this moment, Jane Ferdinand re-entered the parlour, causing an instant suspension of the argument that had broken out. From her demeanour, she'd taken a severe knock. Hilde at once exclaimed, "Heavens, Janey, you look like death! What in the world did that man tell you?"

Jane crossed to the table and sank into Kate's vacated chair. Cecile noted the tremble of her fingers as she passed one hand across her mouth.

"Rob, you are nearest the pot. Pour her a cup of coffee," said Hilde.

"I'll do it." Lewis, who had risen when he became embroiled in the argument with Jasper, returned to his end of the table and seized up the coffee pot. "Though from the looks of her, Janey needs a good dose of brandy."

Both Kate and Jasper converged upon the table at this, crowding to eye the company's matriarch. Whatever opinion the players held of Arthur Ferdinand, Cecile was aware that, to a man, they liked and respected his wife. Jane's eyes were filmy with moisture as her gaze passed along the anxious faces. Her voice held a distinct tremor.

"There is no point in keeping it from you. If it proves to be Dulcie…"

Cecile's breath vanished as the woman faded out.

"If what proves to be Dulcie?"

The sharp demand came from Rob, of all people. A shudder wracked Jane's frame. Her voice was hoarse as she resumed.

"A golden-haired girl has been found murdered. Arthur has gone with the colonel to see if he may identify the body."

Numbness overcame Cecile. She felt peculiarly detached, her thoughts clear and bright while a thick cloud of feeling hovered somewhere out of reach. Observing the silent stupor of those around the table, it struck her how unrealistic was their acting upon the stage. Moments like this they portrayed as violent emotion with histrionic enthusiasm. Much staggering, weeping and wailing would have greeted such appalling tidings, whereas in life each exhibited all the true horror of disbelief.

"It can't be Dulcie," came at last from Kate in a hushed tone. "He must be mistaken."

"Why can't it be?" Thus Jasper on a vicious note. "No need to look daggers at me either. I didn't kill her."

"Jasper!"

"Nobody said you did. Be quiet, you fool!" Lewis turned back to Jane. "Why does that colonel think it's Dulcie?"

"Because she has golden hair, didn't you hear?"

"Jasper, will you hold your tongue?" snapped Hilde. "Though it does seem a trifle precipitate to be supposing any girl with golden hair must be Dulcie, I must say, Janey."

"It is more than that."

"What then?"

A twist at Rob's mouth as he spoke, one he used to good effect for his villains, caused Cecile to shrink a little away from him, wishing she'd taken a different seat.

"The colonel said his sergeant recognised her from seeing her on stage with us."

"Dear Lord! That's why he came here then?"

"Obviously, dear Katharine. And just as obviously he'll be supposing one of us to have done the deed."

Cecile could bear no more. "*Dieu me sauve*! Dulcie may be dead and this is all you think and say?" The cloud was beginning to descend. Her voice went out of control. "Play-actors! You, Jasper, so clever as you think you are, you know nothing of life and death. You, all of you —" On her feet now, she berated them, unable to help glaring from one to another — "making the play with your weeping and your woes as if this is how a person behaves. I have lost all, all! Do you see me making the hysterics?" She flung out accusing fingers. "You do not care if Dulcie is dead, no! You care only to make as much noise and quarrel as you can. This is not the play, *vous savez*? This is life! This is real! Where is your respect?"

Stunned faces only answered her. In a bang, Cecile came to herself, shock and grief churning in her breast. Overcome, she dropped back into her chair and threw her hands over her face, tears seeping as she struggled to hold back the sobs.

Around her the whispering began.

Hilde's voice. "Poor child, she's overwrought."

Then Lewis. "Fetch the brandy, Jasper. You must know where it is."

"Oh, the deuce, why me?" Inaudible hissing. "All right, all right."

Hilde again. "She's right, you know. We are behaving abominably."

"It's my fault." A shrill whisper. "I shouldn't have attacked Jasper."

"Not you, Kate." Lewis again. "It's Jasper who spoke out of turn."

"Will you all be quiet, if you please?"

Jane's authoritative tones cut into the hubbub. Cecile heard the swish of skirts and then an arm came about her shoulders, and a gentle murmur in French she recognised from the early days.

"*Du calme, mon pauvre.* You have suffered with stoic courage, my child. And this hits you harder than most."

Cecile raised her head to look at the woman who had done her utmost to replace the mother she had lost. She managed a wan smile.

"Forgive me," she returned in her own tongue. "I should not have spoken so."

"Yes, you should. Someone had to call this crew to order."

"That is for you, madame."

"I am out of curl, my child. This dreadful news has overset me so that I know not if I am on my head or my heels." She switched to English. "Ah, here is Jasper with the brandy. Drink this, child."

A glass was thrust into Cecile's hand. She eyed the liquid at the bottom with distaste.

"I like it not."

"A sip or two will revive you. Drink."

Obedient to the pressure of the hand that took hold of hers, she brought the glass to her lips and drank. Fire blasted her throat and she coughed. But a second sip was pressed upon her and she found it warming. The ice in her veins began to dissipate.

"Hand over the bottle, Jasper," said Hilde. "I dare say we can all do with a drop. I know I need one."

"Lace Janey's coffee with it, Jasper."

The murmur of voices washed over Cecile as the bottle was passed around, along with the chink of cups and glasses. Ashamed of her outburst, she kept her eyes on the glass still in her hands, sipping at intervals. But the seeping chill of suspicion could not be long dismissed. If Dulcie lay dead, Cecile alone knew why she had been killed. She would not betray her friend's secret, especially now. Despite the lack of confirmation, Cecile began to eye the males of the company askance.

Chapter Three

Confronted with the corpse laid out upon Dr Roffey's long table, the tumble of golden curls incongruous against the lovely face waxen in death, The Grand Ferdinando stood frozen for a space, riveted.

George could scarcely blame him. The atmosphere in the surgery was gloomy, with its sideboard and shelved walls loaded with ominous-looking instruments, banks of medicine bottles, large leather-backed tomes and a plethora of jumbled items to which the layman could put no name. Eerily, the upper windows let in a shaft of light that illuminated the golden head of the sheet-shrouded corpse, creating as macabre a picture as she must have been in the lonely candlelit vigil of the night hours in the graveyard.

Roffey had lifted the corner of the sheet down only enough to reveal the face, which was as well, since Ferdinand's reaction was bad enough. If he were to see the horribly stained stomach with its gaping wound and the blood-spattered clothes, Lord knew what he might do. But the question had to be asked.

"Is this indeed Miss Dulcie, Mr Ferdinand?"

He did not take his eyes from the girl. "Dulcibella ... Dulcibella, no. No, no, no, no, no."

George exchanged a glance with Roffey, standing on the other side, who grimaced his confusion.

"You mean it is not Dulcibella?"

Ferdinand's gaze rose and the shock in his eyes was a contradiction. "Who did this?"

"That I don't yet know, sir, but I must ask you again. Is this or is this not your actress?"

At that, the impresario wafted a hand across the corpse. "This? This cold creature? No, this is not my little Dulcie." His voice took on power. "My little Dulcie is alive, vibrant, warm. You will not make me take in her stead this … this thing."

Exasperation seized George, but Roffey cut in before he could speak, his tone one of cool reprimand.

"Sir, you are not now upon the stage. You are in the presence of the dead. I must beg you to assume a proper deference."

"Quite so, Roffey," George agreed on a snap. "Mr Ferdinand, I brought you here for the purpose of making a formal identification. Can you do so? And pray don't treat me to any more nonsensical flights, which, I may add, give me a poor notion of your true sentiments."

Ferdinand shook his head with a gesture more dismissive than theatrical and his tone dropped. "You are very right, both of you. It is ingrained, I fear, quite ingrained."

"Well?"

"You wish me to say this shell is in truth our dear girl, and it pains me so to do." He thrust his shoulders back but his voice shook. "It must be faced. Yes, Colonel, if you must have it in plain words. These are the remains of Dulcibella Ash." Upon which, the impresario broke down into unmanly sobs, his demeanour far more natural than hitherto.

George signalled the doctor to the far end of the room, dropping his voice to a murmur. "What do you make of him, Roffey? Is he acting now, do you suppose?"

The doctor, a man some years in advance of George's two and thirty, who had already acquired the air of superiority common to medical men, adjusted his spectacles and tutted. "Oh, a consummate play-actor, my dear fellow. I know him of old, for I have had occasion to serve one or other of the

41

players in the past. I believe he cannot help it. These theatrical men appear to me to live in some make-believe world of their own which has very little to do with the one the rest of us inhabit."

"Yes, I rather got that impression. But do you suppose him sincere in his grief, for all that?"

Dr Roffey peered over the spectacles, a little twinkle appearing. "That, my dear fellow, is for you to interpret. My part, I thank God, ends when I have conducted the post-mortem."

"The coroner requires it? Even though we can see well enough how she was stabbed?"

"But with what, Colonel? And there may be other factors to be taken into account. I know Pollicott all too well. Leave no stone unturned is my advice. The meticulous sort, I fear. He will nose out every little detail."

George groaned. "Wonderful. That's all I need." He glanced towards Ferdinand, who was now wiping his eyes with a large spotted handkerchief. "I'd best get back to the lodging-house and find out where all these infernal players were last night. Have you any notion of the time of the murder?"

"Well after midnight. She is cool, but rigor is not yet complete. The cornea has clouded, however, so we must assume a good six hours or more. I should say anywhere between one and three."

George sighed. "I foresee a pleasing time."

It took some moments to extract the impresario and usher him towards the boarding house. George found it difficult to judge how deeply he felt the loss, especially because it had occurred to the fellow that his productions were now in jeopardy. Ferdinand regained a little of his customary manner as he began to bemoan the shoals ahead.

"How shall we manage without the jewel of our company? Alas! Our Kate is comely enough, I grant you, but I fear she will never draw them in as Dulcie does — oh, must I say did?" An eloquent shudder. "It is not to be borne, yet bear it I must." A hand clapped to his brow. "Tomorrow's performance! Oh, disaster, disaster!"

"I doubt you'll be performing anything tomorrow, Mr Ferdinand," George cut in on a prosaic note.

He was treated to a shocked stare. "Not perform? But my dear sir, there is no question of such a thing. The Company of The Grand Ferdinando never, but never fails! Tradition, Colonel. We cannot break with tradition."

"In this extremity, tradition may go hang," said George with acerbity. "Chances are I'll have one of your wretched players under lock and key by tonight."

A gasp of horror greeted this. "You cannot suppose one of our own has done this thing? No, no, Colonel, you are mistaken, I assure you with every power of my soul, you are mistaken. Impossible!"

"Unfortunately, Mr Ferdinand, it is all too possible. What is more, I intend to question every one of them directly."

Ferdinand appeared momentarily bereft of speech. Throwing him a glance, George spied a look of chagrin on his face and his senses came acutely alert. He could not avoid the reflection that the flamboyant nature of the murder, with its open coffin and candles, was perfectly in accord with what he had so far seen of The Grand Ferdinando's manner.

He entered the lodging-house in the wake of a silent and unusually thoughtful host and followed him upstairs with an inward sigh at the task awaiting him.

Nothing was to be done at once, however. Ferdinand chose to make his announcement in a fashion George found both callous and ill-considered.

"Have you told them, Jane?"

When his wife nodded, he glared around the sea of anticipatory faces, which appeared to George to have been augmented since he was last in the room. It looked crowded.

"It is all too true," pursued Ferdinand. "Our Dulcie has been cruelly cut off. She is dead. Murdered." Into the stunned silence, he thundered, "Who has done this thing?"

Watching closely, George saw flickers of fear and dismay pass along the crowd of whitened features turned towards their leader. Except for the fellow's wife, in whom he recognised exasperation. Thankfully, she at once came forward.

"For heaven's sake, be quiet, Arthur! Do you want to cause a riot? Sit down, my dear, and think what you are saying."

She urged him towards one of the chairs by the fire, murmuring indistinctly into the fellow's ear, while the rest began to shift, discomfort and dismay appearing in one or two faces, together with a raft of murmurs.

George found his gaze seeking out the little French émigré. She was seated still at the table, obscured to some degree by the standing figures of two men George did not remember to have seen before. Cecile Benoit had her hands over her face and her shaking shoulders told him she at least had succumbed to grief.

He caught the gaze of a large woman, also seated, who was staring at him, white-faced, with tears slipping down her cheeks though she neither sniffed nor sobbed. George had time only to take in the other female, standing near the young fellow he remembered as the player Jasper. She was biting at one hand, the other clutching the boy's arm. And then Mrs Ferdinand was before him, remarkably cool, if a trifle pale.

"You will wish to know the names of our people, Colonel. They are all here, apart from the fellows who care for our vehicles and the horses. Allow me to introduce you."

"Thank you. That would help enormously, ma'am."

She gave a brief nod and turned at once to two newcomers, a wiry man of small stature, whom she introduced as Wat, and an ape-like giant by the name of Aisling.

"These are our invaluable stage hands, who also take on whatever roles are needed. They have an inexhaustible repertoire."

She was about to turn, when George interposed. "Give me leave, ma'am." He addressed them impartially. "Can you both tell me at once where you were last night?"

The fellow Wat grimaced and shrugged. "We'd a performance. We were at the theatre."

"And after?"

He glanced up at his companion. "Went to The Black Dog with Ais once we finished putting all away."

"What time would that have been?"

"Dunno. Ten, eleven? Ais?"

The big man was frowning. He rubbed his nose. "Couldn't say." His voice was deep, in keeping with his size. "Mebbe eleven. I didn't bide long. I was in bed come midnight, I'd say."

George looked his question at the other, noticing from the corner of his eye how a man of middle age standing close by shifted, looking decidedly uncomfortable.

Wat cast a glance towards him. "I stayed drinking with Lewis here."

"Until what time?"

"What time did we get back, Lew? D'you remember?"

"Lewis Payne," said Mrs Ferdinand with a wafted hand. "Lewis has been with us for years. A stalwart of the company."

The fellow Payne managed a bleak smile. "My thanks, Janey, but I doubt that fact alone will save my neck." And to George. "You're wanting to find out where we all were, I don't doubt."

Choosing a mild approach, George nodded. "Just so, Mr Payne. Can you assist Mr Wat here to establish your return to the house?"

"We were back before Jasper at all events. Rob too, now I think of it."

He nodded towards a dark man seated next to Cecile. Thin-featured with a hawk-like nose, he was grimly frowning. "I was minding Jasper until the young fool disappeared upstairs, as he usually does, with an accommodating barmaid."

The remark, delivered in a sarcastic tone, provoked a flurry of comment.

"Don't be disgusting, Rob!"

"I'll thank you to leave my personal habits out of this."

"Typical! You are the limit, Jasper!"

"What are you, my damned nursemaid?"

Then topping them all, in a commanding voice, Mrs Ferdinand. "That will do! Rob, that was uncalled for. Especially in present company." She turned once again to George. "Robert Collins, Colonel, another long-serving actor."

But no stalwart? There was time for no more as the fellow rose, showing a figure both tall and athletically lean.

"I'm afraid I can't tell you what time I got home. I don't customarily maintain a journal of my daily movements."

Eyeing him with the sort of look ordinarily reserved for an insubordinate trooper, George responded on a curt note. "An approximation will serve, Mr Collins."

The other shrugged, curling his lip. "Then let us approximate it at one, two, or perhaps three. Unlike Jasper here, I did not spend the night outside these walls."

With a snarl, Jasper leapt at the man, but the fellow Payne intervened, catching him back before he could use one of his raised fists.

"No, you don't! Behave, you young hound! We don't need a brawl on top of everything else."

"Jasper."

The warning note in Mrs Ferdinand's voice had an immediate effect. The boy paused, turned his head, his eyes seeking those of the elderly woman.

"Enough," she said, quiet command in her tone. "Sit down."

Sulkily, the boy tugged out a chair from the table and slumped into it, dropping his head on his hand and effectively hiding his face.

George took in the clear implication that it was Mrs Ferdinand rather than her husband who had the mastery of these players. He recalled the landlady saying she was different from her husband, and he'd had ample evidence to support this notion. She exhibited none of the rodomontade he favoured and George began to wonder if he would do best to consult her before conducting separate interviews with his collection of suspects. It occurred to him belatedly that even if they were able to state the time they returned to the house, he would be obliged to seek corroboration, which might be difficult to come by. He made up his mind.

"Mrs Ferdinand, perhaps you would be kind enough to grant me an interview in private?"

At this, an array of consternation mingled with question entered into almost every face. Even Cecile looked up, her face streaked with woe. The Grand Ferdinando, who had been lying back in his chair with his eyes closed, apparently divorced from these proceedings, bestirred himself.

"My wife? What do you want with my wife, sir? You can't suppose she is guilty of doing away with our little Dulcie?"

"Don't be absurd, Arthur," said his helpmeet on a scornful note. "I dare say the colonel is wishful to find out a little more about the company. Or about Dulcie perhaps. Is that it?"

She turned back to George as she spoke, brows raised. He preserved a non-committal silence. The pause was like a stage wait. George could almost hear the suspension of breath, aware every eye was upon him.

Mrs Ferdinand broke the atmosphere, moving towards the door. "Follow me, if you please, Colonel."

George glanced around the company. "I will be obliged if none of you will leave the house."

"But I must dress," protested the large woman, rising. She threw a hand to encompass the rest. "As several others no doubt need to do as well."

"I have no objection to anyone leaving the room, as long as you all remain within call."

Mrs Ferdinand was already in the corridor outside and George made to follow. He was forestalled by the man Rob.

"For how long must we kick our heels at your pleasure?"

"Oh, do stop it, Rob," came in an admonishing murmur from the younger girl. "Have you no feelings? Dulcie is dead." At which she burst into tears and was at once enveloped into the large bosom of the woman Hilde.

"Now look what you've done," complained Payne, throwing a disgusted look at his colleague.

A roar came from the hearth as The Grand Ferdinando rose up in wrath. "I will not have this! Desist, all of you! It is not fitting to the moment to be so quarrelsome and obstructive.

The colonel has a sacred duty —" with a bow towards George — "and I for one have every sympathy with his mission. The perpetrator of this terrible act must be found. I trust and pray that he is not among you all, but my heart misgives me. I cannot deny it, my heart misgives me."

With which he collapsed once more into his chair, to all appearances a broken man. Deeply appreciative, despite the required solemnity of the occasion, George had the greatest difficulty holding back a laugh.

He was once more attempting to leave the room when Cecile, jumping up from her place, called out in urgent tones.

"*Monsieur le colonel!*"

George turned on the instant. She thrust her way through the intervening bodies to stand before him, her reddened eyes and blotched countenance nevertheless determined. Without will, George gentled his tone.

"*Mademoiselle?*"

"You have not said. How did she die, Dulcie?"

George hesitated, once again the cynosure of all eyes, question and apprehension rife amongst them. Ought he to say it? There was no reason to withhold the awful truth, yet he was loath to burden this girl with the worst of the event.

"Colonel?"

Mrs Ferdinand was standing in the doorway, regarding him. George braced, keeping his gaze impartially passing across all.

"Dulcibella Ash was found in a cemetery just outside the town. She was placed in a freshly dug up coffin, from which the remains of another had been evicted. She had been stabbed to death. The coffin was left open with candles burning around it."

The inevitable astonished silence was this time broken by Lewis Payne.

"Good God! No wonder you think it was one of us!"

Cecile uttered a cry and pushed past George without ceremony. He watched her vanish down the corridor, cast a glance back at the rest of the players, apparently petrified, and went out, closing the door behind him.

A murmur of voices broke out at once within the room, but Mrs Ferdinand, awaiting him with a patience he could only admire, gave a wan smile.

"I am sorry we forced you to that. Quite horrible."

"And highly theatrical, ma'am."

She sighed. "Too true. They will be speculating all day."

"One can scarcely blame them when all is said, Mrs Ferdinand. It is quite normal."

A faint laugh came from the lady. "I'm afraid it is nigh impossible to obtain any sort of normality from a company of players, colonel. Trying is the bane of my existence, I assure you. Shall we repair to the morning room?"

George followed her across the hall to the second higgledy-piggledy parlour he had entered earlier, reflecting that where the formidable dame failed, he was unlikely to succeed. Remembering his thought of writing to his friend Fan, he determined to lose no time in so doing once he was able to escape from this house of near lunacy. Although, he belatedly recalled, had not Fan's wife been recently brought to bed? In which case, there was scant hope of persuading Fan to bring her to Weymouth.

Well, if he must manage on his own, he must. He might at least glean from Mrs Ferdinand a more comprehensive picture of the individuals with whom he had to deal. If he recalled correctly, Ottilia had spent her time in discovery of this kind. He might do well to emulate her tactics.

Having read his friend's letter for the second time, Francis refolded it and slotted it into one of the convenient alcoves in his bureau. Closing the lid, he remained seated, staring at the inlaid pattern in the wood without seeing it, his thoughts as disturbed as ever they had been.

Truth to tell, he was torn. Extraordinary — and typical, if Tillie had been her normal self! — that this request came hard on the heels of his discussion with Lister. He had shelved the whole matter, hoping for advice first, but as yet no letter had arrived from the Dowager Lady Polbrook. Weymouth was within reasonable reach. Tillie might undertake the journey without ill effect. But a murder? And a particularly gruesome one, by George's account.

Was it wise to subject her to the trials and tribulations of another investigation? Or could it be just the thing to draw her out?

Upon the last occasion he had sworn, not for the first time, never to allow Tillie to involve herself in another such ghastly affair. Yet there was no denying the bizarre nature of the one his friend described, coupled with the equally bizarre dramatis personae, was precisely calculated to pique the insatiable curiosity that characterised his beloved Ottilia. Under normal circumstances. Dared he hope this promising avenue might pierce the abstraction that had enwrapped her since the fateful miscarriage of the birth?

She'd wept little, which confused Francis. Tears he could have dealt with. This dull acquiescence was so unlike his Tillie, it was anathema. Oh, she made pretence of being affectionate, but her smiles were perfunctory and there was no trace of love in her dulled eyes, usually so clear and true.

And nothing interested her. Nothing! Mistress of his home she might be, but she had left all to Mrs Bertram in the last difficult weeks of her pregnancy and showed little disposition to take up the reins again, beyond agreeing to the menus and otherwise telling Mrs Bertram to do as she saw fit, as his worried housekeeper reported. When he drove her out to take the air, she came with a show of willingness. She even looked when he pointed out views and agreed they were fine. He recalled drawing her attention to some wildflowers of which he knew she was fond.

"Very colourful," Tillie had said, in a tone particularly colourless.

Francis felt inescapably aggrieved, though he tried not to show it. He knew not what to do, or whether to take this step, his indecision compounded by guilt at the dreadful necessity forced upon him to choose between his wife and his unknown son.

He had not hesitated, despite his brother-in-law's doubts. Patrick Hathaway, whom he had called in the moment Doctor Lister had expressed fears of a complicated birth, had put him on the spot at a crucial moment.

"There is no guarantee we can save both, Fan, and Lister agrees. If we are to preserve my sister, we have no choice but to use forceps to extract the infant."

Aghast, Francis stared at him. "Is that dangerous?"

"Extremely so for the child, especially as we are not sure just what is preventing its exit."

"Is there an alternative?"

"To let the birth go ahead naturally, but the blood loss will be hazardous for Ottilia. She might not survive it."

Stark terror blinded Francis to everything but his wife's danger.

"Then there's no choice, Patrick. You'll save my Tillie at any cost."

His brother-in-law laid a hand on his shoulder, gripping it, and giving him a look that pierced Francis to the heart. "What if Ottilia does not agree with you?"

Francis flung off his brother-in-law's hand. "Do it! I allow my wife a deal of licence, as you well know. But not when it comes to her life. I won't take that risk."

The ensuing nightmare had wracked him, but he'd had room only for overwhelming relief when Tillie came through at the expense of their first born. Francis felt a pang when Patrick told him the baby had been a boy, but he could not pretend to anything more. It was not as if infant mortality was uncommon. Patrick, in an unnecessary bid to console him, had said he lost more infants at birth or within a few days or weeks than he could boast of saving.

"There is every hope Ottilia may have better luck next time, though I would advise caution for some weeks. She must be allowed to heal."

Fearful of putting Tillie through this again, Francis was more than careful. He dared not go beyond a gentle caress, which only added to the growing distance between them. He felt it acutely and had no notion how to bridge the gap.

The sound of wheels rolling on gravel brought his mind back and his eyes focused on the coach rumbling down the drive. As it turned into the sweep towards the entrance, he saw the crest on the panel. His heart lifted. His mother had answered the call in person.

Walking quickly across to the door, he left his study and traversed the corridor swiftly to the galleried entrance hall, running down the stairs just as Rodmell sailed out from the nether regions, accompanied by both footmen.

"I apprehend it is the dowager marchioness who has arrived, my lord," said the butler, proceeding in a stately fashion to the front door.

"Yes, and thank the Lord for it!"

Francis beat him to the post, wrenching open the aged arched door and flinging it wide. He crossed the flagged porch and waited only for the carriage to come to a standstill before rushing up to seize the coach door and drag it open. The dowager's features burst upon him in a flood of intense relief.

"You came yourself! Oh, I am beyond thankful to see you, Mama!"

Listless, Ottilia gazed out at the distant hills, counting the peaks created by the treetops. It was as good an occupation as any and Patrick had told her to engage only in restful things. This dictum afforded a convenient excuse to avoid re-entering an existence that felt futile and wearisome. If only Francis would let her alone. Or stop treating her as if she were a china doll he was fearful of breaking.

Truth to tell, all she wanted to do was to lie here in the haven of her parlour and never move again. She did not wish to engage in the petty day-to-day alarums that must drag her out of her comfortable cocoon. She had neither energy nor inclination for anything and it only served to put her on the fidgets when Fan would keep trying to rouse her.

The sound of the door opening made her hackles rise. Not again, please God!

Turning her head, Ottilia beheld not her husband as she expected, but her mother-in-law standing in the aperture, regarding her.

"Sybilla!"

"In person, my dear Ottilia."

The dowager moved into the room and closed the door. In bewilderment Ottilia eyed the elderly creature with features so like her son's strong-boned countenance, but with brows more delicate and grey dappling her hair.

"How do you come to be here? I had no notion you were planning a visit."

Sybilla's black eyes raked her in a critical fashion as she came to stand by the daybed. "No more had I, my child. Francis sent to me."

Quick wrath swept into Ottilia's breast. "Oh, for heaven's sake!"

A wry smile crossed the dowager's lips. "Yes, I suspected you might not be best pleased."

Ottilia suppressed the discomfiting emotion. "Pardon me, Sybilla. Of course I am very glad to see you."

"Liar! But you will be in due time."

Hardly aware how she sighed, Ottilia made to shift her legs to the floor. "I'll ring for refreshments."

The dowager put out a staying hand. "Stay where you are. I've already had tea with Francis."

Which no doubt meant her megrims had been under discussion. With mixed feelings, Ottilia settled back and watched Sybilla pull forward the chair standing near the wall that Francis invariably used when he sat with her, which seemed to happen less and less. A pang smote her and her throat became taut. She fought the threatening tears. She was not going to turn into a watering pot. Nothing was more tedious for a husband than a wife who was forever falling into melancholy.

Sybilla set the chair close beside her and sat down, reaching to pick up Ottilia's flaccid hand. "Now, my precious girl, tell me everything."

It was a moment before Ottilia was able to speak at all as a wave of misery engulfed her. She struggled to suppress it. She did not want to feel.

"There is naught to tell, Sybilla," she managed, aware her voice was husky. "It is only Fan fussing as usual. I'm perfectly all right."

The hand holding hers squeezed tight for a moment. "Come, my dear, you know that is untrue. One glance was enough to tell me you are not yourself, even had Francis not written as much to me."

Ottilia was obliged to suppress an impulse to snatch her hand away, but she could not keep the irritation from her voice. "I wish he would let me alone!"

"He's anxious about you, Ottilia, and no wonder. This is not like you, my dear."

"What is not like me? Merely because I prefer to be quiet for a while is no reason for him to rally the troops. As if the whole household was not already in a plot to force me into doing things I don't want to do."

"Exactly so, my dear child. You need look no further for a reason. You are in general so engaged and interested, you can scarcely blame them."

Ottilia let out an exasperated sigh. "Well, I do!"

"You blame Francis."

The accusation hit home and Ottilia felt the inevitable guilt well up. "I know he only does it because he cares for me, but why can't he see —?"

"Because he cares for you, my dear. He is blinded by his affection." Sybilla gave the hand she held another squeeze. "I believe it has been so with him from the first. You are all the world to him, you know."

"As is he to me." This time she could not prevent the seep of tears and the husk in her voice became pronounced. "That makes it so hard. I try not to be a burden, to deserve his goodness. He is endlessly indulgent and I'm a wretch to treat him so badly."

To her dismay, and indeed irritation, Sybilla fell into laughter at this, releasing the hand she was holding.

"I fail to see what you find amusing."

"Yes, I can see you do, my child. Never mind. When you have been married a few more years, I dare say you will understand."

"I thank you. I look forward to it."

Her sarcasm only made the dowager laugh harder. Ottilia waited in silence for her mirth to abate. All desire to weep had left her, though she was aware how tumultuous and unpredictable were her emotions at this present.

"You've not been two years married, Ottilia," said Sybilla at last. "You have much to learn of the state. An episode such as this is bound to provoke a deal of dissension."

The episode leapt from the back of Ottilia's mind where she had banished it, to the fore. Her stomach tightened, but she was given no opportunity to indulge remembrance.

"Let me tell you what we have decided."

"*You* have decided?"

The black eyes snapped. "Don't dare to object. You are in no case to be making decisions."

"I've no wish to make any," Ottilia snapped back.

Sybilla disregarded this. "Your Doctor Lister suggested a sojourn at the coast and the plan is —"

"What, he means to drag me out —"

"— to take you to Weymouth for a few weeks."

"Weymouth? A seaside resort?"

57

"Sea air is bound to revive you, and you may take ambling walks until you recover a little of your usual energy."

The very thought of ambling walks made Ottilia feel perfectly filleted. "I don't want to go."

"Didn't you express a desire to treat your husband more amiably?"

"I didn't say —"

"Or at least to refrain from behaving like a thwarted child?"

"Sybilla! I never said any such —"

"You will go to Weymouth like a dutiful wife and spare the poor boy from going out of his mind with worry."

Recognising the implacable note in her formidable mother-in-law's voice, Ottilia knew she was defeated. She eyed Sybilla, aware of a faint resurgence of the customary humour that had long been absent from her spirits.

"Well, if you put it like that, ma'am, I suppose I must capitulate."

An amused smile rewarded her. "Excellent. I will tell my son to set all in train for an early departure." She got up and started towards the door, halting before she reached it and looking back. "By the by, Ottilia."

"Yes?"

The black eyes twinkled at her. "You need not suppose you will be permitted to relapse. I am coming with you."

Chapter Four

Francis greeted his friend with pleasure, but a trifle of misgiving crept in when George began almost immediately upon his troublesome murder.

"I'd hoped to have a word with Ottilia at once, my dear Fan. Where is she?"

"Walking on the beach with Hemp in attendance."

"Hemp?"

"Hemp Roy, her steward."

"Ah, Roy, yes. Isn't that the black fellow who came to me with your note to give me news of your projected arrival? Who is he?"

Francis made an exasperated noise. "A whim of Tillie's. He was involved in the imbroglio last Christmas in the house of my mother's neighbour and Hemp ended at something of a loose end. Ottilia chose to succour him and I admit he has proved useful."

He had sent Hemp on to Weymouth on Saturday ahead of the main party, which defied convention to travel down on Sunday, by which time the footman and a couple of maids who had accompanied him had made all ready in the house hired for the duration.

"My thanks, by the by, George, for taking this place on my behalf. My mother is pleased with the location. Is that the famous new Esplanade below us?"

"So I understand. The thing runs for near half a mile, with the purpose of creating an agreeable walk. I am told it has improved the place no end, though you may find the streets sadly dirty and narrow for the most part. If you stick to the fashionable quarter, it is pleasant enough. Where is the dowager?"

"Bullying the master of ceremonies into submission, I imagine. She is at the Assembly Rooms for the purpose of putting all our names down and, if I recall correctly, to get a recommendation for a cook. When I left her, she was just about to descend upon the unfortunate fellow."

George laughed. "That sounds like your formidable mother all right. The matriarch of these infernal players is of the same cut. I'm persuaded Ottilia is going to revel in this lot."

The ever-present shadow crossed Francis's heart, and he felt obliged to nip this optimism in the bud. "Don't get your hopes up, my friend. I'm by no means sure this ruse is going to work."

George's mobile eyebrows rose steeply. "Ruse? What do you mean, Fan?"

A sigh escaped Francis. "I've not told her yet."

"Good grief, why not?"

Rising from his chair, Francis shifted to the window, looking across the new and beautifully wrought street some thirty feet wide, bordered with turf and a grass slope leading down to the sands and thence the ocean. The view was spectacular, providing ample evidence of seaside life, with fishing boats tacking along the coastline, and Francis had already seen a variety of walkers, often accompanied by dogs. A couple of donkeys were trailing along the beach, carrying small visitors, and several children cavorted with buckets and spades, splashing at the water's edge. There was much to entertain, if only Ottilia might begin to take an interest.

"To tell you the truth," Francis said over his shoulder, "I didn't dare mention the matter for fear Ottilia would refuse to come at all. And my mother was in agreement. We got her here on the score of recuperating her health alone."

George rose and came to join him at the window. "But I made sure this is precisely the sort of affair to pique her interest."

"Yes, in the ordinary way. She's been different since the loss of the child."

With some reluctance he gave his friend a few clues as to Ottilia's current state of mind. He had already explained the disastrous birth in the express he had sent in response to George's letter. His friend had replied with concern and assured him he could book a suitable lodging to accommodate the Fanshawes and their entourage.

The house proved to be eminently practical, providing a sufficiency of rooms on the first and second floors to accommodate the Fanshawe party with all its servants, bar the coachman and Ryde, Francis's groom, both of whom were staying at an inn near the stables where the coach and horses were housed. The bedchambers were well-furnished, the parlour done out in blue in the Adam style with the classic white loops and curlicues, oval-backed chairs of simple design, a chaise longue which Francis had caused to be set conveniently for Ottilia to be able to look out of the window, and well-cushioned armchairs either side of the marble fireplace.

The landlord and his family occupied the apartments downstairs, but the kitchen and domestic offices were shared with the visitors. The landlady had offered to cook, but the dowager, after last evening's first meal, determined to find one better qualified to provide food "fit to eat" as she put it. In private, she had confided to Francis she feared Ottilia would waste quite away if there was nothing better to tempt her than the woman's unappetising offerings.

"I see," said George when apprised of the situation. "Well, I should say if anything will rouse Ottilia to action, it's this ghastly mess I'm landed with."

"That is my hope."

The sound of footsteps in the galleried hallway outside attracted Francis's attention. He turned in time to see the door open and then Tillie herself stood poised in the aperture, her gaze moving from him to Tretower. She was looking a trifle windblown, her hair dishevelled and escaping from under a chip-straw hat, her shawl half off one shoulder and trailing behind. But her cheeks were pinker than Francis remembered to have seen them lately, her eyes brighter. She smiled on seeing the colonel.

"George! I did not expect any visitors and have not bothered to tidy up." She came forward with hand held out. "How do you do? Fan told me you were here, but how comes it about you are quartered in Weymouth?"

George bowed over her hand. "I'm commanding the militia down here. Truth to tell, there is only my own company barracked at the moment. But if we do go to war with the French, I've no doubt the powers that be will plant half a regiment upon me."

Ottilia laughed, a sound that lifted Francis's heart. She rarely laughed now.

"You need not pretend with me, George. I've no doubt you volunteered and will be only too delighted to go parading up and down the coast with a band of redcoats, preventing the French from invading our shores."

Laughing, George admitted she was right. "Though there's been little to engage me. Until this wretched business turned up on my doorstep."

Alarmed, Francis caught his eye and frowned him down. George, with a conscious grimace, threw him an apologetic look. Too late Francis realised Tillie had seen the exchange. Her gaze went from one to the other.

"I wish you will sit down, my love," he said hastily, indicating the chaise longue.

Ottilia came towards it, her eyes searching his face, but she did not immediately take her seat. "What am I missing, Fan?"

He essayed a laugh. "Nothing in the world. What do you mean?"

At that a spark lit in her eye. "Pray don't treat me to one of your ridiculous charades, Francis. What is going on?"

He was obliged to bite down on instant irritation. "There is nothing going on, as you put it. Merely George has a tricky situation he is handling at the moment."

"I see." She glanced towards his friend who, to Francis's chagrin, was looking the picture of guilt. "And what is so alarming about this situation, George, that I must be kept in the dark?"

Tretower cast him an anguished glance. "I really can't say, Ottilia." He essayed a grin. "I wish you will sit down, and then I can follow suit."

That made her laugh again and she did sit down, untying the strings of her bonnet and casting it aside. "You need not stand on ceremony with me."

"What, do you suppose I've lost my manners?" He drew a chair forward and dropped into it. "It's a relief to get off my feet for a few minutes, I can tell you. I've been running around like a jack-in-the-box for the last few days."

Breathing a little more easily, Francis crossed to the side table and picked up the hand bell there, sending a summons pealing through the room. "I've not offered you wine, George. Would you care for a glass?" He glanced at his wife. "Or will you drink coffee with Tillie?"

She threw him a faint smile. "Yes, just what I need, Fan, thank you."

"Coffee for me too, Fan. I need to keep a clear head."

Joanie, the younger of the two maids who had accompanied the party to Weymouth, arrived promptly in answer to the bell and Francis put in his request for coffee all round. With Tillie in uncertain mood, he needed his wits about him. The moment the maid left the room, he tried for an innocuous subject.

"How was your walk? I trust you didn't go too far."

A shade of annoyance crossed her face and Francis cursed himself for adding the rider. She hated him to cosset her, as he knew all too well. But she spoke calmly enough, if a trifle coolly.

"It was invigorating. I had to take Hemp's arm on the way back, so I dare say I did go a little beyond my present strength. But don't you go giving him a scold, Fan. It wasn't his fault. He advised me to turn back, but I was enjoying the sea breeze."

How well she knew him. He had indeed formed an immediate intention of telling Hemp to be more careful. He opted to ignore the comment for the sake of peace.

"I'm glad Mama persuaded you to come then. It's obviously done you good already."

He was aware of her watching him as he returned to the window and perched on the seat there, settling himself conveniently between the chaise longue and George's chair.

"Where is Sybilla?"

"Putting our names down at the Assembly Rooms. And finding a cook."

Ottilia nodded and an uneasy silence fell. Francis saw George turn his gaze upon the ceiling in the way he had when he was embarrassed. This would not do. Tillie was far too fly to be taken in. Dared he broach the subject? The decision was taken out of his hands as his wife turned to the colonel.

"Why have you been obliged to take up this jack-in-the-box act, George?"

Tretower cleared his throat and brought his gaze to bear on Tillie. "I've had to go twice to Dorchester to consult with — er — various officials. And my time has been taken up with much to-ing and fro-ing."

A trifle of mischief flitted across Tillie's face and Francis rejoiced to see it.

"If you suppose I am able to form a complete picture from that description, my dear George, I fear my powers of perception have been vastly overrated."

George laughed. "You mean I was not clear enough?"

"Not enough to inform me why Francis is so anxious for you to keep your mouth shut on the subject."

Francis jumped in. "No such thing."

"Oh, come, Fan, do you take me for a ninny all of a sudden? It is patent you are trying to keep something from me."

He might have known it would prove impossible to prevaricate. With a sigh, he capitulated. "Very well, if you insist. George is grappling with a somewhat nasty murder."

To his consternation, distress and dismay both crept into her face. "And you wished to keep me ignorant in case I should immediately throw myself into discovering the culprit? Heavens, Fan, you know I have neither desire nor energy to embroil myself in anything at all, let alone a complex matter of that nature."

"Lord, no, you have it wrong, Ottilia," said George before Francis could answer. "It was I wrote to beg Fan to bring you here, for it's a devilish coil and I doubt I can manage it."

Francis's heart sank as Tillie's gaze travelled from George to himself, quick wrath gathering in her eyes.

"So that was it. You dragged me down here under false pretences. Fan, how could you?" With which she rose and hurried towards the door.

Francis sprang to his feet.

"Ottilia!"

She ignored him, flinging open the door and disappearing, her steps rapid along the gallery.

Francis followed to the door and watched her vanish into their bedchamber. With an exasperated sigh, he turned back into the room and found the colonel also on his feet, a look of dismay in his face.

"I did warn you," Francis said on a rueful note.

His friend came and laid a hand on his shoulder. "If I read her aright, dear boy, it's not the murder that's put her all on end, but the deception."

Gloom overtook Francis. "I thought it best, but it seems I was wrong. I'll have to go after her."

"Shouldn't you give her time to calm down?"

"And postpone the quarrel? It's been brewing for weeks, if you really want to know."

"If I know Ottilia, she'll be only too remorseful presently," said George. "But you know best how to handle her, no doubt."

Francis only wished he did, but the growing estrangement had ruined his abilities in that direction. The maid appeared on the stairs, armed with a tray.

"Here's the coffee. I'll take her a cup."

He moved back into the room along with George to allow Joanie access. She was just placing the tray on the table when his mother's voice sounded in the hall below. Had she commandeered the master of ceremonies to escort her to their lodging?

"Oh, are you back, Hemp? Where is her ladyship?"

Hemp's deep tones answered. "I believe in the parlour, milady."

His mother clicked her tongue. "She ought to be resting."

Relieved the dowager had returned, Francis went to the door as her step sounded on the stair. She could keep George company while he went to face Tillie's fury.

For several minutes Ottilia paced the limited floor space between the four-poster and the two presses into which the maids had unpacked the clothes she and Francis had brought with them, longing for her parlour at home. To be denied the solace of her retreat seemed all of a piece with her husband's perfidious trick.

Oh, she saw it all now. No doubt Sybilla had been party to the scheme. Playing upon her guilt to make her feel obliged to fall in with it. And for what? To force her into doing precisely what she did not wish to do. To use, moreover, the very thing to which in the normal way Francis would have made the strongest objections. A murder forsooth! And he ever the one to do his utmost to stop her becoming involved.

The injustice of this caught at her conscience and Ottilia halted. That was unfair. Even at Witherley, when he'd hated the whole affair from the start, Francis had indulged her even after she had been severely endangered. And he had been glad of her help for his brother's sake when they first met. As indeed for Giles upon the last occasion. But this?

Fury revived as she recollected the deception practised upon her. Was it fair? Was it just to treat her like some idiotic fool who could not be trusted with the truth? What, was she a child to be lured by a package of sugarplums? For that was the sum of it. Get her to the place and shake the sweetmeats in her face to tempt her to eat? Faugh!

Finding herself by the near press, she brought down closed fists and hammered on its surface, making the bottles and jars arrayed along the back edge jump.

The click of the door latch brought her head round. Francis stood there, holding a cup and saucer. "I brought your coffee."

Ottilia's righteous wrath began to dissipate. The very sight of him standing there regarding her with that look of question in his beloved features was enough to waken her conscience once again. She drew an unsteady breath.

"Thank you."

She moved to the end of the bed and sank down upon it. Francis came over and held out the saucer, the dark eyes sombre. Ottilia took it and lifted the cup to her lips, glad of the excuse it afforded not to meet his gaze. She swallowed a mouthful, but her throat felt tight and she put the cup down. His silence goaded her and she looked up.

"Why didn't you ask me? Why didn't you tell me about it when you said George was staying here?"

He eyed her for a moment. "Would you have come if I had?"

Balked, Ottilia looked away. Of course she would not have done. Nothing but Sybilla's prod at her love for him could have persuaded her out of her cocoon.

"Not for myself, no."

"You mean you came to please me?"

The hard edge to his voice hurt her and she hit back. "It's all I cared for."

"Not noticeably."

His tone was decidedly bitter. Ottilia looked up again.

"How can you say that?"

"I don't want you dutiful, Tillie. I want you back to the woman I fell in love with."

Her throat ached and she fought to contain the rising tears. Without thinking, she thrust the cup and saucer at him. Francis took it and crossed to the fireplace, setting it down on the mantel. With pain in her heart, Ottilia watched him lean an elbow on the mantelpiece, his gaze dropping to the empty grate. He spoke without looking at her, low-voiced.

"Weep if you wish, Tillie. I can bear that better than your listlessness."

"I am trying, Francis."

He looked round, a spark in his eye. "Yes, you're extremely trying, my dearest dear, but if you'd only cry at me it would at least be a valid reproach."

Shocked both by words and manner, Ottilia felt the desire to weep begin to ease. "Reproach? For what should I reproach you?"

He straightened. "Oh, come, Tillie, use the intelligence I know you possess. I'm not talking about getting you down to the seaside against your will."

The harshness was pronounced. Bewilderment wreathed Ottilia's brain. "Then I must be stupid indeed, for I have not the remotest guess as to what you mean, Fan."

His dark eyes raked her. "Have you not? Or is this pretence? For pity's sake, don't take a petty revenge because I deceived you over this. I know you blame me."

"Blame you how? What are you talking about?"

He looked away, his gaze travelling from her to the window and back again. His eyes were hard and bright. "For the infant, Tillie. I chose you and you can't forgive me, can you? Patrick warned me you might not agree but I didn't care. I told him to save you at any cost, and we both know who paid the price."

Every word fell like a stone in Ottilia's breast. All these weeks Francis had been carrying this and not a word said. Oh, she had been blind indeed! Without realising what she did, she held out her hand to him, her bosom too full at first to speak. He looked at the hand, then up to her face.

"As easily as that, Tillie?"

She drew a breath. "You have it wrong, Fan. So wrong."

A frown creased his brow. "How so?"

"I never blamed you, not for a minute. That's not..." She broke off as the ache rose up from where she'd tried to banish it, and began again. "That's not at all how it was."

"Then how was it?"

"It is not the loss that troubles me. Our son would not have lived beyond a few days, even had he survived the birth."

She spoke with difficulty, the images that plagued her once again writhing in her head.

"Yes, so Patrick told me afterwards." Francis moved at last, coming to take a seat beside her. "But if you knew —?"

She reached for his hand and it closed over hers. "I knew the moment he said the cord was around the child's neck. Blue

70

babies suffocate, Fan. If they survive, their lungs may be affected and they cannot breathe well enough to build strength." She felt her voice begin to shake, but forced the words out. "But it was too late for our little one, Fan. Even as they cut him free, he was gone."

Francis's arm came about her, and his voice was husky. "Don't, Tillie. There's no need to speak of it."

She turned in his hold to look at him, disregarding the tears that were trickling down her cheeks. "There is, Fan, because you don't understand. I was glad he died, for he was no longer suffering." Her breath became heavy with sorrow and she found it hard to get the words out. "You see, it is — it is what he went through before that I cannot bear. All those dreadful weeks towards the end, when I was so uncomfortable and cross. Remember how he kept moving and kicking? I cursed him so. And all the poor little mite was trying to do was to get himself free and he — he only managed to entangle himself the more ... and I didn't know, Fan. I didn't know."

The grief she had been holding at bay could no longer be contained. Grateful for Francis's silent strength, she wept into his chest as he held her cradled against him.

The storm passed at length. Ottilia lay weakly in her haven, hearing the soothing murmurs as one in a dream, feeling only the warm hands that stroked and petted her into quiet at last.

Francis grasped her shoulders and sat her upright. Then he gave her his handkerchief, smiling as she made use of it. "Feeling better for that?"

She gave him a wan smile. "Much."

He kissed her lips and then hugged her close. "Don't fret any more, my darling. Come back to me, sweetheart."

She broke into a sound half sob, half laughter. "I never left you, Fan. Will you forgive me for —?"

"Do you need to ask? In any event, there is nothing to forgive. It's married life, Tillie. One of the downs and we will weather it together and find ourselves an up soon enough."

She caught her breath and sighed it out. "Yes. Together, Fan."

"It is all I ever want, my dear one. And now you really need that coffee, I should think, and it's probably gone cold."

Ottilia drank it anyway. A little revived, she bethought her of Francis's friend. "I must go and apologise to poor George."

But when she re-entered the parlour with Francis behind her, she found only the dowager, who waved a dismissive hand.

"No matter, Ottilia. I've invited him to dine. An excellent opportunity for him to tell you all about this murder."

Chapter Five

Francis was a trifle dubious when his mother produced a copy of the local newspaper containing a somewhat lurid account of the "Coffin Murder" as the reporter had chosen to dub it.

"Nonsense, Francis. This will save Colonel Tretower a deal of explanation. I secreted it out of the circulating library."

"Mama, for pity's sake!"

"I will return it, Francis, never fear. I can tell you the talk is of nothing else in the Assembly Rooms. It was almost the first thing this fellow Rodber thought to tell me."

"Rodber? Is he the master of ceremonies?"

His mother inclined her head. "A rather pompous fellow, but he will give us no trouble."

"Not if you have cowed him already, ma'am, which I doubt not."

Francis looked across at Tillie, who was perusing the piece in the paper. She had been hustled by his mother into resting on the chaise longue with her feet up, a fresh cup of hot coffee at her elbow. She was looking a degree better in her spirits, if a trifle fragile after the bout of weeping. The revelation had both astonished him and made him wish he had taken the bull by the horns before, when he could have avoided the dreadful distress of misunderstanding and distance. The relief of resumed closeness was such that he wanted nothing to jeopardise it again.

But Tillie appeared to be absorbed. Perhaps the scheme might not after all prove abortive. And there was no doubt she was desperately in need of a diversion to take her mind off the visions that had been worrying her.

She came to the end and looked up, catching his glance with a faint echo of the old mischief in her clear gaze. "Did you know all this, Fan?"

"George gave me the gist, yes. Enough to show me it was just the imbroglio to take your fancy."

"How well you understand me, my dearest. Fascinating!"

He had to laugh. His mother uttered a cry of triumph.

"I knew it. But let you get one whiff of this, Ottilia, I said, and you would be off like a bloodhound."

She smiled. "It is certainly fraught with possibilities." Then she laid the newspaper aside and took up her coffee. "But I will confess it makes me tired just to think of how much work must go into finding out the culprit. I don't envy George, I must say."

"Oh, you will be knee deep in the matter before we know it. Don't tell me, my dear Ottilia."

Francis, a little unnerved by his wife's dismissal, watched her sip the coffee and then set down her cup with a faint sigh. "Well, I will admit to curiosity about potential suspects. I wonder who George fancies for the deed?"

She did not pursue the subject and Francis wondered at it, fretting that it might not answer his purpose. But Tillie had revived by the dinner hour and she made no objection when his mother invited George to open his budget, once the dishes had been set upon the table and Tyler and the maids retired on her orders.

"Well, if you've read one of the accounts in a daily journal," said George, serving himself from a dish of rather sorry-looking fish stew, "you'll know we found the girl in some other poor fellow's coffin. He's been reburied now, but I'll tell you it was a piece of work for our fellows to recover every bit of him thrown carelessly down into the grave. My lad Sullivan was wild with me in the end for making the offer to the parson."

Tillie frowned, her forkful of buttered crab, the only dish to tickle her vanished appetite, poised in the air. "Then it is true the original contents of the coffin had been tipped out?"

"Carelessly done too," said George with a grimace. "The whole thing was macabre in the extreme. Not to say dramatic, what with these infernal candles set alight around the coffin and the girl, looking, I may say, extremely lovely still with all that golden hair flowing about her head and shoulders."

A memory clicked in Francis's mind and he looked up from his plate of roasted beef, having rejected the fish stew with loathing. "That's why you went after the players you mentioned?"

"No. I sought them out because my sergeant recognised the girl from a performance at the theatre here."

"Oh, she was an actress then," said Tillie, betraying an interest faintly reminiscent of earlier times.

"She was," said George, "and I must have seen her myself when I went to the play last month, but I recalled her only vaguely."

"Why, if she was so lovely?"

Pertinent as always. Francis rejoiced. Tillie was growing intrigued. Then he became distracted by the odd circumstance of George's sudden high colour. What in the world —? But his mother was before him.

"Good heavens, Colonel, what is the matter?"

George, rather to Francis's amusement, took refuge in his wine glass. Setting it down, he cleared his throat. "I had my mind on other matters at the time, ma'am," he added with some haste, casting a decidedly apprehensive glance at Tillie.

"To say truth, I noticed none of the players on that occasion except The Grand Ferdinando himself."

A trill of laughter escaped Tillie and Francis's heart lifted.

"The Grand Ferdinando? Dear me, George, is it he with whom you have had to deal? How delightful. Who is he?"

"One of these actor manager fellows."

"Ah, an impresario then. Is it his company?"

"Yes, and I have had to yield to his plaguing me to allow him to hold another performance tomorrow, so you may see them if you care to go."

"If she feels up to it," Francis cut in swiftly with a darkling look at his friend.

George took the hint and swept on. "But I have discovered it is Mrs Ferdinand who has the mastery of these infernal players. And if one of those fellows did not kill the girl, I'm a Dutchman."

The dowager, who had taken fish stew but eaten only a mouthful or two, nodded. "I imagine it must be so, what with the theatrical nature of the crime."

Tillie's gaze was upon the colonel as she swallowed her mouthful. "Is that what you suppose, George?"

"Well, not one of them can fully account for his movements that night. It's my belief they have closed ranks, for I can't get proper corroboration out of any of them, including Ferdinand, although his wife claims he did not leave his bed."

"That won't fadge," said Francis. "What is to stop him slipping out without her knowledge?"

"I don't know that, Fan. You always wake when I slip from the bed."

"Yes, but I'm a soldier. George will tell you one is ever on the qui vive. It's an ingrained habit to wake at the slightest disturbance."

"True, Fan. And most of them had been drinking deep at the tavern. Not that the landlord remembers beyond the fact they were there. He couldn't say who left at what time when Sullivan questioned him. I've spoken to the men severally and together, but to no avail. I learned little beyond their backgrounds."

"Which are?" Tillie asked.

He shrugged. "Not of much interest. Lewis Payne has been acting from a boy and I can't find that he had any particular interest in the girl. The Ferdinands are both seasoned players and have been running the company for some fifteen years or so. Despite the wife's tendency to rule him, they seem a devoted couple, though I would not put it past Ferdinand to get up a flirtation with a young actress."

Tillie was merely toying with her crab, Francis noticed, but her apparent growing interest gave him hope. She pushed for more.

"Who else is there?"

"The young tearaway, Jasper, who was out all night." George coughed in a way Francis recognised as delicacy, glancing at the dowager. "Saving your presence, ma'am, the barmaid at The Black Dog vouches for the boy's whereabouts. He's the son of an actor, I believe, but as he chose to be recalcitrant; I learned nothing more from him. I don't much favour the stagehands, neither of whom seem the sort the girl might go off with, and the only other male is Robert Collins and he's married. I gather his wife holds his purse strings and keeps a tight rein on him."

"Tight, how? Did he say so?"

"He said very little. He's a sullen brute. But Payne mentioned this Trixie has money and, as he put it, 'keeps Rob short'. And that's all. When it comes to sifting through that lot to find the murderer I've drawn blank."

Tillie abandoned her meal, setting down her fork and pushing the plate away a little, and Francis grieved to see her appetite still poor. On the other hand she had listened with close attention to George, as became obvious the moment she spoke again.

"I wonder if this Dulcie had met with someone outside the company?"

George looked struck. "I had not thought of that."

"Well, wherever she performs, a beautiful actress must be plagued by followers, do you not think?"

Setting down his glass, George let out a groan. "As if I have not suspects enough. And who else, pray, would think of leaving the body in an open coffin with candles set alight around it?"

"Someone who sought to cast suspicion upon these theatricals."

Francis's spirits rose. If that was not Tillie all over. George was staring at her with his mouth at half cock, but the dowager struck her hands together, emitting an explosive sound of triumph.

"There, what did I tell you?" She turned to George. "Now are you not glad you wrote to Francis, Colonel?"

Recovering himself, he let out a laugh. "Indeed, ma'am. But, Ottilia, what makes you say that?"

She shifted a little in her chair, a deprecating look upon her face. "From what you've said, I take it the scene was carefully staged. That does not sound much like the artistic temperament to me."

"But it must be exactly what these players know, particularly Ferdinand who manages these productions of his."

"I don't doubt it. But that is pretence. I've no doubt they see false death every day when they are playing a tragedy. It's a very different matter when the death is real, do you not think?"

A shadow crossed Francis's heart. Death was all too real for both of them in the recent past. Was that why Tillie saw the murder in this light? His mother entered the lists.

"You are saying an actor would not be as clear headed as to set it up like a stage set, Ottilia, is that it?"

"I'm saying it is out of character. At least for some, though perhaps not all. The act seems to be particularly cold-blooded. And with no attempt to cover up the crime."

"The reverse in fact," agreed Francis. "I would say it is worth a look, George."

"Of course it's worth a look, but I have no notion where to look, if you want the truth of it. Any number of men could have been enamoured of the wench, for all I know."

"But her friends will know, George."

To Francis's astonishment, this remark had the effect of bringing the darker stain back to his friend's cheeks. He glanced at Tillie and was not in the least surprised to see a look of understanding in the clear gaze. But her words shocked him nevertheless.

"Who is she, George?"

He had been gazing at his empty plate, but his eyes came up fast. "Good grief, Ottilia, must you be so acute?"

The dowager pounced. "Aha! I said there was something. Don't say you've fallen for one of these players, Colonel. That would never do."

"I haven't fallen for anyone, ma'am," he returned on a snap. "And Cecile is not a player. She's an *émigré*. She's with them because her mother approached the players when they were in France and begged them to rescue her."

"Oh, poor child. An aristocrat then?"

"I imagine so, though I have no exact notion of her true status. I met her a few weeks ago when she was trying to pawn a necklace and that fool Throcking took her for a French spy and called me in. She told me her story perforce."

Francis could not resist. "So that's what took you to the play, my friend. And it explains why you didn't notice the golden-haired Dulcie. You were hoping to see your *émigré*."

His colour considerably heightened, George gave him a look of deep reproach. "Traitor! As if it's not enough with the women of your family quizzing me."

Laughing, Francis leaned across and gave him a buffet on the shoulder. "All's fair in love and war, my friend. Besides, it's a treat to see you caught at last."

"I am not caught. And for your information, Fanshawe, I can hardly start wooing the girl in the middle of a murder investigation."

"I don't see why not. I did."

With which, Francis put out a hand to his wife, who set hers in it and gave him, to his inestimable joy, one of her warm smiles.

"Only afterwards, Fan, if you recall." She gave his fingers a squeeze and released his hand. "The point here is that George's *émigré* is, or was, the murdered girl's friend. Am I right?"

He nodded, his high colour fading at last. "I think so, and I'm convinced she knows more than she will tell me. They were sharing a bed, and she knew the girl Dulcie was absent."

"Then perhaps she also knows whom she was with?"

"Cecile denies it. But she knows something. She is peculiarly evasive. And, I may add, inclined to resent any implication she is concealing evidence."

Retiring with her mother-in-law to the parlour, Ottilia took the window seat, which afforded a view of the rolling waves. The days were long and there was still much activity on the Esplanade, where the fashionables walked or paused to listen to the small orchestra playing near the water. Strains of a poorly executed symphony floated up through the open window together with the indistinct sounds of idle chat and laughter. Ottilia's mind roved rather on the details of the murder, however, than the scene below.

The dowager settled in a chair near the unlit fire, out of the direct line of the night breeze.

"I wonder if Francis will manage to get more out of the colonel about this émigré of his?"

Ottilia glanced across. "I doubt Fan will plague him. It is possible George may be more forthcoming in our absence, however."

"But not about the girl?"

"About his findings."

"Why, when he knows very well you are the one who needs to hear it?"

Ottilia gave a faint grimace. "Oh, because Fan has likely warned him not to burden me with the gory details for fear I may be distressed."

"You?" Sybilla gave vent to a crack of mocking laughter. "If the colonel doesn't know you better, I don't think much of his understanding. I don't recall him being shocked by your candour when he was involved with Emily's affair."

"Just so, but did you not note his reticence? He said little about the condition of the dead girl's body beyond the fact she had been stabbed. Yet there must have been a post-mortem."

The dowager's delicate brows rose. "What are you getting at, Ottilia?"

"Motive, Sybilla. Why was she killed? And if I don't miss my guess, George is worried that his Cecile knows."

Sybilla stared. "How in the world do you make that out?"

"He did not say why she was pawning a necklace."

"And so?"

Ottilia pursued her thought. "Does it not seem to you there may be a connection?"

She watched Sybilla's brow pucker as the notion penetrated. But the dowager blew out a dismissive breath at length and wafted a hand. "A trifle far-fetched, Ottilia. The necklace business was some weeks back, I thought he said."

"Yes, but that does not preclude it having a bearing on the murder. Or rather, the reason for the murder. We have it on George's authority that Cecile was a friend of the victim and shared a bed with her — presumably when the girl Dulcie was not sleeping elsewhere."

"What are you suggesting?"

The door opened to admit the gentlemen before Ottilia had an opportunity to answer. Instead she rallied them. "You can scarcely have drunk one glass, either of you. Have you turned Methodist?"

"George has an early start in the morning and wants to keep a clear head."

Francis came across and leaned down to drop a kiss on her forehead. Ottilia touched a hand to his cheek and let it fall as he rose again. It was bliss to be on better terms and her heart swelled with affection.

"Are you leaving us already, Colonel?" Sybilla's voice drew her attention and Ottilia saw that George had taken up a stance by the mantel.

"I must, ma'am."

"Will you not at least take tea first? Ring the bell, Francis."

While her husband went over to grasp the hand bell on the table and sound a summons, the dowager kept her attention on Colonel Tretower.

"You will be pleased to learn, Colonel, that Ottilia has already jumped to one of her startling conclusions."

A riffle of apprehension seized Ottilia and she could not refrain from casting a look at Francis. He caught her glance and quirked an eyebrow.

She gave a little shrug. "It's just a thought." She eyed him. "You won't start fretting, will you?"

"Hardly, when I let you in for this." The expected frown came. "But why should you think so? Is it something horrid?"

Ottilia drew a breath, aware that both the dowager and George had their eyes on her. "Yes, it may be." She transferred her gaze to the colonel and brought it out flat. "George, was the victim pregnant?"

The effect of her question on the assembled company was as troubling as she had anticipated. Sybilla stared at her in a dazed fashion. George's face shut like a door and he shot a look at Francis, whose dark eyes in turn shot fire towards his friend. Ottilia hurried into speech.

"Don't look daggers at him, Fan. Though that is answer enough. I suppose George told you and you said he must not mention it before me." Both men turned to her and Francis came across, putting out a hand which Ottilia seized and squeezed hard. "It is distressing, Fan, but we cannot be forever avoiding all mention of babies. Even —" adding with a little difficulty — "those as unfortunate as our own. Perhaps more so, for if Dulcie was with child, the poor thing never stood a chance."

Her vision misted a trifle, but she swallowed down the urge to weep and tried to smile up into Francis's worried countenance.

"Are you sure, Tillie? I would not have had you hear it for the world."

"I know, my dearest dear, but if we are to help George, it cannot be avoided."

He released her hand as the door opened to admit the footman Tyler and the maid Joanie, burdened with the accoutrements for tea. The business of preparation and pouring afforded a welcome diversion and an opportunity for Ottilia to recover her sangfroid. Truth to tell, her interest was roused, and as Francis brought her tea and handed her the saucer, she was moved to murmur for his ears alone.

"I am glad you brought me, my dearest."

He scanned her face, keeping his tone low. "Are you sure you are all right?"

She smiled. "Don't worry so, Fan. You caused me to discharge a deal of it today."

He nodded and dropped the subject, shifting a little away. Ottilia found the colonel moving in, cup and saucer in hand and apology in his face.

"Ottilia, I cannot tell you how much I regret this circumstance. I was horrified when Doctor Roffey told me, for of course it immediately demonstrated the reason for the murder. I rather wished I had not sent for you, if you want the truth."

"So did I," Francis put in on a rueful note. "Only it was not known when George wrote to me. And we had set out by the time he got the news."

To Ottilia's relief, the dowager took a hand, setting down her cup. "Well, you may both stop being ninnies. I can't bear this nonsensical notion held by the male of the species that their female counterparts are too weak to be given difficult news." She threw up a hand as Francis made to speak. "Yes, I know the present circumstances are delicate, but Ottilia is nothing if not resilient. She will cope. Don't you hold anything back, Colonel Tretower."

He shifted in her direction. "I need not now the worst is out." A laugh escaped him. "I might have known Ottilia would be on to it in a flash."

"So you might. And if you wish her to assist you to unravel this mess, you had better tell her everything."

"I will, ma'am, but not tonight." He supped the last of his tea and went to set his empty cup down on the tray. "I've to post off to Dorchester again in the morning to report to Justice Shellow. But I will call upon you late in the day, if I may." With which, he made his farewells and left them.

Ottilia found the dowager regarding her in mute question.

"You need not look at me as if you expect me at any moment to fall into a heap of melancholy all over again."

"Perhaps not. Yet it will not be easy, Ottilia, despite what I said to the colonel."

"True, and I may not contrive to keep my countenance at all times, nor to refrain from sighing now and then."

"No one will blame you for that."

"Least of all me," put in Francis.

A trifle of mischief filtered into her breast. "No, you are more likely to deprecate my involving myself too eagerly."

Francis lifted an eyebrow. "I know that look. What are you planning?"

Ottilia laughed. "I was wondering how I might contrive to meet this French émigré without going through George."

Cecile sat quietly in the back of the auditorium, sewing to the accompaniment of the actors rehearsing Kate into the role vacated by Dulcie's death. With a performance sanctioned by Colonel Tretower, Mr Ferdinand had lost no time in rounding up his disordered company and harrying them to the theatre at the earliest opportunity, calling upon his wife's aid when too many of them dallied.

If she had not been so oppressed, it would have amused Cecile to see once again how nothing of value occurred without madame's intervention. The players were an unruly lot. None paid heed to their leader's bluster, aware to a man of his tendency to take the art of the stage into his life. In her early days Cecile had been both awed by Monsieur Ferdinand's grand manner and intimidated by his frequent forays into the towering roar which was his stock in trade. But his wife's exasperated responses very soon taught her to disregard him.

"Oh, do stop it, Arthur, for heaven's sake! You are not fooling anyone."

Yet when Madame Ferdinand spoke in command, none dared gainsay her. It was she who had curbed the rising hysteria over the past days.

"That will do, all of you. The colonel has arrested no one and there is no future in quarrelling amongst ourselves and apportioning blame. We must stand together and support each other. Moreover, it would become you better to mourn poor Dulcibella instead of indulging in a disgracefully ghoulish game of casting suspicion upon your fellows. I do not wish to hear one more word of accusation, do you understand?"

The actors were not chastened for long, but thereafter confined their "ghoulish indulgence" to moments when Janey was absent. Cecile would not have engaged in any discussion but that she was continually questioned.

"You must have some notion, Cecily, who Dulcie was meeting," Hilde insisted.

"Of course she has. We all know girls and their secrets in the bedchamber."

"Whose bedchamber knows your secrets then, Jasper?"

"Or yours, Lewis," he retorted.

"Jasper didn't do it," cut in Rob. "We all know Dulcie wouldn't warm his bed for him. Besides, he's never sober enough for aught but a barmaid."

"Which is more than you can boast, my buck," Jasper returned, not in the least put out.

"I've a wife at home, I thank you."

"Well, Kate swears she knew nothing of Dulcie's amorous dealings," said Hilde, returning to her theme, "but I'm sure you do, Cecily."

"Where then is Kate?" Cecile asked in a bid to turn attention elsewhere.

"Either closeted with our esteemed patriarch or learning her lines," said Lewis, once again looking up from the book he was reading.

Jasper groaned. "That means old sobersides will haul us off to the theatre to rehearse at any moment."

Since Kate had not before performed the role of Lucinda, this was inevitable, as Hilde was quick to point out. Their leader had dropped the scheduled piece, *The Country Wife*, as the female characters could not now be covered, in favour of *The Conscious Lovers*. Hilde already knew the role of Indiana Danvers and Jane Ferdinand slipped readily into Isabella in addition to Mrs Sealand.

Rehearsals fortunately kept the actors too busy to plague Cecile. She had fitted Dulcie's costume onto Kate and was stitching the alterations where she had pinned it. Her unofficial role as wardrobe mistress had come about because she was adamant in refusing to tread the boards. But helping Hilde became an exchange for her keep, although her mother had paid handsomely for her rescue. Her domestic skills were few, but she was an adept needlewoman and while she sewed, mended and packed the costumes into the trunks, Hilde supervised the washing and cleaning, employing women for the purpose wherever they went.

She was indebted to Dulcie for teaching her how to maid for herself since they were quartered together. Their friendship stemmed from the intimacy involved and Cecile's grief was genuine, if muted. She knew too much of loss to indulge in despair. Better to find out the cruel offender. From wondering, along with the colonel of militia's clear suspicions, which of the male players could have killed Dulcie, Cecile had passed to a conviction the murderer might be a man unconnected with the company. Why else should she be so cagey about the father of her unborn child?

In vain had Cecile, thinking back to that whispered confession of the night some weeks since, been able to recall any little word that pointed towards any one of the players in particular. But there had been admirers. If only Dulcie had confided in her! Not that she could have prevented this terrible murder, but a sneaking suspicion the colonel of militia meant to question her set her mind running on identities.

She had barely brought a couple of possibilities to mind when the theatre manager came into the auditorium.

Fitzgerald was a darkly handsome man with an aloof manner, rather older than Rob, Cecile thought, but younger than Lewis. She scarcely knew him and was surprised when he paused at the row in which she sat and beckoned. Setting her work carefully over the back of the seat in front, she made her way along the row.

"You want me, *monsieur*?"

He jerked his head towards the entrance. "There's a lady asking for you."

Considerably taken aback, Cecile stared at him. "I do not know any lady."

A rather saturnine look came over his face as he smiled. "She evidently knows you. She asked for the French *émigré*."

Cecile was taken with a wild conjecture. Could this be family? "She is French also?"

Fitzgerald lifted one eyebrow. "Not that you'd notice."

The faint hope died. "Then I know not why she seeks me."

"I suggest you go and ask her. She's waiting in the foyer." With which, he proceeded along the aisle towards the stage and stood watching the progress of the final rehearsal before the evening performance.

Cecile, realising she was foolishly staring after him, gathered her scattered wits and turned towards the auditorium door in a little trepidation. Who could it be? And why should this lady wish to speak with her?

She entered the foyer to find a lady indeed there, engaged in examining a painting of Mrs Sarah Siddons set in one of the niches within the walls reserved for portraits of the great. The foyer was a handsome apartment with much gilding in evidence, a huge chandelier hanging from the ceiling despite the light coming in from high windows, and a quantity of gilt-edged chairs set against the walls.

"Madame?"

The lady turned her head, presenting a countenance unremarkable except for high cheekbones and a pair of clear grey eyes which regarded Cecile with an appraising gaze for a moment. Then a smile appeared and her features lit with warmth as she moved forward, holding out a hand.

"You must be Cecile. How do you do?"

Cecile took the hand and found its grip firm. She nevertheless entered an immediate caveat. "Yes, but I do not know you, madame."

The lady laughed. "That is easily remedied. I am Lady Francis Fanshawe, but more commonly known as Lady Fan."

Mystified, Cecile did not take her eyes from the woman's face. "Yet I do not know what you wish with me, madame."

Lady Fan met her gaze without flinching. "I have heard something of you, *mademoiselle*." She smiled again. "I should mention perhaps that my husband is a close friend of Colonel George Tretower."

A flurry disturbed Cecile's pulse as the image of the colonel leapt into her mind. Then she recalled his present preoccupation with Dulcie's murder and eyed her visitor with rising resentment.

"He has sent you? Why does he not come himself if he has more of the questions?"

Surprise flickered in Lady Fan's eyes. "George does not know I am here. But I do indeed have questions of my own."

"*Vraiment?* And what has the matter to do with you, madame?"

The visitor hesitated, seeming to ponder. Then a sigh escaped her. "You are very acute, my dear, and that is a good thing. Well, let me be frank. You have every right to be wary, my dear Cecile — if I may? — but I assure you I have no ill intention. I would like, if I can, to help you discover who it was who so cruelly killed your friend."

Thoroughly taken aback, Cecile ignored the tiny shaft that went through her at mention of Dulcie's horrible demise. "You, madame? *Mais pourquoi*? What is it to you?"

She found her hand taken in a warm clasp, a look of understanding in the clear gaze. "I have had some success in that line in the past." A rather attractive little gurgle escaped and Cecile's bristles smoothed a trifle. "Officially I am here for my health, but it seems poor George is anxious for a helping hand. Will you not take pity on him, *mademoiselle*?"

Bewildered, Cecile fairly blinked at her. "I? To have pity for this colonel? I do not understand."

"Help me to help him, my dear. I can do nothing without your assistance."

Cecile released herself, stepping back. "You would have me tell you of Dulcie, *c'est ça*?"

"Just so."

"And then you will tell this George?"

"As much as he needs to know. Between women, my dear Cecile, there may be candour unnecessary to be passed along to the male ear, do you not think?"

Cecile could not withhold a crack of crude laughter. "That is seen. For myself, I say nothing with *ces hommes*. They are apt to make judgement, *vous savez*?"

"Indeed they are, as well as supposing we women less capable of making judgements for ourselves," said Lady Fan in a confidential manner. "We will decide together what George should or should not hear, is that agreed?"

Still wary, Cecile eyed her. "I do not know what I can tell you."

Surprisingly, Lady Fan laughed. "Nor do I, my dear, but I feel sure there is something. It often happens that we do not realise how pertinent a little thing we have in our heads may be. I dare say you know a great deal more than you suppose."

"How could that be, madame?"

"Well, think of it a little, Cecile. When one shares the intimacy of a room and a bed, one speaks with a freedom hardly possible in public. Anything Dulcie said to you is likely to be more personal than she might say to anyone else, do you not think?"

Cecile was only too aware of her earlier preoccupation, but she was still conscious of reluctance. "It becomes me not to betray the secrets of my friend."

"Of course not, in the ordinary way." Once again that warm hand clasped hers. "But your friend is no more, and the manner of her loss is a betrayal in itself. If you are able to redress the balance, to give poor Dulcie justice, do you think it is permissible to speak out? Would Dulcie herself not urge you so to do?"

Wavering, Cecile again withdrew her hand. This female was all too persuasive.

"You debate well, madame." She made up her mind. "I will speak. But you will remember your promise."

"To filter what I relay? You have my word."

A small sigh escaped Cecile as an icicle in her heart began to melt. She had hardly realised how painful it was to her to keep in all she knew.

"A moment, madame, while I secure my work, and I will come."

Strolling along the Esplanade, Ottilia kept to neutral topics until the knots of fellow walkers thinned, as she and her companion headed out of the centre of the town in the direction of the bridge. She noticed Cecile cast several furtive glances at Hemp keeping pace a little behind.

"You are wondering about the man? He is my steward. My husband insists I am accompanied at all times, you must know, for my strength is yet uncertain."

The French girl's gaze turned upon her, lifting to Ottilia's superior height. The dark eyes were both large and deep with mystery. Coupled with the lush black locks, Ottilia had no difficulty in understanding why Colonel Tretower was so powerfully affected.

"You are unwell, madame?"

Ottilia chose to waive the truth. "Oh, I am markedly better, but not as robust yet as I could wish."

It was plain the girl would have asked more but was too polite, or too reticent to do so. Ottilia turned her attention to the matter at hand, choosing the direct approach.

"Will you tell me when you learned that Dulcie was with child?"

Startled distress flashed in the eyes before they were veiled. Cecile turned them upon the ocean and her tone became sharp. "I do not know why you ask such a thing of me, madame."

"Come, my dear Cecile, did you suppose Dulcie's secret would remain undiscovered?"

It was a moment before the girl answered, her gaze apparently following the path of a small ship tacking in the bay. "How comes it about that this is known, madame?"

Ottilia became apologetic. "I'm afraid it was inevitable. Perhaps you do not know that in the case of an unexpected death there is usually a post-mortem required by the authorities."

The sudden intake of breath at her side told Ottilia this was news to the girl.

"Ah, no! You would say the doctor cuts *la pauvre* in pieces?"

"With as much respect as he can use, my dear. Doctors are ordinarily sensitive to the perceived cruelty of the undertaking."

A fierce stare was turned upon her. "How comes it about that you know so much, madame?"

"My brother is a doctor, *mademoiselle*. Before my marriage, I learned much of his trade, both by observation and assisting in his work when he would let me. I may tell you with certainty that Dulcie's body will have been returned to its proper form once the investigations had been completed."

Cecile continued to regard her with a look both fascinated and horrified, if Ottilia read it aright. "I did not wish ever to betray this secret of Dulcie. Why can they not permit her to go in peace to her grave? Is it not enough she is killed in this — this fashion of a brute?"

"Would you wish the brute to escape justice?" Ottilia countered. "Especially when Dulcie's secret is evidently the reason she was thus murdered. It is horrible, yes, and perhaps unkind to your friend's memory. But better that than that the man who did this should escape the righteous vengeance of the law."

A blast of contemptuous air escaped the girl. "The law you say? And if the law is itself the murderer? If the vengeance is taken before there is a crime? Me, I know much of vengeance, madame, and of those who ask only to be permitted to live when the law speaks their very life to be a crime."

The words came with vicious emphasis and Ottilia was silenced, recalling Cecile's background. Small wonder the argument for justice made no impression upon one who must have lost all her family to the travesty of justice perpetrated across the channel even now. The scythe of the newly formed

Republique had swept away the lives of many aristocratic bodies in the last couple of years.

She kept pace beside the *émigré*, whose steps had quickened, hoping she would not go too fast for too long. She was beginning to feel the strain when Cecile abruptly halted.

"*Pardon*, madame. I intended not to speak of these things. It is well I accept these customs of my adopted country. *C'est-à-dire*, in regard to Dulcie, it is seen that justice must be done."

Ottilia accepted this without comment, returning to her question. "When did you learn of the babe, Cecile?"

A faint sigh expressed capitulation, and Cecile resumed walking. Ottilia followed suit, not unhopeful.

"It was perhaps since five or six weeks. I woke in the night to hear Dulcie crying. With much persuasion I was able to find out her trouble."

"It shocked you no doubt."

"Yes, but she is my friend. She helps me when I do not know how to wash my clothes or where to purchase necessities of my toilette. Dulcie teaches me many things of which I am ignorant, and helps with my English when Madame Ferdinand gives to me an exercise."

"You felt indebted to her then."

"A debt, no! With a friend, if there is trouble, one must do all one can do. That is from the heart, madame, not from the — how do you say?"

"Duty?" Ottilia supplied. She added in soothing tones, "I understand you, Cecile. It was not an obligation. You did not think of other than how you might succour your friend."

"It was so."

Ottilia went straight for the jugular. "And therefore you pawned your necklace. Did you mean it for a bribe to the man

95

concerned? Or was it in your mind Dulcie might try to be rid of the child?"

Cecile's answer was swift and crude. "Abort an infant? Never! I am *Catholique*, madame. Such is a mortal sin."

"Then you hoped the man would be susceptible to a bribe? Or did you think he would marry Dulcie?"

"I have thought only that with money, Dulcie can do something. Without, she is finished. But I do not know the man. Dulcie gives me no name, even though I plead with her to tell me. I thought perhaps it was Jasper, but he is one who is bad with women, he cares not which. Do you know this, madame?"

"You mean he's a womaniser, what we would call a rake?"

"Yes. Dulcie is romantic. She does not wish to be one of many."

"She wanted love, and who shall blame her? I doubt the poor girl found it."

"Yes, but I believe she did," said Cecile with sudden vehemence. "Or perhaps it is that she thought she found it. Or the man makes her believe."

It was Ottilia's turn to anger. "Yes, that is only too likely. Poor girl. She is not the first to be seduced by false promises, and I doubt she will be the last."

Cecile halted again, earnest demand in the tell-tale gaze. "Think you he has promised to marry her? It is what I fear, madame. She will not say where is she going, but she looks — how shall I say? She is excited, her face it shines like a blossom. She puts on her good gown, the blue satin with the décolletage so low. It is one she had from a role no longer used, she tells me. She pins her hair and uses the colour on her lips and cheeks. She is like a star, that one, always, but this night, she is more. She is *heureuse extraordinaire*, and she does not know she goes to her doom."

The girl's voice ceased, thickened by the end. Ottilia could see the tremble at her lips, the deep distress altogether genuine. The dark eyes were swimming and Ottilia took one of her shaking hands in a warm clasp.

"It is hard for you to speak of it. My thanks, my dear. You have given me a most vivid picture and that helps enormously."

Cecile nodded but did not speak. Her eyes dulled a trifle and she withdrew her hand, turning to walk on. Ottilia reached to stop her.

"Shall we turn back now?"

A frowning gaze swept over Ottilia's face. "You are tired, madame?"

"A little."

Without a word, the émigré turned and together they began to retrace their steps. Ottilia smiled at Hemp, still dogging their steps, and signalled her intention. He came up to her.

"Do you wish to take my arm, milady?"

"Thank you, no. I shall manage."

He glanced from her to Cecile and a look of understanding entered the light brown features. Hemp was nothing if not observant. Evidently realising Ottilia had more to elicit from her companion, he stood aside and fell in behind again. Ottilia hoped he had been walking near enough to hear, for she had every intention of soliciting his help in her quest to find this elusive murderer. She gave Cecile a few minutes grace before putting her next question.

"What did Dulcie do with the money you gave her?"

Cecile's head turned, question in her face. "Why, madame?"

"It may be pertinent. Did she take it with her that night, do you know?"

"You think she proposes to give it to the man?"

"It's possible if, as you say, she was happy and perhaps believed he meant to marry her. I am wondering if a flight was intended."

"Flight? But to where, madame?"

"To Scotland. Or, more probably, to Dorchester where the couple might find a priest to marry them. Was Dulcie of age?"

"She has almost two and twenty years, madame."

A pang smote Ottilia. Only two and twenty and hideously struck down. And for what?

"Then, provided this man procured a licence, they might be married anywhere."

"Is it that you think the man told her they go to be married in the night?"

"I should think it very probable from what you've told me of her mood. Did she take the money with her?"

Cecile's fingers were shifting at her sides, a sign of discomfort. Was this another matter she had thought to conceal? "I see that she puts a heavy purse in her reticule."

"What kind of purse?"

"A purse of leather with strings to hold it tight shut."

"It was heavy, you said?"

"Yes, but all the money is not inside."

"How much did you give her, Cecile?"

"Forty guineas." The girl's intense gaze sought Ottilia's. "She takes only twenty, for I have found the rest hidden in her clothes."

"You thought to look after her murder?"

Cecile flinched at the repetition of the word. "Because I thought to see if one of the players has perhaps taken the money. Then I will know Dulcie has said to him it is there and that it is a player who kills her."

Not that the fact no one stole the remainder of Dulcie's hoard proved the players to be innocent. But that thought Ottilia kept to herself. She bethought her of her promise.

"Is there anything you have said that I may not relay to George?"

Cecile's eyes met hers, wariness in them now. "What shall he do with these matters, madame?"

"I hope he may use them to find out the wicked man who took your friend's life."

Ottilia had spoken with deliberation and she held the girl's gaze, hoping to convince her of the need to tell George everything. That he would be hungry for any words that came from his *émigré* she could not doubt. But the girl surprised her.

"He will be angry that I spoke not before."

Ottilia was betrayed into a laugh. "Not he. Heavens, George is the most even-tempered man I know."

Cecile withdrew her gaze, turning it instead upon a group of shrieking children playing chase with the waves at the water's edge. "He was kind with me at the first. But I believe now he thinks I lie." Her tone became fierce and her eyes too as they once more sought Ottilia's. "I lie, yes. I say I do not know, but for the sake of my friend."

"I feel sure George will understand."

Came a tossed head and an unconvincing airy note. "It is nothing to me, madame."

Amused, Ottilia made a mental vow to discover if George was truly smitten or merely idly attracted to the girl. She might dismiss it for a pipe dream if she was not herself guilty of tumbling into love within a matter of days and Francis likewise.

If she did not miss her guess, both parties here had been affected at their first meeting.

But that was out of her hands and certainly no part of her present remit. She turned her attention to the second of her schemes. "I should very much like to meet the company, Cecile. Do you think that is possible?"

Not much to her surprise, the girl regarded her with a good deal of suspicious comprehension. "You will ask of them such questions?"

"Not directly as I have with you. There are ways of eliciting information without seeming to be other than curious."

Indignation leapt in Cecile's face. "You would make me to be like a traitor, madame, to bring a spy among my people."

Ottilia suppressed a flush of irritation. Really, the girl was prickly in the extreme. "Would you prefer me to explain to them that I am trying to assist George?"

"It is honest, madame."

"Dear me. And have you been entirely honest with them, Cecile?"

Colour rushed into her cheeks, but to her credit she did not look away. "It is better so. They do not behave well, these players. In their heads and tongues it is all making the blame one to one and the quarrels. They think more of this and not of Dulcie." She gave the peculiarly Gallic shrug. "I do not say they are not sorry. Hilde she grieves, I know. Also Kate and Madame Ferdinand, and perhaps Lewis. Also Rob, perhaps a little. But Jasper, I do not think so, or the other two."

"What of Mister Ferdinand?"

Cecile wrinkled her nose in distaste. "He is sorry, yes, but perhaps more because Dulcie is very beautiful and therefore the people come to see her and there is money. Kate is pretty, but now it is only the play and Monsieur Ferdinand is afraid the people will not come. Already the performance does not happen since Dulcie died until today, and Monsieur Ferdinand he worries for the money and that he cannot find another actress *si belle comme* his little Dulcibella."

Ottilia's interest was thoroughly aroused. "I must say your players sound like a most fascinating set of people. I do hope you will think of a way to introduce me."

Cecile frowned and did not answer. They were now back within easy reach of the centre of the town and the theatre. The girl halted almost opposite the house where the Fanshawes were lodging.

"Where do you stay, madame?"

Ottilia pointed across. "Right there." She saw Francis in the window and waved. "There is my husband. I must go." She held out her hand. "Thank you for trusting me. Pray do me the honour of calling upon me when you have the time."

The girl eyed her, still with that mix of wariness and doubt. "I will call, madame, perhaps."

With which Ottilia supposed she would have to be content for the present. Before she could say more, Cecile dropped a curtsey, turned and hurried away in the direction of the theatre.

Ottilia watched her go and found Hemp at her elbow. She lost no time in eliciting his help.

"Do you think you might discover the tavern the players frequent, Hemp? I've no doubt there is one."

Hemp, who had interested her almost from the start of the debacle that occurred in Willow Court months back, looked at her with the serious mien he had worn ever since that fateful time.

"You wish me to make merry with the players, milady?"

Ottilia smiled. Hemp's quickness had impressed her at the outset. "Just so."

"What is it you wish to know of them?"

"What sort of men they are in the main. Which of them are friends perhaps. And if you can contrive to listen in to their private discussions, anything they may say which is pertinent to the murder. From what Cecile said, do you not think they are likely to be loose-tongued?"

One of Hemp's rare smiles crossed his face. "Assuredly, milady. We had a company of players in Barbados who came to perform at the master's plantation now and then. Flora Rum was a favourite with them. And they talked, milady. How they talked!"

Ottilia laughed. "Then you will know just how to do. I rely upon you absolutely."

"If milord is suited, milady, I am happy to serve you in such a way."

Ottilia was tempted to tell him it had nothing whatsoever to do with milord, but she bit off the words. Francis could hardly object to her setting Hemp to spy for her. He was, after all, in her service rather than her husband's. Moreover, Francis had brought her here for this purpose.

Her attention drawn to her spouse, she spoke unthinkingly as they crossed the road. "Francis must have been delayed. I did not expect him to be home."

Hemp had his head on one side, listening as they approached the door. "If I mistake not, milady, this is his lordship coming down to meet you now."

So it proved. The door opened before they quite reached it and Francis left it open as he stepped into the street, his eyebrow quirking.

"I see you managed it as I might have known you would. How did you fare?"

Ottilia had to laugh. "With George's *émigré*? She's understandably cagey, but we learned something, did we not, Hemp?"

"I do not know how valuable it may be to you, milady."

"She'll make use of it, whatever it is, be sure."

Ottilia took Francis's proffered arm, smiling at him. "You forget Hemp is somewhat familiar with my methods, Fan."

"But from the other side, milady," said Hemp feelingly. "This mademoiselle had my sympathy, milord, that I swear to."

Francis grinned. "Yes, she drove you hard, I remember."

Ottilia rejoiced to see him easy with Hemp. He had been a trifle short lately, becoming the lord somewhat while there was that uncomfortable distance between them. It crossed her mind he might have resented the ease of friendship she shared with Hemp. But a more urgent need superseded this notion.

"Francis, we will need tickets for the play this evening."

"Oh, lord, must we go?"

She opened her eyes at him. "Don't you wish to see George's suspects? I've asked Cecile to introduce me, but she is reluctant. And Hemp is going to find whatever tavern they use after the performance and see what he can discover."

"Oh, very well. What is the play?"

"I forgot to ask. But it makes no matter."

Francis sighed. "I had best go and procure a box at once."

"Let me do that for you, milord."

"Yes, pray do, Hemp, for I must see her ladyship settles to rest."

Ottilia paused on the doorstep. "As close to the stage as you can get, Hemp, if you please. Oh, and say it is for the Dowager Marchioness of Polbrook. That should get us the best position in the house."

Hemp nodded and went off on his errand, while Francis ushered his wife into the hall, amusement in his voice.

"Unscrupulous female that you are, my lady Fan."

Ottilia threw him a mischievous glance over her shoulder. "It is always well to use the advantages one has, Fan, and you made Sybilla my mother-in-law." She reached the top of the stairs and turned, caught by a stray notion. "Where is she, by the by? I thought you were escorting her to the Assembly Rooms."

Francis joined her in the vestibule. "We were forestalled. The fellow Rodber turned up with a prospective cook in tow. Mama is interviewing the woman as we speak."

Ottilia was heading for the parlour, but halted at this. "Then we had best not disturb her."

Francis slid an arm about her and drew her into a hug. "I'd as lief you lay down for a space after that long walk."

She snuggled into him, glad of the contact. "Well, I will if you wish it."

He released her, his lip quivering. "So obedient, Tillie?"

She laughed. "Naturally, my darling husband." And instantly frowned as a thought occurred. "Or no, stay! Is Mr Rodber still here?"

"Yes, why?"

"Then we'll go in. From Cecile's description of Dulcie's frame of mind that night, I find it hard to believe she was not in fact going to meet with a man outside the company."

"Isn't that what you said?"

"Yes, and if the man was an admirer and frequented the theatre, you may be sure the master of ceremonies will know of it."

The man Rodber was a garrulous fellow of advancing years in whom Francis espied a leaning towards pomposity, tempered with obsequiousness no doubt induced by his mother's rank. He had evidently reigned for some years over Weymouth's visiting elite and contrived to lard his conversation with references to the patronage of the King, whose sojourn in Weymouth for his health two years before had increased the resort's popularity.

"Her ladyship has kindly consented to give Mrs Horne a trial," he informed Francis once Tillie had been presented. "I venture to think she will be found to be more than satisfactory."

He cast a patronising smile upon the plump little individual he had brought with him, who dropped a curtsey and murmured something only vaguely distinguishable along the lines of doing her best to please. Joanie was sent for and the new cook despatched with the maid, to inspect the kitchens and settle into her temporary position.

Tillie had chosen her usual place on the window seat, to all intents and purposes divorcing herself from these proceedings. But Francis knew his wife too well to be deceived. A certain glint in her eye as she watched and listened to Rodber told him Tillie was assessing the fellow's character to judge how best to tackle him.

As soon as he came to the end of his assurances to the dowager of his confidence in the cook, Tillie drew Rodber's attention, going directly to the heart of the matter.

"We are going to the play this evening, Mr Rodber. One really ought to show support for the company, do you not think? Such a terrible tragedy."

The master of ceremonies at once assumed a mien suitable to the shocking occurrence. "Indeed, indeed, Lady Francis. A dreadful thing. Most distressing to have such a happening practically in our midst. Several of our ladies have been seriously disturbed."

"The girl so young too. And very beautiful, so I have heard?"

The interrogatory note in Tillie's voice invited confidence. Francis's heart soared. His darling wife was rapidly returning to her old self.

Rodber succumbed at once. "Very true indeed, ma'am. Dulcibella Ash was the jewel of the company of The Grand Ferdinando. Such hair! Such a complexion!"

His mother's dry tones entered in. "Are we to understand this peerless creature's acting matched her physical attributes?"

"Ah, your ladyship is in the right of it," said Rodber, shaking a regretful head. "One can scarcely praise the poor girl's prowess in quite the same terms. She was adequate, mind you, quite adequate. Indeed, I venture to think His Majesty himself, had he attended a performance, would have approved her. For you must know she had a — shall we say, a shining quality to her, ma'am, so that one did not notice the lack in her acting, if you understand what I mean."

His enthusiasm was palpable and Francis cast a questioning glance at Tillie. She met his eyes briefly and he read the merriment there, coupled with the unmistakeable gleam of interest he had not seen for some time.

"I understand you perfectly, Mr Rodber," said the dowager, a touch of contempt in her voice. "I take it Miss Ash's admirers were largely of the male sex?"

A dull red crept into Rodber's countenance, but to his credit he did not buckle. A deprecating smile appeared. "Ah, indeed, ma'am, indeed we are a sorry lot."

"It is natural for men to admire a lovely female, do you not think, Sybilla? I protest I am disappointed not to see her myself." Tillie's glance swept the master of ceremonies, her warm smile in place. "I dare say there were gentlemen among your acquaintance who did more than admire, Mr Rodber. Personable actresses do tend to draw a coterie of followers who are eager to waylay them at the stage door."

The master of ceremonies fell straight into the trap, rather to Francis's amusement, his manner becoming confidential as he stepped across to take up a stance near Tillie's position at the window.

"Too true, alas, Lady Francis, too true. Like a moth to a flame indeed when it came to Dulcibella Ash. My lord Charlton was particularly épris and is, I believe, beyond distressed at this horrific taking off."

The name was familiar. Francis cast a look towards his mother. "Isn't he the man who lost his wife a few years back, ma'am? I'm not much acquainted with him, but I believe he frequents White's."

"Quite right, Lord Francis, the very man. He is here with his children, though I believe they commonly reside with an aunt during his absences from home."

"Well, he will not be looking for a new wife amongst a company of players," stated the dowager with a glance at Tillie that spoke volumes.

Surely she did not take Charlton for a suspect? His wife looked thoughtful, but she moved Rodber on.

"Was Lord Charlton favoured, sir?"

The fellow puffed out his cheeks. "I could not say, Lady Francis, indeed I could not. He had rivals enough, that I do know."

"Indeed? Many of them?"

Rodber frowned in concentration. "Let me see now. There is Captain Edgcott. Not that he is presently in the services, but he fought in America, I think."

Tillie looked at once towards Francis and he shook his head. "I don't know him. We must have served in different regiments. George might, if he's in the habit of hobnobbing with the gentry here."

"Ah, you are speaking of Colonel Tretower, sir? An estimable man. We are lucky to have him posted with our militia here. He tells me he has the unenviable task of unmasking the villain of this piece."

"True. Tretower is a friend of mine, sir. He recommended this place to us to speed my wife's recovery."

"Yes, but what of this Captain Edgcott?" Tillie again, ruthlessly dragging the conversation back to the matter at hand. "Is he a young man and personable? Might he attract a female as universally popular as this Dulcibella?"

"You would hardly credit it from his person, but a devil of a fellow with the ladies is Edgcott." Rodber gave a somewhat prim laugh as he turned to the dowager. "If you will forgive me for speaking so free, ma'am."

She waved a dismissive hand in the habitual way she had. "Don't mind me, Mr Rodber. I am not of this namby-pamby generation who refuse to call a spade a spade."

"Indeed, ma'am, indeed, there is a want of candour in these days of mealy-mouthed talk. I myself have been most conscious of the need to curb my natural tendency to talk as I see fit."

No doubt, since he was clearly adept at suiting his utterances to his company. A required attribute for a master of ceremonies, one must suppose. The cynical thought faded as Francis noted Tillie's increasing interest.

"Well, we must certainly include Captain Edgcott. Who else, Mr Rodber?"

The fellow looked startled. "Who else, ma'am? I protest I am at a loss. Include, did you say? Include the captain how, ma'am?"

Tillie raised her brows. "Oh, did I not say? I am trying to discover which of the gentlemen who followed Dulcibella had succeeded with her."

Rodber stared, speechless. Tillie smiled at him. "Come, sir, she was an actress. Sooner or later she was bound to succumb."

"Lady Francis! I declare, ma'am, I do not know what to say."

"Speak openly, man. My daughter-in-law, sir, is not one of these modern misses who pretend ignorance of matters thought to be outside the province of a female."

"No, indeed, ma'am, so I perceive," said Rodber, recovering himself and bestowing an ingratiating smile upon Tillie. "You took me a little by surprise, Lady Francis."

"Curiosity is my besetting sin, Mr Rodber, I confess it freely. Will you satisfy it? Was there any other gentleman quite as assiduous as either Lord Charlton or this Captain Edgcott?"

Rodber gave a rather artificial laugh. "I must say I cannot altogether recall any other." His face changed. "Stay! There is that fellow Paglesham. A young man, perfectly respectable. Ah, and Mr Fawley, rather too old one would have thought for such philandering, but he was used to hang around the stage door some weeks ago. Of course he has gone home now."

"Then we need waste no time upon him. Tell me about Mr Paglesham, if you will."

"Sir Peregrine Paglesham, a mere baronet, and one cannot but wonder how he came by the title. Inclined to give himself airs. I have been obliged to depress his pretensions more than once, but I will admit him to be a comely enough young man."

"How young, sir?"

"Oh, five or six and twenty. Thirty at the most."

Himself only a year or two past thirty, Francis could not help lifting a quizzical eyebrow at Tillie. To a man of Rodber's age, he dared say thirty might appear young. But it was quite old enough to impress a youthful girl like this actress.

Tillie evidently thought the same. "He sounds to be just the sort of fellow to interest Dulcibella. Is he a bachelor?"

"Indeed he is, ma'am. I should doubt of his being able to afford a wife." Rodber gave a discreet cough. "I do not mean to denigrate the fellow, but one cannot help but notice a certain — shall we say shabbiness? — to his vestments on occasion."

Tillie's sharpened gaze told Francis his wife's interest was, for some reason he could not fathom, thoroughly aroused by this, but it was his mother who pounced.

"Do you mean frayed cuffs and a threadbare coat, Mr Rodber? Or are his clothes merely of poor cut and inferior material?"

The visitor threw up his hands, approaching the dowager's chair. "Heavens, no, ma'am, I have given you a false impression of the man if that is what you suppose. No, no indeed. Nothing of that nature. It is merely what one might call a *je ne sais quoi* about his clothes."

"Well, if you don't know, I cannot imagine why you should say they are shabby," came the dowager's tart response.

Rodber bowed in a deferent way. "You are in the right of it, ma'am, I should not have spoken. In my position, however, one acquires an instinct for these things."

"You condemn a man on instinct?"

"No, no, you mistake, ma'am. I express myself badly indeed." Which was all too true, if Francis was to judge by his mother's irritation. But the fellow's pomposity peeped through nevertheless. "It is perhaps a sense rather of a dingy sort of background. Sir Peregrine lodges in one of the less salubrious streets of the town, and although his dress is of quality, it is obvious to me that it is well worn, a trifle stale."

He wrinkled his nose as if the victim of his criticism was a bad smell. Francis wondered what Tillie made of this and, glancing across, saw what he thought of as her absent look in her face, as if her mind were elsewhere. A pang smote him. She had worn the look for weeks past. Or had she? No, not this look. That one had been absent, but empty. This was Tillie at work in her head. She had come back to him indeed.

Without thought, he moved across to her and she looked up, blinking. A smile came and she lifted her hand and brushed a finger across her lips as if to enjoin his silence. Francis's heart warmed. Remarkable how she read his mind as well as he was able to read her expressions. He had forgotten, in the distresses of this period, how attuned they had become in the relatively short time they had been married.

Tillie turned her attention back to Rodber, who had fallen silent under the dowager's sceptical gaze. "Do you think Sir Peregrine is in hopes of securing an advantageous alliance? Is that perhaps his purpose in coming to Weymouth?"

The master of ceremonies returned, with obvious relief, to Tillie's less intimidating company. "I am certain of it, Lady Francis. Since His Majesty chose to honour our little town, we have indeed opened our doors to an increasing number of fashionable persons. Otherwise I dare say he might have chosen Brighton."

"Or Brighton might be a little above his touch if, as you say, he is purse-pinched?"

"Oh, I think we may afford all and more of the amenities provided in Brighton, ma'am. Especially with our particular royal patronage."

It was plain Rodber was offended by the suggestion his little 'kingdom' was inferior to that patronised by the Prince of Wales rather than his father the King, despite the undoubted popularity of the former amongst the fashionable set.

"For my part," cut in the dowager, "I am well suited with your amenities, Mr Rodber. I should hate to be racketing about Brighton at my time of life."

This concession sent the fellow back to her at once and the remainder of his visit was enlivened by a recital of the entertainments on offer and a hope the ladies would take advantage of the next fine day to sample the sea-bathing, which, he ventured to say, was as fine and invigorating as any on the whole of the South Coast.

The moment the parlour door shut behind him, Francis wasted no time.

"What about this fellow he talks of, Tillie? Are you inclined to add him to your list of suspects?"

His mother snorted. "What, only because this Peregrine does not meet with Rodber's approval?"

"Not for that reason, Sybilla, but his situation certainly fits the circumstances of the murder. According to Cecile, Dulcie may have been fooled by a promise of marriage."

"You contrived to meet her then? This Cecile, I mean."

"Indeed I did, and had but just come back from a walk in her company when I heard Rodber was with you. But about Sir Peregrine: if he is hanging out for a rich wife, he would scarcely take poor Dulcibella with her forty guineas. A pregnant actress too. Unthinkable he would see her right if it was his seduction that put her in the family way."

"Is that all the necklace realised? Forty guineas?"

"She pawned it, Fan, she did not sell it. And Dulcie only took half of the money with her."

"But you cannot be putting this Peregrine fellow at the top of your list, Ottilia," the dowager protested, "without discovering if he did indeed succeed with the girl. You have only Rodber's word for it after all that he was courting her."

Tillie smiled. "True, and I had not got as far as that. Merely, I wished to widen the net beyond the members of the company."

"You've done that all right," Francis commented on a dry note. "You may add at least four of these wretched followers."

"Three. I think we may discount the man Fawley, but Lord Charlton and Captain Edgcott will bear investigation. I must contrive to meet all of them."

"There is no difficulty about that, Ottilia. You have only to come to the Assembly Rooms and you are bound to run into the lot."

"But not today." Francis had no intention of allowing Tillie to overdo it. "You'll rest until dinner if we are to go and see this infernal performance."

His mother's delicate brows rose. "Oh, yes, I had forgotten Ottilia spoke of it to Rodber. So we are to go to the theatre?"

"Tillie insists. Hemp has gone to procure a box. Using your name, may I add, since my darling wife does not scruple to employ it for her own ends."

The dowager laughed. "Why not, if it helps?"

"Well, I want to get as close to the stage as I can, Sybilla."

"You will miss the colonel then, unless he reappears before the dinner hour."

Tillie smote her thigh. "I had forgot George." She looked at Francis. "If he is not back in time, Fan, you must leave a note for him, for I must speak with him."

The dowager sat up. "That means you found something out from this *émigré* of his."

"Of no little importance, Sybilla. If Dulcie's purse of guineas was not on her person, it may provide a vital clue."

Having finished his ablutions and tied his hair back in its queue, George was half dressed and in the act of adjusting the stock about his neck when his lieutenant knocked and popped his head round the door.

"Come in, Sullivan, I'm almost done."

His second-in-command, fully dressed and freshly shaved, if a trifle bleary-eyed, entered and closed the door, nodding at Marsh who was brushing George's scarlet coat. "I've four men waiting, sir, and I've sent Puckeridge off with two."

George moved to the bed and sat down to pull on his boots. "You told him to search the houses even if the villagers deny all knowledge of this purse?"

"Yes, sir, though it may take him some time to find out which of them actually got to the coffin first."

"That's why the search," said George, tugging at his left boot. "You don't suppose they'll tell him if they took the damn thing, do you?"

Sullivan gave a short laugh. "Hardly, sir. Seems to me, though, whoever got there first would have been too shocked to go stealing a purse from the body."

"Well, someone did, my boy." George stood up and settled his feet into the boots. "Roffey is adamant there was no purse in the reticule when the body got to his surgery, so where is it?"

He allowed his batman to assist him into the red coat with its multiple trimmings of gold braid and began fastening the brass buttons, casting a glance at his junior, who was frowning. "What's on your mind, Sullivan?"

"Just wondering why the murderer would take it, sir? Seems a bit of a risk. It was bound to be discovered that she had it, and if there was only a matter of twenty guineas in it…"

"That's a lot of money for most, my friend. You could purchase a horse for that. We've no reason to think our man is wealthy enough to ignore it."

"Not if it's one of the players, sir, no." Sullivan gave his chief a dubious glance. "You do know they were performing last evening. I'll warrant none of them will be up yet."

"Precisely, Sullivan. I want to catch them unawares. My shako, Marsh."

His junior looked from the furred and braided headgear to George. "You've not breakfasted yet, sir."

"We'll have it when we get back. I can't stand eating on the run. Besides, I've had coffee. Have you eaten?"

"Just coffee, sir." He grinned. "I'm barely awake yet. Couldn't swallow a morsel."

George laughed. "Wait 'til you're on bivouac, my boy, with a battle in the offing. You'll eat at any hour and sleep on the run instead."

"God help me!"

"Pray the French don't invade and He won't have to. Let's be off."

By the time George and his band, all armed, arrived at the players' lodging, a few hardy souls were already trailing down towards the beach, attired in the customary loose wrappers which were acceptable wear preparatory to bathing. George's imperative knocking with the hilt of his sword brought the landlady, puffing with effort, her eyes popping at sight of the scarlet and white soldiery.

"Gracious heaven! Is it you, Colonel? Oh, dearie me, whatever is it now?"

"Stand aside, madam. We are here on a mission."

The woman's ample form remained in the doorway. "Mission? Oh, no! You've come to arrest them!"

"Stand aside, I said."

The sharp tone had an effect and the landlady fell back. George entered the house and led his men directly up the stairs. In the vestibule, he stood back and signed to his junior.

Sullivan turned to the men. "Knock 'em up, boys!"

The four militiamen at once proceeded through the house, two going directly to the second floor. They worked in pairs, banging on the doors with the butts of muskets and shouting to the inmates to get up and come on out.

Leaving his junior to supervise the attack, George opened the door to the breakfast parlour and looked in. It was empty, but the fire had been lit and covers laid for breakfast. Satisfied, he left the door wide and waited for the players to appear. He disliked using the tactic, but it undoubtedly worked to take his suspects by surprise.

First to appear around the corner of the corridor was an irate Mrs Ferdinand, the colourful huge shawl George had seen before flung around her shoulders and a frilled nightcap tied around her chin. She stopped short at the sight of him and threw up her head.

"Colonel Tretower! Heavens above, sir, what is the meaning of this rude invasion?"

George bowed and indicated the parlour. "Go in, if you please, ma'am."

"I do not stir until you tell me what this is all about."

"My reason is sufficient, Mrs Ferdinand, and you will know it when I am ready to tell you."

He spoke with every evidence of politeness but his words did not appease the impresario's wife. She stared at him in silence until The Grand Ferdinando himself was heard protesting at a roar in the corridor behind.

"This is an outrage! An outrage, I tell you! Don't jostle me, you looby, how dare you?"

A sound of exasperation escaped Mrs Ferdinand's lips and she turned to call out. "Arthur, come here, for heaven's sake! There is no need for you to add to the cacophony."

An apt description, for the voices coming from every direction were growing in volume as one player after another came into sight, variously garbed in night attire with dressing-gowns or coats sketchily thrown over. Two of the actors staggering down the stairs had managed to tug on breeches and George at once resolved to have them turn out their pockets at need.

The complaints were understandably voluble as Mrs Ferdinand, evidently accepting the inevitable, herded them into the parlour. George, standing back at the door and busy counting heads, paid little heed to the chattering hordes, speaking one atop the other.

"What the deuce is going on?"

"Has the colonel run mad?"

"I've never been so insulted … treated like a criminal indeed!"

"Move, can't you, Lewis? I'm trying to get to the fire."

"What we need is breakfast."

"What in God's name is the time?"

And then a straggler halted, drawing George's attention with a flare in the dark eyes raised to his face. Recognition hit and an uncomfortable combination of guilt and want swept through him as his gaze took in the raven locks falling about her shoulders and the long white nightgown under a light wrap, bare toes peeping beneath.

"Colonel?"

It was accented in French and husky. George struggled to respond with his usual insouciance. "*Mademoiselle?*"

"Why do you do this?"

He hesitated. He had formed the scheme upon receipt of the information she had shared with Ottilia. She was bound to realise it in due course and it was evident she was already furious. He stiffened his resolve. Duty came first. He would be obliged to explain himself, but not now.

"That you will learn presently, *mademoiselle*. Go in, if you please."

He kept to English deliberately, refusing to allow his partiality to permit him the indulgence of treating her differently to the rest.

She lifted her chin, a defiant little gesture of pride that could not but touch him, and stalked into the parlour to join the others. George followed her in and raised his voice.

"Silence, if you please!"

It took several moments for the milling players to settle into quiet, one shushing another. Mrs Ferdinand made no attempt to assert her authority. Seated in her chair by the fire, she eyed George with ill-concealed contempt. God help him, he was on his own with these unruly players, it seemed.

"Thank you," he said, when at last the murmurs ceased. "I must request you all to remain in this room until I give you leave to move out of it."

The battery of eyes shifted, looking from him to their fellows and back again. George checked the faces and found one missing.

"Where is your young Jasper?"

"Likely out as usual," offered the dark lean man. Rob, was it?

But at that moment, George heard Sullivan's voice.

"Come along, sir, there's no sense in dragging your feet. All the others have done as they were asked."

"Damn you, get off me!"

The impresario, who was surrounded and had, George now realised, been fending off his people's questions, now thrust his way to the door, emitting his customary roar.

"Jasper, get in here, you slothful muck-worm! If the rest of us have to suffer, you can too. Get in here at once, boy!"

The young man had already appeared around the corner, Sullivan at his back with one hand firmly grasping the collar of the fellow's nightgown. Jasper was red-eyed, pale with lack of sleep and sullen, his hair tousled and his bare legs moving at a stagger.

Ferdinand grabbed him as he reached the door and thrust him into the room. "Wretched boy! If you aren't arrested this day, it will be a miracle."

Jasper all but fell into the arms of the huge man — Aisling, was it? — who lost no time in throwing him off so that he staggered into the others and was passed around like a rumpled parcel, the players collapsing into laughter until Mrs Ferdinand called a halt.

"Sit him down, for heaven's sake, and stop behaving like a set of children in the nursery. Settle down, all of you."

George left them to it and signalled to Sullivan, lowering his voice.

"The men are carrying out the search?"

"I set them to it the moment we had them all out, sir. Except that young rascal." A grin creased his junior's face as he nodded towards the players in the parlour, who were finding seats and settling where they could. "Tried to hide and got himself tangled in his bed-curtains, silly young chub."

George threw up his eyes. "Go and supervise, Sullivan. I don't want them throwing the rooms into total disorder. They can hunt without making a mess."

"Right, sir."

His lieutenant sped off and George was about to go into the parlour when he heard footsteps labouring up the stairs from below. Moving to the bannister, he looked over. The landlady was toiling up, burdened with a heavily loaded tray, an unknown man behind her, armed with a massive teapot in one hand and a large coffee pot in the other.

Reaching the top, the woman halted, eyeing George with fear and doubt.

"I've brought tea and coffee, sir. That's all right, is it?"

George gave permission at once, feeling that it might do something towards appeasing the players for being routed out of their beds at an early hour. The response was gratifying.

"Annie, you treasure!"

"God, the woman reads minds! I'm gasping for a cup of tea."

"Move, Aisling, so Annie can set it on the table."

"Any chance of a bun or something? I'm starving."

George remained outside the parlour while the hubbub of setting out the accoutrements for the beverages ensued. The large man, having set down his pots, came out again, hesitating as he looked at George, who raised his brows.

"Yes? You're the landlord, I take it?"

The man nodded, touching his forelock. "That's right, sir. Annie — me wife, that is — has got hot rolls ready. Can I bring 'em for the company, sir?"

"By all means."

With a word of thanks, the man hurried off and was soon followed by his wife. George moved a little away from the door, listening to the sounds from above and along the corridor that betokened the search was underway. He hoped with fervency that Sullivan managed to stop the men from making a pig's ear of the business. The last thing he needed was a barrage of complaints about bedchambers having been rendered uninhabitable, although his men could scarcely turn them over without making something of a shambles. Well, if they did, they did. It was in a worthwhile cause and he would just have to endure the consequences.

His unruly mind slipped to the single consequence he had failed to anticipate. How the devil he was to make any sort of headway with Cecile after this was a bugbear of the worst order. Especially as he must needs question her further, since her discussion with Ottilia showed she clearly knew a great deal more than she had admitted at the outset.

The owners of the property reappeared in a few minutes with a batch of new-baked rolls, butter and pots of jam and honey, accompanied by a large fruit cake. The players, already occupied in drinking, fell upon the proffered food with a good deal of relish. George found his stomach grumbling, but when the matronly female they called Hilde came across to ask him if he wished to partake of the refreshments, George refused.

"Thank you, ma'am, but not on duty."

Reminded of his purpose, she gave him a questioning look.

"What is this duty, Colonel? Where are your men?"

George looked her in the eye. "Searching your rooms, ma'am."

Her gaze widened and she let out a gasp. Then she turned back into the parlour and burst out with the news on a note of screeching hysteria.

"They are searching our rooms! Turning the place upside down!"

An exaggeration, but what could one expect from players? The instant cacophony of protest and comment that broke out presently returned the atmosphere to one of suspenseful anticipation that gave George some satisfaction. He did not want them complacent. He wanted them scared enough for the murderer to make a slip and give himself away. If indeed he was amongst them.

Within a short time, the men hunting the first floor rooms arrived with fists full of purses. George signed to them to wait out of sight and at last entered the parlour.

Ignoring the players, who rapidly fell silent to stare at him, he looked around the room. The large table was scattered with cups, plates and the rest of the paraphernalia brought in by the owners. He spotted a smaller table in a corner and headed for it, Lewis and Wat moving hastily out of his way.

Watched by his audience, George felt rather as if he were on the stage himself as he hefted the table and carried it nearer to the door, setting it down in an open space. For the first time this morning, a faint amusement lightened his sombre mood as he recognised his action was inducing both fear and bewilderment. Leaving the table in place, he left the room again and was gratified to see Sullivan coming down the stairs from the floor above, the two men detailed to search those rooms behind him, similarly carrying purses.

"Is this the lot?"

"All they could find, sir."

"Right. Have them set them all down on the table there, Sullivan."

With which he went back into the parlour and watched the reactions as the men came in and dumped their finds in a pile on the table.

"That's my purse!"

"Damnation, they've taken all our purses!"

He lost track as Sullivan came up to murmur close. "Sir!"

George kept his eyes on the men's work. "What is it?"

"We found the stash of guineas among the dead girl's things."

"The purse?"

"No, sir, I mean the rest of the hoard. But I wouldn't let the men bring it."

"Quite right. We're not concerned with that. Only with what was in the purse."

"Well, I counted it and it's all there, sir, so no one's had a go at that."

George had no chance to answer. An arctic voice interrupted him.

"Colonel Tretower!"

He turned to find the matriarch at his elbow. She was last seen in her chair by the fire, but the appearance of the purses had roused her to evident wrath.

"What in the world is all this, Colonel?"

He did not flinch under her fiery stare. Nodding at Sullivan, who stepped back, he moved to the table again. "It is, as you can see, ma'am, a collection of purses."

"Yes, but why? What do you want with them?"

"I am going to check each one, ma'am, and its owner may watch me do it."

He could not forbear glancing at Cecile, who was sitting at the big table, her pose rigid and her features tight with strain. She caught his eye and flashed him a look of deep reproach. The sense of guilt swamped him all over again. Wrenching his gaze away, he buckled the feeling down. Duty first. Presently he would deal with the aftermath.

He seized the first purse that came to hand and held it up. "Whose is this, if you please?"

None responded at once. And then the little fellow Wat stepped forward with obvious reluctance, raising his hand.

"It's mine."

George beckoned him over, opened the purse and emptied its contents onto the table. The coins were of small denominations, only one golden guinea among them. George scooped up the coins, slid them back into the purse and handed it to the obviously relieved Wat. George gave a grim smile as he reflected the fellow must think himself now safe from suspicion. Let him think it. It was possible it was so, if Dulcie's purse was found in amongst this lot.

He picked up a second one and the girl Kate scurried across, making a grab for it. George held it out of reach.

"Not so fast, ma'am."

"But it's mine! You've no right to look at what's inside!"

George spoke on a gentler note than he had yet used. "I'm sorry, miss, but I am investigating a murder. Or had you forgotten?"

Her mouth fell open and a look of horror entered her eyes, mingling with despair. Her voice became a squeak. "But you can't think I killed Dulcie!"

"I am making no accusations, Miss Kate. I am merely trying to ascertain what these purses contain and who they belong to. Now then."

Without further ado, he emptied the purse onto the table. A few coins fell out, along with a crumpled handkerchief, a little gold ring, and several silver containers. Kate scrabbled to seize them all up, dissolving into tears. George made no attempt to stop her, merely handing over the purse so she could stuff everything back inside. No doubt the little hoard was of personal significance, but it was of no use to him.

The next purse belonged to the impresario, who took a high hand and demanded whether George expected to find Dulcie's severed finger in it. A remark which drew several sniggers and an admonition from his wife.

"Stop it, Arthur! Is this humiliation not enough without you making foolish jokes?"

The purse was full, but not with Dulcie's missing coins. George returned his property to Mr Ferdinand and the exercise carried on. The players rapidly became bored, those who had their purses back recovering their sangfroid sufficiently to be able to return to refreshing themselves. Talk became general as the pile diminished and George's disappointment grew.

At last every purse was claimed. Dulcie's golden guineas had not materialised. Either his men had not found all the purses or the murderer was cleverer than he had hoped. He recalled that Aisling and the fellow Rob were wearing breeches. Both had already claimed a purse, but that did not preclude them having Dulcie's.

"Sullivan!"

His lieutenant stepped back into the parlour. He had waited outside the door with the men at ease in the corridor. "Sir?"

"You see those two gentleman wearing breeches?"

The fellow Rob's head shot up and Aisling's gaze widened, his ears going red.

"I do, sir."

"Turn out their pockets for them."

Rob leapt from his chair, his cheeks darkening as his eyes sparked. "What the devil is it now? If you think I'm letting that fellow dig into my breeches —"

Sullivan was practically in his face. "Turn out your pockets, sir, or I'll do it for you."

Rob glared with defiance, but the man Aisling hastily thrust his hands into his breeches and pulled his pockets inside out, showing them empty.

"Nothing, see. Nowt in 'em, sir."

The lieutenant nodded at him. "Thank you, sir. Now then," he added, turning back to the other.

"Oh, for God's sake turn them out, Rob, and let's be done with this farce."

This from the middle-aged Lewis. Jasper, seated now at the table near the window after recovering his own purse, bare of anything but a couple of small coins, began to giggle.

Rob cast him a glance of dislike and folded his arms, glaring at Sullivan. "You want to know what's in them, you turn them out."

His junior glanced at George, who nodded. With obvious reluctance, Sullivan plunged a hand into one pocket and brought out a handkerchief. Searching next in the other, his own face a trifle high-coloured, he came out empty-handed.

"Ha! Disappointed, eh? Well, you can't win 'em all, captain."

"I'm a lieutenant, sir," snapped Sullivan, retreating.

"Now what?" demanded Mrs Ferdinand, looking decidedly triumphant. "I presume you did not find what you were looking for?"

"No, ma'am, unfortunately we did not. However, the exercise was necessary." George cast a look across the players' faces, most of which looked relieved rather than showing the contempt evident in both Rob and the matriarch. "You will be glad to learn no doubt that suspicion does not rest solely with the company. That does not mean any of you are out of count, but you may rest easier for knowing that I did not find the purse I was seeking." He bowed. "I apologise for the inconvenience. I have no further need of you. However —" He paused, looking towards Cecile. "If you will be good enough to give me a moment of your time, *mademoiselle*, I have a few matters with which you may be able to assist."

All eyes turned to Cecile, whose dagger glance was unlikely to be missed by anyone. Mrs Ferdinand intervened.

"If you mean to interrogate the child —"

"Ma'am, I do not interrogate," George snapped, losing his grip on his temper for once. "Nor have I any intention of subjecting *mademoiselle* to annoyance."

He became aware his clipped tone was having a deleterious effect upon the company who were, to a man, staring with ill-concealed surprise or dismay, which was not helpful if he wanted to get any sense out of individuals he might have to question again later. Moreover, he did not need Cecile too frightened to speak to him. He tried for a milder note.

"Since Miss Benoit knew Dulcibella Ash better than anyone here, she is best placed to give me the information I need."

Mrs Ferdinand looked from him to Cecile and back again. "Then I insist upon being present at this interview."

It was the last thing George wished for, but he saw no way of preventing it. "Certainly, ma'am, if *mademoiselle* desires your presence."

He looked at Cecile as he spoke and found her watching him, her gaze narrowed and a furrow between her brows. Was she wondering what he wanted? She rose and came not to him, but to the matriarch. She spoke in a low tone, in French, but

George just caught the words under the murmurs that had started up again among the players.

"I will see him alone, madame."

"It is scarcely convenable, my dear. A young girl like you and in a state of undress. You ought to have a chaperon."

"Who is to know outside of our people? Besides, he is a militiaman, madame, and I do not think he proposes to make advances."

Mrs Ferdinand eyed George and he attempted to appear unconscious. Then she turned back to Cecile. "I don't like it, but I see you are determined. Are there secrets you have to tell him?"

Cecile's cheeks flushed a delicate shade. "Perhaps."

"Well, I will not pry. Dulcie's ugly demise is punishment enough, poor girl."

Relieved, but a little apprehensive of what Cecile might say to him, George led the way out of the parlour, crossed to the room designated as the players' workroom and opened the door.

"*Mademoiselle?*"

Cecile passed him with lowered eyes, her small figure stiff with resentment. George braced.

Smarting with embarrassment and hurt, Cecile could barely endure the sight of the colonel's grave countenance. Yet his very presence was disturbing to her in a way she had forgotten in the press of anxiety and grief. She determined no inkling of that should show in her face and moved to the window, looking out into the street below where the usual straggle of early risers were heading towards the Esplanade and the beach or the fish market.

All too aware of the brooding colonel somewhere behind her, Cecile waited for him to speak. When he did not, she felt compelled to turn and confront him.

He was standing by the mantel, leaning an arm along it, but his gaze met hers across the plethora of grouped chairs between. Cecile could read nothing in it, but there was expectance in his silence.

"*Eh bien, monsieur?*"

"Won't you sit down?"

He nodded towards the sofa, ranged to catch the heat from the small fire in the grate. It was becoming chill in the mornings and Madame Ferdinand had requested of Annie that fires be laid.

Cecile did not choose to be disadvantaged by his standing over her. She threaded a way to a position behind the sofa and faced him across its barrier, finding its high back a useful grip to prevent her shaking hands from being noticed.

The colonel's eyes did not leave her face and a muscle twitched in his cheek. He switched to French. "You may as well say what you have to say, *mademoiselle*. I believe you have reason to be angry."

That was enough to loosen her tongue. "I am betrayed."

He flinched but he did not speak. Perversely, Cecile's righteous fury began to dissipate. She whipped it up again.

"I told this Madame Fan of Dulcie's purse only yesterday and you use my words in such a way? How does it make me to look, *monsieur?* I am now a traitor to my people and if I will confess it, I must lose the only friends I have in the world."

His face changed and he sucked in a breath. "I had not thought of it in quite those terms."

Cecile released the sofa back and banged closed fists on it instead. "Naturally you do not. You think only of your need, your duty. Oh, I know how it is, *monsieur*. It is duty which drives the informers to denounce my father, no? A man who did no harm in the world, but much good. But duty needs sacrifices, yes?"

There was a flare at his eyes. "Your father's fate bears no comparison to these circumstances, *mademoiselle*. I seek to right a wrong here."

"So also did they. Or so they believed. That makes it not just or fair. Nor is it just that you took my words for this — this humiliation."

He flung away from the mantel, an expression of severity in his face though his tone was quiet, if clipped. "What would you have me do, *mademoiselle*? Ask them to show me their purses? Do you think if one of your players had stolen Dulcie's gold that he would produce it for my inspection?"

Ignoring the bulk of this very reasonable demand, Cecile pounced on the one thing that caught her attention. "How do you know it was stolen?"

"It wasn't in her reticule. I checked with the doctor."

"But how do you know she did not give it to the man?"

"Whether she gave it or he stole it, the point is whether he has it, is it not?"

Triumph lit in her breast. "But he has it not, that is seen. You did not find it."

"Unfortunately not."

"Then you have wasted your time and embarrassed me to no purpose," she accused with relish.

His eyes, usually so mild, kindled. "Is that all you care for? I thought your grief was genuine, Cecile, but it appears I was mistaken if it is nothing to you that Dulcie's murderer is caught."

Heat flooded her face and her bosom raged with a fury she knew was born of guilt. Her voice turned husky. "You have no right to say this of me."

For a moment the spark held. Then it died out of his eyes and he sighed, throwing out a hand. "No, I have not. I apologise." His hand turned, the palm now an invitation. "Come. Sit, if you please. Let us begin again."

She felt grudging, but her innate sense of justice would not permit her to maintain her recalcitrant attitude. She came around the sofa and, pulling her wrap about her, sat on the edge of it. Looking up, she found the colonel's large frame all too intimidating and pointed to the chair opposite as, without thinking, she switched to English.

"Please to sit also, *monsieur*. It is uncomfortable for me to have you tower like this."

He dropped into the indicated chair and grinned suddenly. A sliver like the shock of ice shot through Cecile's veins.

"All too apt a word, Cecile. My name is Tretower."

It was a mild coincidence, but she could not prevent the tiny smile. His use of her name had an odd tingling effect upon her senses.

"But I wish you will call me George."

She did not at once avail herself of the invitation, though the name echoed in her head as he said it. She knew she would find it difficult to manage the hard "G" and was conscious of a fleeting hope he would not mind her using the French pronunciation.

"It is for this you wished to see me?"

The humour died out of his face. "That, and a few details you neglected to tell me before."

Her warmer feeling towards him vanished. "Yes, you would have me betray Dulcie."

131

He eyed her in a fashion she could not read. "You set an inordinate store by treachery and betrayal, *mademoiselle*. I dare say you have reason enough."

She did not know whether to be annoyed or placated. "It is of all things what I detest."

"Understandably. But I must beg you to consider this. The more you withhold, the more difficult you make it for me to discover who killed your friend."

Again she could not prevent herself from smiling. "*Eh bien*, it is a difficulty for me, Monsieur Georges, that your common sense makes me to become hot inside when I know the words you speak ought instead to make me reasonable."

He laughed, the lines creasing at the corners of his eyes in a way she found peculiarly attractive. "I am sorry if that is the case. I'm afraid my commonplace mind jumps always to the reasonable response."

She was conscious of softening within her. "I do not think your mind is common, Georges. I would say it is keen."

To her amusement he reddened. "Well, I must thank you for that concession at least."

"Concession?"

His mouth twisted in a wry fashion. "I had not looked for compliments from you, Cecile, matters being as they are."

All vestiges of resentment had left her, rather to her own surprise. "But did you not say we must begin again?"

"I did and I am glad you are willing."

"*Peut-être.*"

"I'll take perhaps. May I ask you what I wish to know?"

She was touched that he made it a request. There was no denying he was a gentleman in the true sense, even if duty forced him into a tougher mould. Truth to tell, she was not wholly averse from the strength that mould depicted. He was a man one might rely on, that was seen.

"I am ready, *monsieur*. Ask as you will."

He cocked an eyebrow. "French or English?"

"As you please. I am good with English. Madame has made me learn and Dulcie..." She faltered, drew a breath and spoke in a firm tone. "Dulcie has helped me. She is very much my friend, even that her conduct is against those principles I have myself learned from a child."

Why she told him Cecile did not know. It slipped into her mind she could not bear him to think her morals were of the ilk of the players, although she did not despise them for it. It became imperative to make this clear.

"I would not have you to suppose I blame Dulcie. Nor the others. Even the players who behave without care of their reputation, like Jasper. This life of the vagabond, it is difficult for them. They live strangely and do not have opportunity as do people who stay in one place. *Alors*, and men, they have a bad idea of the *actrice*, you understand? Even that they do not fall, the men suppose they will do so and they do not scruple to make the seduction."

To her surprise, George made no derogatory remark. "That's exactly what I wanted to ask you, Cecile. I have learned of several gentlemen, followers we call them, who favoured Dulcie. It is possible one of these seduced her. Is there anything you remember that might help me? Anything at all. Something she said perhaps? A name she may have mentioned. Or did you ever see her leaving the theatre with a man?"

Flashing images sang through Cecile's head. Without pause for thought she caught at them, spilling their content.

"Ah, *oui, y voilà*. The one with the nose large, I think of the military as you, but he wears no uniform. A big laugh he has and makes words well so that Dulcie is flattered. Once I heard him, but Dulcie does not answer, only blushing and she hurries me away. She whispers then that he tries to make her go with him but she will not."

She looked across to find George intent, frowning. "When was this, do you recall?"

She shifted her shoulders, unable to place the time. "I do not remember *précisement*, but perhaps some weeks since."

"Did Dulcie meet him at any time after that? He is here in Weymouth at the moment."

Startled, she stared. "I cannot say. If she does, she does not tell me. But he is here? What man is he then?"

"Captain Edgcott, though I should doubt of his ever having seen active service."

There was contempt in the tone and Cecile's interest caught. "Ah, you do not like this man."

Surprise flickered in his eyes. "No, I don't. He's a Captain Sharp, if I don't miss my guess, as ready to inveigle young men into dangerous play as to use his dubious military title to flatter and seduce women. I should be delighted to pin this murder on him."

Cecile warmed to him, the more pulled by this evidence of right thinking. The man had integrity. She could not let it pass nevertheless.

"*Alors*, it is not proven Dulcie was with him at all."

"No, more's the pity. Anyone else?"

She smiled. "But yes, *mon colonel*. You have said, no? Dulcie, she is *si belle* and the gentlemen will try for her, is it not so?"

He gave a sigh that sounded quite exasperated. "Unfortunately, it is so. Can you think of any individual in particular other than Edgcott?"

Another flash of memory cut in. "I do not know the name, but Dulcie speaks of one who is kind, as she says. Perhaps older? I remember she said if she was of a better birth perhaps she becomes *belle-mère* — I do not know the English word."

"Stepmother?" He snapped his fingers. "Charlton! Yes, I understand he was an admirer. A good fellow. Not my first choice for a murderer, I must say."

She smiled at that. "You would say this wicked one cannot be a man you like? In this case, Georges, how will I bear it if it is one of our people?"

His brows snapped together. "These players? You are fond of one of the men?"

Quick to hear the note of jealousy, Cecile's pulses quickened. Then this colonel liked her more than a little. She opted for truth. "Not in such a way, Georges, as you think."

"You don't know what I think."

She met his eyes, unblinking and direct. "Yes, I know it."

He did not drop his gaze, but his colour darkened slowly and a rueful look overspread his countenance. "Feminine intuition, I suppose?"

She did not answer, feeling perfectly certain for the briefest moment that George Tretower was her future. And then the certainty left her and her heart hammered a rapid retreat as she dropped her gaze. She felt acutely conscious of his maleness, all at once remembering her unconventional state of undress. Unable to help herself, she folded her arms across her breasts and pushed back into the sofa.

He sat in frowning silence for a moment, and she watched him from under her lashes, taking an odd pleasure in the strength in face and body both. His figure looked well in the regimentals. She could not help wondering how he would look in civilian clothes. Decidedly inviting, she would guess. She banished her inappropriate thoughts as he spoke again.

"Did you ever hear of a fellow named Paglesham? Or perhaps only Sir Peregrine? Not well to do, but assiduous in pursuing Dulcie, as I understand it."

Puzzled, she stared at him. "How is it you know these things?"

He gave one of his sudden grins. "I am indebted to Ottilia — Madame Fan as you call her — for the information. She found it out from Rodber. You know of the master of ceremonies?"

She shrugged. "I know only the players, *monsieur*. I do not mingle with any other. Madame Ferdinand she keeps me close, you understand? She does not wish that any should know me for a player. When Monsieur Ferdinand he tries to make me go upon the boards, it is madame who tells him I will not. It is not my wish to do so, and I have said, but only madame makes him to stop."

His brows were drawn together as he studied her, as it seemed to Cecile.

"She supported you because of your rank? She did not think it fitting?"

Cecile gave an unhappy little sigh. "She thinks one day perhaps someone will come for me. She says it cannot be that all my family are taken. We travel, you understand, and she hears much news. Madame Ferdinand says there are more who escape, *émigrés* as you say. She supposes one may look for me."

"But you don't think it, do you?"

His voice was curiously harsh and Cecile all but flinched. She answered with truth.

"*Non.* Me, I think all are gone. I know of my father, my brothers, cousins, all. Men, women, children. They do not care, the canaille. They take everyone. That is why my mother tries to save me. She has seen what happens in the chateaux nearby. *Immediatement*, she packs for me a valise and she dresses me in the guise of a servant and she takes me to the players. *Me voici.*"

"And thank God you are here, Cecile."

The low-toned comment was accompanied by a hand put out towards her. She laid hers into it and it closed warmth about her fingers. She did not dare look into his eyes until the pricking in her own subsided. He did not say a word more, only held her hand with gentleness and she was again struck by his innate kindness. Impelled, she looked up at last.

"You are not a man upon whom this duty sits well, Georges. You do not like it that you must catch a murderer, *n'est-ce pas?*"

His grip tightened all at once and he let her go. "I don't at all. Nor am I equipped for the task. That's why I asked my friend Fanshawe to bring his wife here. She is practically an expert."

Astonished, Cecile stared at him. "How can this be?"

He grinned. "Ottilia will have it she falls into these things by accident. But if you ask Francis, he is convinced she hunts them out by some sort of mysterious sixth sense."

She was amused. "But she is a lady."

"An unusual lady. Rather like you. One does not expect to find an aristocrat among a company of players."

Shock threaded through her. "How is it you know I am of them?"

"I know your class has been targeted. At this time I believe the citizens of France are prepared to denounce anyone at all, but they were originally after the elite."

"It is true. You will not speak of it if I tell you my name?"

"Certainly not, if you will entrust it to me."

"I am Mademoiselle de Benoit-Falaise. My father he was le Marquis de Falaise. But now I am only Cecile Benoit, you understand."

"I understand perfectly." He rose and gave her a deep bow. "*Mademoiselle.*"

Cecile took his proffered hand and rose to her feet, feeling ridiculously as if she was in a ballroom instead of bare-toed in a shabby lodging in a seaside resort.

George smiled, that warm smile that crinkled the corners of his eyes and sent a flush of heat through her veins all over again.

"I must go." He half turned and then frowned, snapping his fingers. "The deuce! You did not say if you remembered anything of Sir Peregrine Paglesham."

Regretfully, Cecile shook her head. "I do not think so. They were many, these men who admired Dulcie."

The colonel looked a trifle cynical. "So I would suppose, given the general praise for Dulcibella's beauty."

A faint stirring of dismay prompted her tongue. "And you, *mon colonel*? You have been in the theatre, is it not? Have you also an admiration for the beautiful Dulcibella?"

His expression softened and a look positively tender entered his eyes.

"I hardly noticed her for hunting instead for a dark-haired beauty with speaking eyes who made no appearance upon the stage, much to my disappointment."

Heat flooded her face and she uttered a strangled laugh. George smiled, picked up her hand and dropped a kiss on her fingers. Then he turned for the door and was gone, leaving her trembling and alight with anticipation to match Dulcie's on the night she was killed.

Chapter Six

Listening to Hemp's report with interest, Ottilia began to feel anxious to know how George had fared. He had caught the party upon the point of setting out for the theatre last evening and Ottilia had delayed their departure to give him an account of her conversation with his émigré. He had fastened upon the question of the purse with alacrity, vowing to find it if it took all day and formulating a plan to take the players by surprise in the morning.

It was odd to hear what Hemp had to say of their carousals in the tavern after the performance, knowing the poor things must have been routed out at an ungodly hour. Ottilia had herself risen late, finding the exertions of the previous day had tired her more than somewhat. She was glad to acquiesce in Francis's decree that she rest at home today, leaving Sybilla to begin the hunt for Dulcie's named followers at the Assembly Rooms. He had escorted her thither after breakfast, with a promise to return once his mother was settled.

Ottilia, feeling buoyed by an increase of appetite which enabled her to do justice to the fresh fish, prepared with excellence by the new cook, seized the opportunity to send Joanie for Hemp.

"Did you manage to engage any of them in conversation?"

Hemp's curled lip was answer enough, though he amplified it readily. "Easily, milady. That young spark will speak with anyone, I think." A wry look entered the light brown features. "He took me for a pugilist and would keep challenging me to a bout, no matter how many times I said I had no interest in or experience of the ring."

Ottilia laughed. "Poor Hemp. What did I let you in for?"

A rare smile came. "He is an amusing scamp for all that, milady. I think there is no harm in him, for all he likes to pester and drink and womanise."

"A rebellious scapegrace, is that it?"

He nodded, leaning in a negligent fashion against the edge of a chair, his arms folded. A casual pose, which he would never have allowed himself to adopt if Francis were in the room. Although he certainly would not sit in her presence and Ottilia wished, not for the first time, she could persuade him to drop the pose of servant. It was not as if he was not a man of means in his own right, even if the dilatory legal settlements had not yet delivered up the whole of his patrimony. She set the fleeting thought aside and returned to the matter at hand.

"Did you have any luck with the others?"

"Jasper introduced me, but not all were forthcoming. I spoke a little with Lewis Payne. He is the fellow with the paunch, milady, who played the disappointed suitor last night."

Startled, Ottilia blinked at him. "You saw the play?"

"I thought it wise, milady. I took a ticket when I secured your box."

"You could have taken a seat with us, Hemp. There was plenty of room."

His face closed in the stern way he had. "It would not be fitting, milady."

"But what could you see in the gods, Hemp?"

He grinned. "I was not in the gods, milady. I was in the pit."

"Oh." Ottilia eyed him. For all his insistence on the dictates of propriety and position, he was decidedly independent. She abandoned the argument. "This Lewis then portrayed the coxcomb Cimberton? What had he to say for himself?"

"Not much. He was more inclined to worry over Jasper and try to keep him in line. The boy was loud and slapping the posterior of every barmaid who came near."

Ottilia's insides curled with distaste. "I see. Too indiscriminate then to have been Dulcie's secret lover."

"But he spoke of her, milady, a great deal. Not, I regret, from a sense of grief at her passing, no. But for the loss of her beauty on the stage. He says — and the others agree — they will lose custom without her."

"Yes, that's what Cecile said too, if you remember. She attributed it to the impresario Ferdinand. Was he there?"

"Only for a few moments, milady, and that was before I managed to edge in to speak with Jasper. I heard him enjoin Lewis to see the boy did not disgrace them all."

Ottilia's mind was still on the notion of Dulcie's demise losing the company its customary audience. "The theatre was full last evening, though I dare say the sensation of the murder is responsible for that."

Hemp's wry look appeared. "I think that is so, milady, for the players drew interest from all in the tavern. Jasper enjoys the attention, I think. But not Rob. Robert Collins, milady, the tall one who depicted the friend of the hero; the one with whom he quarrels and fights the duel, if you remember?"

"Ah, yes. Cecile thought he was grieving a little for Dulcie, if I remember rightly."

"That is so, milady, and I remarked him particularly therefore."

"Did you manage to snatch a word with him?"

Hemp shook his head. "He is not communicative. He kept his eyes in his tankard and gave me no more than a nod. Morose he was, milady."

"Did he not join with the general agreement about losing audiences?"

Hemp lifted his chin as if he thought back. "I do not think so, milady. I heard it from Jasper and Lewis. Also Wat and Aisling. They are the lesser players, milady. Those who came and went in many guises on the stage."

"Oh, you mean the little fellow and the giant? Yes, I noticed both and I cannot think this Dulcie creature would have been in an excited frame of mind at the prospect of marriage to either."

"You discount both?"

"I think we must. Dulcie was young and extraordinarily lovely by all accounts. And according to Cecile, she was incandescent that night. I think we must look for a prepossessing male, don't you?"

"Then you will look at Robert Collins, milady." Hemp straightened, unfolding his arms to gesture. "He is tall, with those devil looks females seem to find irresistible."

Ottilia laughed. "You know the sex, Hemp. Or are you thinking of Miss Ingleby and young Simeon Roy?"

The two had been of particular consequence in the debacle in which Hemp had been involved. But he frowned at the notion. "Not them, milady. I do not think Simeon had this kind of devil look. He was more like Jasper perhaps. No, I have seen the type in Barbados, the women, black and white both, sighing over them as if the sun picks them out."

Ottilia could not but wonder at a faintly bitter note. Had he lost a sweetheart to some passing wolf? But the matter was scarcely germane.

"You think Robert Collins is a candidate for the murderer?"

"I do, milady. Jasper rallied him on missing Dulcie because he did not speak. But Lewis shushed him. And then Jasper whispered to me that Rob would have taken her if he could, only that he has a shrewish wife who would beat him with a cooking pan for it."

"Interesting, Hemp. Then he could not have married Dulcie had he been the one to get her with child."

"That is my thought, milady. More, he must be doubly anxious to be rid of her for he cannot avoid being found out as her pregnancy progresses."

Ottilia gave it some thought and found a flaw. "But Dulcie must have known he was married, Hemp. Cecile was certain she thought she was going to her wedding that night."

His brows drew together. "That is so, milady. But it is not certain she thought of a wedding. Perhaps he deceived her to think they would run away together."

"And leave a wife and children behind? Not to mention losing both their employments. No, I cannot credit it."

The rise of disappointment in Hemp's face amused and touched her. She put up a finger.

"One should never jump to conclusions, Hemp, before considering all the options. I do not say this Robert is not the man, but if he is, Cecile must have read her friend incorrectly."

"And you do not think she did, milady?" He gave a reluctant sigh. "No, me neither. It is a pity. I did not like the man."

She had to laugh. "Well, we cannot, unfortunately, condemn the people we do not happen to like merely because it suits us to do so."

His rare laugh rang out. "Very true, milady, though it would be a convenience if it were possible."

"Yes, our murderer took the convenience to its conclusion too. Poor Dulcie. Bad enough to be murdered, but the deception rankles, Hemp."

He nodded but said no more. "Do you wish me to pursue these players?"

"If you don't object to it. I am unlikely to find means to talk to the men myself. See if you can find out any more about whom Dulcie might have been seeing outside the theatre. I cannot think she was able to keep her assignations entirely unremarked."

"Then I must cultivate Jasper of the loose tongue."

Ottilia made a moue of distaste. "Loose living too, by the sound of it."

"Loose everything, milady," said Hemp, preparing to leave the room. "He trades upon his looks and his talent and behaves like a boy who has been let out of school. He would be the better for a sharp lesson. Perhaps I will give him a bout after all."

"No, don't, pray." The last thing Ottilia wanted was a damaged actor complaining of Hemp to Francis. "Besides, we need him garrulous and he can't talk if you knock him about."

A wry laugh came. "True. I will curb the urge, milady." He bowed briefly and opened the door. Muffled voices came to Ottilia's ears and she was gratified when he looked back. "It is the colonel, milady."

He withdrew and moments later George walked in unannounced.

"Forgive me, Ottilia, but your steward fellow suggested I should come in directly."

"Quite right," she said, waving him to a chair. She was herself comfortably ensconced, with her feet up, on the chaise longue which she had caused to be moved and set to catch the heat from the fireplace where the small fire that had warmed the room in the early hours now merely smouldered. "How did you fare? Any success?"

George dropped into the chair opposite which Hemp had been leaning against. "None. The only thing we discovered is the rest of the girl's money hoard among her things. Properly speaking, it is Cecile's and I forgot to say she ought to repossess it."

Ottilia disregarded this for the moment. "The purse was not there?"

"No, and before you ask, it was not in any of the villager's houses either. Puckeridge searched three in the end, but no luck."

"How disappointing." She regarded him with a good deal of sympathy. "You look decidedly grumpy, George, and I am not surprised."

"It's not the purse." A faint colour stole into his cheeks and his amendment came with haste. "At least, of course it is, but…"

"You talked with Cecile?"

His cheek darkened the more and his tone was defensive. "I had to see if she had any notion of her friend's having been with Edgcott, Charlton or Paglesham. Or any other, come to that."

"Did she have any such notion?"

"She recalls the fellow Edgcott, but says Dulcie had no interest there. Charlton was kind, as she phrases it, and she knew nothing of the other fellow."

Ottilia digested this for a moment, but with half her mind on George's evident dissatisfaction. She liked the colonel and knew how much Francis valued his friendship. She did not care to see him thus. She ventured a probe.

"What is it, George? Did it go ill with your *émigré*?"

He shot a frowning look at her. "No! Or rather, yes, but briefly. What do you mean, Ottilia?"

She smiled at him. "You're not a happy man, dear George."

A conscious laugh escaped him. "Under these circumstances? How could I be?"

"Ah. Does she not favour you?"

"Ottilia!"

She spread her hands in a deprecating fashion. "Well, there must be something to put you in this unaccustomed mood."

He sighed. "I suspect she does, that's the trouble. Only as things stand..."

"You cannot pursue it, is that it?"

He gave her a wry look. "I swear you are a witch, Ottilia. And if you dare speak of this to Fan —!"

She threw up her hands. "Idiot man! Do you think I would betray you?"

He winced. "I wish you won't use that word. Cecile keeps on saying it and I can't say I blame her. She was wild with me for using her information in such a way."

"Yes, I can see why. You persuaded her of the necessity, I am sure."

He shrugged. "I think she forgave it in the end." He looked pensive. "She's an odd mix, that girl."

"How so?"

"She's fiercely loyal, both to Dulcie and the players. But their general conduct goes against the grain with her. I suspect she is strictly strait-laced. She says the matriarch — Mrs Ferdinand that is — has kept her close in the hope of restoring her to a member of her family in due course. But Cecile believes they are all dead." He looked up. "It's tragic, Ottilia. But she's unbelievably courageous although it's also clear she has been badly affected."

There was no doubting his intensity of feeling as he spoke about his émigré. Ottilia was both touched and concerned for him. A happy outcome was by no means certain, for the shoals in his way were plentiful. Better not to dwell upon it. But he had touched on something that made her think.

"If she is so strait-laced, perhaps Dulcie did not confide in her as readily as she might to someone a little more of her own milieu."

George frowned across. "What are you getting at?"

Ottilia put up a finger. "Cecile shared a bed with Dulcie, yes. But with whom did Dulcie share a dressing-room?"

Ottilia saw George's attention snap in. "There are only three other actresses, so it should not be difficult to find out."

"Who are they?"

"Mrs Ferdinand, the eldest. Then there's the woman Hilde, who is of middle age. The youngest is Kate, who, according to Cecile, has a *tendre* for young Jasper. By her reasoning, Dulcie would thus not have succumbed to him at least."

Ottilia was eager. "Kate must be our target, I think, George. If she is young enough to be a confidante, she may know a deal more than Cecile."

"You think I should question her?"

"No, I think I ought rather to do it." She gave him a deprecating smile. "That is, if you don't object."

"Object? Do you think I have the slightest desire to engage in such a discussion? Besides, you'll do it much better than I ever could. I can see myself!"

"You asked Cecile."

"That's a very different matter."

She was amused. "Yes, it would be."

"Ottilia, desist!"

She laughed, but was prevented from saying anything more by the entrance into the room of her husband, who hardly paused to greet his friend before breaking into an impassioned complaint against his mother.

"No notion of subtlety at all. She's even more ruthless than you, Tillie, except that she goes at it like a bull in a china shop."

"Well, you would scarcely expect Sybilla to employ subterfuge," Ottilia said, rather amused than otherwise. "It is not in her nature."

"Subterfuge? Lord above, she might as well have shouted her intention to the whole room. I would not mind but that she dragged me into the business, calling on Rodber to find those fellows and present them to me on the instant."

"And did he?"

Francis did not answer at once, instead eyeing his friend with disfavour. "Either you stop grinning, George, or I remove Ottilia back to Flitteris and leave you to your own devices."

George was impenitent. "After what I've been through this morning, I need a diversion."

"Divert yourself on this then: Sir Peregrine Paglesham is a bumptious upstart who looks like one of these Greek statues. You may as well arrest him at once, for any young female in her right mind is bound to prefer him to either Charlton or the bluff idiot calling himself a captain."

"Edgcott? A Captain Sharp, if anything," said George on a contemptuous note.

"More like, I should think. Not that I exchanged words with the fellow, but I heard him and that was quite enough. If he's seen active service, I'm a Dutchman."

"There we are at one. Tell me about Paglesham."

Francis threw up exasperated hands. "How should I? I'd barely blinked at sight of the fellow when Mama edged in, introduced herself and bore him off. Lord knows what she's saying to the man, but I wouldn't put it past her to be subjecting him to a fearsome interrogation."

A gurgle escaped Ottilia. "Then we may safely assume Sybilla will know everything there is to know about him. What of Lord Charlton?"

Francis shrugged. "Nothing. Do you suppose I asked him if he'd done away with this wretched actress?"

Ottilia tutted. "Don't be facetious, Fan."

"Well, for pity's sake!" He threw up his eyes and gave out a resigned sigh. "Coffee!" Crossing to pick up the hand bell, he shook it with vigour.

Perceiving her husband was seriously discomposed, Ottilia set herself to soothe, holding out an inviting hand. "My poor darling, you must have had a wretched time of it."

He crossed at once to the sofa and perched beside her, taking her hand and drawing her towards him. "What I need is a comforting hug from the woman of my dreams."

Ottilia set her hands against his chest, holding him off as her cheeks warmed a little. "We are not alone, Fan."

"Don't fret, it's only George."

"Only George? I thank you for the compliment, Fanshawe."

"My pleasure. Turn your back and stop complaining."

"If you're going to start fondling, I'll leave you," said his friend, mock-severe, but he turned to face the other way anyway.

"Pay no heed to him, my dear one. He's merely jealous."

Ottilia chuckled as she was dragged into a convulsive embrace which she returned with fervour. A knock at the door made her husband release her, just as Joanie entered the room. Francis put in his request for coffee and the maid left.

George had turned on her entrance and now cast a disgusted look at Francis. "Have you done? Or should I withdraw before I am subjected to another such revolting spectacle?"

Francis, whose mood, Ottilia was glad to see, had lifted, merely cocked an eyebrow.

"Wishing you were similarly engaged with this Cecile of yours?"

Seeing his friend's colour begin to rise again, Ottilia intervened. "Don't tease him, Fan. Poor George is sorely beset."

Francis laughed. "Very well, I'm dumb."

"Not so dumb you won't tell us of Charlton, I hope. Did you perhaps think to introduce the subject of the murder with him? It is everywhere talked of, after all, by Mr Rodber's account."

Francis was playing with her fingers, but he looked up at this. "I didn't have to. Charlton spoke of it himself." He looked at George. "I don't think he's your man. He said it was a bad business and spoke of this Dulcibella in an impersonal fashion, I thought."

"Come, Fan, elucidate, if you please," said Ottilia with a degree of impatience. "What did he say of her?"

"That she was very easy on the eye, but less adept on the boards. He thought it a great pity she should be taken off in such a way. He would not wish it on any female. He seemed more interested in the grotesque nature of the crime than the victim herself, to be frank."

Ottilia did not think this necessarily proved disinterest, but George forestalled her before she could say so.

"All well and good, Fan, but if he did the deed, he is bound to draw attention away from the girl, wouldn't you say, Ottilia?"

"I think he would take care to sound impersonal, as Fan puts it. I would not say it exonerates him. And since we know for a fact he was one of Dulcie's followers, his reticence appears somewhat disingenuous."

"Well, I don't see how one can say so without appearing to accuse him," Francis objected.

"Nobody is as yet accusing him."

"No, but I will if I have to," said George.

"But not before we have found out a little more from this Kate." A trifle of irritation attacked Ottilia. "I must say it is an inconvenience you were obliged to do this hunt for the purse, George." She saw her husband's look of question. "No, he didn't find it, Fan. But the nuisance is that I dare say Cecile will not now visit me as she said she might."

The words were scarcely out of her mouth than the door opened to admit the footman Tyler. "Mademoiselle Benoit, my lady."

Cecile tripped into the room, cast a glance around and stopped short at the sight of George.

The flurry of greeting as George presented his *émigré* to Francis, who took time to express his condolences, was at once followed by the entrance of Joanie with a tray. Her husband undertook to dispense coffee, affording Ottilia an opportunity to observe the way Cecile's gaze strayed, under her lashes, to the colonel when his attention was engaged elsewhere. There was hope then, given her sojourn with the players did not overshadow the suitability of her birth. Would George care? Ottilia was inclined to doubt it would weigh with him. And if, as he said, she had been kept close…

Her thoughts faded as the girl herself turned on her a hardening gaze and then rose from the chair George had vacated and brought her cup and saucer across to the chaise longue.

"I may sit with you?"

Ottilia shifted her feet to make room. "Pray do. Forgive my unconventional pose. I am resting at my husband's command."

Cecile cast a glance across to where Francis and George were standing as they sipped coffee. She lowered her voice and turned reproachful eyes upon Ottilia.

"It was not pleasant what this colonel did *ce matin*."

"And you blame me, I take it?"

The girl's eyes dropped to her cup and a tiny sigh escaped her. "You must speak of the purse to him, *bien sûr*."

"I wish it had not been necessary."

The dark gaze raked her. "Also without result."

"Which is a pity, but at least it lessens the suspicion that rests with your players."

At that, her eyes flashed. "They are not my players."

Ottilia smiled. "I should have said friends perhaps." She changed tack. "How well do you know Kate?"

Cecile shrugged. "Not so well as Dulcie. She is strong with passion, that one."

"She behaves like a grande dame?"

Cecile considered. "Perhaps it is more that she desires praise for her acting."

"Ambitious? She would like to be taken for a Siddons?"

Cecile brightened. "*Oui*, you have it, madame. She would like that the world speaks of Katharine Drummond the great one, you understand?"

"Then she was not jealous of Dulcie's beauty, but of her popularity?"

"Perhaps a little. But me I believe she despises Dulcie, who is not very good with the acting but even so the people come to watch her."

Which did not augur well for the beauty having confided in Kate. Nevertheless, Ottilia seized opportunity. "I should like to meet this Katharine Drummond. I must say I found her acting impressive."

Cecile smiled and Ottilia was interested to see how much her features softened. Had George been privileged to see the smile?

"In this case, madame, I do not think Kate will object to meet you."

An interruption came from George, stepping in towards the sofa.

"Cecile!"

The tiny shock in the way she turned and a faint rise of colour in her cheek were decidedly tell-tale. But the tone was discouraging.

"*Oui, mon colonel?*"

George's eyes registered the rebuff and his voice hardened a shade. "I want to ask you again about Paglesham. You recall I mentioned him earlier?"

Cecile's brows drew together briefly and then smoothed out again. "I remember."

"I had forgot, but my friend Francis here reminded me that Paglesham is a handsome fellow. Are you certain Dulcie did not favour him? Did she not speak of him at all?"

The *émigré*'s look became wry. "Dulcie she does not trust men of this kind. She has told to me she believes they are like Jasper."

"In what respect?"

153

"Jasper he is a man so pretty he thinks all women must like him, therefore it needs not that he is kind. Nor is he keeping faith with a woman, and Dulcie she says all such men are the same."

George let out a frustrated breath and Ottilia came in for his irritation. "What do you make of that, for heaven's sake?"

"Well, she isn't going to put every good-looking man out of count, I can tell you that much," said Francis, setting his cup on the mantelpiece.

"By no means." Ottilia put her attention back on Cecile, whose gaze had gone from one to the other in a puzzled look. "You are wondering why the gentlemen defer to me, I dare say."

Cecile shrugged. "Georges has told me you are with experience in such matters."

"It's more than experience." Francis, as ever, jumping to his wife's defence. "She has an instinct and a mind more than capable of outfoxing any cunning murderer. She does not just investigate. She solves."

"Oh, Fan, pray don't. You will give Cecile a perfectly false notion of my capabilities."

"There's nothing false about it. Didn't George beg me to bring you?"

To Ottilia's relief, the colonel intervened. "I've already told Cecile as much, and that I'm trusting to Ottilia to untangle this mess."

"Well, let us concentrate on the mess then," said Ottilia in haste, turning back to the *émigré*. "Cecile, would you say that Dulcie might therefore choose a man who is not good-looking?"

"But not of an ugliness." The girl waved her hands. "*C'est-à-dire*, she likes a man who is kind, or who is — what is the word in English?" She switched to French, looking to George. "I would say *raffiné*."

"Ah, you mean refined, sophisticated."

Ottilia pounced on this. "Now that I can credit. An older man, with a worldly air, who shows her both kindness and admiration. Flattering to a young girl perhaps."

"Do we include Charlton and Edgcott in this category?" asked George.

Francis gave a scornful laugh. "Edgcott? Sophisticated?"

George nodded, turning to Cecile. "True. And you told me Dulcie paid him no attention. Paglesham does not fit, so who else?"

"That reminds me," cut in Francis. "I left Mama quizzing the fellow. I had best get back to her or I'll be having a peal rung over me." He came across to lean down and drop a kiss on Ottilia's forehead. "I'll leave you for a space, my dear one, since you are well enough attended."

She smiled up at him. "Indeed I am. See if you can discover more about Charlton, will you? He must surely fit the particulars."

Francis grimaced. "I'll do what I can, though he is scarcely forthcoming."

With a word of farewell to the other two, he left. Ottilia at once reverted to the question at hand. "My steward, who was talking with the men of the company last night —"

"A spy again?"

Cecile's indignant tone amused Ottilia, but she hastened to smooth her over.

"I confess it freely, my dear, but you see I do not expect to talk to your male actors myself, though I hope you will help me talk to the women. Hemp was by way of being my deputy."

"Thus he spies for you, no?"

"Yes, but in a good cause, Cecile. He has made friends with Jasper." She gave a gurgle. "That young man annoyed my steward by asking him repeatedly to box with him."

George laughed out. "What, merely because he is black?"

"Indeed, yes. And poor Hemp is not a pugilist."

"Ah, *c'est ça*. This is the man who goes with you on this Esplanade?"

"Just so. And he thinks the actor Robert Collins has the right sort of attraction. Devil looks, he calls them."

"Rob?" Cecile's tone became sharp. "I thought this at the start. The day you came to say, Georges, and madame tells us of this horrible news."

"You suspected him?" George, who had retired to the mantel, was eyeing the girl in a frowning fashion that Ottilia deprecated. That would not win him her affection. "You never said so before."

Her chin went up. "Do you think I will aid that you arrest one of my people?"

"If he was guilty of killing your friend, I should hope you would."

The dark eyes flashed. "I would not. I do not betray my own."

George's dagger look did not bode well, but Cecile spoke before Ottilia could intervene.

"*Alors*, I do not think Dulcie will go with Rob, even if it was that he is not married. Rob is not kind and he speaks in a way of making one feel *idiote*, you understand?"

"I know just what you mean," said Ottilia, jumping in fast. "Is there no other who fits this notion of older sophistication?"

Cecile gave that peculiarly Gallic shrug. "Of the men older? Lewis, no. Nor can I think of Monsieur Ferdinand, for though he is sometimes kind, he also is cross and he complains too much. *Eh bien*, there is Monsieur Fitzgerald, but I think he does not mix so much with the players."

Ottilia's ears pricked up. A new name? "Who is Monsieur Fitzgerald?"

"The manager of the theatre," supplied George, who was staring at Cecile rather hard. Had she not mentioned this man before either? "A very respectable man, so far as I know. I'm not well acquainted with him, but he frequents the Rooms when he does not have a company in the town."

"What manner of man is he?"

"You have seen him, madame."

Ottilia raised her brows. "Indeed?"

"He it was who told me you wish to see me, when you visit me at the theatre, do you not remember?"

A face floated in the back of Ottilia's mind. "Rather stern-featured? Tall, I think."

"That is he, but I do not think he speaks with Dulcie more than any other."

"But he knows all the players well, I presume? You — or rather they, have been performing in Weymouth for some time, I imagine."

"Each year they come, yes." Cecile was both frowning and eyeing George under her lashes again in a manner that struck Ottilia as furtive.

"You've visited Weymouth in previous years then." George was looking altogether stern. Suspicious? Ottilia remained silent, alert to the unspoken battle. Would it break?

Cecile's chin lifted. Defiance? "The last year only. Before, I remain with the sister of Madame Ferdinand for that I may learn better the English. I did not come then to this place."

"But you were here last year," George persisted.

157

"I have said."

"And still you don't know which gentlemen in particular have courted Dulcibella Ash? Every man mentioned, apart from Paglesham, was here last year."

Interest burgeoned in Ottilia. "Is that so indeed, George?"

"That much I ascertained from Rodber. As a matter of precaution when the season began, I had a list from him of last year's visitors. Charlton and Edgcott were both on it."

"But not Paglesham?"

"No, which gives one to think, if Cecile —" with a glance at his *émigré* which spoke volumes — "noticed no assiduity in the other two last year."

In one swift movement, Cecile rose from the sofa to confront him.

"Of what do you accuse me, *mon colonel*? Think you I lie when I say I do not know which man it is who makes Dulcie *enceinte*?"

George did not flinch. "I think you have omitted to say a deal that you do know. You have stated categorically that you will not betray your friends."

"*Eh bien?*"

"That I understand. What I cannot understand is why you persist in denying what must have been obvious to you. Whether Dulcie confided in you or not, you know more than you are saying."

Cecile's complexion had paled and her eyes glittered. "You are very clever, *mon colonel*, but you do not make me to speak by this means."

He did not back down. "I've tried a soft approach. I hoped, evidently in vain, that your affection for Dulcie would induce you to assist in the discovery of her murderer."

"This I have done," Cecile protested. "I answer your questions."

"Briefly, and holding back, deciding whether or not you wish to answer. Nor did you mention Fitzgerald, which you might very well have done." He threw up a hand. "Oh, you don't choose to trust me, I know. But —"

"*Voyons*, you are a fool, Georges!" Cecile turned on Ottilia. "See you, madame? Why is it the men say always this thing of trust?" And back to George, on a note of near contempt. "Trust, you must earn it, Georges. It is not a thing one may give at the first instant. Madame expects not that I will trust, is it not so?"

Ottilia had to smile. "I certainly had no reason to think you might trust me."

"*Et voilà!*" Triumphant, Cecile lifted her chin at poor George once more, staring boldly up at him, despite his infinitely superior height and the breadth of his shoulders. He looked decidedly overgrown at that moment as a trifle of defeat formed in his face, along with a wry twist of the lips.

"Well, that has put me properly in my place," he said.

A slow blush crept up Cecile's cheek and her belligerence collapsed. A sheepish smile was cast upon George. "*Alors, mon colonel*, it is that I do indeed trust you more than you suppose."

"Do you? Truly?"

She let out a sigh and sank back down onto the sofa. "I wish it, *tu sais?*"

George relaxed back, clearly softened by the intimacy of the 'tu'. "But?"

Cecile nodded. "It exists, this but of yours, Georges."

"Tell me then."

She glanced towards Ottilia and gave a deprecating smile. "You, I think, will not judge of this Dulcie."

"But you think I will?" Thus George, his brows snapping together.

"Yes, I think it."

"Try me."

Cecile spread her hands. "It is to me most shocking, but she is my friend. I do not say what I think when I see that she allows the liberty to such men as these who come to the door of the stage."

"How much liberty?" Ottilia asked.

"Last year, I do not think she permits the thing most intimate. It is like the test to see who will be the best. And perhaps she does not love them. She meets with them only in the day, perhaps to dine, and she returns and chatters of the food or the gift. But this time it is different. This time she is in the glow almost from the first. She speaks of nothing, even that I ask. And then she goes to have supper at night, when the performance is finished, and she comes not back until it is very early in the morning."

"As she did that night," Ottilia put in, "only she did not come back at all."

Cecile's eyes darkened the more as they misted over and her lip trembled. Her voice became husky. "Yes, but I did not fear for her. I have thought instead the man will marry her, as she hoped. She told me of the *bébé*, as I said. I gave her money. I knew the man is here, for she did not stay out at night in the other towns where the players go to perform. It was in May, when first we came here. But Dulcie did not tell me who is the man."

George had watched her throughout this recital, a softened expression in his face, though Cecile had kept her gaze on Ottilia. But this loosened his tongue.

160

"If you knew he was in Weymouth, you knew he could not be one of the players."

Her gaze went to his. "But no, Georges. I cannot be sure of this, for Dulcie she allows also the liberty with the players. They are *comme ça*, *tu sais*? They hug and kiss and touch. And sometimes, the men touch where they should not. And Dulcie she only laughs at them, even that she might push them away. But she does not mind the way Kate minds. They do not dare to touch Kate like this."

Ottilia could not be surprised Cecile had not confided all this. It was evident her upbringing had imposed a very different morality upon her than she found amongst the players. Horribly embarrassing, to be obliged to speak of it to the colonel of militia investigating the murder. That she did so now was an indication of a growth of feeling towards George, which must gratify him. If he realised it.

But she was at one with him that this piece of the puzzle threw suspicion on a man resident in Weymouth rather than one travelling with the company. Yet one with knowledge of it, enough to set the scene in a distinctly theatrical fashion. The thought led her back to the earlier exchange.

"Tell me more of this Fitzgerald, Cecile."

She shrugged again. "I cannot. It is better you should speak with Monsieur Ferdinand. Or perhaps Madame, for she it is who helps him with arranging matters of the theatre. Moreover, I think he is like a friend with both."

Ottilia looked to George. "Too much older than Dulcie then perhaps? Is he of an age with The Grand Ferdinando and his wife?"

"Good Lord, no. I should not think Fitzgerald is much above forty. Perhaps a year or so less."

Ottilia was dubious. "In which case, he would need to possess a deal of charm to beguile a girl as youthful as this Dulcie." She saw a shadow cross Cecile's face and reached to lay a hand on hers where it rested in her lap. "Whoever he is, we will find him out, I promise you."

Cecile looked from Ottilia to George and gave a tiny sigh. "You desire to meet with Kate, madame. Is it that you will also speak with Madame Ferdinand?"

Cheered by this ready acquiescence, Ottilia agreed. "There is also the older actress, is there not. Hilde, was it?"

"It is for Hildegard. She has been for many years with the players."

In which case, she might well be a useful resource. "Do you think all three ladies would accept an invitation to drink tea with me? You may say you met me by chance perhaps."

The fire leapt back into Cecile's eyes. "But no, madame. I will ask them, but I will tell them why it is you wish to speak with them."

With which Ottilia was obliged to be content, reflecting that it might after all save a deal of awkwardness.

Chapter Seven

The dowager Lady Polbrook was found to have abandoned her prey in favour of a rubber of whist with several valetudinarians of advanced years. Francis, with his wife's request in mind, hunted for Lord Charlton.

The spacious Assembly Room was fairly crowded, with sea-bathing and breakfast well over for the day and the weather being a trifle inclement for excursions. The Room's lofty and elegant proportions allowed the noise of chatter to dissipate somewhat. A good deal of light came in from the windows, which made it easier to look among the patrons, either promenading, standing in shifting groups or sitting in the chairs provided about the walls or, like his mother, at the card tables in the adjoining room.

He spotted Paglesham, who was talking with a young lady chaperoned by a dragon of a female, and then saw Charlton just coming in from the door leading to the entrance hall. Francis moved across to intercept him.

"A little chilly out, is it?"

Lord Charlton was older than Francis by a year or two but had an air about him of middle age. His figure had begun to thicken, although he carried it well, and a slight plumpness to his cheeks did not detract from a countenance generally held to be well-looking, if unremarkable. He appeared ready enough to talk.

"Yes, there is a trifle of breeze. I was checking to see if their nurse has taken my girls back inside."

Francis registered the anxious note. A good subject to begin with. "How many girls have you?"

"Just the two. Delightful monkeys they are, but young yet. I would not trouble my head over Sophy, she's a robust creature, but little Lizzy is susceptible to colds."

Struck by the fellow's evident affection for his daughters, Francis was conscious of an impulse to dismiss any possibility of his being Dulcie's murderer. But he had not witnessed Tillie in action for nothing. She would say, and rightly, that fondness for his children did not preclude an act of callous disregard for the life of an importunate lover. A sneaking regret for his own loss crept into Francis's breast, but he suppressed it. Time enough for him and Tillie to beget another babe.

"How old are your girls?"

"Five and seven."

Sadly young to have lost their mother. But Francis did not say so. He took the bull by the horns. "I imagine you would be glad to give them a stepmother."

Charlton shot him a narrow look. "Yes, if opportunity offers."

Francis threw up a deprecating hand. "I meant no offence."

"None taken, Fanshawe." A wry smile came. "It is not for want of applicants, you understand."

"I imagine not," returned Francis with a laugh. "You are scarcely ineligible."

"And thought to be hanging out for a second wife, since I have no direct heir. I would, however, be loath to inflict the wrong sort of female upon my girls."

Like Dulcibella Ash? Although no man of Charlton's stature would marry an actress. Unless he was besotted and heedless of her reception amongst the ladies of the ton. There seemed no way of introducing the subject without speaking of it directly. Francis abandoned pretence.

"I wish you will tell me what attraction there was in this deceased actress."

Charlton's pleasant expression changed. "You raised this subject before, Fanshawe. May I ask why?"

"I will tell you," said Francis, giving him look for look. "Let us retire to somewhere more quiet."

Frowning, the other followed him as he threaded a path to the main doors and slipped into the entrance hall beyond. It was occupied, but large enough to admit of a degree of privacy in a quiet corner by the window that let onto the street outside.

Charlton's eyes held a less friendly light and a trifle of challenge. "Well?"

Eyeing him now with interest, Francis took the plunge. "You know Colonel Tretower of the militia here, I take it?"

"What of it?"

"He's a friend of mine."

A riffle of something — dismay? — passed across the fellow's face. "Hence your interest? I had not supposed a civilian might be called upon to assist Tretower in his task."

Unwilling to throw his wife to the lions by spreading her involvement abroad, Francis prevaricated. "Hardly that. He merely supposed a discreet word between equals might clear up a couple of details."

Charlton's air remained distant. "Such as?"

Checking with a swift glance round that they were not overheard, Francis lowered his voice. "You are known to have been one of the girl's admirers, sir."

"Among many, sir."

"But only a few who ventured to approach Dulcibella Ash via the stage door."

The man's face hardened and his tone was icy rage. "Are you accusing me, Fanshawe?"

"I am pointing out that you would do better to reveal the extent of your involvement with the girl."

"Or I may find myself standing trial for this singularly unpleasant murder, I take it?"

The confrontation began to feel dangerous and Francis's soldierly instincts kicked in. He was not here to do battle. "I did not say so. Nor did I imply any such outcome."

"Then?"

"You may prove a valuable witness."

The other's rigid pose relaxed a trifle. "How so?"

"Your candour, if you will allow me to say so, will likely exonerate you. Remaining obdurate can only make it more certain Tretower will be obliged to approach you directly. I cannot think you would relish an official request."

There could be no doubt, from his expression, that this rang with Charlton in no small degree. Nevertheless, he hesitated, his mouth pinched, his cheeks sucked in. Francis held his gaze, waiting.

At last he blew a resigned breath. "What do you wish to know?"

Relieved, and a little surprised at his acquisition of a trifle of the ruthlessness Tillie employed in such circumstances, Francis reverted to a tone of friendly interest.

"You are spoken of as having been kind, a quality this Dulcie appreciated, which suggests you spent time with her. When and how much time?"

The direct question flustered Charlton. "How the devil should I remember how much time?"

"An approximation will do."

The other shifted his head in irritation. "An hour or so perhaps. I gave her a supper after a performance."

"Where and when?"

"Good God, I don't know. A few weeks ago? There's a neat little coffee house situated out of the way of the fashionable quarter, if one can call it that. Weymouth is a dirty little town once you move away from the Rooms and the vicinity of this famous Esplanade. But if you are prepared to negotiate ill-lit streets you may find the odd gem amongst the dross."

"Where is this gem and what is it called?"

"It is Mrs Horniman's place. You'll find it a few houses down from the pawnbroker's shop."

Francis asked for no more directions since George was bound to know the place. "Did you take the girl there more than once?"

Charlton's annoyance grew. "Yes, if you must know. I had met her last year, by accident. She was running in the rain and nearly came to grief and I happened by. I recognised her from the theatre and … well, one thing led to another."

Deeply suspicious now, Francis pressed him further. "How far did it go, Charlton? You had much better speak out."

"How the devil do you suppose it went, man? Lord knows I'm no saint, but I'm no lecher either. I sought no favours, if that is what you seek to discover."

"Never? She was, as I understand it, eminently desirable. And, by all accounts, available."

Charlton bristled, speaking in a low but vibrant tone. "That's where you're wrong, Fanshawe. Dulcibella was an innocent. Oh yes, I know there are men who consider actresses fair game, but I'm a father of daughters. I know what I would do to any man who defiled one of mine. As for that poor girl, she was little more than a child. I tell you, I'd like the chance of a dark night to meet the villain who killed her. I'd send him straight to hell!"

167

There was no mistaking the fellow's sincerity. His face had turned ruddy, his breast heaving with emotion.

"God willing, that is exactly what Tretower will do," said Francis lightly. "I must thank you for your frankness."

"I'll be franker still, sir. I tried to discourage Dulcibella from going apart with any of her so-called admirers. I would not trust that fellow Edgcott to hold the line. And as for Paglesham —"

"Why do you say that? What do you know of him?"

"More than I wish to, I can tell you. A jackanapes lionising among the ladies, who encourage him merely for his pretty face."

Was this jealousy? Had he cut Charlton out with a prospective leg-shackle? But that was scarcely germane.

"Do you suppose Paglesham was granted favours by this Dulcibella?"

A troubled look came into Charlton's features. "I fear it. She was a trifle dazzled, I believe. And there is the old adage, like to like. She was not a female of great intelligence, though one could hardly expect a chit of her age to recognise a coxcomb's flattery."

"But you don't know for a fact that she spent time with the fellow?"

Charlton shrugged. "I saw him hanging around the theatre on more than one occasion. He was by the stage door when I escorted Dulcibella the night we had supper. But Edgcott was quite as assiduous. Of the two, I thought she preferred Paglesham, and who can blame her?"

Who indeed? "This was when you tried to get some sense into her head, I take it?"

"With little success, I fear. She laughed and blushed and protested she could take care of herself." A deep sigh escaped the man. "A manifestly false assertion as it turns out, poor child."

It was worse than he thought perhaps, since he did not appear to know about the pregnancy. George had evidently kept that piece of scandalous news out of the public consciousness. A wise move, since it could only increase the sensationalism of the murder.

Francis was inclined to eliminate Charlton from the list of suspects. Either he was sincere or he was a better actor than Dulcibella had been an actress.

"I will thank you again, Charlton. An enlightening discussion."

The man's gaze narrowed. "May I take it that Tretower will not pursue me?"

"I cannot answer for him, but I will relay all you have told me."

A shrewd look came his way. "You are a cautious fellow, Fanshawe."

Francis thought it prudent to refrain from comment. "Shall we return to the main room? I must ascertain whether my mother has need of me."

The other took the dismissal in good part, which rather enhanced Francis's opinion of his innocence than otherwise. He decided, as they returned to the crowded assembly, to refrain from treating with Paglesham until he knew just what the dowager had discovered. She was forthcoming enough once Francis had managed to extract her from her absorption at the whist table, which he did with a fictitious reminder.

"If you wish to take that walk along the Esplanade, ma'am, it will be well to do so before this breeze gets up any sharper."

The dowager gave him one of her eagle looks and Francis returned it with a meaning one of his own. She nodded.

"Presently." Then she addressed her companions. "This must be my last rubber, gentlemen."

"Just as well," barked the crusty old general who was playing against Lady Polbrook. "Ruining me you are, m'lady Syb."

His mother's black eyes regarded the fellow with irritation. "I wish you will not address me with that ridiculous appellation, Leo."

"Address you any way I choose, m'dear girl. Earned it at my time of life."

"I am not your dear girl either."

"Yes y'are. Always were." He threw a twinkling look at Francis. "I might have been your father, boy, if this stubborn female hadn't turned me down an eon ago."

"That will do!"

"Hoy! Back to the game, if you please."

This from his mother's partner, another of the elderly trio who, as she had told her son, had hailed her with enthusiasm upon her first visit.

"A set of rascals I had the misfortune to know in my youth."

Francis had laughed. "What, your cicisbeos?"

"One of them was. As if your grandfather would have countenanced a marriage with a mere captain of the guards, even had he not already arranged an alliance with Polbrook."

But Leo Godfrey had risen high in the ranks and was known to Francis by reputation from his soldiering days. His gallantry towards the dowager would have had Francis bristling if it was not touching, for the old man suffered from an arthritic condition and depended upon an attendant who wheeled him wherever he wanted to go. He was a regular in Weymouth and it occurred to Francis he might know something of the dubious Captain Edgcott.

"Why do you not accompany us, General?" he suggested when the rubber came to an end with his mother and her partner triumphant.

The dowager cast him a black look, which he met blandly. She frowned as the losers emptied their pockets and counted out the shillings owing into a convenient receptacle in the table. The general dumped his coins and signalled to his flunkey.

"No use waiting on me, m'boy. Lidsey will get me out. Catch you up on the Esplanade, Syb, m'dear."

No sooner had his mother exited the Rooms on his arm, than Francis found himself under fire. "What in heaven's name possessed you to invite that wretch, you ninny? Do you suppose I wish to encourage him?"

Francis cocked an eyebrow. "Are you not enjoying his attentions, Mama?"

"Don't be ridiculous. Attentions indeed. Besides, I thought all this jockeying was because you wished to speak to me alone."

"I do, but it occurred to me I could usefully pump the general about Edgcott."

His mother gave him a shrewd glance. "Ottilia has set you on to sound out the men, has she?"

"Charlton, yes, which I've done. And he directed me to Paglesham, but I wanted to know what you found out before I tackled him."

His mother gave out one of her rude explosions of contempt. "A sycophantic coxcomb, who suits his tongue to his company. You know the type."

"All too well. What did he tell you?"

"Nothing to the purpose, the young saucebox. He turned everything I said to suit himself and gave little away."

171

"But did he admit to having courted this Dulcie girl?" asked Francis, impatient.

"Readily," said his mother, preparing to step onto the wide spread of the walkway and releasing his arm to pull her shawl more securely around her against the salty wind. "Is that idiot Godfrey on his way? I'll not remain here to be buffeted at his convenience."

"No matter, ma'am. I can take you back to the lodgings, if you prefer, and meet him on my own."

The dowager, settling herself once more with a hand on his arm, dismissed this suggestion. "Let me tell you of this Paglesham fellow first. Or rather Sir Peregrine. He had the temerity to correct me, if you please, on the pretext of supposing I had it wrong."

Francis grinned appreciatively. "Did you give him pepper?"

A wry glance came his way from her black eyes. "I would have if I was not on a mission to extract information."

"Well, and what did you find out?"

His mother puffed out another snort. "He would like me to think he was favoured, but he admitted to having a rival or two and was unsurprised at it. According to Paglesham, the girl had few equals."

"In looks?"

"So he claimed. But she had also a deal of charm, an air of innocence — I am quoting the man — which would have done credit to any debutante."

Francis jumped on this. "So also said Charlton. At least, he called her an innocent and tried to discourage her from falling victim to Paglesham. Did you get the impression she did so fall?"

He felt her shrug beside him. "That I cannot swear to. He lamented her ineligibility to be courted in earnest. Any man must be proud, he said, to be able to show off such a prize."

This began to look grim indeed. "As his wife, did he mean?"

"So I took it. He was perfectly frank about his wish to establish himself and had the gall to ask me what I thought of his prospects."

At any other moment Francis would have laughed at this. But his mind was racing. If Paglesham had succeeded and discovered Dulcie was with child, he would not have risked his future by marrying her. Might he have led her to believe he would, on purpose to make away with her? But had he the kind of mind to prepare the scene to cast suspicion upon the players?

"Did he strike you as cunning, Mama?"

"He struck me as an oily flatterer out for what he could get. Cunning? Perhaps, inasmuch as he cuts his cloth to suit his company. He was almost as obsequious as Rodber to begin with."

Setting himself up in his own conceit because he was singled out by the highest ranked lady in the town? Yes, very likely. Could he get more out of the fellow?

"It sounds to me as if he will bear further investigation. I must see Tillie before I talk to him, however."

"To get your instructions, no doubt."

Francis laughed. "Of course." He heard the sound of wheels on the flagway. "Here comes General Godfrey." Halting, he turned to his mother and spoke low-toned. "I haven't thanked you for persuading Ottilia to come here, Mama. It has changed her immeasurably already."

173

The dowager, her eyes on the approaching wheeled chair, nodded. "Yes, while this business lasts. But don't imagine the megrims won't return afterwards. The grieving process takes time, Francis."

He hesitated. Tillie's tearful confession of the cause of her misery was too personal for sharing. There was an element of grief, though he hoped it had lifted.

"I think she is over the worst," he ventured.

The dowager gave him a sceptical look but said nothing since the old general, his attendant pushing him along at a cracking pace, was almost within earshot.

"Deuced windy, eh?" he called. "Say your piece quick, Fanshawe, for I'm damned — saving your presence, Syb — if I stay here to be blown about like a sailor up a mizzen mast." It was evident the old man was as shrewd as they come if he had divined Francis's purpose in the invitation. He craned his neck to look over his shoulder at his brawny attendant. "Stand off, Lidsey. Call you when I need you." He waited until the flunkey had wandered some feet off down the turfed slope towards the beach and then looked under his brows at Francis. "Cut line, boy. What d'ye want of me?"

Francis grinned appreciatively. "I should have known you would see through my subterfuge, sir."

"Wasn't born yesterday, young feller me lad. Seen service, haven't you? America, your mother told me."

"That is correct, sir. With my friend Tretower."

The general gave a nod of approval. "Good lad that. Sound as a roast."

"Exactly so, sir, but neither he nor I believe as much of Captain Edgcott."

"Captain Pah!"

174

"Precisely, sir. I wondered if you might be better informed?"

The general made a rude noise. "A half-pay officer, if any. A drill ground is all the soldiering he's seen, if that. And if we do go to war with the Frogs, won't see Edgcott in a landing boat."

"Unlikely, I agree, sir."

"None of which is to the purpose, Leo," interrupted his mother on an exasperated note. "The man was after this dead girl. Do you know anything about that?"

Her elderly admirer poked his head up as he gave her an irritated look. "How the devil should I know, Syb? Ain't the fellow's keeper."

"Don't tell me. You're a worse gossip-monger than the tabbies, Leo. You hear things."

His eyes twinkled. "Have to amuse myself somehow, m'dear girl."

"No doubt. Come, out with it, you wretch. What do you know?"

Amused by the interchange and the way his mother's slight flush belied her acerbic tongue, Francis was unsurprised when the general capitulated.

"If you must have it, word is Edgcott was cut out by Paglesham. Made no secret of it. Complained of his rival to any who'd listen. Not the women, he ain't as ill-bred as that. But he steamed off in the coffee houses and taverns. Said it was his belief the beauty preferred to dispense her favours among her own and Paglesham would get nowhere."

Francis jumped on this. "You mean he thinks she was involved with one of the players?"

"That's the story. No use asking me if she told him so, for I've no information of the kind."

"Then it looks as if Edgcott is not our man."

"What's this, Fanshawe? Joined the Bow Street Runners, have you?" The jocular tone was nevertheless accompanied by a knowing look.

"Merely assisting my friend, sir. He has to live here and he doesn't want to upset people unnecessarily."

"He can upset Edgcott with my blessing. Man's a menace. So is the Paglesham court card. Can't abide these jumped up toadies. Won't find me objecting if Tretower arrests the feller."

"He won't arrest an innocent man, however."

"Francis, I'm cold. If Leo has nothing more to tell us, let us go in."

The general gave a whistle and his man loped back up towards them. He gave Francis another of his shrewd looks from under his brows. "I'll keep my ears open, lad, and pass anything useful along to Syb." The tease came back into his gaze as it turned on the dowager. "Don't you forget our rendezvous tomorrow, Syb, my lovely."

She made an explosive sound. "Be silent, Leo! Rendezvous indeed."

The old man grinned and waved. "Get me out of this wind, Lidsey."

He was wheeled away and Francis gave his arm to his mother, who was muttering under her breath. "What is this about a rendezvous then, my dear and flighty mama?"

"Don't you start. He means the whist table, wretched man. I declare, he'll drive me to distraction before the week is out."

Sorely tempted to tease but all too conversant with his mother's temper, Francis held his tongue. He was inclined to think she was secretly enjoying the old man's attentions and suspected she was a deal less dismissive when he was not there to witness her blushes.

Tillie was found to be sipping yet another cup of coffee in her time-honoured fashion. She was alone, and imparted the intelligence that George had insisted on escorting Cecile to her lodging before going off to beard the theatre manager.

"For what purpose? Does he mean to close the place?"

"Ah, you do not know, Fan," said Tillie with a gleam in her eye. "We have another possibility for Dulcie's lover."

His mother groaned. "As if there are not men enough already. Who is the fellow?"

"His name is Fitzgerald and, unfortunately for him, poor man, he fits the criteria. Older and sophisticated. We have yet to learn if he is kind, but personable he most certainly is."

Having settled his mother into a chair, Francis edged onto the chaise longue as Tillie shifted to make room for him. "How do you know? You've seen him?"

"Briefly, when I went to find Cecile at the theatre." She set down her empty cup and stretched out a hand. "Tell me what you managed to discover. I can see you are big with news."

Francis clasped the hand with a rise of pleasure and held it loosely between them as he related his discussions, leaving his mother to tell her part with Paglesham again. As was her wont, Tillie listened with close attention, a tiny frown coming and going between her brows. Francis guessed her brain was busy and wished he might see into her thoughts. She was ever quick, revolving complex issues in her head and coming out with conclusions he rarely arrived at for himself.

His mother seemed as anxious for Tillie's opinion as was he.

"What do you think, Ottilia? For my part, everything points to Paglesham. And he, I surmise, would be most damaged by an alliance with an actress."

Francis quashed this without hesitation. "I can't agree there. Though I no longer believe Charlton did the deed, that motive must be stronger with him. Who is Paglesham after all?"

"A nobody, and that is just the point," argued the dowager. "Many a man of title has forced the world to accept an unsuitable wife in the teeth of disapproval." Her eyes snapped. "Nor need we look far for an example."

Francis threw up his eyes. "Not this again, ma'am, for pity's sake!" He had heard enough from the dowager on the subject of his brother's ill-timed second marriage to last a lifetime. "Besides, Violette is not an actress."

"No, she was my son's mistress and don't tell me all the world does not know it, for even Leo dared to twit me on the subject."

Which explained a great deal in her attitude towards the general. "The more fool he then. He ought to have known you better."

Conscious of the bitter note in his voice, he was relieved when Tillie intervened, dragging the conversation back to the main issue.

"You make a valid point, Sybilla. If, by all accounts, this fellow Paglesham has only a precarious foothold in Society, then a marriage with Dulcie must inevitably bring him down. It is the way of the world sadly."

"Then you would put him at the top of the list?"

"I am not sure, Fan. Cecile is adamant that Dulcie did not trust good-looking men, remember?"

To Francis's annoyance his mother let out a snort. "I would not allow that to weigh in the balance. I tell you, the man is a practised flatterer. Any young girl might well be fooled into supposing his affections were engaged. He knows just how to beguile and cheat."

"Then I think we must indeed keep him to the forefront of our minds," said Tillie in a soothing tone.

The dowager rose. "I am going to my room. All this nonsense is singularly fatiguing."

Francis watched his mother stalk out and turned to find Tillie watching him with a rueful look in her eyes.

"That was unfortunate. I am so sorry, my dearest. As if you had not had enough to bear from me."

He gripped her fingers tighter. "Don't say that. I'll endure anything from you, Tillie, and you know it. But I'd hoped Mama was over the business of Randal's untimely nuptials."

"My poor darling. You were sorely beset, I know." Tillie leaned forward and lifted their joined hands, planting a kiss on his fingers. "I doubt she will ever get over it completely. It was a severe blow and quite ruined her relationship with your brother."

He might have said a great deal on the subject, but Francis held his peace. He had no wish to burden Tillie when she was still in a delicate state of health. He reverted to the murder.

"If you wish me to question Paglesham, I need guidance."

Tillie smiled at him. "Sparing me, Fan?"

He was betrayed into a laugh. "Yes, you wretch. I have no wish to rake all that up again in any event. I had much rather concentrate on the consequences of this murder, I thank you." Her clear gaze shifted and Francis knew at once her mind was back on the problem confronting them. He released her hand and instead ran a finger down her cheek. "What is it, Tillie? I know that look. You have fathomed something, have you not?"

Her gaze came back to him. "I am still wondering what happened to the purse."

"Is it so important? Won't you find it with the murderer when we catch him?"

There was a frown between her brows. "I doubt it. Too incriminating. I am persuaded the man who was clever enough to lay a trail to the players would not have made so foolish an error."

"But George's men found nothing," Francis pointed out. "Neither the players nor the villagers were in possession of the thing. The murderer must have it."

The look she always wore when she had something worked out persisted. "No, I think not."

"What, then? There is no doubt it was taken from the body."

"Yes, but not by the murderer."

He eyed her with some degree of impatience. "Well? If you will have it so, you must have some notion in your head."

A faint smile flitted over her face. "You know me too well."

"This is not one of those things you are going to refuse to speak about until you know more, is it?"

She shrugged. "I can't know more, nor do I dare to hope I may."

"Tillie!"

She laughed. "Pardon me. I am being exasperating, am I not?"

"Yes, you impossible female!"

"Very well, I won't tease you, but don't blame me if you think I have taken leave of my senses."

"You did that an eon ago and you are fortunate I happen to love you or I should have had you clapped in Bedlam long since."

The gurgle he had not heard in an age sounded and Francis was moved to kiss her. Her smile faded as he released her, and the look he recognised was back.

"Fan, I think someone did take the purse, long before anyone else came upon the scene. If I am right, there may have been a witness to Dulcie's murder."

Chapter Eight

The manager was discovered in his poky office in the recesses behind the public façade of the theatre. Chagrined to find him in conference with The Grand Ferdinando himself, George was the more hampered when the impresario hailed him in a fashion as irritating as it was affected.

"Ah, look who it is, Fitz, look who it is. The arm of the law yet again, by heaven! If you have come to arrest me, Colonel, I must remind you that you found no incriminating evidence among my personal accoutrements, none whatsoever, sir. Oh, the humiliation! The shame of it! My purse turned out before all my people, my standing impaired, my —"

"Would you have me discover Dulcie's murderer, or would you not?" George cut in, stemming the flow.

"I would, I would, of course I would. Ah, my poor little Dulcibella, yes indeed, we must flush out the villain, we must indeed. But, Colonel, in such a fashion?"

"In whatever fashion appears to me expedient, Mr Ferdinand, your sensibilities notwithstanding."

A muffled snort drew George's attention to the man Fitzgerald. So he was alive to the flourishing affectations of the impresario, was he? Ferdinand did not appear to notice. He clapped a hand to his heart.

"You speak sooth, Colonel, indeed you do. I am lacerated, sir, lacerated. I have not been right since the dreadful event." A great sigh came and he shook his leonine head. "But the show must go on, Colonel, the show must go on. Such is the life of a player. We halt not for the best or worst that life may throw at us. Let thunderbolts fall where they may, we go on."

"Very commendable, I am sure." George glanced past the impresario to Fitzgerald. "Forgive me if I interrupt your conference, sir, but I would be glad of a word."

The manager's mien, which had been one of indulgence, changed. His brows snapped together, giving his face a piratical look. George had not before noticed how his very dark hair, smoothed back from his brow and resting on his collar, together with the slanting brows, the lean nose and cheeks and a somewhat swarthy complexion, added up to a whole to which an impressionable female might well be drawn. Sophisticated it certainly was. A certain aloof air might add to the attraction. But before any enquiry, he had to rid himself of Ferdinand, who chose to be astonished.

"You want Fitz? But my dear sir, what in the world do you suppose he can tell you that I cannot? Not that I mean to suggest you are not well acquainted with us all, my dear friend, but you cannot know my people as I do."

"There is no reason to suppose the colonel wishes to question me about your people, Arthur." Fitzgerald's tone was measured, although his eyes held on George in a calculating way as if he sought to determine just what he did want. "I am at your service, Colonel. Arthur, we may resume presently. I have the dates down and we may go over the receipts in due course."

The impresario appeared far from satisfied, his gaze going from George to Fitzgerald and back again. He adopted a grumbling tone. "It's deucedly inconvenient, but I suppose I know when I am not wanted. I will see Hilde instead. Not that I can afford a new costume for Kate, with audiences dwindling as they must without our little Dulcibella. As for Rob's elaborate scheme of staging for *Love's Last Shift*, that is utterly out of the question. You will find me in the Green Room,

Fitz." With which, he got himself out of the place by dint of squeezing past George, and making a production out of his exit with a valedictory reference to the importunities he was obliged to endure from sundry players and others, unspecified.

George waited for the door to shut and then turned to the man behind the desk, who at once gestured to the one chair available other than his own.

"Shall we sit?"

"By all means."

The desk between them was a large receptacle, leaving little space for much else beyond a set of filled shelves, a dresser crammed against the back wall, which was covered in playbills, and a corner stove, presently unlit but giving evidence of emitting smoke at every opportunity by the blackened walls either side.

"I wonder you don't remove to a more convenient apartment to conduct your business, sir," George remarked.

Fitzgerald cast a disparaging glance about his little kingdom. "It serves me, sir. Space is at a premium in a theatre, Colonel. However, you did not come here to discuss my function."

"I did not."

The mouth twitched. Discomfort? The man's gaze did not waver.

"Let me guess. You wish to ascertain the extent of my involvement with the fair Dulcibella, is that it?"

His cool assumption took George aback. But it made him suspicious. Too clever by half, if he was the man. He chose to be direct.

"Were you involved with her?"

Fitzgerald gave a mirthless laugh. "As much as I was with any of them. I no longer aspire to the lifestyle, though I am obliged to have dealings with the tribe."

184

"The tribe?"

A cynical smile increased the piratical look. "A law unto themselves are players. Like gypsies. They are not dissimilar. The life lends itself to loose morality and unprecedented intimacies."

An image of Cecile's countenance leapt into George's head. Youthful, lovely, yet marked by suffering, her innocence eroded, scarred by the harsh realities of vagabond living. He dismissed it, along with the pang it cost him. He must concentrate on the matter at hand.

"Be plain with me, Fitzgerald. How much had you to do with these players?"

"Very little, apart from Ferdinand and his wife. Janey has a shrewd head on her shoulders. It is she, rather than Arthur, who holds the purse-strings."

"But you must know them all fairly well?" George persisted. "The company has been coming here for years, as I understand it."

Fitzgerald pursed his lips. "I have known the Ferdinands for many years, but latterly we see them more often. They were used to tour the continent."

"Until the troubles in France made such excursions untenable," supplied George. "So I gather. They picked up Cecile Benoit there."

He was subjected to a sharp glance. "An odd acquisition, yes. She earns her keep assisting Hildegard with the company's wardrobe."

George set his teeth. The notion of Cecile slaving at sewing was no more welcome than the thought of her caught in this unsuitable trap.

"Mademoiselle Benoit is not in question. Beyond Dulcibella —" He noted a twitch of the fellow's eyebrow and added swiftly, "to whom we will return shortly, what can you tell me of the actors? Are you aware of any liaison with the dead girl?"

Fitzgerald's gaze travelled to the ceiling and there stayed as he evidently pondered. George found it oddly suspect. Was it as much of a pose as the impresario's ingrained flourishing manner? He waited, regarding Fitzgerald with growing scepticism.

After a moment, the man's gaze dropped down again and he met George's eyes. "I think not."

"It took you an inordinate amount of time to work that out."

Fitzgerald's brow lifted. "A swift review of a number of memories, Colonel. I did stop at one of young Jasper briefly, but though the boy is a notorious womaniser I cannot see him troubling to make such a performance of the business. Had he killed Dulcie, one would expect him to do it in a fit of temper or a drunken brawl. I doubt he would even try to conceal the deed, unless to claim he remembered nothing of it."

This rang with what George knew of the young actor, but argued a more intimate acquaintance with the players than Fitzgerald claimed.

"What about Robert Collins?"

The brows snapped together. "Is he suspected?"

"Why do you ask?" George countered, his senses alert.

"My dear Tretower, is it not obvious? However, one should not fall into the error of supposing the man to be a true villain merely because he is cast in that role more often than any other."

"Is he?"

Fitzgerald spread his hands. "What would you? He looks the part. He is also a fine actor, though one would not have supposed any female might warm to him. A morose type. He is said to be ruled by a shrewish wife, but on that point I am going by hearsay. I have never met her, though I believe she resides in Dorchester with their two children."

So much George already knew. More than Fitzgerald probably, since he had sent Sullivan to verify the fact when they rode to Dorchester the other day. Mrs Collins had proved as sullen a creature as her husband, disinclined to answer questions. The only noticeable interest, to Sullivan's disgust, was in the intelligence that Dulcie had met her end.

"Dead, is she? Good riddance."

Her attitude so much shocked his lieutenant that Sullivan came away without asking anything more. George followed an inclination arising from this memory.

"If his home life is uncomfortable, he might well console himself elsewhere perhaps?"

"Since he rarely goes home," said the other on a cynical note, "one doubts he is much disturbed by it."

"Yet such a pretty armful as Dulcibella Ash might be a temptation."

The man's face thinned as his lips pursed. "But not, I surmise, in reverse. A liaison with Robert Collins would indicate poor taste on Dulcibella's part."

"Ah, but there is no accounting for the whims of women, wouldn't you say?"

A bark of laughter greeted this. "Very true, sir. Even Kate, of whom one would expect a deal more common sense, has a marked penchant for Jasper."

Was there an edge to the words? George took an oblique path. "You've noticed it?"

"It is common knowledge in the company and my friend Ferdinand is apt to bemoan her preoccupation in that direction. He thinks it mars her performance when she is paired with him, as she will be more now. Unless he can find another Dulcibella, which is debatable."

George took due note of an odd look in the fellow's eye as he spoke of the girl. Was it regret? He probed a little.

"Was she truly irreplaceable? I admit she looked a beauty, even in death, but there must be others personable enough."

A tell-tale quiver of the lip attacked Fitzgerald, for the first time showing unease. His fingers were peculiarly rigid where they lay on the desk and his voice sounded forced. "Beauty is not everything. Talent, real talent…" He faded out and looked up. "Dulcibella had something more than beauty, a quality more unusual, unfortunately, than talent."

George recalled what Charlton had said. "Innocence?"

"Not that, though that too. She had a glow about her. It came from within. One can't explain it, but for such a quality to shine through on the stage is rare." Was it regret in the man's eyes? "Ferdinand is unlikely to find such another. She was a magnet and her presence has done the company proud. They have prospered these two years."

Was that all he cared about? Or did it go deeper with him? How to phrase it without setting the fellow on his guard?

"I gather her acting did not match her looks," he said lightly. Fitzgerald made no immediate response beyond a flick of an eyebrow. George persisted. "I confess I scarcely noticed her when I attended a performance upon their last visit to the town."

The man's gaze sharpened. "Did not notice her? Singular, Colonel. Most men had eyes for no other."

"You include yourself in that category, sir?"

A dismissive laugh. "Hardly. As old a hand as I am, I have seen too many performances to be riveted by any one individual."

"Even one with this glow you speak of?"

Fitzgerald blew out a sighing breath and this time George was sure he detected regret. "It is strange, is it not, how memory can play one false? I see her in my mind's eye, animate and warm, yet it is not an image upon the stage that haunts me."

"What then?" George regarded him with close attention. Was this genuine grief, if muted?

Fitzgerald's fingers moved in a restless fashion, caressing the leather-backed blotter on his desk and then shifting to the ink stand to lift a quill from its place. He brushed the end across his hand. When he spoke again, his voice was low.

"I saw her leave the lodging."

The implication zinged in George's head. "That night?"

A nod came. "She entered a coach."

Questions tumbled through George's mind and he rapped them out. "What time was this? How did you come to be there to see it? Why did you not come forward? Do you not realise how vital this may be?"

Fitzgerald dropped the quill and raised both hands palm up in a placatory gesture. "Your pardon, Colonel. I confess myself at fault, but not with deliberation. I believe the image has been sitting at the back of my mind. Until you began to harp upon the business, I did not realise I had it there."

"You began by saying it haunted you." Furious, George thought he had never heard anything so disingenuous in his life. For two pins, he would arrest the man on the instant.

But Fitzgerald appeared unmoved by the snapped reminder. He shifted his shoulders and spread his hands. "What would you? One is not always master of these things. Had I been asked if I had seen her, no doubt it would have jumped to the forefront of my mind long since."

"How was it you came to be there at that exact moment?"

"I was walking home from the tavern. Near midnight, I think, but I cannot be certain. It may have been earlier. My way takes me past the players' lodging. Oftentimes I accompany Arthur, but he had left earlier."

George controlled his temper with an effort. "Very well, and what exactly did you see?"

Fitzgerald peered into the middle distance as if he conjured the picture. "A coach was waiting in the lane. I paid no heed to it at first. But then a girl came out of the lodging. She was cloaked but her glorious gold hair cascaded over her shoulders. One could not mistake. Before I could think or do anything, she had stepped up into the coach."

"Did you see a man with her? Did not someone help her up the steps?"

Fitzgerald frowned. "Not that I recall. But I was on the other side of the street. Perhaps the fellow was inside and leaned out?"

George regarded the man with a mixture of exasperation and sheer disbelief. "You do realise you are at least a witness in this business?"

The piratical look became pronounced as the fellow's brows snapped together.

"Damnation! Yes, I suppose I must be, to that extent."

"Moreover," pursued George, driving it home, "you have no apparent means of proving your story."

The brows shot up. "Good God, that is so too! You mean I may have made it up for the purpose of swinging suspicion away from myself?" He frowned again. "Singularly stupid of me, had I done the deed. Or merely careless. Why draw attention to the matter at all?"

George could not deny the truth of this. Unless the fellow was being doubly clever. He began to feel pressured and to wish for Ottilia's peculiar ability to sift fact from fiction. But he could make use of the introduction in other ways.

"Which of the players did you leave behind you at The Black Dog?"

Fitzgerald pondered again, setting his gaze upon the playbills plastered to the wall. George could willingly have planted the fellow a flush hit to the jaw. He felt as if he had lost control of the interview. Was he being played for a puppet?

The man's eyes returned to give George a concentrated look. "Jasper, certainly. Lewis, I think. I cannot be sure of Rob, but I think Wat and Aisling had gone. Like me, they were late to the tavern after setting things to rights at the theatre. I waited to lock up after them."

So he meant to foist the blame off on to Robert Collins, did he? He would catch cold at that, for Rob had already stated he remained to look out for young Jasper. George reviewed the man's words.

"Have you any reason to think either Wat or Aisling might have gained Dulcie's affections?"

A spluttered laugh greeted this suggestion. "My dear Colonel, do pray keep a steady head. Can you honestly suppose either one a suitable prospect? In any event, you must realise the two are mere jobbing actors, pressed into service where needed. They are stagehands, sir."

"Too lowly for Dulcibella?"

A patronising shrug. "One would say so, though perhaps it is a little unkind. Good men, both, but scarcely of a type to appeal to a girl of Dulcibella's multiple attractions. You have only to look at them."

George had come to much the same conclusion, and he had Cecile's notion to support it. But he had no mind to trust anything Fitzgerald said at this point.

"What about Lewis Payne?"

Fitzgerald's eye gleamed. "Now you are clutching at straws, Colonel. No, no, Lewis is no candidate. I have known him long and, if I must stoop to tale bearer in this cause, gossip has it he and Hilde have an established and comfortable arrangement."

This was news to George. Nor had he seen any evidence to support it, though he was bound to admit it was not unlikely. The two had been members of the company for many years and neither was married. Leaving Lewis, he took up the last option.

"I dare say you will dismiss this out of hand, but I must ask you."

He was treated to an enquiring look and an air of willingness. "I will try to satisfy any query of yours, sir. It is the least I can do."

Was it indeed? For which particular reason? Or was it spurious?

"Ferdinand himself."

The man's eyes widened. "Arthur? Arthur kill his golden goose? You must have windmills in your head, sir."

"Every man of the company must be considered, sir. Not one can prove his having remained all night in the lodgings, including Ferdinand."

Fitzgerald waved his hands, his lip curling. "Oh no, nonsense, Colonel, this cannot be. What possible motive could he have? The reverse, as I have stated. Besides, he is devoted to Janey. Unutterably and irrevocably devoted to her, I assure you."

"Indeed? Even though she is apt to rule him?"

"Yes, yes, but he enjoys that," said Fitzgerald on an impatient note. "He has said to me I don't know how many times that he relies upon Janey to keep him from taking the stage too much into ordinary life."

George played his ace. "But the fact is, Fitzgerald, there is a cogent motive for any married man."

The manager's figure stilled. His gaze narrowed. "What do you mean?"

George kept his eyes glued to the man's face, determined not to miss his reaction.

"Dulcibella Ash was with child."

Shock, disappointment, rage? The emotions flitted so rapidly across Fitzgerald's face that George had difficulty interpreting them. And then the oddity akin to regret was back, just as he'd looked when he spoke of feeling haunted. His words were unexpected.

"Poor little Dulcibella. How tragic. How horribly cruel is fate." A frown came. "It is not generally known, I take it? Arthur never said a word of this. You have not told him?"

George shook his head. "And I will be glad of your word that you will not mention the matter outside this room, Fitzgerald."

The fellow's shock appeared genuine, though how could one judge? He gave a poignant sigh. "You may rely upon me. I should not care to be the one who carries such tidings to either Arthur or Janey. Good God, Janey! She will be distressed beyond measure. She is a mother hen to those young girls, for all her strictness. And to think the child managed to conceal it from them all."

"Not quite all," George said drily, and received a sharp look.

"You mean the man who killed her for it. An unpleasant thought, sir, to say the least. A hideous thought in fact."

"Quite so." He did not mention Cecile's knowledge of the pregnancy. It was of no value to this interview. The niggling thought he would have shielded Cecile even if it was germane snagged at his mind. He put it aside and stood up.

"I thank you for your frankness, sir. You have been most helpful. Keep your observation of Dulcie that night to yourself also for the present."

"Certainly, if that is your wish."

"I thank you. And you may expect to be called to stand witness in due course. The more details you can dig up from your wayward memory, Fitzgerald, the better."

The other's brow lifted. "I dare say you are bound to retain an open mind on that score, Colonel. I can only hope further discovery will eliminate the need for me to fear the rope."

Upon which note, George took his leave, feeling that if Fitzgerald was the murderer, he was a very cool villain indeed.

Ottilia listened with close attention to George's tirade, delivered as he strode up and down the parlour, his tall person in the military rig dwarfing the place.

"I've been played, I'm convinced of it, Ottilia. First the wretch points the finger at Collins, having done his best to pretend otherwise. Then he introduces this spurious memory, which he claims evaded him previously, of seeing Dulcie get into a coach. For my money, Fitzgerald was, if anything, in the coach. From there to the cemetery is a mere couple of miles."

At this, Ottilia entered a caveat. "Would he take her there directly? He has first to render her into a suitable state for the killing, do you not think?"

George halted by the mantel, setting a hand on it as he looked frowningly down at her.

She had been watching the tumbling waves out of the window when he arrived, hot from his interview with the theatre manager and bursting with spleen. Her curiosity aroused, Ottilia had taken Sybilla's seat by the fire, which Tyler had coaxed into life at her request. Her mother-in-law was still in her room and Francis had slipped out to warn the dowager's cronies not to expect her since she had the headache, no doubt brought on by yesterday's reminder of her quarrel with her elder son.

Seeing George's temper sadly frayed as well, Ottilia had invited him to unburden himself, which he did with a vengeance, clearly by no means pleased by her interrupting question.

"What are you getting at, Ottilia?"

She spoke in a soothing tone. "You may have better information from the doctor who performed the autopsy, George, but it seems probable to me the murderer must have administered a drug to Dulcie to render her insensible."

George's frown did not abate. "Before killing her, you mean?"

"Just so. She looked beautiful, you said, which argues against any sort of struggle. Nor do I think it likely he would have stabbed her in the coach. Only think of the mess."

She had the satisfaction of seeing George break into a grin. "Ottilia, you wretch, how can you?"

She smiled. "Well, it is a consideration, do you not think? What did your doctor say?"

"Roffey? He thinks she was killed in situ, but he can't be sure."

"Well, if the blood was contained within the coffin, it seems probable. Imagine trying to lay a body already covered with blood into it. Then too, he clearly had his intentions already set and Dulcie was hardly going to get into the coffin herself."

George threw up his eyes. "I might have known you would upset my conclusions at the outset."

"Not at all. It may well have been that Fitzgerald was indeed in the coach. All I am saying is that, whoever picked Dulcie up, he could not have taken her directly to the cemetery. He might wine and dine her first perhaps."

"Why, if he was pretending an elopement?"

"You have only Cecile's supposition for that. All we know for a fact is that Dulcie was in all that night."

"Why should she be if her desperate problem was not going to be solved?"

Ottilia put up a finger. "We don't know that either. A promise of marriage might have been made, perhaps to lull her fears. I must say it seems unlikely to me the girl would dress in her best for an elopement at dead of night. Nor did she take any change of raiment, or so much as a toothbrush."

George looked struck and his frown reappeared. "Very well, but what of Fitzgerald? Are you saying he administered a narcotic?"

Ottilia opened her eyes at him. "I am not saying Fitzgerald did anything, George. That is an assumption on your part."

He uttered an exasperated sound, his protest both curt and irritated. "But it fits, Ottilia. He knows the players and he knows theatre. It's a bagatelle to him to set the scene in such a way to point to the company and he tried to make me suspect this Rob fellow. He suddenly comes up with this fairy tale of seeing Dulcie, which I don't believe for a moment. And to cap it all, he has the right sort of looks and personality."

"Is he kind?" Ottilia countered. "What time was it when he saw her? Does it fit with the time Dulcie left the lodgings? Moreover, does it fit with the time of death?"

"Lord knows!" George drummed his fingers on the mantel. "Roffey places the killing somewhere between two and three in the early hours. Midnight or thereabouts for the coach, Fitzgerald claims. I'd have to check if Cecile noted the time."

Ottilia pounced. "The approximation is enough, George. It may well fit, whether or not Fitzgerald is lying. Let us say Dulcie enters the coach around midnight. The murderer takes her somewhere convenient to ply her with refreshment in order to introduce the drug."

"Yes, and then what? He's got to carry the unconscious girl into the coach without being seen."

"Just so, which is why he waits until a later hour. Indeed, he must wait, because he wants to set the scene so his candlelight will be spotted."

George smote his own forehead. "Of course. Why didn't I remember that? He judged it a trifle off, however, because the candles had mostly burned down by the time the villagers saw it and it was near dawn."

"And there is the business of digging up the grave and extracting the coffin."

George dropped into the chair opposite, resting his arms on his knees and clasping his hands together between them. "We believe he had help for that, though we have not yet discovered from whom."

This was of interest and Ottilia allowed herself to be distracted for the moment. "What have you done to find out?"

"I set Sullivan to make enquiries of all the official grave-diggers round about. Without result, I may say."

"Well, they are not going to confess to it, are they? The murderer would have paid them well, though it seems a deal too risky to trust such a man." Her mind leapt to the obvious. "What about grave robbers?"

"I thought of that too, but how do we find them?"

"Difficult, I agree, when you are militia."

He sighed. "A handicap, I don't mind telling you, when it comes to questioning suspects."

"I am sure it must be," said Ottilia with a sympathetic look. "But you have gleaned a deal of information nevertheless."

"Evidently not enough to convict Fitzgerald," he retorted on a gloomy note.

"You may yet do so, although we have still to find out more of this fellow Paglesham."

"I thought Lady Polbrook was going to talk to him."

"She did, and she is quite as convinced of his being the murderer as you are of Fitzgerald."

George perked up. "Indeed? Why?"

Ottilia laughed. "No, George, you can't go and arrest the fellow at once. It is merely that Sybilla thinks he, of all men, is the most likely to have his ambition thwarted by Dulcie's pregnancy, and so he rid himself of an unwelcome encumbrance."

"Ah, but so it is with Fitzgerald. He is unmarried, but I can't see him taking an actress to wife."

"But he could have done," Ottilia objected, "so we may have to give him the benefit of the doubt." George did not look as if he wanted to give the man the benefit of anything, to her amusement. She returned to her hypothesis. "It would be well if we knew the contents of Dulcie's stomach, George."

"I'll check with Roffey." George stirred restlessly. "A pity we can't get hold of this grave robber. We would have our man in a moment."

Ottilia pondered whether to mention her notion of there being a witness other than the grave robber. It was not to be supposed that whoever dug the grave would have been encouraged to linger, which made it unlikely he might be the thief who had purloined the purse. On balance, she thought George had enough on his mind without adding to it at this present. She changed the subject.

"Let us see if I manage to glean anything from the theatre ladies, George. If Fitzgerald is a likely candidate, you may depend upon it one of them will know."

Had it not been for Mrs Ferdinand, who was perfectly gracious and self-assured, Ottilia would have despaired of the success of the gathering for tea. She had called upon her mother-in-law to preside, but Sybilla's presence clearly overawed Katharine Drummond, who sat mumchance for the first ten minutes. Hildegard Larkin was plainly flattered to be invited to hobnob with a lady of so high a rank as the Dowager Marchioness of Polbrook, and Ottilia was amused to find herself almost as exalted a personage in the actress's eyes.

"Honoured, I'm sure, my lady," she said, executing an accomplished curtsy when Cecile presented her as Milady Fanshawe.

Ottilia scotched this at the outset, for she was relying upon the creature to gossip her head off. "Oh, pray call me Lady Fan. Everyone does, you know. I never stand upon ceremony, if I can avoid it."

Miss Larkin visibly rejoiced. "What a relief, my lady, for I'm a plain woman myself. Not that I can't put on airs if I must, for I hope I'm a good enough player for that."

Ottilia smiled. "Certainly you are, from the performance I was privileged to see, Miss Larkin."

The woman dropped all reserve, leaning in and going so far as to touch Ottilia on the arm. "Hilde will do, my dear Lady Fan, if you don't object. I can't abide formality."

"Then we are at one, Hilde. Do, pray, sit down by me a while."

Nothing loath, the creature took a seat beside her on the second chair in the window embrasure where Ottilia had stationed herself, precisely for the purpose of taking her chance with each of the actresses in turn. Sybilla had pledged, not without persuasion, to entertain the rest while she conducted her enquiries.

"So you have seen our rendition of *The Conscious Lovers*, I take it?" Hilde began. "What did you think of us?" She then waved expressive hands. "A terrible question, of course, for how can you do otherwise than praise us all to the skies? I wish you won't, however, for the truth is we are nothing without our Dulcie's magic touch."

Genuine regret sounded in the woman's voice, but Ottilia was happy to find her so ready a talker. Not to mention an early reference to the topic of the day.

"I must admit I am sorry not to have seen her. I hear on all sides of her beauty and this gift she had of appearing to advantage on the stage."

Hilde sighed. "A lovely creature, she was, but such a silly little fool too." A grimace came. "Horrid of me to say it now, but poor Dulcie had less than common sense."

Ottilia leapt on this. "You are speaking of her dealings with men?"

"Oh, it wasn't her fault, Lady Fan. She was badly brought up, poor child. Janey did her best, but there is no doing anything with a girl whose head can't help but be turned by all that attention."

"I understood she was something of an innocent," Ottilia suggested, watching the woman carefully.

"Too innocent. Any man might have taken her in, and of course one did. But I'd stake my oath it wasn't one of ours."

This was said with an air of suppressed violence. As Ottilia eyed the woman, the maid Joanie entered, followed by Tyler, both bearing trays with the accoutrements for tea, together with a selection of little cakes and dainties.

The business of making the tea, which Sybilla undertook while the servants dispensed plates and proffered the treats on offer, took some time. The conversation became necessarily general for a space and Ottilia seized her chance to take stock of the visitors.

In the presence of the others, Cecile was peculiarly self-effacing, speaking very little and seemingly content to watch and listen. Was it her habit to take a back seat with members of the company? Once the girl Kate's initial shyness wore off, she contributed willingly, responding to Sybilla's query about her favourite roles in the expressive voice with a timbre Ottilia remembered from her performance.

As for Mrs Ferdinand, she was both gracious and graceful, yet had a confident way about her that argued as strong a personality as the dowager, if less forceful. She listened with clear indulgence to Kate expressing her desire to play the great female Shakespearean roles, like Juliet, Lady Macbeth and her namesake Kate the Shrew.

"But such opportunities are rare," she said in her musically modulated tones. "Audiences won't come for Shakespeare."

"We are besides too small a company," Mrs Ferdinand added with a smile. "We would have poor Wat and Aisling running around like flies in a tar-box, trying to play a dozen different characters."

Ottilia seized opportunity, lowering her voice. "Your stagehands, I believe. They at least could scarcely have time for dalliance with the female players, I surmise."

Hilde showed her a face both astonished and amused. "Lord, no! Are you thinking of our poor Dulcie? Neither Wat nor Aisling could have hoped for a chance with her, I assure you, Lady Fan."

"Who could then, Hilde?"

Hilde threw a glance at Kate and dropped her voice to a murmur. "I shouldn't care for Kate to know it, but if you ask me Jasper would have whipped Dulcie's skirts up in a minute, if she'd let him."

The descent to vulgarity rather amused Ottilia than otherwise, besides serving her purpose. She similarly dropped her voice even further, adopting a conspiratorial tone. "I understood Kate has something of a yen for Jasper. Is it so?"

Hilde rolled her eyes. "She is besotted. She knows well he is the worst possible match for her, but she can't help herself, poor love. Mind, she tries. She pinches at him with the best — we all do so, you must know, Lady Fan, for he is the most annoying boy. Arthur despairs of him and I don't blame him."

"But Dulcie did not indulge him? You are sure of that?"

Hilde shook her head with vehemence. "Wouldn't touch him. Or let him touch her where it matters. There's no stopping him from fondling, of course. The boy has hands like an octopus."

Ottilia moved her off the unprofitable subject of Jasper, who appeared to be the bane of the company. "I gather your other fellow — Rob, is it? — was a little *épris?*"

"Which of them was not?" Hilde tossed her head. "Galling for poor Kate, though she was as fond of Dulcie as any of us. You would think us females would be jealous as sin, would you not? If I still had my youth, likely I would have been. But Dulcie was such a sweetheart, you couldn't do anything but love her."

There was a catch in the woman's voice and Ottilia saw her eyes rim with moisture. Genuine affection? Ottilia tested it.

"You must miss her sorely."

Hilde sniffed, but her voice had turned a trifle husky. "We are all trying to carry on, because there's nothing else to do. Besides, we are mostly old troopers. But it's hard, Lady Fan, very hard."

"I am sure it must be." Ottilia took a deliberate measure. "Harder for the murderer in some ways, never knowing when his guilt may be discovered."

Shock rendered Hilde silent for a space. She eyed Ottilia as if she was a dangerous animal who might at any moment make a fateful leap. Then she drew a tight breath.

"You can't believe it's one of ours, you simply can't."

Ottilia held her gaze. "It's a possibility we cannot set out of count."

Hilde's eyes became frantic. "But who? Not Lewis. It wasn't Lewis, that I can swear to."

"How can you swear to it, Hilde? Do you know for a fact he was at the lodgings that night?"

A deep flush crept over the woman's features and she threw an apprehensive look at Mrs Ferdinand, deep in conversation with Sybilla. Ottilia noted Cecile was engaged in a low-toned discussion with Kate. Opportune. She turned her eyes back to her quarry.

"Hilde?"

The actress's gaze came back to her, becoming intense. Her voice was a murmur. "This is to go no further, Lady Fan."

Ottilia hesitated. "I can't promise that if what you want to tell me is pertinent to the case."

Hilde's hand came up, fidgeting with the neckline of her gown. She appeared to make up her mind. "Lewis was with me." She gripped her fingers together. "We — we don't flaunt it. We try to be discreet."

"Can you keep it secret? In such a close-knit company?"

Her mouth worked a little. "They suspect, I dare say, but I'd swear none knows for certain. Besides, we prefer the informality. Neither of us is tied to the other." She eyed Ottilia in a sly fashion. "Now tell me I've shocked you."

She had indeed, if Ottilia was honest. She could not approve a liaison which evidently left both parties free to seek amusement elsewhere. On the other hand, where there was no promise of fidelity, one might argue there could be no betrayal. She found it personally distasteful, but who was she to pass judgement? She smiled.

"A little perhaps."

Hilde's mouth twisted. "But it's what you expect of actresses, is that it?"

"I did not say so."

"You don't have to, Lady Fan. I'm used to it. And I've no doubt it's what made poor Dulcie a target."

"No doubt." Glad of the return to the point at issue, Ottilia took instant advantage. "You think she was targeted by one of her admirers?"

Hilde shifted her shoulders. "She had so many." A spasm crossed her face. "You asked about Rob."

Encouraged, Ottilia looked a question. Hilde sighed. "No use denying it. Rob was smitten with Dulcie. Nothing he could do about it, for Trix would have his bollocks." She then threw a hand to her mouth, consternation entering her eyes and her cheeks flying colour. "Oops! I do beg your pardon, ma'am, it slipped out."

Ottilia gave her a wry look, but avoided commenting on the vulgarity.

"Trix is his wife?"

"Yes, and she's a tartar of the first order. Can't call his soul his own, our Rob. She's the only woman I've ever thought ought to be muzzled in one of those scold bridles. Scratch, scratch, scratch, like a bad-tempered cat."

"She sounds a very shrew," Ottilia said, keen to keep the woman talking of this particular player.

"Oh, hideous. Lewis tells him he ought to give her the back of his hand, but Rob's terrified of the woman. She nagged him constantly about abandoning his apprenticeship for the theatre. Now if Trix had been murdered, I'd be telling you to look at Rob, no question. It's no wonder the poor man lusted after Dulcie. She was the sweetest little thing. Mind, she couldn't act to save her life. No one cared though. She made a pretty picture and both Arthur and Janey coached her to say her lines with the right inflexions so she passed muster, but that's about it."

"She could not conjure the emotions needed?"

"Oh, a semblance of 'em. The audiences did not care, for they were too dazzled by her. Or the men were. But the real stuff?" Hilde shook her head. "Nothing. Not the way Kate does it. Or Jasper, for the matter of that. That's why Arthur puts up with him. The rest of us are competent. I don't count Arthur for he's old school, with his roaring and posturing. But Jasper and Kate are supreme."

It was said in a matter of fact manner that drew Ottilia's admiration. "You do not sound as if you envy either, Hilde."

She shrugged. "Why should I? I'm content with my lot. I've got regular work and I enjoy my roles. I'm fond of Janey and Arthur." She dropped her voice. "And I have Lewis for a friend." Another shrug. "I had my time, Lady Fan, and it was good. I'm lucky to be still able to work in the profession. And what would I do else?"

What indeed? Ottilia warmed to the woman, despite her tendency to go off the subject. She took her firmly back. "And you have no notion who Dulcie might have favoured outside the men of the company?"

"None at all. I paid no heed, to be honest. There were ever hopeful males hanging around the stage door. I'm always too busy making sure the costumes are put away in good order, and then I want nothing more than a nightcap and my bed." She laughed in her hearty way. "I'm a dull creature, Lady Fan, when all's said."

"It's not the adjective I would use." But Ottilia had no desire to continue the conversation. She was hunting her mind for an excuse to exchange Hilde for Kate, when she remembered the theatre manager.

"How well do you know Mr Fitzgerald, Hilde?"

"Fitz? Pretty well, why?" Her eyes widened. "You're not thinking to couple Fitz with Dulcie, are you?"

"Why not?"

Hilde stared. "Why not? Heavens above! It's ridiculous, that's why not."

Ottilia held her gaze. "Why is it ridiculous?"

The actress blew an impatient breath. "Fitz, of all things! A confirmed bachelor. I've never known him to hanker after any female. Not that I think he's one of those types if you know what I mean. In fact, I did hope at one time…"

She faded out, a faint flush creeping into her cheeks. Had she had designs on Fitzgerald herself? Ottilia probed gently. "You thought at one time?"

Hilde looked decidedly uncomfortable. "He's quite a catch, is Fitz. When he first took over as manager, some years ago now, I tried — well, I threw out a lure or two, let's be honest. But he wouldn't bite."

Ottilia was conscious of feeling rather sorry for Hilde. She had evidently settled for a less than lawful alternative, having failed to secure a more permanent and solid investment. On impulse, she reached out to lay a hand over the pudgy one lying in Hilde's lap.

"Why don't you marry Lewis?"

Colour swept into the woman's face. "He hasn't asked me. Besides, it wouldn't answer. He could no more secure my future than I can myself. No, Lady Fan. We're better off muddling along as we do."

Ottilia left it there, feeling anxious to tackle Kate instead. As if she read her mind, the girl rose from where she had been sitting with Cecile on the chaise longue and came across to the window. Wholly ignoring her senior, she fixed Ottilia with a pair of candid dark eyes.

"Cecily says you want to talk to me, ma'am."

Ottilia smiled. "Indeed I do."

"Suppose you want me to give place," Hilde grunted, picking up her cup and plate and shoving to her feet. She patted the younger girl. "Good luck, dear. Lady Fan is nothing if not shrewd. Don't bother prevaricating." With which, she threw

Ottilia a wink and moved off to join the others, breaking into their conversation without ceremony. "Well, she's done with me. Your turn after Kate, I expect, Janey."

Kate took the vacated seat, treating Ottilia to a moue of distaste. Her tone was almost waspish. "It didn't take Hilde long to revert, I see." She brought her gaze to bear on Ottilia, faint apology in it. "Janey told us to be on our best behaviour."

"Acting a part for my benefit?"

A tiny laugh escaped Kate. "Yes. Or more for Lady Polbrook, for Cecily told us you are easy to talk to." Her voice changed, a trifle of apprehension entering in. "She said you are helping that colonel and you have solved murders before. You must be very clever, ma'am."

Ottilia was beset with her usual embarrassment. As ever, the tribute felt undue.

"I am not particularly clever. Merely observant. It is a knack, if you like, which has proved useful in the past, yes."

Kate eyed her with a look of interest. Genuine? Or was it assumed? "You might have made an actress then."

Astonished, Ottilia was betrayed into a disbelieving laugh. "I hardly think so. I am no hand at mimicry. Besides, I should be terrified."

"It is not mimicry, ma'am. But it is observation. You have to study humanity. Not just how we walk and talk, though that is part of it. More, you must look for what is inside that may be revealed upon the outside. People give their thoughts away in all sorts of ways and a player must be alert to that."

Impressed, Ottilia regarded the girl with increasing interest. "Then it is something like perhaps. But you go further, Kate — if I may? — for you must reproduce these things upon the stage."

A sudden smile lit the girl's unremarkable features, lighting them up. "That is the trick of it. But it should not be a conscious thing once you are in play. You must live within the skin of the role and the rest will follow."

"You are giving me a remarkable insight into your trade, Kate." Ottilia was genuinely interested, almost to the point of forgetting her purpose. "I take it Dulcie did not have this attribute of bringing the role to life?"

A spasm crossed Kate's face. "She did not have to. Her shine and beauty were sufficient."

"You did not like that?" A surprised look made Ottilia amend this. "I do not mean to imply that you were jealous of her success."

"Not of her success. I should much dislike to be lauded merely for my looks."

"Then?"

Kate sighed. "Oh, for being overshadowed by her, if you wish to know. While they were being dazzled, audiences could not note my skills."

"You are forgetting the feminine element in your audiences, Kate."

She shook her head. "I am not. She had that quality of drawing the eye, you see. Females were as much taken with her. I was myself."

It began to seem as if Katharine Drummond might benefit from Dulcie's death. But to do her justice, she had made no such leap herself. Or she had the grace not to say so.

"What I am wondering, Kate, is whether Dulcie confided in you?"

A tiny frown settled between the girl's brows. "About her admirers?" Her gaze strayed to the French girl. "She was more likely to tell Cecily, if she told anyone."

Ottilia scotched this at once. "Only to a degree. Since I am sure you know it, I don't scruple to say that Cecile is much too strait-laced to be the recipient of that sort of confidence."

Kate's brows rose in an unexpectedly haughty look. "The sort that marks us for little better than prostitutes?"

"I did not say so. Nor did I imply any kind of judgement, Kate."

There was no sign of consciousness. The girl continued to regard her steadily. "Everyone makes that judgement. It is a risk of the profession. But we do not all succumb." She drew a sharp breath. "I thought Dulcie would. She chattered of the men who pursued her."

"That is just what I am after, Kate. Who came up in her chatter? What did she say of them? You've spoken of observation yourself. Such details may reveal a good deal."

Kate look struck. "Of course you are right. Only I don't know if I can remember much of it. I like to run my lines in my head while I prepare, you see, and I paid scant attention to Dulcie's inconsequence."

Ottilia could have screamed with vexation. Must the girl be so single minded? She tried for a coaxing note. "Try, Kate. Any little thing tucked away in your head may be of use."

The actress hesitated, not as if she sought to prevaricate, but with a look of concentration as if she gathered her memories. Ottilia waited, taking opportunity to observe how the girl's thoughts became mirrored in her face, yet without grimace or apparent change in her expression. It was fascinating to watch. When a pertinent thought arrived, Ottilia knew it at once by an abrupt change.

"Yes, there was a peculiarity now I think of it." The dark gaze came to rest on Ottilia. "The night she died Dulcie spoke of her good fortune. Or did she say good? Fortune certainly."

"Do you recall just what she said?"

A tiny frown settled between Kate's brows. "Not exactly. Something about change. And having played the roles she had done fitting her for her fortune. She kept making a curtsey before the mirror and plying her fan. 'My lady,' she said. 'My lord.' I paid no mind at the time. Dulcie was always posturing."

"Did she say a name? Or speak of a particular person?"

A shrug came. "If she did, I did not notice." Then her eyes widened. "Stay! She did mention someone. Perry? Not that night. Earlier, I think."

Alert, Ottilia pressed her. "How much earlier?"

"Oh, before we came back to Weymouth. We may have been in Exeter or Lyme for all I know. We make a circuit through the month. Sometimes as much as six weeks if Arthur has managed to secure an extra booking."

Impatient of this divagation, interesting as it was, Ottilia probed for more pertinent detail.

"Wherever it was, can you remember just what Dulcie said of this Perry?"

Kate gave a tiny laugh. "Oh, yes. The naïve little idiot supposed he was in love with her. She seemed to think she had only to decide. Imagine it! I think she had some notion she was in the position of a debutante in society. I dare say she took it from one of her roles. She was apt to confuse real life with what we did on stage, believing it to be a true reflection."

"Did she have others in mind besides Perry when she thought to choose?"

"I imagine she must have done. There was no shortage of admirers wherever we went. Indeed, one or two were apt to follow her from town to town. I could swear that army captain turned up at the stage door in Exeter."

Startled, Ottilia caught her wandering gaze and held it. "When? When was this, Kate? Please try to pin it down. It may be particularly important."

The girl's face reflected surprise back. "Indeed? Is he the man?"

"I don't know that, Kate. But he is known to be one of her admirers in Weymouth. Think back, if you please."

For the first time, a hint of consternation entered the dark eyes. "It was weeks back."

"How many?"

"I don't know. Four to eight perhaps? We have visited The Exeter Theatre since, so it must have been the time before. Janey will know. She keeps track of these things for Arthur."

The impulse to shift at once to Jane Ferdinand was strong, but Ottilia curbed it. Whether or not this put Captain Edgcott back in the running, she had still to sift the matter of this man Perry. Sir Peregrine?

"Kate, I must ask you to think carefully, if you please. When was it — or where were you, if that is easier — when Dulcie spoke of believing Perry was in love with her?"

The little frown reappeared and Ottilia saw the girl fall into the same concentrated attitude. Not unhopeful, she waited out the effort, and was rewarded.

"I believe it was in Lyme Regis."

"Was Perry in evidence there?"

"Not that I noticed." Then her tone became confident. "No, he wasn't. Dulcie said she must decide before we came back to Weymouth."

"Decide what? Whether to accept an offer? Could the choice have been whether to marry or stay with the theatre?"

Kate's face showed a trifle of anguish. "I don't know! I wish I did. I wish I had listened more closely, truly I do. But the truth is, I found her assumption so nonsensical, I shut her chatter out of my mind and concentrated on my lines."

Her agitation would not help to recover the memory. Ottilia backtracked. "Never mind it. I dare say it is of less importance than I suppose."

Kate did not answer. "How can it be? You are thinking this man Perry might have killed her, are you not?"

"Any one of her admirers must be suspect, Kate. We do not yet have any firm evidence to show just who it was, which is why I wanted to talk to you all. The more we know of these men, the closer we may come to finding out."

Kate put her fingers to her mouth in a gesture that made her seem vulnerable all at once. "I see that. I am sorry not to have been of more help."

"You have been of immense help, Kate, and I cannot sufficiently thank you for being so open with me."

The girl nodded and rose. "You will want Janey, I expect."

Ottilia smiled and raised her voice. "Yes, but I think we might all take a refill, don't you? Sybilla!" Her mother-in-law, who was looking a trifle bored, glanced across. Ottilia gave her a little gesture of apology. "Is the tea still hot, do you suppose? Should we send for another kettle?"

The conversation became general for a while as Tyler was sent for to refresh the tea. Ottilia moved to stand by Sybilla's chair from where she was able to observe the players. It was noticeable that both Hilde and Kate had become more relaxed, the latter cutting into a discussion under way between Cecile and the older woman concerning a new costume.

"But I beg you won't do it in blue, Hilde, for I believe a dark red would suit better."

"You mean it would suit you better," returned the matron. "Arthur doesn't want it changed."

"I'll talk to him then," said Kate. "Or Janey will. Janey!"

Mrs Ferdinand, who was responding to some question of the dowager's, looked round with an admonishing frown. "Hush, Kate! I am talking to Lady Polbrook."

The girl did not flush, but her eyes showed dismay and she threw an apologetic look at Sybilla. "I beg your pardon, ma'am. I did not mean to interrupt." A smile of great charm appeared. "Only you and Lady Fan have made us feel so much at ease, I'm afraid I forgot my manners. Pray forgive me."

It was, to Ottilia's mind, both prettily expressed and very much a sample of Kate's acting skills. She convinced Sybilla, who became at once gracious.

"Think nothing of it. I am glad to know you feel comfortable."

"You are very kind, ma'am, thank you."

With which, Kate smiled again, shot a look at Mrs Ferdinand as if she sought approval and turned back to her companions. Ottilia noted Hilde's raised eyebrow and knew she had guessed aright. Kate was acting a part.

Cecile seemed not to notice. "Is it not that there is red cloth in the trunk, Hilde?"

Or was it an attempt to smooth over the little faux pas? Recalling the *émigré*'s origins, Ottilia thought it likely. She must have been well versed in social ease before she had been obliged to fall in with a company of players.

Her attention was claimed by their matriarch as George had called Mrs Ferdinand. "I understand you may wish to converse a little, Lady Francis?"

"If you are willing, ma'am."

Sybilla intervened. "When we have a fresh pot, Ottilia. You will be interested to know that Mrs Ferdinand is acquainted with Lord Charlton and this captain we hear so much about."

This was said with a meaning look and Ottilia was at once interested. "Is it so, ma'am? Do you know either of them well?"

"Not well at all," responded the matriarch, her voice low-pitched and pleasing. "Lord Charlton sought me out for the purpose of warning me of Dulcie's innocence. He was concerned she would be taken in by a man of less integrity than himself."

"Which she clearly was," stated Sybilla on a dry note.

A shadow crossed Jane Ferdinand's face. "I should have been more alert. Dulcie was scarcely more than a child."

Sybilla glanced up at Ottilia with a look she recognised. If the players had not been present, the dowager would have snorted. She plainly had no belief in Dulcie's innocence. A pragmatic creature was her mother-in-law. She called a spade a spade and had no truck with subtleties.

Hilde, however, abandoning the resumption of a discussion on costume, was quick to leap to Mrs Ferdinand's defence. "You can't blame yourself, Janey. With so many after her, it's hardly surprising Dulcie lost her head."

"I can blame myself, and I do." Jane Ferdinand's head came up and she met Ottilia's gaze with a clear one of her own. "I did not take Lord Charlton's warning with any seriousness. I believed I had a close enough eye on the girl, and I suspected besides he might be trying to flummery me into chasing off his rivals because he wanted the girl for himself."

"Good heavens, why?" Sybilla was staring at the woman in disbelief. "Would he not instead have tried to persuade you of his honourable intentions?"

"Towards an actress? Hardly, Lady Polbrook."

"There is that, I suppose."

Ottilia cut in without ceremony. "What made you suspect his motives, Mrs Ferdinand?"

Her lips worked a little before she spoke. "I knew Dulcie had been seeing the man. I taxed her with it last season, but she protested he was only being kind. Kind! He took her to Mrs Horniman's late in the night and plied her with dainties and toys. Tokens of what, may I ask? Affection? Mere friendship?"

Ottilia broke into the rising distress. "Did you ask him?"

"Certainly not. I asked Dulcie. She said he was like an uncle to her. Well, I beg your pardon, ladies, but I have good reason to know how so-called uncles may behave towards young girls. Especially girls labelled with the stigma that dogs women of our profession. We may be as respectable as any lady of repute, but the world persists in believing otherwise."

Sybilla, with a scorching glance at Ottilia, kept her mouth firmly shut. But the low-toned tirade required an answer.

"You are perfectly right, Mrs Ferdinand, and I am sorry for it. In this instance, such prejudice has proved tragic. You are understandably and justifiably upset and I applaud your sentiments."

The woman blinked a time or two, and Ottilia realised she was winking tears away. Her voice came huskily in the surrounding silence.

"That is generous of you, Lady Francis. Thank you."

Since Tyler chose this opportune moment to enter the room with a freshly steaming kettle and a clean teapot, Ottilia was spared having to answer. By the time tea was once again made and served, an easier atmosphere had been restored and Ottilia drew Jane Ferdinand out of the circle to her improvised eyrie by the window.

"Pray tell me more of this man Charlton, if you will, Mrs Ferdinand."

The woman met her gaze with an oddly hardened expression in her eyes. Her voice remained low. "Tit for tat, Lady Francis. Pray tell me more of this Colonel Tretower."

Ottilia eyed her, wary. She had divined George's interest, had she? Did this mean she knew Cecile was enamoured? It felt distinctly odd to be requested to trot out George's credentials. She opted for frankness.

"If you wish to gauge whether he is a suitable sort of man to be courting Cecile, ma'am, you had better ask my husband. They have been friends far longer than I have known either. Comrades in arms too, for my husband was a sometime soldier."

Mrs Ferdinand gave her a shrewd look. "Then he is bound to be biased. I wish besides for a woman's judgement." A smile flitted across her lips and vanished again. "I have lost one lamb to the slaughter, ma'am. I do not intend to allow another to be gobbled up by a marauding wolf."

The thought of George in such a light was too ridiculous for Ottilia. She could not withhold a gurgle of merriment. The affront in the elder woman's face sobered her at once. She put out a hand.

"Pardon my ill-timed mirth, ma'am, but your epithet applied to poor George simply will not do."

A reluctant smile appeared. "Well, it ought to allay my qualms that you think so, I suppose."

Ottilia's amusement faded. "My laughter was out of place. It is a besetting sin of mine, I'm afraid, to be merry at the wrong moment. It has got me into all sorts of awkward situations, I assure you."

Mrs Ferdinand visibly relaxed. "A sense of humour is never out of place. We could not get through the exigencies of life without one." Then she drew a tight breath and the distress returned as she glanced across at the *émigré*, who had retired from the conversation and was sipping tea in a meditative fashion. "I have stood in place of her mother to that girl. I promised Madame Benoit I would use her as if she had been my daughter. But that was of course nonsense. Any daughter of mine would have trodden the boards."

"I understand you have kept her close and tended her with the utmost care, ma'am."

"Not close enough since she did not see fit to inform me of Dulcie's condition."

Ottilia all but gasped. "You know?"

The matriarch's features became tighter still. "If I had known earlier, Dulcie would not be dead. Cecile's confidence came too late."

"When did she tell you?"

"After the colonel routed us out of bed to search for a missing purse." There was wrath in the woman's eyes. "I questioned Cecile since she clearly knew all about it and she confessed the truth."

"You have not told the others, I trust?"

"Cecile begged me not to, and I did not wish to add to the general upset besides. My people are distressed and bewildered enough, and the men cannot be wholly comfortable until the murderer is discovered. Nor any of us indeed."

"Which, I presume, is why you were willing to allow me to question you all."

The woman's chin came up in a gesture both proud and touching. "The sooner the business is cleared up, the sooner we may recover a semblance of normality."

"It is both distressing and uncomfortable for everyone, I agree. I do know just how it is, Mrs Ferdinand."

The woman regarded her with the first show of interest in other than the matter at hand. "It is said you have experience in these matters."

"Yes, and in no case has it been either easy or other than horrid for all concerned. Murder is a painful business for those left behind."

Mrs Ferdinand nodded, but sighed too. "We have wandered far from the point. What of Colonel Tretower, Lady Francis?"

Ottilia began to realise why this woman was indeed the matriarch of the player company. She was nothing if not persistent. What could she say? "George is a good man, ma'am. But I really think your questions would be better addressed to him."

"That won't help me." The voice was almost a snap. "I am less interested in whether he can support a wife than in the type of man he is. He is obviously a gentleman and a man used to command. He seems to be just and, to a degree, considerate. But is he kind? Is he sensitive? Will he comfort my poor lost little waif? If he takes her away from us, she will have no one, for we are her family, unworthy as we are. This George of yours must be all in all to Cecile, don't you see?"

The suppressed agitation of this speech moved Ottilia to clasp the creature's hand and give it a comforting squeeze.

"If you suppose George would influence Cecile to reject her friends, you misjudge him. He is far more likely to encourage her to keep close contact with you all. Nor do I think Cecile would dream of abandoning you. George himself spoke of her as being fiercely loyal."

"Has he affection for her? Does he truly care for her?"

Ottilia was obliged to smile. "If you ask me, I believe he was smitten with Cecile from the outset. But he will not commit the solecism of proffering his suit until this matter is settled. He is charged with finding the murderer, after all, and he considers it would be inappropriate."

"Then you've spoken with him on this subject," accused Mrs Ferdinand quickly.

"I've tried, but George is too discreet to discuss his personal affairs at length, even with me."

A long sigh escaped the matriarch. "You paint a worthy picture, ma'am."

"I am relieved if anything I have said has helped to ease your mind."

The other woman nodded, becoming brisk all at once. "You wanted to know about Lord Charlton."

"Indeed I did. Also Captain Edgcott. Kate told me you would remember just when and where it was that he was hanging around Dulcie some weeks back, and outside of Weymouth."

"The military man? He has been something of a fixture but, to my belief, Dulcie did not encourage him."

"My mother-in-law said you knew him?"

"An acquaintance only. He greeted me by name as I left the theatre."

"When he was waiting for Dulcie?"

"I presume so. He was apt to delay me with effusive praise of our performances. I suspected he was merely trying to curry favour but I did not encourage him."

"Can you pinpoint where and when he appeared other than in Weymouth?"

"I recall seeing him both at Lyme Regis and Exeter."

"When, Mrs Ferdinand?"

"I could tell you more precisely by examining my books, but certainly in both June and July. We perform each play in every location, so we have been three times to the Marine Theatre in Lyme and twice to Exeter during those months, although we began the season here at the Theatre Royal in May for two of the plays."

"As long ago as that?"

Ottilia made a rapid mathematical calculation in her head. The victim had been around two months gone, according to George's surgeon. She could have been impregnated at any one of the locations, although everything pointed to the deed having been accomplished in Weymouth.

"Did your company return here in between those two engagements?"

"Indeed, for we brought *The Rivals* here a month since. Or rather, nearly five weeks now."

"Was Captain Edgcott in evidence at your opening visit?"

Jane Ferdinand looked regretful. "That I cannot tell you with any certainty. The opening of a season demands a great deal of my time." Her tone became tart. "We were here preparing for several weeks, but I had little leisure to be noticing which stage door followers might be pursuing our leading female player. I had enough on my hands ensuring our male juvenile was fit to take the stage."

"Jasper?"

An exasperated snort almost worthy of Sybilla escaped the matriarch. "The bane of my poor husband's life, Lady Francis. If I was not so extremely fond of the boy, I should urge Arthur to throw him off the payroll. Not that he would, of course. One does not wilfully cut one's own throat."

Amused, Ottilia yet took the chance to shift attention to the male players. "I gather he can account for his movements that night, but what of Rob?"

Mrs Ferdinand's gaze became hard and fixed. "I thought you wished to ask me about followers. I won't believe any of our lads capable of this horrific crime. Against one of our own? Unthinkable."

Ottilia did not pursue the subject. It was evident she would get no help from the matriarch. She changed tack. "Let us talk of Lord Charlton then, ma'am. You did not trust him."

"No, I did not."

She had lost the woman's cooperation, Ottilia realised. Touching on the players had been maladroit. She persisted nevertheless.

"Charlton has two young daughters. He contends that his concern for Dulcie stems from how he would feel if either were subject to such importunities as she suffered."

"Does he indeed? I have yet to learn of a gentleman who equates his female kin with the lot of actresses. We are considered a race apart. We have foregone our entitlement to the courtesies accorded to ladies."

It was plain this aspect of her profession was a thorn in Jane Ferdinand's flesh and she could not think beyond it. Ottilia settled for plain facts.

"Can you say if Charlton was in evidence at either of the two resorts where you saw Edgcott?"

"He was not. Nor did the other young man appear."

"Sir Peregrine?"

"Is that his name? A good-looking boy. Rather a temptation, I thought, but Dulcie claimed she had no *tendre* for him."

"Had she one for any of these men?"

Mrs Ferdinand shrugged. "I cannot say. She hid it well, if she did. From me at least."

From everyone, it would seem. Which suggested Dulcie did believe the affair was serious. It had been too much to hope she would have confided in Mrs Ferdinand, since she did not take her desperate situation to the matriarch.

Ottilia felt she had gleaned food for much thought, but nothing to set her firmly on the track of the murderer. If there was only some way to elicit a description of the man. It was a pity George had no means of tracing the person or persons who had dug up the grave.

Chapter Nine

Banished from his lodgings and charged with a message to General Godfrey cancelling his mother's engagement to play whist, Francis took opportunity to pursue the man Paglesham. Primed by Tillie before leaving the women to their tea with the female players, he was hopeful of eliciting more pertinent detail.

"He may perhaps be more forthcoming talking man to man."

"Not if he's such a coxcomb as my mother claims," Francis objected.

His wife had given him one of her mischievous looks. "He might if you affect to be admiring of his conquest."

"Tillie, you wretch!"

She had laughed and set her hand to his chest in the intimate gesture he had grown to find tender in the extreme. "You need not fawn and flatter, Fan."

"You may be sure I won't."

"But you might say how you envy his having seen the beauty upon the stage perhaps?"

He had regarded her warily. "I might."

"And that you had heard he knew her personally. If all Sybilla says is true, that will be enough to loosen his tongue."

Francis took her hand from his chest and kissed her fingers. "Ingenious, my dear one, but you are nevertheless a manipulative schemer." He regarded her with wry amusement. "It's well for you to giggle, woman, but if I hadn't brought this on myself, I should refuse point-blank to do your bidding."

"As if I would dare bid you to do anything."

"Ha! That's all I have to say to that fatuous statement."

He had left her chuckling, insensibly cheered. She was blossoming under the necessity to pit her wits against a murderer once again and Francis cherished the returning warmth and the charm of their banter. Her mischief and wit in the face of disaster had been the attribute that first attracted him. Francis had forgotten how much he valued it until his Tillie had lost it utterly in the dark days just gone. He hoped his mother was wrong and she was truly over the tragedy.

Having delivered the dowager's excuses and exchanged pleasantries with the general and his cronies, he caught sight of his quarry just leaving by the main door. Francis followed, rather pleased than otherwise at not being obliged to accost the fellow in such a public place as the Assembly Rooms.

Paglesham left the building and headed along the street in the direction away from the beach. Where the devil was he going? Should he overtake the fellow now?

The man slowed and stopped, pulled out his pocket-watch and checked it. Francis was about to accost him when he slipped the thing back into his pocket and stepped to the door of the building next to where he had halted. The circulating library? Excellent. Francis had only been in the place a couple of times and on neither occasion had it been as crowded as the Rooms.

He followed Paglesham inside and saw him head for the table where the day's newspapers were set out. There was one elderly fellow seated nearby with an open journal on his lap, gently snoring. Francis glanced along the shelving to find only a female with a male escort, both browsing books. He crossed to the table and saw Paglesham had picked up one of the newspapers. He wasted no time.

"Ah, you have the *Gazette*."

The man turned his head and Francis surmised a peevish expression in the fellow's pretty features. He had the sort of looks Francis rather despised as unmanly but which most females found irresistible. The bow lips, the classic nose, the round cheeks and somewhat flaccid chin gave the face a feminine aspect, but he must concede the fellow's figure was well set up. He had dark hair and a pair of large dark eyes, just now exuding annoyance, which was also in his voice.

"Did you want it, sir? I am before you, I fear."

Francis affected to consider him. "Sir Peregrine Paglesham, is it? I fancy I saw you in discussion with my mother yesterday."

It was quite a comedy to see how the fellow's expression changed as he eyed Francis, his brain clearly backtracking to determine who accosted him. The instant he realised was obvious as he assumed delight and his tone became obsequious.

"Good gracious me, sir, I do trust you will forgive my incivility. You must be Lord Francis Fanshawe. I cannot sufficiently apologise for speaking in so dismissive a fashion. My abstraction must be my excuse, sir. I was miles away, I fear."

The task his wife had set him became almost anathema to Francis. The fellow inspired him with both disgust and acute dislike. He suppressed it.

"No apology is necessary, sir."

Paglesham held out the newspaper. "Take it, my lord, I insist. My need can wait."

Francis waved it away. "Not at all. I am in no hurry."

"But I could not concentrate, Lord Francis, knowing you were wishing to peruse it. Do, I pray you, take it!"

There seemed to be no other recourse open to him but to acquiesce. Francis accepted the *Gazette* but did not look at it. How in Hades was he to introduce the subject of his mission?

"Had you a particular interest in today's news, sir?" He saw an odd look flicker in the man's eyes and produced a smile. "I ask because I was just behind you and noticed you looking at your watch. It does not seem to me that a man in a hurry will interrupt his progress unnecessarily."

Sir Peregrine gave a laugh that sounded false. "No, indeed. You are singularly observant, my lord."

"A trick of my wife's, sir. I have learned of her."

The fellow looked baffled, but he was not slow to pick up the social nicety. "Are we to have the pleasure of seeing Lady Francis in the Rooms?"

"Perhaps. It is not certain. We are here for her health, you must know. She is recovering from a recent indisposition."

He had no intention of committing Tillie to any sort of excursion. She had gone for an early walk along the Esplanade this morning, accompanied as usual by Hemp, but she was far from strong as yet. It was a question whether she could tolerate the noisy crowding of the Assembly Rooms.

"I am sorry to hear it, my lord. But at least I had the inestimable pleasure of conversing with the dowager marchioness. She is quite a character, is she not? And most condescending to be so kind as to single me out."

The sycophantic note was beginning to irritate. Francis ordered himself to cut line and get on with what he had come to do. He glanced at the *Gazette* in his hand and inspiration hit.

"I wonder if there is any more in here about this plaguy murder?"

Did Paglesham's face go a shade whiter? He certainly looked a trifle sick. "A terrible business." His gaze searched Francis's

227

face briefly. "Worse, perhaps, for me. I knew the girl, you see." Astonished, and gratified at having the subject so readily introduced, Francis stared at the man. "You are surprised, my lord."

"Well, yes, I must say that I am."

The other's tone became deprecating. "As a man of the world, I dare say you know how it is. Miss Ash's beauty was extraordinary."

"So I have heard." Mindful of his instructions, Francis set the *Gazette* down on the table and leaned a little towards the fellow, lowering his voice and adopting a confiding air. "You are to be congratulated rather than censured, sir. As I understand it, the fair Dulcibella stunned all beholders."

Sir Peregrine sighed deeply. "She did, sir, she did. As for congratulation, I was by no means her only favoured cavalier."

"But you were favoured, that is the important thing. More than the rest perhaps?"

He despised the archness of his own tone, but Tillie had been right as usual. The fellow could not wait to boast.

"I flatter myself I did have the preference, my lord." He preened a little. "I dare say I might be forgiven for thinking I had a trifle the advantage over my most assiduous rivals. Of age, you must know, for Dulcie was youthful. And if I may dare to say so without conceit, my lord, my mirror suggests I have a little more prepossession than either Edgcott or Lord Charlton."

"They were your rivals?" Francis could not bring himself to comment upon the fellow's disgusting vanity.

"My chief rivals, sir. I cannot speak for Edgcott, whose chances must be counted negligible. But Charlton had all the advantage of title and position and yet Dulcibella's preference settled upon myself."

Francis returned him to reality without compunction. "Then you must feel it indeed, sir. A tragic loss."

Paglesham's features assumed a grief-stricken air. Undoubtedly false in Francis's judgement.

"Too, too dreadful, my lord. I confess to have been thoroughly unmanned when I heard of it."

"When did you hear?"

Sir Peregrine's fingers kneaded at his forehead. "When we all did, sir. Upon the day following as rumour hit and was swiftly followed by lurid accounts of the business in the newspapers."

"You must have been severely shocked, Sir Peregrine."

The fingers shifted to his temple and his eyes rimmed with moisture. Was it genuine? Or was he something of an actor too?

"Appalled, dismayed, numbed, sir. It seemed impossible. That loveliness, that warmth and vitality, all gone. And for what, my lord? That is what haunts me. Why should any man destroy a thing so beautiful?"

A thing? Was that how he saw the poor girl? But this was not getting him to the point of finding out the extent of Paglesham's involvement. Vital to discover, if he could, whether the fellow had been intimate with Dulcibella Ash.

"I am sure it must have been a shocking blow to you, sir. Particularly when you had known the girl in the flesh, so to speak."

The man's hand dropped, his eye suddenly keen, all trace of distress vanishing. "What are you saying, Lord Francis?"

Francis pretended surprise, spreading his hands. "Why, nothing untoward, sir. I assumed, from your words, that you had succeeded with the wench. Forgive me if I presume too far."

Sir Peregrine appeared to recollect himself. His mien of dismay returned. "No, no, you are right, of course. Perhaps I should not feel it quite as strongly had I not taken matters to their natural conclusion." He looked apologetic. "Villainous to have done so, as it now seems."

Villainous indeed, if his was the hand that wielded the fatal knife. But he was at least confessing to having bedded the girl. If he spoke truth. Francis fired a broadside.

"It would appear you were not the only man to make the conquest, sir."

It missed the target. Paglesham sighed. "Yes, that rather leaps to the eye. Is it callous of me to feel chagrined? I believed she had developed a *tendre* for me alone, but the wiles of women can never be fully plumbed."

"You think she played you false?"

"I would have kept her, sir."

Evading the question? "As your mistress?"

He sighed again. "She would not give up the stage. Dulcibella enjoyed the adulation, you must know. My persuasions fell upon deaf ears, I fear."

Francis dared a step further, adopting a confidential manner as unpleasant in the doing as the whole of this conversation was proving to be. But needs must.

"You don't suppose she was holding out for a ring upon her finger, do you, Paglesham?"

There was no mistaking the fellow's distaste. A haughty look overspread his features. "My dear Lord Francis! As if I could contemplate such a union."

"Though such has been before known, sir."

"Not by me, I assure you, sir."

"Yet would your Dulcibella have known that? Might she not have cherished hopes, once she was certain of your regard?"

Discomfort entered the fellow's eyes. He blustered a trifle. "Well, there is no accounting for the whims of females, after all. No, no, I cannot think it. She was naïve, yes, but not as foolish as all that."

"Foolish enough to trust someone ill-disposed, however," Francis said on a tart note before he could stop himself.

Sir Peregrine's round cheeks flew colour and his gaze veered between fear and fire. "I do not know what you imply, sir, but —"

"Good God, sir, you take me up wrong," Francis cut in swiftly. "One cannot but be dismayed at the manner of this poor girl's having been taken in. You, sir, have said how deeply you feel it."

Paglesham relaxed again. "I do, my lord." He seemed to gather his dignity. "I, too, have wondered, as do we all. Who did this thing? I venture to think it must have been one of her colleagues."

"Because of the theatrical nature of the undertaking?"

Sir Peregrine gestured in a vague way. "Jealousy can be a powerful urge, Lord Francis. You must be conscious of it."

"Not personally, no."

The fellow's mouth worked and a faintly bitter note entered in. "It is unlikely you would, sir, dare I say? With all your advantages."

Francis produced a spurious look of sympathy. "I have been fortunate perhaps. It is certainly unlucky for you that such a promising liaison was cut short in so brutal a manner."

A return to the murder appeared to afford Paglesham little satisfaction. His discomfort became apparent when he once again dug into his fob pocket for his watch. He consulted it and gave an apologetic cough.

"You must excuse me, Lord Francis. I have stayed beyond my time." He managed an obsequious smile as he replaced his pocket-watch. "I must count myself honoured by your lordship's kind interest in my affairs, but I fear I may have been indiscreet."

Francis gave a slight bow. "You may rely upon my discretion, Sir Peregrine."

He received a punctilious bow in return. "I do not doubt it for a moment, my lord. I will wish you good day."

Francis replied suitably and watched the man hurry out of the library. He was certainly rattled. Was he regretting having admitted so much? Whether the man was a fool or a murderer remained a question. No doubt Tillie would have an opinion.

It was likely too early to return to the lodging. His wife had warned him to give them a couple of hours. Having no desire to waste his time in the Assembly Rooms, Francis opted to search out a coffee house. He bethought him of the place mentioned by Charlton. Mrs Horniman's? He might with advantage discover how to find it.

With this end in mind, he left the library and headed for the nearest tavern, which proved to be The Black Dog, a little way along the road from the theatre. Entering the taproom with the intention of asking for directions, Francis was brought up short as he spied his employee Hemp, deep in conversation with a set of men he vaguely recognised. He recalled Tillie's scheme for her steward to befriend the players. Had he found out anything of value?

At that moment, Hemp turned his head and saw him. A slight frown creased Hemp's brow and Francis gave him a nod. He turned away, murmured to the good-looking young fellow who was engaging his attention and, rising from the settle, came across.

Francis saw the youth's eyes follow and catch upon him with a look of blatant interest.

"Did you want me, milord?"

Francis turned his attention to Hemp. "Is that insolent young fellow one of the players?"

A slight smile appeared. "Jasper Jefferies, milord. A miscreant boy, but one cannot help liking him. He is a major talent and an enfant terrible at one and the same time."

Francis regarded Hemp with a rise of reluctant interest. Hitherto, although he had known the man was both intelligent and educated, Hemp had not been forthcoming, treating him with the distant deference due to his employer. Was this how he spoke with Tillie? Francis was obliged to suppress a faint resentment. There could be no occasion to be stupidly irritated because his wife enjoyed a comfortable relationship with the fellow. Tillie had never thought of him as a servant. Easy to forget he had means of his own and had agreed to take the position for reasons that escaped Francis. He changed tack.

"I came in to ask directions to Mrs Horniman's coffee house."

Hemp's frown reappeared. "I know it, milord. I cannot think it an establishment milord could enjoy."

Francis cocked an eyebrow. "I thought as much. I'm not going there for enjoyment. It figures in this business and I might as well inspect the place."

Hemp gave a slight nod. "Would milord wish me to take him there?"

"Why, do you suppose I need protection?"

Hemp cracked a smile. "I doubt it. I am certain milord could give a good account of himself at need."

Irritation pushed Francis into speech. "Will you cease this oppressive punctilio, Hemp, for pity's sake! You'll drive me mad."

The grin widened. "As milord pleases."

Francis threw up his eyes. "Very well, if you are done with these players, you may as well show me this coffee house."

"Let me make my excuses, milord, and I will be with you."

Relieved he had dropped the affectation of extreme servitude in his address, Francis watched him take leave of the group, with evident bonhomie as he slapped the boy Jasper on the back and shook hands. Exchanging banter? The laughter suggested as much. He had clearly taken Tillie's request to heart and seemed in danger of becoming the life and soul of the party.

Hemp led him into the back streets of the town, which, like certain areas of the capital, were dingy, dirty and ill-kept. So far he had known only the fashionable end and it was quite a revelation to see how Weymouth changed within a couple of streets.

"You would hardly think it the same town," he remarked.

"True, milord. We approach the belly of an underworld in this district."

"How far down? Thieves and prostitutes? Or is it merely the haunt of lesser men?"

"Mrs Horniman's is respectable, milord, but within a short distance there are taverns of less repute."

"You have visited them?"

"One or two, where it is best to keep your purse well down in your pocket. I would not advocate your venturing there, milord."

"To make myself a target? I doubt I should find what I was looking for, in any event."

Hemp gave him a curious glance as he took a turn into a narrow street, its kennel unkempt and dirty, the huddled buildings smoke-stained with grimy windows.

"May I ask what it is you wish to find, milord?"

Francis looked about him with disfavour. "Is Mrs Horniman's here?"

"No, milord. I took a short detour to show you this tavern."

He stopped by a dingy building with a swinging sign proclaiming its calling. The Old Fiddler looked to be just the place where one might expect to be robbed or cheated.

"How in the world do you come to know this appalling establishment, Hemp?"

Hemp grinned. "The boy Jasper led me here. He is ripe for any mischief and the barmaid is both pretty and accommodating."

"Good God! Disease-ridden too, I should think."

"Indeed, milord. I advised him to leave well alone, but he's a reckless lad and hot at hand."

"He'll come to grief soon enough if he follows that path." But his interest in the player Jasper was but tepid. "It's providential you know the place, Hemp. Her ladyship wants to find the fellow who dug the grave for our murderer."

Hemp eyed the tavern. "I could try, milord, but later perhaps. I would think such persons are more likely to slip in under cover of darkness."

"Very well, but don't run your head into danger, my friend."

"The one advantage of my colour in this country, milord, is that I fright the lower orders."

Francis had to laugh. "So you may, though by my reckoning few would care to tangle with a young fellow of your height and obvious strength, Hemp."

"Except Jasper, who has not given up his ambition to take a few punches from me." He began to retrace his steps. "Mrs Horniman's is on the main street a little farther down from where we turned off, milord."

The coffee house proved to be a reasonably well-kept establishment with a large, open area in front of the fireplace as well as a series of booths along the walls, several of which were occupied. The proprietress cut a matronly figure, bustling to and fro with pots and platters and exchanging the time of day with patrons of the middling sort, tradesmen and the like. Smoke wafted from a couple of elderly fellows seated on a settle near the fire, sucking long pipes and engaged in desultory discussion. Behind the counter, a thin man of middle age took orders, calling out to a couple of waiters who toiled in and out of a green baize door with kettles and filled trays.

It was a comfortable scene which lacked the formality of places he might in general frequent, and Francis understood why Charlton chose it for a discreet rendezvous with an actress.

He picked a booth near the centre and slid onto the bench on one side, signing to Hemp, who was hovering, to do the same on the other. "Don't stand on ceremony, my friend. I'm no slave master and you're a man of independent means, are you not?"

"I am still your servant, milord." But he slipped into place opposite.

"In fact you are my wife's servant, if anything. It was her idea to offer you a place."

"For which I am ever grateful, milord. I owe milady more than I can say."

"That's why you stay, I take it."

Hemp gave an odd laugh. "Also because it is good to be part of a family again, milord."

Francis warmed to the man. He had not taken time before to draw him out. He had given in to Tillie's request with reluctance, but perhaps Hemp was more of an asset to his household than he had supposed.

Their arrival in the coffee house had not gone unremarked, but there was a perceptible pause before Mrs Horniman, if the bustling woman was she, stepped up to enquire their pleasure. Was it Hemp who caused the hesitation? Some people were inordinately wary of persons so obviously different from themselves.

"Good day to you, sir, and how may we serve you?"

The practised words tripped off the woman's tongue with ease, but her eyes slid from Francis to Hemp and back again. Wondering at their being in company together?

"Coffee, if you please. No cream or sugar. Hemp?"

His dark gaze slid to the proprietress. "I will take the same, madam, I thank you, but with a little sugar."

The deep voice with its cultured accent visibly took the woman aback. She blinked, turned back to Francis with an obvious effort, and dropped a curtsey.

"Would you care for anything with it, sir? We have a variety of cakes and buns."

"Nothing, I thank you." Francis seized his chance. "Are you Mrs Horniman?"

Surprise flickered in a pair of pale blue eyes. "I am that, sir."

"Lord Charlton recommended your establishment."

Her face showed immediate consternation. "Did he, sir?"

A trifle tart? Interesting. Had she disapproved of Charlton's liaison? Or was it the murder she was thinking of? Before he

237

could decide how to bring up the subject, Mrs Horniman cut off the opportunity.

"I'll fetch the coffees, sir."

She bustled off and Francis looked across at Hemp. "She knows about the girl's death."

"Indeed, milord. A few days since there was nothing else talked of in here."

"I forgot you had been here before."

"Not to drink, milord. Jasper showed me the place because Lewis Payne — he is the older player — said he would not come here again until the murder was forgotten. He and another called Aisling were subjected to much question and a good deal of lurid speculation."

Francis regarded him with some severity. "I trust you have not repeated such to her ladyship?"

A wry look crossed the other's face. "Only what is pertinent, milord. I do not trouble milady with unnecessary detail."

"Thank the Lord for that." Not that Tillie would turn a hair, but he could well imagine the gist of that sort of gossip. Despite her ease with people from all walks of life, his wife had a prudish streak. He knew also from their whisperings in the night, when Tillie's guard was down, that the unfortunate fate of the dead girl's unborn baby was distressing to her.

With his mind back on the murder, he seized opportunity. "Have you gleaned anything valuable from the players?"

Hemp's gaze narrowed in thought. "My suspicion still runs on Robert Collins, milord, although milady does not credit his involvement."

"So I understand, and her reasons are sound. Why do you think him guilty?"

"He alone of the players cannot move on from the death. Wat tells me he is habitually morose, but his mien is woeful to my mind."

"That may mean only a strong attachment to Dulcie," Francis objected.

"Or strong remorse. He is also shaky and nervous. I remarked it particularly. Lewis did also, for he jibed at the fellow to take his own counsel and dose himself with something."

"Laudanum?"

"I do not know, milord, but Lewis tells me it is Rob who quacks the company for any minor ill or injury. Apparently there are unseen hazards behind the façade we see upon the stage."

"Do not all the men realise they are under suspicion?" Francis asked, pursuing his own thought.

"The others tend to dismiss the possibility of the colonel bringing the deed home to them, milord. Rob alone fears his claim of being in bed at the time cannot be proven."

Hemp's harping on Rob, whom he clearly disliked, was interrupted by the arrival of Mrs Horniman, who set down on the table between them a coffee pot with two cups, a jug of cream and a bowl of sugar. The woman curtsied and her tone was more mellow.

"I hope you will find it to your satisfaction, sir. Pray call me if there is anything amiss."

"I thank you, I shall do so, though it does not look as if we will want for anything." A bonhomous smile was cast upon Francis and the woman was about to turn away. "Stay a moment, if you will."

She turned an enquiring look upon him. "Sir?"

"Are you acquainted with Sir Peregrine Paglesham?"

The name appeared to make no impression. "If I am, sir, I do not know the name." Her tone became pointed. "Not all my patrons see fit to tell me who they are."

Francis gave a wry smile, but did not enlighten her. "But you know Lord Charlton, I think?"

Mrs Horniman sucked in her cheeks. "I cannot be expected to keep note of all who come here. We are a busy house, sir." With which tart utterance she nodded, unsmiling, and moved away.

Having served Francis, Hemp dropped sugar lumps into his cup. "May I ask, milord, why you enquire of this man? Paglesham, was it?"

"Why, do you know something of him?"

Hemp shook his head, stirring his coffee. "Nothing, milord."

"He's a suspect, Hemp. One of the girl Dulcie's admirers. I talked with him just before I met you." He saw surprise in the other's face. "Did you think I had no task to perform as well as you? I am detailed to question the gentleman falling into my own sphere."

Hemp regarded him steadily. "I remember you participated before, milord."

He had almost forgotten the occasion of their meeting when Hemp was of the household where Tillie had become involved in a suspicious death. Francis grinned.

"I get dragged in willy-nilly, my friend. However, on this occasion I can blame none but myself."

A large shadow fell across the table, interrupting them. A heavy-set man had paused by the booth.

"Lord Francis Fanshawe, is it not?"

Francis looked up into a harsh-featured countenance with wide jowls, a jutting nose and a pair of thick brows over deep-set eyes. Recognition flashed, and his interest flared. He feigned ignorance.

"I am he."

The cautious response was met with a sudden smile that at once dispelled the harshness. "I thought I could not be mistaken, sir. You were pointed out to me upon the Esplanade."

"Indeed." Francis set down his cup, his tone discouraging. He might need to talk to the man, but he was not going to pander to his vanity. "You have the advantage of me, sir."

The other man did not appear to be in the least disconcerted. He thrust out a hand. "Edgcott, sir. Captain Edgcott, sometime of the military. Always a pleasure to encounter one of our own, sir. The general tells me you have seen service."

Somewhat taken aback by Edgcott's determined friendliness, Francis rose. Needs must, he shook the hand. "You are acquainted with General Godfrey?"

"Acquainted with everyone, sir. I am a regular at Weymouth, you must know."

He spoke without a trace of boastfulness and in a welcoming spirit which could not readily be dismissed. The fellow's mien matched none of the assumptions Francis had made upon catching first sight of him in the Assembly Rooms.

Also on his feet, Hemp picked up his coffee. "Allow me to make room for you, sir."

Edgcott showed surprise. "Good of you, my man, but I don't stay."

That would not do. Francis adopted an easy tone. "Nonsense, sir, take a pew." He gestured to the opposite bench. "You have only just come."

"On the contrary, my lord, I have been here an age. I saw you come in and thought I must take opportunity to make myself known to you. But I am in no mind to make a nuisance of myself."

But Francis was not going to lose the opportunity. Hemp, with a tact Francis could only admire, was already shifting out of the way. A few persuasive words saw the captain settling himself in Hemp's vacated place, protesting he would stay but a moment or two.

"I will obtain a fresh cup from the landlady, milord." With which, Hemp went off towards the counter, taking his unfinished drink along with him.

Francis took opportunity to take better stock of the captain as he refreshed himself from his own cup. The rough look of the first instant had entirely dissipated. The eyes held bright interest and the relaxedness of the smile took away from the effect of the prominent nose. His figure, though broad in the shoulder, was not quite as bulky as Francis had first supposed, an impression caused perhaps by an ill-fitting coat he wore, its collar and cuffs too large for present fashion, and the three-cornered hat which belonged to an earlier age. Hardly the kind of man one would expect to attract a lovely young girl.

"May I know where you were in service, my lord Francis?"

"America, sir, in the main, but that was a long time ago."

Edgcott nodded in a knowledgeable way. "Ah, then you will know Tretower. He told me he was there."

"Indeed. We were in the same regiment and are still friends. As it happens, I brought my wife here to recuperate upon his recommendation."

"A wise move." Captain Edgcott gestured with his finger. "The air is invigorating and the company merry. You could not do better, sir. And to have a friend readily in situ. Could not be better, my lord."

"I thought so," agreed Francis, wondering how he might introduce the subject of the murder.

"The South Coast is particularly fine, I would say," pursued Edgcott, "but I would not recommend Brighton. Our esteemed prince has turned the place into a haunt of the best and worst of society, my dear sir. No, no, one is best to keep to Weymouth and those resorts towards the west. I like to ring the changes a little myself, but Weymouth calls me every time."

Mrs Horniman arriving with a clean cup and saucer at this moment, he broke off to thank her, with a merry laugh.

"You see I have been waylaid, dear lady. As if one could readily leave your establishment when the coffee and the company is so very welcoming."

The proprietress simpered a little. "It is good of you to say so, Captain. I am sure I hope we may always make you comfortable."

"Impossible to be otherwise, dear lady, quite impossible."

To Francis's mingled astonishment and interest, he reached an arm about the woman's hip and delivered a hearty slap to her ample rump. She gave a little shriek of laughter, coloured and protested.

"Ooh, you are a terrible man, sir!"

She waddled off, the captain looking after her with his smile fading as he turned back to Francis, lowering his voice. "Pays to treat such women with a trifle of familiarity, my lord Francis. Such a small thing to yield so much by way of excellent treatment. Why withhold it when it costs me nothing, that's what I say."

His better opinion of the man rapidly disintegrating, Francis took refuge in pouring out the coffee. "I will leave you to doctor it to your taste, sir."

"Ah, you will find me a cream and sugar man every time, my lord. I like it sweet and I like it rich. Just as I like my women." A leering look came Francis's way and he could not forbear a flicker of distaste. Edgcott's manner changed in an instant. "But I should not say so to you, Lord Francis, a happily married man. I hope you will excuse my unruly tongue. Monstrous of me to lapse into vulgarity. You will forgive it, I know."

How he should know any such thing Francis could not fathom. He began to think the fellow was as accomplished an actor as any in The Grand Ferdinando's company. What impression was he trying to create? Or was he merely testing the ground? Francis put out a feeler.

"I am very happily married, as it chances, sir. But I have not forgot the joys of bachelorhood. Nor am I unable to appreciate the charms of other women without wishing to take advantage of such."

Edgcott was sucking up his coffee in a manner both uncouth and as indicative of an older style as his costume. Was he in fact older in years than he looked?

"And why should you not, sir? It is unnatural after all for man to be tied to just one of the delicate creatures, do you not think?"

"Whether it is natural or not, sir, does not interest me. I have no desire to tamper with any other than my own wife."

Regretting the tart note at once, Francis hoped he had not made his disapproval of the man too plain. But Edgcott was evidently more thick-skinned than he had supposed.

"Well, well, you are a lucky fellow, my lord Francis. I lost my wife a good few years ago, but I cannot aspire to a like abstention. Appetites may be stirred by an object of attraction, you know."

"Such as Dulcibella Ash?"

He brought it out with a ring, hoping to confound the man into giving himself away. To no purpose. Edgcott gave a heavy sigh.

"Ah, the little actress. She was a beauty indeed. A lovely girl. A sad loss to the world."

"So I have been led to understand."

Edgcott shook his head, his lips pursing, his eyes registering a distress Francis found it hard to believe in. "Such a pity, my lord, such a great pity. You may count yourself unlucky to have missed her. Or should I say lucky to be spared the unhappiness of knowing her only to lose her?"

Francis seized on this. "When you say knowing her, sir, what exactly do you mean?"

Edgcott looked across the rim of his cup as he slurped at the brew. There was no guile in his eyes, nor in his voice as he replied. "Alas, not in the fashion I should have chosen, I confess. I tried my damnedest, you may believe it, sir, but dismally I failed." He shook his head again, almost with the exact same level of disturbance in his countenance as when he spoke of her death. "She would not yield. To my mind, she had higher game in view and therefore chose to spurn me." Then his friendly smile brightened his face again. "Or, if honesty is to be served, let us suppose she found my person disagreeable to her. Never ready to dismiss ourselves as too ugly and ill-favoured to be desired by the lovelies of the fair sex, eh, my lord? Coxcombs all, we men, would you not say?"

A hearty laugh accompanied this assertion and Francis knew not how to answer. Was the man's bluff manner real or assumed? He passed so easily from self-deprecation to confidence, it was hard to judge. Francis chose to turn the question back.

"You had rivals then, I take it?"

"Past counting, sir, past counting. That lovely could have had any man she wanted."

Recalling what General Godfrey had said of this fellow's complaints of Paglesham, Francis pressed for more. "Galling for you, sir. Especially if you were acquainted with them yourself."

This elicited a snort. "Couldn't but be otherwise, sir, in a place such as this. But no use now to be cursing pretty boys and men of better means." He downed more coffee and then gave a rueful smile. "I tell myself I am well out of the business, sir. She would have cost me a pretty penny first to last and I am not a warm man. Such trinkets and toys as I bestowed upon her were received without return of any kind. Wasted, sir, quite wasted."

Francis's dislike was growing. The military attracted all sorts and conditions of men with whom he had been obliged to hobnob in his younger days. Yet he had rarely met with a man as openly vulgar in his speech, as ready to talk to a stranger of matters he would have done better to keep to himself. Convenient for his present purpose it might be, but it was scarcely endearing. Suppressing his distaste, he tried for more pertinent information.

"Do you not wonder who despatched her in so brutal a fashion?"

Edgcott threw back his head. "But without cease, sir. A crime too barbaric to be contemplated." He leaned a little across the table in the confidential way he had. "Although, sir, there was homage of a sort in the act, I thought."

This was a new turn. "How so?"

Edgcott opened wide his eyes. "But the candles, my lord Francis, the candles. I thought at once when I heard of it that the fellow had at least the decency to set the poor girl in a bower to illuminate her loveliness. And he coffined her, which must be set to his credit."

Startled, Francis could not forbear a sharp retort. "To his credit? No, by God! What, so macabre a scene?"

A protesting finger gestured. "No, indeed, my lord Francis, on the contrary. Think how it might have been otherwise, how it too often is. So indecent and untidy to be throwing her carelessly in some alley or left to marauding creatures in a wood. No, sir, to my mind, villain though he is, whoever did the deed had a shred of mercy left to him to be serving the dignity of the corpse."

This novel view of the matter could not but astonish. "Next you will be ready to shake this murderer by the hand."

Edgcott laughed as if Francis had made a jest. "Not I, sir. I'll see him damned first. Especially as I must suppose he succeeded where I did not."

"Why must you suppose it?"

"Why dispose of her otherwise? No doubt the girl grew importunate, pressing for more than he was willing to give. I knew her for a grasping filly since she did not see fit to return my gifts with any token of affection. No, no, I am persuaded, sad as it is, the girl must have brought it on herself. Women, sir, are all too ready to seek advantage. You must have remarked it."

"You take a severe view of the sex, Captain Edgcott."

"Not I, sir." A leering look and a wink was bestowed upon him. "Love the dear creatures too much, that is the long and the short of it. But there is no denying they are all the same when all is said and done. Out for what they can get, and never satisfied when they get it."

Francis cocked an eyebrow. "You might say the same of men, sir."

A loud guffaw made several heads turn in the adjoining booths. "Ah, you've hit it, my lord Francis. Terrible set we are, and that's the truth. Take me, sir. A rough old fellow am I and no mistake. But do I think myself unfit to be rolling a girl like Dulcibella Ash in my bed? No, sir, I do not. I'd take her and ten like her, if I could." Picking up his cup, he drained it and stood up, shoving his large person out of the booth. "My compliments to your wife, sir. I've seen your esteemed mother, of course, but she won't deign to notice me, and who shall blame her? My dear lord Francis, it has been an honour."

Rising to take the hand held out to him for all the world as if he was the wretched man's friend, Francis summoned a look he hoped was sufficiently complacent.

"It has been interesting, sir."

"Always delighted to make the acquaintance of a fellow soldier, sir, even if the life is long behind me."

"How long behind you, Captain Edgcott? I have not asked where and when you saw service."

"Here and there, sir, here and there. You know how it is. They post you off up country and send you back down again without compunction. I'd be sorry to have sold out now the French are threatening our gates, but I'm getting too old for these tricks these days. Can't be riding up hill and down dale at my time of life. I'll say goodbye, Lord Francis. Or perhaps *au revoir*. My compliments to Tretower when you see him."

With which, he raised his hat in a jaunty fashion, gave a final wink and smile, and headed for the door to the establishment. Francis heard him begin to whistle as he went and slowly sat down again, his hackles up and unable to decide whether he was more suspicious or bemused.

Chapter Ten

As he hesitated outside The Old Fiddler, the boy fingered the cloth of his new coat. He was unused to the thickness of an article with so much wear still in it, and it felt as alien to his body as the decent shirt beneath. The breeches were a different matter, though they chafed a trifle in the groin, for the old pair he'd stuffed with the rest of his rags between some rocks in the cove where he'd changed had not been as worn as the threadbare coat. They would have done him another year at least, if he weren't to grow too fast. But he were well set up now. What should stop him figging himself out from top to toe? Not that he were nodcock enough to buy it all in one go. Folk were apt to question. An' old Throcking were a downy one.

Perkin picked his moments with care, when the pawnbroker was haggling over a purchase and his bored son was serving, sliding into the shop and buying one piece of clothing at a time. He did not make the mistake of proffering his guineas in payment. He had exchanged two of them for lesser coin with Grain, who knew him of old. The fence asked no awkward questions, though he'd given the boy a narrow look when he saw the gold.

Once he had his outfit complete, carefully hidden away in his secret cache tucked in a convenient recess at the back of St Mary's Church, Perkin took his bag containing the motley suit of new clothes down to the cove, plunged naked into the waves to freshen his malodorous person, allowed the sun to dry him and then dressed himself in togs the like of which he had never worn before. He had wished for a mirror and spent some time admiring his reflection in any window he passed when he got back into town, dwelling particularly on the boots which made him look like a swell, he thought, even if they were a little large for his feet. He'd get a second pair of socks to make 'em snug, that was it. And one of them neck-cloths the nobs wore. That would really give him polish.

Only trouble was, these new togs of his would spoil if he slept nights in St Mary's graveyard. It weren't nowise as safe as his old haunt. He shivered involuntarily. Not as he'd go back there, not if he were to be hanged for it.

St Mary's graveyard was small and too central for his liking. Dodging the verger was a nuisance he could do without, for it weren't restful. But would Missus Tetsy give him a room?

She'd not balked at feeding him leftovers, telling the denizen of the kitchens at the Old Fiddler to let him have the end of a loaf, a heel of old cheese, or, on a good day, a half of yesterday's pigeon pie. But what would she say if he walked in, bold as brass, demanding a room where he could board until he found a proper lodging?

Perkin had his story ready, but she had one of them eyes as saw things as they shouldn't, did Missus Tetsy, and he was dubious of being believed. What was more, he'd never dared venture in by way of the front before. He'd have been chased out in his old rags. It were different now. He looked respectable, didn't he? He thrust out his thin chest. Standing here was getting him nowhere. He stepped up to the door and pushed it open.

The fug of smoke and stale liquor from the taproom permeated the narrow hall, together with a murmur of desultory talk, the clink of utensils and the aroma of burned meat. The latter caused Perkin's mouth to water and his empty stomach clenched. Perhaps he'd fill his belly first. Missus couldn't object to that. Drawing a breath for courage, the boy swaggered in, trying to look as if he belonged.

The taproom was busy, every bench and stool seemingly occupied and a wall of backs stood between the boy and his glimpse of the counter. No one paid him the least heed as he slid between a couple of chairmen he vaguely knew and edged around the big-bellied form of Moses the ship's-chandler, for whom he'd run errands in the past. To his relief, he went unrecognised and was able to reach the counter without being accosted.

While he waited for the tapster to notice him, he searched surreptitiously for the two faces he hoped never to see again. But there was, to his heartfelt relief, no sign of either Truggery or Stowe. It was his considered belief both must have scarpered soon as they heard of the horror at which they'd assisted. If they'd been still in Weymouth, The Old Fiddler was where they'd be this time of day, dining on beef and onions no doubt.

"Hoy! Do'ye want owt, boy?"

Perkin started, turning to face the tapster. "Ale, if it p-please you, sir," he stammered, the beat of his heart quickening.

The tapster grabbed a quart jug and drew off a foaming tankard, slamming it down before him and grunting the price. Then he held out his palm for the money, eyeing the boy the while as if he suspected he was unable to pay.

Perkin dug a hand into his pocket and brought out a fistful of coins. The tapster's eyes widened.

"Mighty well off fer a sprig your age, ain't yer?"

He didn't know the half of it. Though this was only silver and copper. The boy shrugged with a nonchalance he was far from feeling and handed over four pence.

"I earned it, din't I?"

"Aye, just about you did."

The tapster's disbelief was patent. One or two pairs of eyes turned their way and Perkin began to wriggle. His instinct was to run, but that would give him away. He countered with a hope of deflecting the fellow.

"Where's Missus Tetsy?"

"Who wants ter know?"

The boy lifted his chin. "Perkin. Missus Tetsy knows me, she does."

The tapster's lip curled. "Does she now?"

"She does too. You call her and you'll see."

Doubt partially obscured the tapster's sceptical look. Perkin held his ground, staring the man out despite the attention he'd attracted from nearby drinkers.

"Be here in a minute, she will. Then we'll see." The tapster closed his fist about the coins and moved off to serve someone else.

Breathing more easily, Perkin buried his nose in his jug of ale and took a deep draught. By the time he emerged, those who had been watching had turned their attention elsewhere. The boy's unease grew. He'd made a mistake, showing too much silver. Missus Tetsy might prove as suspicious as the tapster. He was more than half inclined to finish his drink and leave. Find another tavern, where he weren't known. He hadn't the knack of doing it right, that was the trouble. He'd scratched a living all his life. Until the night he still could not recall without a shudder.

He swallowed half the contents of his jug and set it down. Best leave now while he still could.

"Gracious goodness, it is you!"

Missus Tetsy! He glanced wildly round and found that stout dame had planted herself, arms akimbo, before the counter.

"What's all this then, young Perkin? John here tells me you're waving silver about. And how did you come by those clothes, I should like to know?"

Perkin swallowed, the rhythm of his pulse in disarray. "I had a bit o' luck, missus."

"Looks like a pailful of luck to me, my lad. What have you been about?"

Aware his voice was shifting up in register from nerves, the boy embarked upon his well-rehearsed explanation. "I done a job fer a gennelman, missus."

"Some job it must've been to get you enough to fig yourself out like a beau and have money over."

"Well, it were that, missus. I toiled fer days."

"Doing what, may I ask?"

The sceptical note was not lost on Perkin. He could not sufficiently regret having taken this route, but it was too late now. He had either to convince the woman or make good his escape. The patrons closest had fallen silent, watching the byplay with interest. To the boy's chagrin, old Moses took a hand.

"You ain't got no silver off of me, that's sure, my lad. He done a job or two fer me, Tetsy, but nothing like." He nodded towards Perkin, indicating the clothes. "Never seen you in other than rags, boy. Where'd you get them togs?"

"Off of Mr Throcking, sir. They ain't nowise nowt but old 'uns."

The landlady seized Perkin's shoulder, looking him up and down. "Are you telling me you got money enough to pay for them from a job for a gentleman?"

"I did, missus, I promise."

"And what gentleman would employ a scrawny rat like you, I'd like to know, for you looked no better nor a beggar when last I saw you, young Perkin." She shook a finger in his face. "Tell the truth now. You taken to thieving?"

Perkin shrank away, heart thumping and feet itching to run. "I ain't never, missus, honest. The gennelman give me a guinea or two is all."

A huge guffaw emanated from old Moses. "A guinea or two? Why, yer ain't worth a groat, yer young varmint. Lying 'e is, Tetsy, that's sure."

"I ain't, I ain't, I swear it!"

By this time, the surrounding clientele were dividing into two camps, one seemingly as amused as old Moses, the other siding with Missus Tetsy in scandalised disbelief.

"Turn 'im upside down and shake 'im," suggested one of the chairmen, his broken teeth showing in a grin. "Soon find out 'ow rich 'e really is."

Perkin made a spirited bid for freedom, but Missus Tetsy had him fast. "No, you don't. You ain't going nowhere until we get to the bottom of this. Come on, lad, where'd you get the money?"

Desperate, Perkin improvised. "The gennelman had me dig an 'ole, that's what."

"Dig a hole? And he paid you two guineas for it?"

"That's a loud one, if ever I heard one," said old Moses, chuckling. "Two guineas to dig an 'ole! Yer'd best come up with summat better nor that, lad."

"It's true," Perkin's voice was a squeak as the submerged memories began to surface, the image of the dark hole he'd watched opening up looming in his head. "I dug and dug fer days, I did."

Amid the laughter and raucous comments, a deep and cultured voice penetrated.

"Excuse me, sir. May I come there, if you please?"

Missus Tetsy's stern tones distracted the boy. "Now, you listen to me, young Perkin. I've had about enough of your lies as I'm prepared to listen to. Tell me the truth, or so help me I'll hale you off before that colonel of militia."

Perkin blenched. As if he hadn't seen enough of the militia to last him for years, stamping about the town like they had been. And out at the fatal cemetery too. The images were roiling in his head as he glanced about, looking for a way of escape. There were too many between him and the door, and most far too attentive to his altercation with Missus Tetsy.

"You, boy!"

It was the deep voice again. Perkin looked up. A huge man had pushed his way in. Tall, broad in the shoulder and his face blacked out.

Remembrance swept into Perkin's mind. It was him. The man in the mask. Stark terror gripped him and he lost all power to think.

The man's hand reached out towards him, black like his face. Spots danced in the boy's vision and his ears buzzed. The world went blank.

The Reverend Duddenhoe was coming to the end of his eulogies over the coffin. Throughout the service, George, standing at a little distance so as not to intrude in his military capacity, found his gaze straying to Cecile, alone among the mourners dry-eyed and stoic. She did not look much at the lead-lined elm box that contained the sad remains of her friend, but rather kept her gaze upon the skies as if she sought the spirit of Dulcie in the heavens. A fanciful notion struck George that perhaps his Cecile looked also for the decimated souls of her family, ranged in support alongside the murdered girl.

His mind shifted, catching on a detail. When had he begun thinking of her as his Cecile? She had given him no encouragement to suppose she returned his regard. Or had she? One or two instances he cherished when he thought she looked or sounded tender, but he wavered between certainty and doubt.

As if she felt his preoccupation, Cecile abruptly turned her head, briefly caught his eye and as swiftly dropped her gaze to the coffin. The fillip of response in George's breast sank along with his spirits. Someone twitched his sleeve and he was almost relieved to find Sullivan at his elbow. A low murmur reached him.

"Had a little set-to with the coachmen, sir, but I silenced them by all but accusing them of the murder."

George snapped back to duty. "Unless one of them drove the murderer here, I doubt they'll be of use to us."

"No use at all, sir. Nothing found in the carriages, Puckeridge says."

"No drop of blood?"

"A few old stains, but Puckeridge tasted 'em and swears they are nothing like. They smell mouldy, he says. I don't doubt him. Musty old chariots they are, sir."

The players had arrived in two ancient lumbering coaches. Along with a wagon, so The Grand Ferdinando had told him, these constituted the company's transport in their journeys from town to town. Ferdinand had instructed the livery stables to fig them out for the occasion and taken opportunity to harangue George.

"We ought by this to be preparing for our departure to Poole, my dear Colonel, for our engagement in Bournemouth. We cannot be delayed in this. I must insist you let us go, sir, I must indeed."

George was in no mind to permit the players out of his jurisdiction until this wretched murder was solved and he said so. The impresario was more than chagrined.

"This cannot be, Colonel, indeed it cannot. We are promised, sir, promised. The company of The Grand Ferdinando always, always keeps faith. It is an unwritten law of the theatre, Colonel. Would you have me break it for this?"

"This, Mr Ferdinand, is the murder of your actress, who, I may remind you, is about to be buried here."

The brutal truth had its effect. Ferdinand blenched and threw his hand to his head. "You are right to censure me. If my brain was not so full, if my heart less so, I might realise the unintended callousness of my preoccupation. My dear Colonel, I must beg your indulgence." Nevertheless, he leaned in close, lowering his voice. "But think of it, I pray you. We must be gone early next week or we will renege on our contract at Bournemouth which, as I am sure you must appreciate, Colonel, is bad for business. Very bad indeed. Think on it, I implore you."

He had then reassumed his woeful mien and moved away to his wife's side, re-joining the cavalcade moving slowly towards the designated graveside. George had immediately detailed his second-in-command to have Puckeridge and his men take opportunity while the service was in progress to make a surreptitious search in the coaches for anything that might indicate one had been used for the purpose of bringing Dulcie to this place on the fatal night.

"Afforded a rare treat for the curious, sir," observed Sullivan. "At least it gave them something to do besides sticking their stupid heads through the railings. It's a good thing you thought of detailing the men to keep them out."

"Inevitable the villagers would come crowding the place."

Mrs Ferdinand, when informed the Coroner had released the body for burial, had requested his aid to ensure the funeral was private. George had done more, offering to make the arrangements on her behalf.

"Will you? Can you? I confess it is a task that fills me with dread."

"Leave all to me, ma'am."

She had been a trifle shocked when he told her the burial would take place in the very cemetery where the murder had been committed. However, as George pointed out, there was no other convenient burial ground within the parish where a non-resident might be laid to rest. The grave chosen was at a far end, well away from the fatal spot, and within a pretty tree-lined grove with a number of flowering shrubs along its edge.

George was glad of the opportunity to observe how the male players reacted as they entered through the gates. He was looking out for one who might be tempted to cast his eyes to the place where Dulcie had lain, for the murderer would know just where it was, despite all having been made good in the violated grave.

Yet though each glanced around in a manner that suggested they all knew this was the fateful cemetery, none displayed the furtive hunt for which George was alert. Fitzgerald was the only outsider present, aside from the militiamen and ghoulish onlookers beyond the railings, and he merely nodded in recognition of George and passed on, walking with the Ferdinands. But the impresario had detached himself and come across, distracting George's attention. He hoped he had not missed any little giveaway in the rest.

"Dust to dust, ashes to ashes…"

The weeping rose in volume as Dulcie was delivered to the earth and George instinctively looked to Cecile. She was not sobbing like the other women, but the sun picked out a glistening upon her cheek. George yearned for the right to give comfort.

Within minutes the ceremonial side of the business was over and the tableau began to break up as Jane Ferdinand moved to talk to the officiating cleric. Lewis Payne had an arm about Hildegard Larkin, who was applying a pocket handkerchief to her eyes. The girl Kate, still weeping, leaned heavily on the arm of Robert Collins, of all people, who was red-eyed and woeful in the extreme. Genuine grief? It certainly looked like it.

George's gaze shifted to Fitzgerald, conversing a little apart and in low tones with the impresario. Nothing to be learned there. The giant Aisling, together with Wat and young Jasper Jefferies were already moving swiftly in the direction of the gates, talking in a manner that looked to be already shifting away from the solemnity of the occasion.

"*Monsieur le colonel?*"

A jerk in his pulse threw George into disarray for an instant. He turned fast.

"Cecile!"

A tremulous smile trembled on her lips and he flooded with warmth.

"I have startled you, I think. Forgive, I beg."

George struggled for composure. "Not at all. I'm sorry. I was distracted." More so at sight of her continuing distress evident in the speaking eyes that had first struck him. "This was hard for you, I fear."

"It is so." She looked away and back. "But better I have this chance to say farewell. This was not granted me with — with *ma famille.* Even my mother when she left me, all was confusion in my mind and I did not say it."

Scarcely surprising, and the trace of regret affected him not a little. Yet he forbore to speak of it, tactfully keeping to the present event.

"I am glad if it has helped you."

Her gaze remained upon his face, a questioning look appearing. "It would help more, Georges, if you can lay to rest the pain of suspicion."

"I cannot, Cecile. Not yet. I wish I could, for your — for all your sakes," he corrected himself.

"This Madame Fan she has not found the truth?"

George wished it was within his power to allay her fears and remove the tiny lines of discontent from between her brows. But one thing he could say with confidence.

"She will. She has not failed yet."

The frown persisted and puzzle came into her eyes. "It is strange that a woman can do this thing. How is it she may find who killed Dulcie but you cannot?"

A rueful laugh escaped him. "I wish I had her insight. I don't know how it is but Ottilia has a knack. She sees things that escape a mere man."

"Even this her husband?"

"Ah, Fan — or Francis rather — is her champion. He shields her and comforts her and does his part as she requests." He could not resist a speaking look. "I would I had a like pleasurable duty for a deserving woman."

To his intense delight, a trifle of colour crept into Cecile's pallid cheeks and her glance flicked away as the tip of a pink tongue came out to wet her lips. George was obliged to tamp down a demon of longing. To relieve her embarrassment, he changed the subject.

"I understand the company is supposed to leave for Poole and Bournemouth. Ferdinand is anxious for my permission to depart Weymouth."

Cecile's colour faded as her gaze came back to him. "And you will give it?"

"I suppose I must in the end." An idea occurred and he glanced across to where the impresario and Fitzgerald had begun to follow Hilde and Lewis, who were walking towards the coaches. Mrs Ferdinand had fallen in behind, still deep in conversation with the vicar.

"May I escort you, Cecile? I must speak with Ferdinand."

She set her fingers in the proffered crook of his elbow. "You will tell him we may go?"

"Upon conditions." He looked down at her. "How long will you be away?"

Cecile swept him a speculative look. "Better you ask when we may return, *mon colonel*."

"It's the same thing, isn't it?"

"Ah, no." A secretive little smile curved her mouth. "Not in the mind of a woman, *tu sais?*"

The intimate version of the French "you" gave him a leaping hope. He lowered his voice to a murmur. "As a mere man, I can hardly be expected to interpret such finer shades of meaning. Enlighten me, I beg."

A tiny laugh escaped her. "I do not think I will do so." An unprecedented look of mischief was thrown at him. "You may ask of your Lady Fan what it means, Georges, *mon pauvre homme*."

Greatly intrigued, his ambitions buoyed, George determined to get her alone before the players left the town. But the pleasant little interlude was brought to an end as they closed with the impresario. Cecile released herself and went directly to Mrs Ferdinand, who caught her in a convulsive embrace.

"In good time, Colonel. Have you thought on the matter I raised with you, sir?"

With reluctance, George pulled his attention off Cecile and turned to Ferdinand and Fitzgerald, who had both halted. "I have thought of it, Mr Ferdinand. I propose, if this matter has not been resolved, to send a couple of my men along with you."

"Your soldiers? Good heavens, sir, are you serious?"

George ignored the affronted note. "Perfectly serious, sir. Either my lieutenant, or more likely my sergeant, will be with the men."

Fitzgerald's brows were raised. "Guards, Colonel? For what purpose?"

"To ensure none of the party absconds."

"Absconds? Absconds?" Ferdinand all but spluttered. "What do you mean, Colonel? You cannot be still suspecting this murderer to be among my people?"

By this time, Mrs Ferdinand had come up with Cecile and the Reverend Duddenhoe, who was looking astonished. None spoke, but George was conscious of both the matriarch's keen regard and the impassioned eyes of his inamorata. Damnation. He might have guessed she would be infuriated by this move. Well, it could not be helped.

"Those are my terms, Mr Ferdinand. My men go with you or you stay here." He executed a formal bow and threw his hand up in a salute. "If you will excuse me."

Straight-backed, George strode back towards the graveside to where Sullivan was overseeing the men filling in the grave. He seethed at the exigencies of his duty as the headway he thought he had made with Cecile dissipated.

"He's coming round, I think."

A vague memory of fear pushed into the boy's swimming head and he struggled feebly.

"Easy, boy. Easy now."

The voice thrust into his mind as remembrance surfaced. Perkin opened his eyes and found the room was going round. He closed them again, but not before he saw the black face again. He tried to push away the hand that was gently tapping at his cheek.

"No … get away…"

"It's all right, boy. No one's going to hurt you. Drink this."

Cool glass at his lip made him open his mouth. Fiery liquid burst into his throat and he choked.

Someone pulled him up. "Sit up, boy, come. Try again. Sip it."

Presently the boy was able to do as he was bid. This time the liquor went down more smoothly.

"Pale as a sheet he is, poor lad." Missus Tetsy? The voice was back to the old sympathetic tone he knew. Perkins struggled to open his eyes. His gaze, still hazy, fell upon the landlady's well-known features, creased with concern. "There, lad, that's better."

It was better. His head was no longer swimming and though he still felt weak, Perkin was beginning to revive. He glanced about and found he was in a pantry he found vaguely familiar.

263

Missus Tetsy's bulk obscured most of a pattern of shelving and he was sitting on a bench or box.

"A little more and you'll do."

It was the deep voice. Memory hit. Perkin turned his head and found the black face still there. The man's arm was around his shoulders, holding him fast, a glass in his other hand which he brought close to the boy's mouth.

"Drink, boy."

Perforce, he took another sip, feeling the strength in the arm that held him. He was too weak yet to run. There was no escape. Perkin began to whimper.

"Don't, sir … please don't kill me! I didn't mean nothing by it."

"Lord 'a mercy, what's he saying? He's lost his mind!"

Perkin was beyond making sense of this. He was crying now, unable to think of anything except the hideous nightmare of the visions that had come back to plague him.

"Don't kill me, sir … I won't tell no one, I promise. I ain't said nothing to no one and I never will. Please, sir…"

"Hey, hey, what's this? No one is going to kill you, boy." The deep voice was soothing. "There's no need to be afraid of me. I won't hurt you."

Perkin struggled in his grasp and the hold about him relaxed. The boy tried a leap for freedom. His legs buckled and he almost fell.

"You'd best sit down again, lad," said Missus Tetsy. "You ain't fit to go anywhere yet."

Sniffing, Perkin allowed himself to be recaptured by Hemp and sank back onto the hard wood with a sob in his throat.

"What do you want with him, sir?" A trifle of belligerence had entered Missus Tetsy's voice, but it did not appear to be directed at Perkin. "I'm thankful for your help, yes, carrying him and all, but it seems to me as you ain't cutting in for his sake."

"No, madam," came the calm reply. "From what he was saying back in the taproom, I believe the boy may have valuable information."

This struck at the heart of the boy's nightmare and he began to tremble.

"What, Perkin? What could he possibly know that might be of use to anyone, I should like to know?"

A hand was rubbing at the boy's back, but the tremors kept coming.

"I can't tell you that, madam. But milady will wish to question him."

Perkin's rising fear and astonishment was echoed in the landlady's voice.

"Milady? Gracious heaven, whoever do you mean, sir?"

"Lady Francis Fanshawe, madam. I am her steward. I cannot swear to the boy's usefulness, but I must insist upon taking him to milady."

A strangled cry escaped the boy. "No! I won't go!"

The arm came about him again, but this time it was a cuddling hold. The deep voice was gentle. "Come, boy. I mean you no harm. Milady is very kind. There's nothing to be afraid of. She'll likely give you a meal. Are you hungry?"

He was in fact starving, Perkin realised, as the smell of cooking permeating the pantry from the nearby kitchen curled into his nostrils. His mouth watered and he found himself nodding.

"Excellent. You come along with me, then, and we'll feed you first."

Missus Tetsy laughed. "Fattening the lamb for the slaughter, eh?"

Perkin wriggled and whimpered again.

"Don't frighten the boy more, madam. It's nothing of the kind. Milady will ask him a few questions, that's all. See, boy? Will you go with me quietly? I don't want to have to drag you there."

"I won't have him bullied, sir. He's not a bad lad. Or leastways, he wasn't before he took to thieving as I'm certain sure he has."

Feeling as if he was between the devil and the deep blue sea, Perkin began to lose all sense of purpose. He was for it, whichever way you looked at it. No point in battling. If he wasn't for the rope, or if the black fellow didn't mean to kill him, he'd get a beating for sure. Wouldn't be the first time.

"Can you stand, boy?"

The black man was urging him onto his feet. Perkin sniffed, dragged his sleeve across his nose and got up. He was a trifle shaky still, but the grip on his arm seemed like to keep him from falling over. Giving himself up to fate, Perkin allowed the man to lead him forth.

Listening with only half an ear to Monsieur Ferdinand's voluble protestations, Cecile struggled with a recalcitrant conscience. With hindsight, the abrupt change in George could not but pique her vanity. Had he an inkling of how easily she read his moods? Or how she knew on the instant each effect she had upon him?

No, poor George could not be aware how two years' association with the players, watching them work, had honed her ability to see behind mere words to the thoughts beneath. Both Kate and Jasper had this trick of subtle change in voice, in look, in face and manner to convey a swift alteration of mood or intention. She had known upon the instant how the flush of shocked ire in her had made George turn stiff and cold. He cared more for her opinion than Monsieur Ferdinand's, that was seen.

It was true she was enraged. What, to be hedged about with soldiers in uniform wherever they went? It was *affreux*. An embarrassment scarcely to be borne. Moreover, it was hard to forgive that still he suspected one of their own to be guilty. After she had fallen in with Lady Fan's request to meet with the women, she had hoped concentration had turned upon outsiders. All questions, much discussed afterwards, were of Dulcie's beaux. But it shocked her to realise George still suspected the players enough to be sending gaolers to keep any from running away.

"Cecile, are you all right?"

The murmur came from Kate in the seat beside her. She turned her head, forcing a smile.

"*Merci*, yes. And you? It was painful, no?"

"Much worse than I expected." Kate's mobile features half crumpled. "I had not realised how much I miss Dulcie. It was not fully real to me that she is…"

Kate's voice failed and Cecile sought for her hand. It gripped hers and she was grateful for the shared support. Presently the other girl's hold relaxed and she spoke again.

"I wish that colonel of yours would solve this and put us all out of our misery."

Cecile stiffened, withdrawing her hand. "He is not my colonel."

"Well, if he isn't, he would like to be."

The sly note made Cecile turn to look at her again. Kate was smirking. Indignation rose and Cecile could not withhold a whispered protest. "You speak of this, all of you?"

Apology flashed in Kate's face. "Only with Janey and Hilde."

"Pah!"

The explosion was involuntary and drew Madame Ferdinand's attention from across the carriage. Cecile sunk further into her corner in the forward seat, glad Hilde had elected to travel in the other coach with the rest of the men. All well for Kate to say only the women spoke of it, but from Hilde to Lewis was but an ear away and from there to the other male players no distance at all. She twitched Kate's sleeve.

"Do they all know? Tell me true."

Kate opened wide eyes. "There is no need to sound so fierce, Cecile. If you want to know, it was obvious from the first, only we were all so shocked by the horrid news and the idea your wretch of a colonel had that one of our boys had done it, none of us took notice to begin with."

"I desire you would cease to take notice," said Cecile with some heat. "*En effet*, there is nothing to see, nothing to be thought at all."

A giggle emanated from the girl at her side and Cecile eyed her with annoyance. To her relief, Madame Ferdinand took a hand, her tone an admonishment.

"Kate!" Cecile watched Kate take her underlip between her teeth and turn her gaze to the opposite window. Chagrined, she looked across to find Madame Ferdinand's gaze upon her. "I don't know what she's been saying to you, Cecile, though I suppose I may guess." A frowning glance at Kate accompanied this, but her quarry did not react. "Rest assured, child, none will interfere."

Now Cecile could not doubt but that the colonel's interest in her was common property. She seethed in silence, but was honest enough to acknowledge her own conduct must be partially to blame. She had not thought of how it would look to accost him as she had done in the cemetery. If she was honest, the only thing in her mind had been to snatch a moment in his company. She had not failed to note his observation of her during the service, and been gratified by it. She was glad to think it had not held her attention to the exclusion of Dulcie's obsequies. She was not so far gone as to have the colonel incessantly in her mind. At the back of it, yes perhaps. But to know the players watched her, laughed perhaps, was galling. Worse to realise she disliked the thought of being away from Weymouth and out of his reach.

Ah, this was too much. She must appear wholly unconscious if she did not desire to be unmercifully teased. Once Hilde knew Kate had spoken, Cecile could not doubt she would prick at it. Hilde could never hold her tongue.

For an instant, Cecile wished she might magically move ahead in time, to be removed from this period of uncertainty and upset to an era of safety in the comfort of George's charge.

Shocked at where her thoughts were tending, she made an effort to suppress them. But a niggle of remembrance crept into her head. 'I would I had a like pleasurable duty for a deserving woman.' Her toes curled in her shoes and warmth cascaded into her bosom. Such words! Who could doubt their portent?

Yet her spirits drooped as she recalled George's demeanour at the last. He would not seek her out. What excuse had he? There could be no more questions for her. But she might find questions, might she not? Was it not within her right, before they departed for Poole, to seek to know the progress of this Lady Fan? Such a visit might be permissible? And if so, might she not contrive to let it be known she would welcome a chance to bid George farewell?

Weaving and discarding a variety of messages in her head occupied Cecile for the remainder of the trip back to the lodgings where Annie, serving refreshments suitable to the ordeal of the funeral, greeted the company with a startling piece of intelligence.

"My man overheard a commotion in The Old Fiddler with that black fellow." She nodded to Cecile. "You know, miss, the one who serves the lady who's making enquiries about poor Miss Dulcie's murder. Something's afoot, I'll warrant."

Chapter Eleven

"How in the world did you find him, Hemp?"

Ottilia observed the boy as her steward told his story, noting his evident fright in the intermittent tremors that shook him and the darting fearful glances at Francis and herself.

"Sheer luck, milady. I had not meant to go back to the tavern, for I spent hours in there last night without result."

"Do you mean that seedy place you showed me yesterday?"

"That's right, milord. Young Jasper forgot his hat and I said I would check for it since he had to go to the funeral today. I was waiting to ask the landlady when I heard Perkin here talk of being paid to dig a hole."

The boy shrank back, as if he would conceal himself behind Hemp. Ottilia smiled at him.

"Pray don't be afraid, child." She patted the cushions on the chaise longue. "Come, sit here beside me."

The boy Perkin appeared reluctant. He glanced up at Hemp, who had a firm hand on his shoulder. "Milady won't hurt you, boy, I told you." He gave Ottilia an apologetic look. "He's scared witless, milady, say what I might. He bolted the food I gave him and tried to run off again."

"Well, I don't blame him," said Ottilia, returning her gaze to the boy's white face. "We must be altogether alien to the poor child. What is all this about digging a hole, Perkin? What sort of hole was it?"

The boy's features whitened visibly and he twisted his fingers together. He opened his mouth, but no sound came out. Hemp let out an exasperated sigh.

"He said he dug it as a job for a gentleman, milady. I'm bound to state, however, that the landlady, who knows him well, did not believe he got the money doing any sort of job."

"What money?"

"He's plump in the pocket with silver. The woman Tetsy thinks he stole it." At this, the boy gave a whimper, pulling away from Hemp, who grabbed his arm. "What is more, milady, much was made of his new clothes, which he says he got at the pawnbroker's."

The boy twisted as he tried to get away, his face agonized. Ottilia, her pity aroused, but her mind afire with conjecture, intervened.

"Let him go, Hemp." She lowered her voice. "Stay by the door."

Released, Perkin shot backwards and fetched up against the wall as Hemp moved quickly to the closed door and took up a stance before it.

"It doesn't look to me like you'll get anything out of him, Tillie," Francis murmured. "Skinny little runt, isn't he? He can't be much older than your nephews."

"He is probably older than he looks." Ottilia rose and went swiftly across, dropping down before the boy and taking hold of his hands. She smiled at him. "My poor boy, I am so sorry you have been frightened. I promise you will come to no harm in this house."

He made no attempt to pull his hands away, but his chest rose and fell in clear agitation. He shot a glance at Hemp.

"I thought it were 'im! I thought as he'd kill me."

"That is so, milady," her steward cut in. "As I told you, he swooned at sight of me."

"Hush, Hemp! Let the boy speak." But the child, shaking again, said nothing. She encouraged him. "What man is it you fear, Perkin? Who is it you think will kill you?"

"Him!" It was a cry, the terror potent. "The gennelman. Nor I never thought he seen me, fer I were well hid."

Excitement rose in Ottilia's breast, but she concealed it, gently drawing the boy towards the chaise longue as she picked up on his words. "Why did you think Hemp was the man? Did he look like him?"

"It were 'is face. Black it were. Leastways the top half."

"Then he was not a black man like Hemp?"

"Dunno, missus."

An idea occurred. "Could he have worn a mask perhaps?" Ottilia released one hand and gestured. "To here, so you could not see his eyes?"

"Mebbe. I dunno. He were big like this 'un."

"Tall, you mean?"

"Aye, and big too."

"Broad in the shoulder?"

"Dunno. He were big is all. Had a cloak on and one o' them old hats all corners."

Ottilia saw her spouse start, and threw him an admonitory glance before he could open his lips. She made a mental note of his interest.

Pressed onto the chaise longue, Perkin perched on its edge, still shaken with tremors. Ottilia sat beside him, in such a position to oblige the boy to turn towards her so he would not see either Hemp or Francis. She signed to both to keep silent, passing a finger across her lips. She kept the boy's hand in hers.

"Is that the man who paid you to dig a hole?"

"I never done it, missus." Perkin's breath came in gasps. "It weren't me as dug it, I swear. It were Truggery and Stowe. I seen 'em. Them noises o' digging woke me."

Ottilia kept her tone soft, infusing sympathy into her voice. "How dreadful for you. What did you do?"

"Watched 'em at it. Heard 'em saying as how the gennelman wanted the grave dug up, 'cos Stowe were arsting fer why. Nor Truggery didn't know neither, nor he didn't care long as he were paid fer it." The boy shuddered and his eyes became rimmed with moisture. "Don't fink even Trug 'ud have done it if he knew. Nor Stowe don't 'old wiv violence, tho' Trug 'ud beat me blue if he knew I seen 'em."

His tongue loosened, the boy's words poured out. Ottilia hesitated to put her urgent questions, fearing to stem the flow. She chose simplicity.

"What happened after they dug up the grave?"

Perkin began to shake again. "He come, din't he? Mean he were, like as nowt 'ud trouble him."

"How did he come there?"

"Come in a coach." Another shudder. "If I knew as she were in it and what he meant to do, I'd have scarpered quick, 'cept as I dursn't show meself for fear of Trug. An' after, I dursn't utter a squeak nor move 'til he'd gone. He'd 'a done me in and thrown me in that there grave, for two pins he would."

Elated, Ottilia listened with rising hope. To stumble on a witness to the murder was unbelievably fortunate. It was evident this boy had seen everything. But she must tread with care. Let him tell it in his own way.

"It sounds to have been worse than a nightmare, Perkin."

The boy dipped his head several times. "It give me bad dreams, missus. Nor I dursn't go back there, an' St Mary's ain't safe neither, being as it's in the middle o' town. Nor I din't want to spoil my new togs. I were hoping as I could get a room at The Old Fiddler, only Missus Tetsy —" He broke off in sudden consternation, throwing a leaping look across his shoulder at Hemp by the door and Francis standing by the fireplace and leaning an elbow on the mantel. The boy's pointed elfin features flushed and he snatched his hand out of Ottilia's, huddling into himself and whimpering.

"Hush, child, hush now." She leaned across and stroked his lank hair. "You are doing very well. You need not fear retribution, I promise you. I won't allow anyone to harm you, do you understand?"

The boy's lip quivered. "Do yer swear it, missus?"

Ottilia smiled and put a hand to her heart. "On my life, Perkin."

He eyed her with uncertainty. Ottilia kept her gaze steady upon his. Then a long sigh escaped him and his thin shoulders relaxed a trifle.

To lend colour to her assertion, Ottilia addressed Hemp. "Pray ask Joanie to see a truckle bed put up for Perkin in one of the servant's rooms. Tyler's perhaps. He must stay here with us for the moment."

Her spouse's brows shot up. "Have you run mad, Tillie?"

"For his own safety, Fan. If this story is accurate, and we have no reason to suppose otherwise, you know very well how vulnerable that will make him."

Her husband's frown told her he had taken her point, recalling she hoped as she did, though it was never far from her mind, the fate of the only witness to the murder of his sister-in-law nearly two years back.

Perkin's sharp glance was following the direction of her gaze. Ottilia hoped he had not understood all, though it was evident he got the gist.

275

"Stay here, missus? In yer house?"

"Why not, Perkin? Would you object?"

His glance swept the elegant proportions of the room and came back to her. For the first time, a beam lit his face. "Not likely, missus. Bang up I calls it!"

"I will arrange for him to sleep in my room, milady," said Hemp. "Best if I keep an eye on him."

The boy did not look to be enamoured of this scheme, but he said nothing, beyond casting another of his darting looks at Hemp.

"You have not told me what happened when this man arrived after the grave had been dug," said Ottilia in as matter of fact a tone as she could find, judging Perkin's initial fright to have subsided a good deal.

He frowned. "Trug were peeved as he made 'im open the coffin and throw them bones into the grave. He ain't one ter waste bodies, Trug ain't. Sells 'em ter them orspital surgeons he does down Dorchester way."

"He and Stowe are resurrection men, I take it?"

Perkin confirmed this with one of his jerky nods. "Aye, an' Stowe din't think them old bones 'ud be of use to no one, least of all the gennelman. Nor they weren't neither."

"No? Why then did he want the coffin?"

The boy's breath caught. "For to put the leddy in, missus. She were in the coach. I seen him carry her and put her in."

"Was she asleep?"

"Dunno. She weren't dead yet, fer I heard her sighin' and mutterin' after he put her in."

Ottilia's stomach clenched for the coming relation of the fate of the wretched Dulcibella. But her task must be to keep the boy talking.

"Did he light the candles before he brought her to the coffin?"

Perkin's eyes flew to hers and he gasped. "'Ow come you knowed that, missus?"

Though she was far from feeling like smiling, Ottilia forced a curve to her lips. "That is why Hemp wanted you to come to see me. I am trying to find out what happened to the poor lady you saw in the coffin."

"He killed her. He had a big knife and he — he lifted it up high like this —" demonstrating with his hands making a fist — "and then he brings it down and sticks it right in her pudding house!"

Plunged it into the girl's stomach? Ottilia could picture it all too horribly. Unsurprising the boy was shuddering again.

"Horrible it were, missus. She bounced like a ball, and it were enough to make me cast up me accounts, what with the noise and the blood and all, only I dursn't. An' them candles burning so's I could see it clear as clear. Nor I din't hardly dare shift a muscle, missus, for fear as he'd find me and serve me as he served the leddy."

"Very sensible, Perkin. But did you stay there all night?"

"Not me, missus. Waited 'til I couldn't hear the coach no more, an' made off fast as I could."

But his gaze, which had been steady up to now, had turned shifty. Moreover, he was fidgeting where he sat, his fingers fiddling in a manner as telling as it was involuntary. Ottilia had not spent years minding her two lively and mischievous nephews without learning to know the signs of prevarication. An inkling of the probable nature of his lie could not but obtrude, but she must tread warily.

"Perkin, did you get a good look at the lady in the coffin?"

He bit his lip and would not meet her eyes. Ottilia persisted in a gentle tone.

"I ask because you may be the only person to have seen her at night. You see, by the time she was found, the candles were burning down and it was beginning to be light. No one can tell me just what she looked like lying in the coffin there."

An inaccurate statement, for she'd heard George's impression. Might it lend importance to the boy's participation and appeal to his pride?

"I understand that she looked very pretty," she pursued.

"Aye, missus," the boy agreed, his voice jumping, "only I never seen her afore. Folks say as she were one wi' them players, but I dunno."

"She had golden hair, I believe. It must have looked particularly lovely in the candlelight," Ottilia prompted.

"Ay, if she weren't all over blood," the boy blurted, and then threw a hand to his mouth, his eyes popping at her over it.

Ottilia lowered her voice to a whisper. "Did you take a closer look, Perkin?"

He nodded, his hand fixed firmly across his lips as if to stop any more incriminating words from coming out.

Ottilia hesitated, not yet willing to pounce. She must draw him out a little more. "What did you see?"

He began to shake again, bringing his hand down and gripping it together with the other, shoving both between his unquiet knees. A timorous whisper came.

"Blood ... all over. Turned her dress red it did. It were even in her hair."

"But you saw something more, did you not?" Ottilia probed with care, hoping not to break his confidence. He was kneading his fingers in his thin thighs. "Her reticule? A bag she had?"

The joined hands dropped suddenly as he jerked. His head came up.

"I din't open it. Seen it ready open, I did, I swear it. Wouldn't 'a looked otherwise."

"I believe you." Ottilia drew a breath and set a hand on the boy's knee. "Come, Perkin, it is useless to deny it. You found her purse, did you not?"

Sudden rage flared in the boy's eyes and he threw off her hand with violence, shooting to his feet. A concerted movement from the men made Ottilia throw up a hand to stop either from interfering.

"It were jus' lyin' there," cried Perkin, sobs catching in his throat though his eyes blazed. "No one din't want it. He never took it. She din't need it no more. But I did, missus, I did! Never 'ad nowt my whole life long and there it were ... more gold than I never did see. I 'ad to take it, missus. I couldn't nowise leave it, could I? Walk away from good fortune? More'n flesh and blood could stand it were."

He was sobbing as he sank to the floor, knuckling his eyes. Her heart wrung, Ottilia glanced at her husband, who gave a wry smile.

"Poor little devil. He's likely more terrified of the rope than the murderer."

"Between the hammer and the anvil," said Ottilia.

She looked down at the pathetic heap the boy made, clearly too desperate now to be further questioned for the present. Before she could decide how to act, Hemp left his post by the door and came across to the boy.

"Hey, boy, get up now."

His tone was gentle as he plucked the child bodily from the floor and set him on his feet. To Ottilia's astonishment, the boy flung his arms about Hemp's thighs and clung. An image swept into her mind, of the pitiful mad girl Tamasine, who had clung to Hemp in a similar fashion, as if he was her whole dependence and support.

Hemp pulled the boy off and hoisted him up into his powerful arms, settling him there as he looked at Ottilia. "I will look to him, milady."

"Thank you, Hemp. Try if you can get him to tell you where is the rest of his hoard. But don't let him run off, if you please. I mean to keep my promise to him."

Hemp nodded and retired with the boy, murmuring soothingly to him the while.

Ottilia watched them leave as her husband came across and sat down beside her, pulling out his pocket handkerchief. To her astonishment, he applied it to her cheeks and the corners of her eyes.

"Good heavens, Fan, was I weeping? I did not know it."

"Yes, so I gather." He kissed her and slipped the handkerchief back into his pocket. "I doubt you know how in the world you are to keep your promise either."

Ottilia sighed, tucking her hand into his. "Will George insist on our handing him over, do you suppose?"

"What, when he is a material witness to the murder? I imagine he will want to take him into his own custody."

"But he won't hang him, will he?" Despite herself, she caught a breath on an escaping sob.

Francis rubbed a soothing hand across her back. "I can't speak for George, but I should think he will be loath to proceed to criminal charges, as long as the money is returned."

Ottilia let out a shaky breath. "Poor child. He can scarcely be blamed for the theft. He must have been petrified and shocked. No one could wonder at it that he crept to the body to have a closer look."

"Morbid curiosity? I noticed you pressed him on it."

"Because he was clearly concealing something. And it would be a natural thing to do, for anyone."

Francis cocked an eyebrow. "Natural to steal a purse full of guineas?"

Ottilia met the scepticism in his eyes. "For Perkin, yes. In the circumstances. His collapse shows him to have a conscience. I doubt he is a habitual thief. How he lives I know not, but you heard him. It was more than flesh and blood could stand, he said. I wonder if you or I could resist, had we lived as he does?"

Her spouse smiled. "You have no need to argue the point with me, my love. Save your eloquence for George."

"I am persuaded he will understand how it was. How could he not?"

She was unable to help an anxious note and was grateful for the hug she received. Releasing her, Francis rose and went to pick up the hand bell.

"Coffee!" He gave it a vigorous ring.

Ottilia had to laugh. "Coffee is ever your remedy for me, is it not, dearest?"

He gave a mock bow. "I am merely serving your addiction, my lady Fan."

She smiled and held out her hand to him. "I need you, my darling lord."

He grinned. "You want me to pave the way with George?"

Ottilia clicked her tongue. "Wretch! Have you taken to reading my mind?"

He came across to sit beside her again, putting an arm about her. "It's not very difficult, my loved one. You are all too transparent on occasion."

"I love you," she said, leaning her head on his shoulder.

"Gratifying, but if you are hoping to persuade me into taking that boy into our household on a permanent basis —"

Ottilia sat up in a bang, indignant. "Did I say so?"

"I know you too well, Tillie. And I tell you here and now I won't do it. Hemp is one thing. A ragamuffin boy is something else again."

Ottilia sighed. "Well, perhaps George will have a notion of how to help him. He ought to be set to some trade, but…"

She faded out as the door opened to admit Joanie, who curtsied. Releasing her, Francis rose from the sofa.

"Coffee, if you please, Joanie."

"Yes, my lord. Only there's a visitor, my lord. Mademoiselle Benoit, my lady."

She stepped away from the door to reveal Cecile waiting without.

Out of breath, Cecile could barely stand to wait for the maid to leave and close the door before breaking into agitated speech.

"Is it that you have news, madame? *La concierge* she speaks of a boy *et cet homme qui vous* —" She broke off, struggling for her English, registering in a vague way the astonishment in Lady Fan's face. "*Pardon!* I forget. It was in a tavern, you understand?"

"You heard this from the landlady, you say?" cut in Lady Fan.

"Good God, we might as well inform the town crier!"

Cecile had not taken in the presence of her hostess's husband. She dropped a curtsey. "*Pardon, monsieur*, I did not see you."

He waved a hand, crossing to take up a stance at the mantel. "It makes no matter, *mademoiselle*. But I wish you will explain how this landlady of yours comes to be first with this news."

Cecile drew an unsteady breath and advanced into the room. "Forgive, I beg. I cannot wait to come, though Madame Ferdinand obliges me to eat first, but of little use is this for the food it chokes me when my heart is on fire to know."

"Won't you sit down, Cecile?" Lady Fan patted the seat beside her. "The maid will bring coffee presently. You will take a cup, I hope? It will help to calm you."

Moving towards the sofa, Cecile thanked her. "It is well, madame, but all my desire is to know what has transpired."

"Wine, perhaps?" offered Lord Francis as she passed him, an eyebrow cocked. "Brandy?"

She let out a tiny laugh. "*Merci*, but it is not necessary for the liquor, *monsieur*. I will remain calm."

"Coffee it is then."

He smiled and Cecile caught an inkling of why he and George were friends. Just that amused twinkle in the colonel's eye had caused more than one little disturbance in her breast. Another came as she recalled the uncomfortable way he had frozen as they parted company earlier at the cemetery. Taking a seat, she was glad when Lady Fan dragged her mind back to the present moment.

"May I know just what the landlady said, Cecile?"

"It was not she, but the husband who was in the tavern. It was he who heard and saw. There was a boy, is it not? An argument, I think? He saw the boy carried in the arms of this man. And after, when he went out, he saw again the boy was with your servant and he followed."

"Ah, he saw the boy brought here?"

"It is so, madame. Thus his wife thinks there is news."

"And you are anxious for news, no doubt."

Cecile could not withhold a shiver. "We have buried *la pauvre* today. And next week we must go to Poole for Bournemouth."

"What, do you say George permits the company to leave Weymouth?" demanded Lord Francis.

Resentment returned. "He sends soldiers with us that the villain shall not escape. But me I do not believe it is one of our people and therefore I come to you, madame, with hope that you may assure me it is so."

The Lady Fan looked regretful. "Alas, I cannot, Cecile. What we have heard today is extremely interesting, but so far it does not identify the murderer."

Lord Francis spoke again, his tone curt. "We've not had time to sift the information, *mademoiselle*. You have come upon us when we have only just ourselves heard what the boy has to tell us."

Eager now, Cecile ignored the clear dismissal in his words. "But something he has told, no? It is of use? It may assist to find the man?"

"Perhaps."

He glanced at his wife as if for corroboration. Cecile at once turned to her, unable to help a trifle of irritation creeping into her voice.

"Madame? You do not speak. Is it that you do not trust in me? You ask of me the questions and I answer, no? You wish to speak with the women and I bring them. Why then am I to be left in ignorance?"

Lady Fan's brows rose. "Have I said I will not tell you?"

"*Non*, but there is that in your face which tells to me you do not wish to speak of it," said Cecile frankly.

"Dear me. I appear to be less adept at concealment than I had realised. My husband was saying so only a moment ago."

Lord Francis exchanged a glance peculiarly intimate with his wife, causing Cecile to suffer a curious pang. She watched as he crossed to the window.

"Perhaps Cecile is also a mind reader, my love."

"Evidently." Mischief flitted across Lady Fan's face. "Or perhaps you have been studying Kate's player tricks?"

Cecile had to laugh. "Without intent, madame. But tell me, I beg."

A sigh escaped her hostess. "I ought to reserve it for George's ears first, but as you are so nearly concerned —"

"Do not wait, madame. It is not certain Georges will tell me what I wish to know." Realising from the other's look that she was giving herself away, Cecile amended her tone. "For Georges, it is a duty, which I understand. He may not speak of it. But you, madame, you have not the duty *militaire*."

"True, but I am acting for George."

"Don't disturb yourself, Tillie," came from her husband at the window. "If I mistake not, this is George approaching our door at this moment."

A flurry in her pulses sent Cecile to her feet. "Ah, *non*, is it so? He is here?"

Lord Francis turned a questioning face upon her. "Yes. Do you not wish to meet him?"

She did not. Yet the urgent image of his features in her mind belied her. She headed for the door. "I will go now."

Lady Fan was on her feet. "Don't go, Cecile. Of all people, George will least wish to prevent you knowing what has transpired today. Besides, it is too late for escape. You will run into him on the stairs."

The patent truth of this struck Cecile with some force. Veering away from the door, she fetched up at the mantel and gripped its edge with one hand. "He will wish to know why it is I am here."

"He will understand your reasons, I am sure," said Lady Fan, her tone soothing. "Will you not sit down again?"

Cecile shook her head, the suspense tightening her breast. It occurred to her she would give a ridiculous impression of disquiet if she remained where she was. Without thought, she dropped into the nearest chair, gripping the arms with her fingers and staring at the door.

George accepted the cup and saucer Francis handed to him without comment, his eyes on Cecile. She was sipping with delicacy, avoiding his gaze. He could see she was agitated and did not doubt his presence was the cause.

"You are come opportunely, my friend."

Because Cecile was here? George eyed Francis with question and received a cocked eyebrow in return and an amused look.

"I am not referring to the obvious, George." He looked to his wife. "Shall I tell him, or will you?"

His attention caught as Ottilia waved a nonchalant hand. "Do so, by all means."

The air of mystery was potent, augmented in Cecile he realised. Urgency broke in him. "Good God, Fan, what's to do? Is there some development?"

"It is a very breach, George. We have a witness to the murder."

In astonishment and rising hope, George listened to Francis's account of Hemp's discovery of a boy called Perkin and a story Ottilia had dragged from him of the night of Dulcie's murder. His awareness took in Cecile's eagerness, and he could not doubt she was equally avid for the details.

286

"Then this boy can identify the man?" He turned to Ottilia, who looked regretful.

"I doubt it, George. From what he said, I suspect he wore a mask."

Cecile broke in. "Black? And in the night. It is perhaps why he is afraid of your steward?"

"Just so. He fainted clean away at first sight of him, Hemp said. Although he has taken to him now as if Hemp is his protector, poor child."

George waved this away. "Nevertheless, can you cobble together a description, Ottilia?"

She exchanged a look with Francis, who raised an eyebrow. "You think I jumped to a false conclusion?"

Ottilia gave that knowing smile of hers. "Not necessarily false. Perhaps premature."

Impatience claimed George. "Ottilia, for the Lord's sake, speak out!"

"Pardon me, George. Yes, to answer your question, I think we may safely suppose, from Perkin's observation, that our murderer is tall and well built. Strong enough at least to carry a dead weight from the coach to the grave."

"She was already dead then?"

"No, indeed." Ottilia threw an apologetic glance at Cecile. "Perkin gave a horribly graphic description of the killing. But Dulcie was unconscious."

"Drugged," said George on a grim note. "I checked with Roffey as you suggested. He said there was a narcotic substance in the stomach."

He could not help a glance at Cecile. She was still, but peculiarly rigid, her hands white where they gripped the cup she was holding. George cursed inwardly. She ought not to hear all this.

"For the rest," Ottilia went on, "we know the man was cultured. Perkin speaks of a gentleman. And he employed two resurrection men to dig the grave. They go by the names of Truggery and Stowe, although the boy has not seen them in Weymouth since the murder. He says they sell bodies to the Dorchester surgeons."

Hope flickered in George's breast. "Then if we can find them, they must certainly identify the man."

"But can you?" Francis asked. "I should think they must be long gone."

"I can set the Dorchester militia to make a search at least. They will leave no stone unturned if there is a chance we can locate these men."

Movement caught his eye and he turned to see Cecile setting her cup down. She did not look at him, but fixed her dark gaze on Ottilia. "It is well, madame. This man cannot be of the players, that is seen."

"Why not?" George demanded. "I am sorry to be obliged to say it, Cecile, but I do not see that this description exonerates them."

Her lustrous eyes turned on him, reproach in them. "But these are not gentlemen."

"But they may assume the carriage and voice of gentlemen, Cecile," said Ottilia, expressing his thought. "Moreover, I am afraid the actor Robert Collins fits the description."

"Rob? Ah, no! He is tall, yes, but also he is thin. *Alors*, I do not believe he is strong, for he cannot prevent that his wife strikes him."

George was sceptical. "Cannot? Or dare not attempt it?"

She gave him a furious look which could not but slice at his heart. He was grateful for Ottilia's intervention.

"I wish I might rule him out, Cecile, but if it comforts you, I would put him at the bottom of the list."

George's attention was caught. "And the list? Who is on it, Ottilia?"

She turned to her spouse. "You have met them, Fan, not I. Which of them fits, would you say?"

Francis, who had taken a seat beside Ottilia, pursed his lips in concentrated thought. George waited, mentally reviewing the three he knew to be under consideration.

"Not Charlton," said Francis at last. "He is not of superior height and I would call him stocky rather than a big 'un, as the boy had it. Edgcott is big, but only in the shoulder. I suppose he might look tall to a boy. But he wears a three-cornered hat and Perkin specifically spoke of one."

"Did he? That's interesting indeed." George looked to Ottilia again. "Was he wearing anything else of note?"

"A cloak. Yet I would have thought he might have removed it. Would it not hamper his movements?"

"Well, did you ask the boy?"

Ottilia raised her brows. "My dear George, the child was in no condition to think clearly enough to give me such details. His guilt about stealing the purse made him far too distressed, and he was already altogether terrified from thinking Hemp was the murderer and intended to kill him."

George curbed his irritation. "I'll have to interrogate him thoroughly myself."

"You had better let Tillie do it if you want to get anything out of him," Francis said.

"Very well, very well, but what of the other fellow?"

"Paglesham? Oh, he fits perfectly. Except that I doubt of his having the necessary authority to employ these resurrection men."

George took this without comment. "Then we need only add Fitzgerald to the list."

Cecile started. "Again you seek to accuse a man of the company?"

"He's not of the company," George snapped, and at once regretted his tone. He softened it. "Fitzgerald is the theatre manager, and I am sorry to say his testimony is highly suspicious. Besides which, this description fits him like a glove. Personally, I would put him at the top of the list."

Cecile rose with a swish of her skirts, a flash at her eyes that made George's heart sink.

"Will you bring Monsieur Ferdinand to ruin, Georges? To lose Dulcie it is not enough? He must lose also another player in Rob, or if not, he must lose this venue where he brings his people every year."

The hurt would not be contained. "Is it my fault, Cecile? Am I to blame for the murder? What would you wish me to do? Leave the man who killed your friend to roam free?"

She did not flinch. "That is not reasonable, no. But you can look to these men not of the theatre, is it not?"

"Naturally I will do so. I would be very happy to be able to say neither Robert Collins nor Fitzgerald had anything to do with this affair, but I cannot. My duty is to the truth. If it ruins The Grand Ferdinando so be it. Though I cannot suppose it might for the man is nothing if not resilient. I think you are unnecessarily pessimistic."

She stood before him, uncertainty in her face, together with a look at the back of her eyes he could not identify. George was swept with a yearning to take her in his arms and kiss away the trouble. Forgetful of his surroundings, he dropped his voice to a murmur.

"Cecile, don't do this, I beg of you. Why do you wish to quarrel with me?"

Her lips quirked and a smile came into her eyes. "*C'est imbecile, non*? I do not know, Georges."

He found her hand and raised it to his lips. Colour crept into her cheeks but she did not look away. She addressed him in French. "Settle this quickly, Georges, I pray you. I cannot endure the pain. These are my family now."

"I know," he returned in the same language. "I will do my best. At least we are further forward. Think of it like that, if you can."

A rueful look came into her eyes. "I can think only that I will soon be absent from Weymouth, Georges. Too soon."

He held her gaze. "Weymouth is at no great distance from Bournemouth, *ma cherie*."

She blushed at the endearment and withdrew her hand from his, switching to English as she turned to Ottilia. "Madame, I will go now. You do not object if I tell them of this boy?"

George intervened swiftly. "No! For the lord's sake, don't mention that we have a witness."

"No, indeed, Cecile, pray do not speak of it," said Ottilia, rising in an urgency George understood. "You may put the boy in danger of his life."

Cecile's face was a study. "*Quel horreur*! You would say the evil one will seek to kill him also?"

"It has been done before, Cecile, to my everlasting shame and guilt."

A jerky motion from Francis reminded George how he hated to hear Ottilia blame herself for that episode. He had himself been a party to that particular investigation. All three of them must take a share.

"It's true, Cecile," he said, moving to flank her. "A young man lost his life because we were all indiscreet. Say nothing of this, I charge you."

"But what shall I say? All know why I came here. Madame Annie has said to them about this boy."

Ottilia was frowning. "Yes, of course, that is why you came." She set a hand to Cecile's arm. "I have it. Tell them it was all a mistake. The boy proved to be innocent of any connection with this business. You may say he was employed to dig ditches and that he believes black men are the devil."

The rare little laugh escaped Cecile and warmth crept into George's chest.

"*Voilà une bêtise*, but it may serve."

She made her farewells but refused the escort he offered, once again becoming a trifle agitated. "Ah, no, Georges, *merci*. I go alone."

He watched her leave and turned to find both Fan and Ottilia eyeing him. Too intent to care why, he threw up a hand. "Don't say a word, either of you! I'm going after her, but I'll be back in a moment."

In the periphery of his vision as he headed for the door he saw them exchange a glance, but he was past making anything of it. The need to speak with Cecile was paramount.

He caught her up as she was opening the front door. "Wait!"

She turned, her fingers still about the handle. George covered them as he reached her, possessing himself of her hand.

"What is it, Cecile? Why are you shy of me all of a sudden? Is it this business of my wishing to send my men with the company?"

She made no attempt to recover her hand, but her fingers quivered in his. Those eyes, so dark, so expressive, met his gaze, uncertainty in them. "It is not this, no."

He dropped his voice. "Tell me."

She sighed a little breath. "The players, Georges. They tease me because of you. I did not know. I did not think, but Kate…"

She faded out, the colour again in her cheeks, her fingers shifting in his so that he could not but tighten his hold as his blood began to heat.

"I have caused you embarrassment. I am sorry for it." He tried to steady his voice which had become unprecedentedly shaky. Lord, what had this girl done to him? "Cecile, I did not intend to speak until this is over, but you cannot doubt of my regard."

At that, her chin went up and she pulled her fingers from his, a flash darkening her gaze.

"Regard? *C'est tout?* I thank you, *monsieur le colonel*, but me, I have no use for your regard!"

He felt as if she slapped him. He drew back a little. "Have I then been mistaken? I thought — Cecile, I was sure you returned my regard."

"Then you have thought it wrong, monsieur."

Confused at the fury in both face and voice, George fairly blinked at this turn. He could not help the hurt in his tone. "Why do you say that? It is not how you have behaved towards me."

To his further confusion, Cecile tossed her head. "Then me, I have been mistaken also." With which, she turned from him, wrenched open the door, passed through and slammed it in his face.

George did not know whether he was more infuriated or bewildered. Without thinking what he did, he walked slowly back up the stairs and into the Fanshawe's parlour, where he found Ottilia and Francis with their heads together on the sofa. Exasperation seized him.

"If you are going to bill and coo, the two of you, I'm done. Women!"

Chagrined to see his friend's amused look, he was relieved when Ottilia surveyed him with her usual warm sympathy.

"What happened, George?"

He was too wound up to withhold it. "I told her of my regard and she spurned me." Memory hit. "*C'est tout?* Is that all? That's what she said. And then she lost her temper and left me."

"Dear me, George, is that what you told her? You have a regard for her?"

To George's further chagrin, Francis put his oar in, throwing up his eyes.

"Good God, man! Even I know better than that."

His bewilderment increasing, George looked from one to the other. "What the deuce do you mean, either of you? What should I have said?"

Ottilia's gurgling laugh came. "Poor George. Don't tease him, Fan. Can't you see he is upset?"

"You are not helping, Ottilia. And while I am about it, what in the name of all the gods is the difference between asking how long she will be away and when they might return? Cecile said I should ask you, Ottilia, but if you can unravel that, you're a genius."

"She is," said Francis, giving his wife a fond look. "Well, Tillie?"

The answer came without hesitation. "One is personal and the other is not." Ottilia's look was speculative. "I suspect she was teasing you, George."

"Oh, Lord! Then why is she being so unkind to me now? She actually said she had no use for my regard."

Ottilia exchanged just such a glance with Fan as proclaimed the understanding he would wish to have with Cecile. It was evident his friend had learned more of women than he had. Ottilia's gaze came back to him.

"The next time, George, speak rather of your affection or, if you will forgive me, your love. Regard has a colder ring."

Relief flooded him. "Good God, is that all? But she must know I am talking of affection."

"Knowing and hearing are two different things, my dear George. You have chosen a passionate girl. Moreover, she is French. Your English reticence will not do."

Goaded, he could not withhold a retort. "Well, she'll have to take me as I am or not at all."

Ottilia tutted. "George, this is not worthy of you."

Conscious of being demonstrably in the wrong, George regarded his friend's ill-concealed mirth with acute disfavour. But before he could express his mind, a knock at the door produced the steward Hemp, who gave him a slight bow.

"I am glad you are still here, sir, for this nearly concerns you." He turned to Ottilia. "Milady, I have been talking with the boy. He remembered more of what the gentleman said."

"What was it, Hemp?"

The tease was quite gone from Ottilia's voice and George felt his irritation dissipating as his attention returned to the murder.

"The man was threatening the gravediggers, telling them not to say anything of their work for him. He had a pistol, Perkin says. This Truggery threatened him right back, saying he knew 'summat of him', as the boy put it. But what is more pertinent, sir," added Hemp, turning his gaze upon George, "the murderer told them he was very well acquainted with the colonel of militia here."

Chapter Twelve

"The difficulty is I know all the suspects."

"But how well, George?"

Ottilia sipped her refreshed cup of coffee as she watched the colonel's restless striding about the room.

"For pity's sake, sit down, George! You are fidgeting, Tillie, and I won't have it."

"Hush, Fan," Ottilia admonished, but she was relieved when George flung himself into the opposite chair. She still found vigorous action difficult to tolerate, despite the undoubted improvement in her health and spirits. George's disquiet was patent, more so for the earlier contretemps with his inamorata. "I am sure he would much prefer to go a-courting than think about this horrid murder."

The colonel flung up his head. "I should. Infinitely. Though much good would it do me if I cannot give Cecile the satisfaction of knowing the murderer of her friend is behind bars."

"Then let us consider our options. You have been in Weymouth some months. Which of these men, do you suppose, might count himself well acquainted with you?"

Francis eyed her. "What do they think? You suggest our man would claim more than his fair due for the purpose of frightening the gravediggers?"

Ottilia could not withhold an appreciative smile. "Just so, my dearest quicksilver husband."

"Then it leaves us no further forward," said George on a note of dissatisfaction, ignoring her spouse's amusement.

Ottilia put up a finger. "Don't despair yet. The murderer may have spoken the exact truth."

A crease appeared between his brows. "Well, I don't see how. I did not know the actor before this business, though I have had occasion for discussion with Fitzgerald once or twice. As for Paglesham, I've had little to do with him, and I may say I have studiously avoided Edgcott."

Francis snorted. "Not a man easily snubbed, if you ask me. He cuts his coat to suit his cloth, of course, but he struck me as adept at making himself agreeable. Or else he is almost as accomplished an actor as these Ferdinando players. I don't know whether I was more disgusted with him or with Paglesham's sycophancy."

He spoke with some distaste and Ottilia, who had listened to his accounts of both conversations with intent interest, picked it up at once.

"Why did you dislike him so much? Edgcott, I mean."

Francis made a face. "Apart from his vulgarity, he was altogether callous about Dulcie. He was quite open that he had tried and failed, as I told you, but his attitude rankles."

Ottilia regarded him thoughtfully. "Is it because he is the only one to take a different view towards the candles?"

With a surprised look, George demanded enlightenment.

"He spoke of them as an homage to Dulcie's beauty," Francis said. "Better than leaving her body lying around to be half consumed by wild animals, or some such thing."

"Good God, you mean the fellow said that?"

"He has a foul mouth on him and no respect for women. I should not be surprised to learn he had forced the girl or rendered her drunk for his purposes."

George's face was a study and Ottilia had to smile. "Do not go thinking you had best arrest the fellow without more ado,

George." But she seized opportunity. "However, it occurs to me it might be well to check for these illicit gravediggers in Lyme Regis and Exeter."

His frowning gaze turned on her. "Why?"

"Because Mrs Ferdinand recalls seeing Edgcott at both places."

"He told me he prefers the resorts to the West," Francis chimed in. "Do you suppose he followed Ferdinando's travels to have a touch at Dulcie when no rivals were by?"

"Or he may have had other occasion to make such visits, Fan. If he has sold out, how does he live?"

Francis shrugged. "I assume he has some means. He said he is not a warm man and complained of frittering his money on toys for Dulcie without result. He specifically mentioned he thought her mercenary and flying at higher game."

"Putting the scent on Charlton," said George on a derisory note.

"Yet according to Kate Drummond," Ottilia put in, "Dulcie was debating whether to take 'Perry'."

"Peregrine?"

"Just so, Fan."

"The devil!" George threw up his eyes. "That throws it back on Paglesham."

"Perhaps."

"He boasted of conquest," Francis reminded her.

"True. And crucial. We must not forget she was enceinte. Whoever was the father had motive. Why kill her unless to be rid of the difficulty?"

"Jealousy?"

"A possibility, Fan, but a little far-fetched, I think."

He gave another of his snorts. "The reason was extremely far-fetched in Witherley, if you recall. There is no saying what will set off a murderous mind. You should know that better than most."

Ottilia frowned. "But character was key on that occasion. Your Edgcott sounds to be a man of stable mind at least, but is he so ruthless?"

"Where women are concerned, yes."

"Ruthless enough to kill merely for jealousy?" demanded George with scepticism.

"I've already surmised he is capable of forcefully overcoming Dulcie's reluctance."

Ottilia set a hand on his arm. "We cannot rule it out that he did so, but would Dulcie wish to marry such a man? We know from Kate she was possessed of a conviction she was to enter society and mingle with this or that ladyship."

George jumped on this. "She spoke of Perry not Edgcott. She thought Paglesham would marry her?"

"He wouldn't," Francis cut in. "He was specific on that point."

Ottilia felt obliged to quash this line. "He said so to you, Fan. That does not mean he did not lure Dulcie with false promises."

"Any of them could have done that," George objected. "Including Charlton, though Fan does not think he fits the description."

"Except Robert Collins," Francis pointed out. "He is already married."

"Yet I think we can be certain one of them did indeed make some sort of promise," Ottilia went on, "whether of marriage or some other solution to Dulcie's desperate problem. Dulcie at least believed that night she was destined for happiness. We also know she was drugged. If we take Fitzgerald's story for truth, we know the man took her off in a coach around midnight."

"Which," said George with obvious reluctance, "becomes more plausible since this boy told you the murderer came in a coach."

A stray thought made Ottilia throw out a hand. "Coaches, George!"

"I beg your pardon?"

She clicked an impatient tongue. "Who owns a coach?"

"How the devil should I know? I doubt either Edgcott or Paglesham has the means, and Fitzgerald does not need one. And I had Ferdinand's coaches checked while the funeral was going forward and there was nothing untoward discovered."

"But anyone might hire a coach," said Francis. "Is that what you had in mind, Tillie?"

"Just so. You must discover from the livery stables, George, if one was hired within the timeframe."

The colonel became brisk. "I'll set Sullivan on to it. We may have to check outside of Weymouth. I'm going to see Shellow tomorrow so I'll drive across to Lyme and possibly Exeter too. It'll mean staying over, which is a nuisance, but it can't be helped."

"You mean to check for Edgcott at those two theatres?"

"I'll question the locals there, but I'm hopeful Shellow will have his men hunt for the gravediggers."

"Excellent. And we should discover whether Fitzgerald owns a coach."

"Easy enough."

Ottilia found her husband's eye on her. "Would Fitzgerald bring up the business of seeing a coach at all if he had been the man?"

"A fair point, Fan."

"Unless he thought to throw suspicion away from himself because George clearly had him in his sights?"

"From what George says of him, I am inclined to think him too level-headed to make so foolish a mistake."

"He's overmuch level-headed, if you ask me," said George in mordant fashion. "Conveniently so."

But Francis continued to keep his attention on Ottilia. "Then upon whom are you focused, Tillie? And pray don't fall into your usual practice of refusing to say anything until you know more."

She could not resist throwing him a look of mischief. "I might, but I will not since I am reliant upon you for my discoveries."

"You need not be. It's too late today, for I must go and fetch Mama directly. But if you feel up to it tomorrow, I could escort you to the Rooms to see these fellows for yourself."

"All well and good," George cut in, "but at this present, if you please, Fan, I must insist upon her answering your question."

The demand was just. Ottilia smiled upon George. "Everything points to Paglesham or Edgcott. The trick is to discover which of them is lying."

Chapter Thirteen

It was, to Ottilia's dismay, still an ordeal to her to endure the crowding chatter of the Assembly Rooms, although her husband said the place was quieter than usual.

"The fine weather must have drawn off a number to attempt one of these expeditions they talk of."

Ottilia did not respond. She felt disoriented, aware of many eyes that scrutinised her as Francis guided her towards the entrance to the card room in which she glimpsed Sybilla in a foursome. Her mother-in-law had attended at her usual time, leaving Francis to return to the lodgings to bring his wife at her leisure.

A face loomed up before her in which she recognised the master of ceremonies.

"Ah, Rodber, you have already met my wife."

The man was bowing with a flourish. "Indeed, my lord, and may I say it gives me great pleasure to be permitted to welcome your ladyship at last to our little assembly."

Ottilia thanked him, though she was tempted to decry his notion of 'little'. The room seemed to her vast, with high ceilings and a good deal of light splashing the tiled floor. She replied suitably and was glad when Francis evaded Mr Rodber's efforts to take over. She caught a wave from her mother-in-law, accompanied by a narrow look of question, which Ottilia returned with a smile of reassurance. Sybilla had been dubious of the wisdom of the outing, although she understood the need for it once brought up to date with the state of the investigation. She gave a nod and returned to the game.

"The devil of it is," said Francis in Ottilia's ear as he guided her to a quieter part of the large room and found her a chair, "that neither of our fellows is in the place at this moment."

"Perhaps one of them will come in presently."

"Unless they have gone off on this infernal expedition. Well, if they don't turn up, I'll take you home again." He was eyeing her with a frown. "You look decidedly peaky."

Ottilia tried for a measure of her customary self-possession. "I admit I find it a trifle overwhelming, but I dare say the feeling will pass."

"I don't want you tiring yourself unnecessarily, Tillie. We can very well find another way."

"We may have to if neither of them come in." She allowed her gaze to wander around the visitors and found most of the curious faces had returned to their occupations. "I never thought I should have occasion to be glad of your rank, Fan."

He cocked an eyebrow. "Thank my mother's rather. She is senior among Weymouth's visitors."

"Except for the King, should he appear to gratify Mr Rodber."

Her spouse laughed and she smiled, relaxing a little. In general, she loathed the social convention that dictated none would approach her, in such an assembly as this, without invitation or a formal introduction. Francis and the dowager being already known, her identity must be obvious. The drawback could not but obtrude.

"It is of scant use either Edgcott or Paglesham appearing here, Fan, for how in the world are we to draw them apart?"

"The deuce! I had not thought of that."

Ottilia sighed. "I shall have to mingle."

"No need. You may observe just as well from here. Ah, there's Charlton just coming in from the entrance hall. Do you want to try him?"

"By all means."

While Francis waited his chance to attract the man's attention, Ottilia took opportunity to observe the stocky fellow who had entered, trying to put herself in Dulcibella's place. He was certainly possessed of a good countenance with a patrician nose and a confident air, but he looked his years. What could attract a young beauty except for his rank and status? Yet she would be naïve indeed to suppose such a man might marry her.

Charlton had caught Francis's eye and was coming in their direction at his signalled invitation. Ottilia saw how a few eyes took note of this preference and was both amused and flustered at the exigencies of the social niceties.

"Does the whole world know I am convalescent?"

The agitated murmur drew her spouse's attention and he laid a consoling hand on her arm for a brief moment. "I had to account for your absence."

Aware the undue interest lay in her belated appearance, Ottilia accepted this and turned her attention to Lord Charlton, who was bowing as Francis performed the introductions.

"May we hope you are a little recovered, ma'am? I need scarcely say it is a pleasure to meet you at last."

Ottilia summoned a smile, wishing she might bypass the necessary preliminaries. "Thank you, sir, yes. I have found the sea air invigorating."

"Find a chair, Charlton, and join us for a moment, if you will."

A faint frown crossed the other's face, but he complied, taking one of the empty chairs set around the walls and bringing it across. He sat down with his back to the room, which afforded a neat way of excluding others from disturbing them. An enquiry from Francis as to his daughters elicited a chuckle.

"My little devils, you mean? They are grown as brown as berries and wild enough to drive their nurse demented. I shall be obliged to act the stern papa before daring to present them before their aunt and the governess."

The change in the man's demeanour caused Ottilia to revise her first impression. He looked younger and an attraction of vitality possessed him as he talked.

"Do not, I charge you, Fanshawe, allow anyone to tell you daughters are easier to bring up than sons. Deadlier by far than the male — saving your presence, Lady Francis." He turned laughing eyes on Ottilia. "I adore them both to their little pink toes, but I quite dread the moment they begin upon flirtations. Both are already perfectly wicked in that line. A mere father is no match for them, I assure you."

Francis looked amused and Ottilia could not help laughing. "I had charge of my nephews for years, sir, and can vouch for it that boys are a perfect handful and quite as expert at getting their own way."

Charlton smiled. "Then I must hope to have that pleasure in store."

"Indeed I hope you will." Ottilia gave him a speculative look. "I imagine you must be besieged, sir, in a place such as this."

He grimaced. "There are few eligibles, ma'am, and in truth, I come here for the pleasure of my girls rather than my own."

"But you contrive to enjoy your sojourn nevertheless," Francis cut in, his tone deliberate, "when it is not interrupted by unnatural events."

A frown snapped in between Charlton's brows and his sombre mien returned. "Are you at that again?" He glanced at Ottilia. "Scarcely a suitable subject for feminine ears, sir."

A mischievous gurgle escaped Ottilia and her spouse grinned.

"You are mistaken, Charlton." He lowered his voice. "I beg you will not spread it abroad, but it is my wife rather than I who is assisting Colonel Tretower."

Astonishment spread across the man's face as he stared at Ottilia. "Is it indeed so, ma'am? I cannot think it possible."

She kept her gaze steady. "Quite unfeminine of me, is it not?" She seized on her usual excuse. "You see, my brother is a doctor and I have had occasion to see him at work, so nothing shocks me very much."

"What is more, she has solved murders several times in the past," said her husband on a note of pride that could not but gratify her.

Enlightenment entered Charlton's features. "Good God! Do you mean —?" He broke off and cleared his throat.

"Yes, I do mean the scandal in my family," Francis said doggedly. "And other events since."

Charlton now looked upon Ottilia with a new eye, she thought. Interest mingled with wariness. He glanced from her to Francis and back. "You questioned me at your wife's instigation?"

"Correct."

His cheeks darkened and his eyes glinted. "I must confess myself somewhat insulted, ma'am, but no doubt that is neither here nor there."

"It is a pity, sir, and I am sorry for it," Ottilia said. "Yet as I understand it, you were as anxious as any to have Dulcibella's murderer brought to justice."

The fire died out of his face and he sighed. "I could not help but think of how I would feel if either of my precious babes was in her place."

"Be content, my lord. We have reason to judge you out of the running."

"Ottilia!"

She cast an apologetic look upon her spouse. "Well, but it is true, Francis, and I had rather Lord Charlton worked with us than went off in a dudgeon, for which I could not blame him."

She turned a questioning gaze upon the man as she spoke, noting his frowning puzzlement. Did he believe her? Imperative he did not feel threatened if he was to be of use. She was fairly certain he was not the murderer, although she would not hesitate to name him should evidence come to light to say he was.

He relaxed a little, a faint smile crossing his lips. "Well! You are an original, Lady Francis, I'll give you that."

She was aware of her spouse's ironic eye upon her, but she chose not to acknowledge it, merely waiting to see how Charlton decided to play it.

He straightened in his chair and nodded. "How can I help you?"

She began without preamble. "When was the last time you met with Dulcie, sir?"

He did not look best pleased with the question, his eyes narrowing a trifle. Ottilia neither flinched nor gave sign she noticed, holding her gaze steady. She felt tension beside her and knew Francis was gearing to intervene should the man speak to her with less than the respect he considered her due.

Charlton broke first, glancing away and back again. He cleared his throat. "How is this relevant?"

"It may be."

He pursed his lips and dropped his eyes to the fingers of one hand, drumming on his knee. Ottilia waited, flicking a warning look at Francis to enjoin his silence. Was the man thinking of times, or forming an evasive reply?

"It was an afternoon two or three days before she died. A Saturday, I think. I met her by chance as she came out of the theatre and walked with her along the Esplanade."

There was a constricted note in Charlton's voice, which had dropped to a pitch low enough to be inaudible to any outside the little circle. Ottilia matched it.

"How did she seem to you then?"

He looked up and met her eyes, a faint frown in his own. "Distrait. A little troubled, I thought. That's why I persuaded her to walk with me."

"Was she content to do so?"

The frown intensified. "I did not think so. She seemed a little shy of me."

"As she had not been before?"

Charlton gave a tiny sigh. "I thought she trusted me. Hoped it. But she denied being either anxious or distressed." His hand curled into a tight fist. "I ought to have persisted, forced her confidence. I might have prevented…"

He closed his lips, a burn at his eyes. Ottilia was seized with a clutch of compassion.

"You could not have stopped it, sir. Dulcie was lured with a false promise of some kind. She expected a happy outcome."

"And was deceived?" The bitter note was marked. "Worse yet. Had I known who threatened her, I might have offered protection."

"My dear fellow, she did not know who threatened her," put in Francis on a dry note. "Or even that she was threatened."

"Except," said Ottilia with deliberation, "for the menace of becoming a mother without being a wife."

Shock leapt in Charlton's eyes and his countenance whitened. "Oh, dear God! The very thing I warned her of!" A trace of horror entered in. "That was why? He disposed of the infant as well?"

Francis reached across to lay a hand on Ottilia's and grip it, his tone minatory. "Careful, Charlton. It is not generally known."

Ottilia gave her spouse a reassuring smile, suppressing the shadow that brushed her heart. "I am afraid it is just as you say, sir. An inconvenience cruelly removed."

"Inconvenience? God, I wish she had told me! Inconvenience! It does not bear thinking of."

"Yet someone did think of it, sir, with a vengeance."

Charlton seemed too taken up with the horror to turn his mind to identities. "Why go to that extreme? For the Lord's sake, there are ways enough to secure a female in that condition, are there not? A man of honour ought to pay for his mistakes."

"With marriage perhaps?"

He waved this aside with impatience. "An ineligible female? Of course not. But provision may be made. Accommodation, an allowance and so forth."

Francis gave the man a wry look. "You are talking as a man of means, Charlton. A trifling expense for such as you or I perhaps. To others, keeping a mistress and child may be a luxury."

"Added to which," put in Ottilia, "Dulcie was no country wench to be readily shut away in some corner of a man's estate. She trod the boards and was a beauty of note throughout the South Coast."

The corners of Charlton's mouth turned down. "The fear of scandal operated also? Well, he chose a mighty peculiar way of avoiding it."

"Oh, the sensational nature of the murder was quite deliberate, do you not think?"

"Was it? Why?"

"My dear sir, because it concentrated attention upon the company of The Grand Ferdinando. Although we have discovered Dulcie had neither interest in nor intention of dispensing her favours to any of them."

To her surprise, Charlton nodded. "That is so, ma'am. I lectured her on the evils of her situation and warned her to be circumspect. She laughed at the very notion of succumbing to her fellow actors. I believed her sincere."

"Interesting. Did you also warn her against the gentlemen posing as your rivals?"

The startled look in Charlton's eyes was accompanied by a swift in-drawn breath. His tone became taut. "You assume too much, Lady Francis. I did not seek her affections."

A restive movement from her husband told Ottilia his choler was rising and she hastened to smooth over the moment. "I did not imply as much, sir. One may be pardoned, perhaps, for imagining an interest in a girl whose repute of beauty is legendary and with whom you are known to have associated."

A rueful laugh escaped the man and he threw up a hand. "Touché!" He turned an eye on Francis. "I admit I'm a thought ready to take umbrage. When one's motives are purely avuncular, it is galling to be tarred with a common brush."

Francis cocked a sceptical eyebrow. "Purely avuncular? Would you have us believe you never once saw the female in the light of conquest?"

Charlton's cheek darkened and Ottilia could have cursed. She threw an admonitory look at her spouse, but he returned it with an impenitent frown. Yet this sudden ruthlessness proved salutary.

"I admit," said Charlton in a heavy tone, "that my first impulse deserved censure. But it dissipated rapidly. Had you known Dulcibella, you would not doubt me. She was little removed from the schoolgirl and had none of the sophistication one might expect of an actress."

Seeking to encourage this turn, Ottilia kept her tone light. "She was naïve?"

"Naïve? She had no notion of her vulnerability. She supposed men wished to court her for some fairy-tale ending. Her charm lay in her innocence and a total lack of conceit."

"If you befriended her, I must suppose you took note of those who did regard her with a predatory eye."

"Of course he did," Francis put in on the edge of a snap. "He said as much to me, did you not, Charlton?"

The man's eyes narrowed. "You are talking of that fellow Paglesham. An upstart puppy. I had reason to curse his pretty face, for Dulcie did favour him. She blushed at mention of his name, insisting this 'Perry' of hers meant her no harm."

"Then you did warn her against him," pursued Ottilia.

"I tried. She assured me she had taken my lessons to heart and would let no man take unwanted liberties with her. She claimed she knew how to keep a man at arm's length. So much for that."

"It was true. She would not permit her fellow actors to go beyond the line." Ottilia gave a faint smile. "Though her notion of where the line stood left a little to be desired, I surmise."

Charlton's jaw tightened. "As we see."

Ottilia's sympathies veered towards the unfortunate Dulcie. "Come, sir. She paid dearly for succumbing. It is not for us to judge her now."

He drew in a taut breath and nodded, throwing a considering look from her to Francis and back again. "You suspect Paglesham of the deed?"

"He is on the list," said Francis.

"As was I, I thank you."

The clipped tone told its own tale. Ottilia began to despair of making further headway. She tried for a lighter note. "Well, you have confirmed he had the preference, sir."

"Moreover, he makes no secret of his conquest," put in Francis.

"Then, Good God, why does not Tretower arrest the fellow?"

Ottilia received an exasperated glance from her spouse and very nearly gave way to merriment. "My dear sir, one cannot arrest a man merely upon supposition. There must be substance if a charge is to stick."

"What more is needed, if he admits to having defiled the poor girl?"

"For pity's sake, man, a fellow is not to be thought guilty of murder merely because he had his way with the wench! Where have your wits gone begging, Charlton?"

The other man threw up his head, staring at Francis. "You suggest he was not the only one? I won't believe she peddled her wares to Edgcott, if that is what you mean." He blew out a disparaging breath. "Not that the fellow had not the gall to try. At his age! Disgraceful. Mind, I dare say he is as chary of being suspected as any of us."

"He seemed insouciant to me," said Francis on a frown. "What makes you say so?"

"He's taken to hobnobbing with Paglesham. Comparing notes, I shouldn't wonder."

Ottilia's mind jumped. "You've seen them together?"

"In a coffee shop just the other day."

"Mrs Horniman's?" asked Francis.

"No, some other. I don't know the name. An obscure little hole. I was walking by with my girls, whom I had taken to a doll's hospital for a needed repair for Lizzy's favourite, and Paglesham and Edgcott came out of the place together."

A new possibility was rearing in Ottilia's head. "Did either see you?"

"I don't know. I paid scant attention at the time, for Lizzy was plaguing me to know how long her doll might be obliged to remain there. Indeed, it only came back to me just now."

Ottilia found her husband's eyes on her, in a questioning look she knew well. She gave him a speaking glance in return and set her gaze on Charlton.

"I must thank you for being so frank, sir. You have been immeasurably helpful."

He gave a small shrug. "I could do no less. Don't hesitate to call on me if I can do aught else."

He rose and Francis followed suit. A bow and a curt word of farewell and he was gone. Ottilia was not in the least surprised when her husband sat down again and fixed her with a commanding eye.

"Out with it, my woman of wonder. And no fobbing me off."

She could not resist a spurt of mischievous laughter. "You know me too well."

"I do, and I won't be denied. What is afoot?"

She sobered, watching for his reaction. "What do you say to a conspiracy? Paglesham lures Dulcie with promises and Edgcott carries out the deed."

Having set his second-in-command to the task of seeing what he could discover at the livery stables in Weymouth and its environs, George betook himself to Dorchester to confer with Justice Shellow. The elderly squire had agreed with the two other landowners and designated justices of the peace in the area that he would oversee this particular murder and requested George to report to him.

"For I don't mind telling you, m'boy, that I've more gumption than the two of 'em put together, though I trust you won't tell 'em I said so."

The twinkle that accompanied this request had drawn George and he'd been relieved to be dealing with a fellow of ordinary common sense.

"Won't tell you how to do your business, Colonel, but keep me informed, m'boy, and let me know what you need from me."

It was therefore with every hope of receiving the necessary assistance that he approached Shellow. His quarry was at home and eager for news, pausing only to pour them both a glass of sherry before requesting George to open his budget. He whistled when he heard of what had come to light.

"A witness, you say? More than we could have hoped for, m'boy."

"Yes, sir, but his description does not help us to identify the murderer." He explained the difficulty and moved swiftly on to the resurrection men. "What we do have from the boy is an identification of the men who dug up the grave and extracted the coffin."

315

"There's a piece of luck, Colonel. Well done."

George gave a hollow laugh, but refrained from pointing out that it was scarcely his doing. Shellow naturally had no notion Ottilia was toiling on his behalf.

"Unfortunately, sir, our witness has not seen the men in Weymouth since the murder. They were despatched from the scene before it took place, so I surmise they — er — scarpered, as the boy has it, the moment they learned what the gentleman they helped had done."

Justice Shellow set down his empty glass on a little table beside the comfortable leather-covered chair he was occupying in his bookroom. "But they can point the finger, m'boy, if we can trace 'em."

George set aside his own glass, the wine barely touched. "That is the difficulty, sir. Truggery and Stowe operate outside the law."

"Resurrection men?" George received a shrewd look. "Thinking of the hospital here, are you?"

"Indeed, sir. The boy specifically states they sell to the surgeons in Dorchester."

"Then you may leave that to me. Happen to know old Keymer well. Runs the place."

"Excellent, sir." George leaned forward in his seat. "I was hoping you might be able to set your constables to hunting these fellows down. It's possible they might operate in Lyme Regis and Exeter."

The elderly man looked at him rather hard. "Reason to think so, eh?"

"One of our suspects was seen in both places, hanging around the theatres there. I'm off to Lyme after I leave you, to see what I can find out from that angle. Also to check the livery stables for this coach."

"You said a gentleman, Colonel?"

"It looks that way from what the boy said. But a player could assume the necessary voice."

"But would he know how to get hold of these resurrection men of yours, m'dear fellow? Sounds to me to be a shady character. Who's this suspect who haunts the theatre?"

"A Captain Edgcott." The justice lifted his gaze in a suddenly intent look. "Do you know him, sir?"

"Heard of him. Something of a fly by night. Settles in one place 'til they get his measure and takes off again to find another set of pigeons for plucking."

"A Captain Sharp then?"

"Not that kind. He don't cheat unwary lads in gaming hells and bully them to pay up. More of a go-between. Helps out young fellers who get themselves in a fix and daren't tell their sires. Edgcott makes it all go away — for a fee or a promise or favour in return."

George heard this with a leap of surmise. "Then he could well be our man."

Shellow raised his brows. "Got reason to think so?"

"If his stock in trade is as you say, sir. At present we are focused on Edgcott or the pretty young fellow Paglesham, but this gives me to think, sir. If Paglesham, who says he did succeed with the victim, was responsible for her condition —"

"He engaged Edgcott to murder the wench on his behalf? Hm."

Shellow's regard was tinged with scepticism as he pondered, steepling his fingers. George waited with a thread of rising impatience. He was half inclined to drive straight back to Weymouth and arrest both for conspiracy to murder, but Ottilia's caution was rubbing off on him. He needed proof first.

At length, his elderly host sat back, dropping his hands to the arms of his chair. "Possible. Seems a trifle over the odds for Edgcott. Fellow's morals are dubious. Might indulge in actions on the edge of the law, what you might call petty crime. But outright murder?"

"You don't think so?"

"Think he's got too much regard for his own neck to put it in jeopardy. Not the sort of man to go to such lengths. Would've thought he'd arrange to pay off the female."

"Ah, but this is a female of renown, sir, a recognised beauty and an actress to boot."

The justice still looked dubious, but he nodded. "See what you mean. Drastic measures called for, you think?"

"There seems no other recognisable motive for the deed, sir."

Shellow shook a finger. "And we won't forget there are two deaths to be accounted for."

"The infant, yes. We will charge him with both murders when we catch him."

"There's the rub." Shellow pushed himself to his feet. "Do your part, m'boy. No saying what you may find out from these other theatres. Rely on me for the hunt for the gravediggers. Can't do anything now until Monday, but I'll see Keymer then. He might have a clue as to the whereabouts of these resurrection men of yours. What were the names again?"

"Truggery and Stowe, sir. The former is likely the ringleader."

Shellow moved to an escritoire set to one side of the room and opened it. "Make a note of that now. M'memory is not what it was. Don't you fret, m'boy. I'll set the search going for these fellows and send to you at once if we find 'em."

318

George thanked him and, after detailing where the investigation stood otherwise, left in a more hopeful frame of mind. He was gratified by the intelligence of Edgcott's habits, which chimed well with Ottilia's concentration on him or Paglesham. The business looked to be in a fair way to being settled, which augured better for his chance of making his peace with Cecile.

As he drove the gig he used for longer journeys onward towards Lyme Regis, he could not help dwelling on yesterday's contretemps. The Ferdinando company were due to give their final performance on Tuesday, which meant Cecile would be out of his reach afterwards. He had told her Bournemouth was not far, but the truth was he could not leave Weymouth until this damned murder was resolved.

Nor did he feel it politic to be pressing his suit upon Cecile until he could do so with the knowledge of having assuaged her grief and upset at her friend's distressing demise. His whole desire was to go to her and mend his fences, but his present duty held him captive.

The one excursion to the Assembly Rooms had tired Ottilia unduly and Sunday found her ensconced on the chaise longue, watching the world go by outside the parlour window. She had adjured her husband to remain with Sybilla for the duration of the service at St Mary's Church, and to accompany her to the Rooms afterwards if she wished it.

"With luck, you may get a sight of Paglesham. Try, if you do, to find out what he was up to with Edgcott at that coffee house."

"Certainly, if the fellow shows his face. Though I should doubt of getting anything out of him, assuming your theory holds."

Ottilia was not sanguine either, but she felt it was worth his remaining for a space on the off chance, even though Sybilla would no doubt be engaged with her three gentlemen cronies and admirers. She was glad to think her mother-in-law was finding some amusement in their stay, since she had come purely on Ottilia's behalf.

From what she could see from the window, it looked to be a trifle windy outside, with the waves showing choppy. The Esplanade was all but deserted. She spotted a couple hurrying along, the man holding his hat and the woman's petticoats blowing close about her legs. Several children were braving the surf, their shrieks tinny on the distant air. Ottilia watched them with a curious mixture of pleasure and pain. A little sigh escaped her and, as she withdrew her gaze, her eye caught on a cloaked figure standing on the Esplanade side of the cobbled street below.

Ottilia felt a catch at her breast. A three-cornered hat shadowed the man's face, but it was evident from his stance that he was watching the window. Perkin's description jarred in her head and she stared down, struck by a creeping sense of trepidation.

It was he! The murderer. She was sure of it. And he knew of her involvement. Why else would he seek to frighten her? Was that his intent?

A flare of defiance rose up. She would not be intimidated in her own home. Without a thought of the danger, Ottilia rose up and went swiftly to the door and out into the hall. She ought to call for Hemp or Tyler, but her feet were moving too fast to think it through. In a moment, she was in the hall, wrenching the front door open.

Caution kept her on the threshold as her gaze hunted the opposite side of the road. The man was no longer there. Where had he gone so fast? Did he guess she was coming down? Her pulse was out of true, but she crept a couple of steps beyond the door, glancing this way and that along both sides of the street and down the Esplanade. No cloaked figure rewarded her search. She made out a distant form with a cane limping in the direction of the pier, a dog gambolling beside it. The children were still chasing waves, a nursemaid calling from the shore. But there was no one else within sight. For a moment Ottilia wondered if her debilitated condition had caused her to imagine it, but she breathed more freely nonetheless.

As she turned to go back into the house, the cloaked figure loomed up before her, blocking the doorway, and grasped her by the throat.

Chapter Fourteen

Instinct sent Ottilia's hands up to clutch the man's wrists as she gazed up into a face disguised by a half-mask under the concealing three-cornered hat. A voice, guttural and low, spat vicious words into her face.

"Desist! Look no more, if you know what's good for you. Understand?"

The blood drummed in Ottilia's head and a fleeting thought of Dulcibella's fate sent fear pulsing through her. Yet her innate common sense kicked in, despite the clouds beginning to thicken in her mind. It was a threat, no more. She must answer before she lost consciousness. She tried to utter, but the constriction at her throat would permit no words to form.

As she struggled for breath, she felt herself roughly shaken and the voice came again.

"You hear me?"

Ottilia was near to swooning and she tried to nod. Anything, if only he would let of her throat. But his grip was too strong and it passed through her mind that she was going to die as Emily had died. And Francis would lose her after all.

"Milady!"

The shout from within was followed by immediate thumping footsteps on the wooden stairs. Ottilia was released so abruptly, she lost her balance. Flailing for a purchase that did not exist, she fell to the cobbles. The impact left her gasping, struggling for breath. She heard feet running and knew the murderer was making his escape. And then Hemp was kneeling at her side.

She tried to point in a bid to have him go after the man, but if he understood, her steward ignored it.

"Milady, are you badly hurt?"

Ottilia gestured at her throat, still dragging her breath in and out. Now she was freed, the pain of the fellow's grip began to impinge. To her annoyance, wetness seeped from her eyes. Hemp set an arm under her shoulders.

"Come, milady, let me help you up. We will attract notice."

Highly undesirable. The thought gave Ottilia courage and she tried to help as the steward lifted her to her feet. Once there, she found her knees shaking and leaned heavily into his support. But the late contretemps filtered into her consciousness.

"Did you see who it was?" Her voice was a croak and she cursed in her head.

"No, milady. I saw only that he had you by the throat."

He sounded distressed and she struggled to express her observations. "Cloak … three-cornered hat … mask. What Perkin said."

He hissed in a breath. "The murderer?"

"I am certain it was he." He began to urge her into the house and she summoned the effort to walk. "I hoped you might have … recognised him."

"You are not well, milady. I can carry you."

"I may be slow but I will manage if you give me your arm," she croaked, although her voice came a little easier now despite the soreness inside.

It took all her strength to cope with the stairs, even with Hemp taking most of her weight. She was obliged to grip the bannister and pull herself up step by step. She had no room for speech and heard only in the periphery of her mind Hemp's voice calling for Joanie. He helped her into the parlour and she sank, with gratitude, back down onto the chaise longue.

"You should lie down, milady."

"In a moment." She took several deep breaths as her lungs began to work more normally. But she was glad at last to lie at her length, resting her head on the rolled end. She put her hands to her throat, massaging gently. "Drat the man. He has bruised me to pieces."

"Yes, I can see, milady. You are severely marked." His tone changed. "Here is Joanie, milady. She will take care of you while I go for his lordship."

A hitherto unforeseen danger leapt in Ottilia's mind. Francis would be outraged. Furious with her for foolishly going out alone. She spoke without thinking.

"No, pray! There is no need, Hemp. I am better now. Or I will be."

But Hemp, poised to leave, looked down at her with a frowning countenance. "Milady, I have seen how milord is with you. I would not for my life delay in bringing him to you upon such an occasion."

With a few swift words to the hovering maid, he was gone. Ottilia's heart plummeted and tremors shook her frame. The aftershock, she told herself, but anticipation of the coming thunder gave the lie to this comforting thought. Not that it was in the least comforting. She truly was in shock. She could feel the blanket of numbness descending.

"Water, Joanie." The words came out shakily and the maid did not immediately obey the request.

"Hemp says a ruffian set upon you, my lady. You look terrible, if I do say so as shouldn't."

Ottilia could not withhold a choke of laughter, which hurt her throat. She put up a hand to hold it. "I thank you, Joanie. That is all I needed to hear."

But the maid was not paying attention. "Here's Tyler, my lady. He'll fetch water for you. Though if you ask me, it's a dose of brandy you need. I know as his lordship would say so if he were here."

"My throat is already on fire, I thank you. I will take water only."

Tyler was already out of the door and Ottilia relaxed back again, striving for calm. But the thought of what Francis would have to say to her kept her pulse in disarray, even as she tried to bend her mind to the problem of the identity of her attacker.

He was tall and very strong. The cloak gave an impression of size, but she thought he was not a big man beneath it. That he dared to come out into the open thus argued a member of the Ferdinando company. Although that was not necessarily the case, she decided, recalling her suspicion of a conspiracy between Paglesham and Edgcott. According to Francis's description, the man could not have been the captain. But Paglesham was tall. As also was Fitzgerald, the theatre manager, according to George. He might well have heard of her involvement. Indeed, who knew how far that information may have travelled?

Tyler arrived with a jug of water and Joanie poured out a glass and gave it to her. The relief of its cool descent was palpable, even though it hurt to swallow. She had not downed more than half the contents when the sound of pounding footsteps outside sent her heartrate into high gear. Francis! She set down the glass in haste.

The steps thundered up the stairs and seconds later her husband burst into the parlour. He stopped in the doorway, his gaze shooting across to find her. Ignoring everyone else, he flew across the room, dropped to his haunches beside the chaise longue and seized Ottilia into a fierce embrace, holding her close enough as almost to deprive her of breath all over again. His voice came hoarsely in her ear.

"My darling, my darling. Oh, dear Lord, my precious one!"

Moved beyond words, Ottilia caught her breath on rising sobs, feeling her bruised throat constrict as she tried to croak out a response. His hold loosened and he leaned back, looking intently into her face, his own white and strained.

"How badly did he hurt you? My dear one, why? What possessed you to leave the house without me?"

Ottilia found her voice, albeit quivering with tears. "Don't be angry with me, Fan, pray. I know it was foolish of me, but —"

"Angry? I'm far too upset to be angry!"

"— I swear I only took two steps outside. He came at me right in front of our door. Don't scold me, Fan!"

"My darling heart!" He found her hand and pressed it to his lips. "I never want to leave you again. You must promise me now, this instant, that you won't again go outside these doors without an escort."

She was weeping, but she disregarded the tears seeping down her cheeks. "Fan, I'm so sorry. Forgive me, pray."

He paid no heed, gripping her fingers. "Promise me, Tillie! I can't bear it if you don't promise."

She threw herself back into his arms. "I promise, I promise. Oh, Fan, I love you so very much."

Presently he drew her away from him again. "Don't weep, sweetheart." His fingers brushed the wet from her cheeks, but his gaze was shifting down. "Let me see. Oh, dear Lord in heaven, he bruised you, the villain!"

Gently he touched the wounds, bent his head to set his lips first to one side, then the other, and gave her a smile quite as shaky as her own. She sank into him, allowing her limbs to go limp. Presently, as the murmured words of tenderness calmed her, Ottilia recalled that the servants had been in the room and she pulled back.

"Oh, they have gone, thank heaven." She relaxed against the rolled end of the daybed, allowing her hand to rest in her husband's protective grasp. "I see now how poor Emily must have suffered."

She told him how it had felt briefly, but moved on to her description of the man which tallied so well with what Perkin had told them. Francis cursed softly.

"I would give much to know which of them did this to you. I should know how to deal with him."

"He did worse to Dulcibella, my dearest. We must let the law give him his due."

"If the law can catch him."

She squeezed his hand. "We will find him out. I am now doubly determined."

His brows lowered a little. "But you won't run your head into danger again. You gave me your word."

"I did, and I will not go back on it, Fan. I promise my role will be entirely passive from this moment."

For the first time since his entry into the room, he laughed, his eyebrow quirking. "If I believed that, my dear one, I should count myself a looby."

She was obliged to smile. "Well, I will confine myself to thought without a vestige of action. Will that content you?"

"It will, but I shall make sure George knows of this. He may add it to his indictment when the scoundrel is behind bars."

George arrived back at the barracks on Monday afternoon after an abortive journey which had yielded little or nothing by way of result, either at the theatres or the livery stables, and cost him two nights and a whole day away. The theatre manager at Lyme had been away in Exeter, which gave him no choice but to follow, by which time it was too late to do anything but find a suitable inn for the night. When he finally ran the two men to earth in a tavern on the Sunday, neither could recall anything more than that Edgcott was a regular visitor. He was, however, pelted with questions since the news of the murder had spread to both towns. He was thoroughly out of temper and wishing he had never been saddled with the riddle of Dulcibella's demise.

He left his vehicle in the charge of a groom and headed for the officer's parlour, with the intention of demanding coffee, and found his junior already partaking of the beverage.

Sullivan jumped up on his entrance. "You're back at last! I've been waiting to catch you, sir."

George eyed the coffee pot. "Is that still hot?"

"I'll ask for some fresh." The younger man went to pull the bell, but his gaze remained on his senior. "Sir, I've had the devil's own luck."

Dragging his mind from his own failures, George recalled the man's mission. "You've found something out? I hope to God it's of use because I don't mind telling you I've wasted my time. Is it about the coach? Did someone hire one for the night in question?"

"Not exactly, sir, no."

Eagerness showed in the young face, but he paused as the batman entered to ask for a fresh pot of coffee. George, too hungry to wait for dinner, put in an additional request for beef slapped between slices of bread in the manner of Lord Sandwich at the gaming tables and waited with impatience for Marsh to remove the tray and leave the parlour.

"Well?"

"One of the ostlers at the livery stables here saw our man's coach standing outside a private house."

"But how can he know it was our man's?"

"I'm coming to that." Sullivan's excitement was manifest. "He saw the murdered girl carried out of the house and set into the coach."

George fairly started, his tiredness evaporating. "Good God, is it so indeed? Why did he not come forward before? This damned murder has been talked of all over the town."

"Just what I thought, sir, but I didn't ask him, fearing to set tongues wagging."

"Yes, fair point. But if he recognised this Dulcie —"

"He didn't. Seems he was pretty owlish at the time, having spent the better part of the night in a tavern. And this was in the early hours, around two or thereabouts."

George cursed. "But such an odd occurrence? He did not think to question it?"

Sullivan grinned. "Well, he says it did seem odd to him, which was why he mentioned it when he heard me asking about coaches on that particular night."

"Well, what exactly did he see?"

The lieutenant's eyes sparkled. "A fellow in a cloak and a three-cornered hat carrying a blonde girl who looked to be asleep."

There could be no doubt it was the murderer. Questions teemed in George's head, tumbling out of his mouth. "Does this fellow remember which house? Can he identify it? Do we know who lives there? Did he notice anything about the coach that might help us? Did he see the man's face?"

Sullivan threw up a steadying hand. "None of all that, sir, unfortunately. He has a vague recollection of staggering home via a different route than normal and losing his bearings, but he claims all those houses look the same."

"All which houses?"

"The ones towards the edge of town, heading out towards the coast road."

"Which is the one leading to the cemetery also," said George, his mind running over the suspects. "But why there? None of these fellows lodge that far out, for we've checked their directions." Grimness settled in his mind. "Damnation. I was almost sure we had it settled, but this throws out all our suppositions."

Sullivan looked crestfallen. "I'd hoped it would help, sir."

George threw up a hand as Marsh entered bearing a replenished tray and a full plate. "Of course it helps. It's another eyewitness."

He held his tongue while his batman was in the room, seizing upon the food with relish and watching his second-in-command pour black liquid into two cups. Accepting one, George swallowed down his mouthful of beef and took a draft of the sustaining brew, setting his mind to cogitation. He thought aloud as soon as they were alone.

"We'd best find out if there are any lodging houses out there. I suppose it's possible our man took another place for the purpose. Rodber will know, so I'll take that."

"What can I do, sir?"

Sullivan was plainly eager and George regretted having quashed his find.

"I didn't mean to disparage your contribution, lad. You've done extraordinarily well. We've just got to think again."

His junior eyed him over the rim of his own cup. "Will you put this to Lady Francis, sir?"

George raised his brows. "Why, do you doubt her ability to bring us off?"

Sullivan shifted his shoulders. "From what you've said, sir, I can't really tell."

"Ah, but what you hear, my partner in arms, is my dilution of her observations," said George with a grin, picking up his beef and bread again. "Left to myself, I'd have arrested one or other of those fellows days ago. Ottilia has a knack of noticing details and she understands how people think. She's something of a student of human nature, which I freely admit I am not."

The younger man frowned a little. "It's odd, sir, that's all."

"Because she's a woman?"

"Well, yes."

George wagged a finger, speaking a trifle thickly through a mouthful of beef. "Never underestimate the sex, Sullivan. It's a fallacy we men live under to imagine ourselves better thinkers. Women are far superior in that line, especially when it comes to what goes on in the male mind as regards females." He winced as he recalled Cecile's insights. "You'll find it out when you become attached, I warn you."

Sullivan coloured and laughed in a self-conscious fashion. "I can't say I've noticed it."

"Then you've not been in serious pursuit." He pulled his mind from the image of Cecile's furious eyes and took another draft of his coffee. "However, that's neither here nor there.

I've another task for you, Sullivan. I need this boy Perkin under my protection."

"Isn't he better where he is, sir?"

"Not once it's known he's there. Moreover, I can't risk him taking off. You'll come with me tomorrow and fetch him away. Choose one of the older fellows to take care of him here, and detail others to take it in turns to guard him at all times. Make him comfortable, but give him something to do to keep him from thoughts of escape."

"Well, I suppose he could polish boots or brass, sir," said his junior doubtfully, "though from the sound of it he's not skilled at much of anything."

"We'll train him up. Rig him out with a uniform and turn him into a soldier. He doesn't know it, but it's that or be hanged for thieving."

"Poor little beggar."

"That's why he gets a choice. Lady Francis's steward has him in charge at present and was detailed to get him to give up the purse he stole, so if he has done it, you'll take care of that too."

"Right, sir."

"And once you've settled Perkin, see if you can get this ostler to lead you to the house in question. Or at least the street or the general area."

His junior was doubtful but willing enough to try. George toyed with the notion of going to see Cecile and dismissed it. Much as he longed for a sight of her, it was late, she was likely busy and he was uncertain of his reception.

The bustle of the final preparations provided Cecile with a semblance of normality. The impresario had determined to finish at Weymouth after all with *The Country Wife*, making some drastic cuts, having his wife double up her roles. While

Cecile pinned and tacked, adjusting the bodice of Dulcie's costume to fit Kate's smaller bosom, those intrusive regrets could be relegated to the back of her mind. They scarcely penetrated the hubbub, what with Kate running her lines with Rob as Cecile worked, Jasper protesting Monsieur Ferdinand's various prohibitions against excess before the night of departure, Lewis and Hilde involved in some sort of altercation and the stagehands bumping scenery across the wooden boards.

Yet she could not entirely suppress the sneaking dismay. Where was George all this time? She had found herself missing him all through the incessant grumbling rehearsals on Sunday and Monday while her hands were busy with sewing, but her mind unoccupied. Why had he not attempted to see her? To try at least to placate her wrath? It had dissipated all too rapidly, leaving her with a yearning for a chance to retract her hasty words. She cherished the endearment he had used, but it alone had not power to assuage the fear she might have alienated his affection.

She brushed the thoughts aside, concentrating on her stitchery. Difficult enough, when Kate kept moving as she spoke the words of her performance.

"I pray you, Kate, remain still," she said, on an exasperated note.

The actress glanced at her. "What is it, Cecily? You've interrupted my train of thought now."

"It is that I wish not to prick you with my needle, but you move too much."

"Oh. Well, I'm sorry, but I've no time to waste if I don't want to look nohow tonight."

Cecile threw up her free hand. "*Eh bien*, I leave it if you desire also that your gown may look not tidy."

Kate's tone softened. "No, don't. Pray forgive me. I am nervous, Cecily. I've not played Margery Pinchwife before."

"You have no need to be nervous," came in an alien voice from a few rows away from where they were standing in the pit below the stage. "You will be magnificent."

Flicking a glance over her shoulder, Cecile saw the theatre manager had entered the auditorium with Janey, who came down the aisle.

"Fitz is right, Kate. You will play it to admiration. Are you firm on the words now?"

"Rob is helping me run the lines." There was a flurry in Kate's voice. "Where were we, Rob?"

The actor's usual sullen mien came over him. "We can stop and let Cecily finish sewing. You have it fully down in any event." He flourished the printed folio of the play.

"No, I want to go over it all, if you please."

Rob sighed, but found his place, gave Kate her cue and the run continued.

Cecile tuned it out after a moment, and her ears pricked as she heard instead a snatch of a discussion between Madame Ferdinand and Fitzgerald.

"What came of the rumour about this boy then?"

"It proved void. Apparently the boy was merely terrified of Lady Francis's black servant. Though I could wish it had portended something. This uncertainty is distressing."

"I notice everyone is a trifle on edge. No doubt it will be easier away from here."

"I cannot imagine it will ever be easier, Fitz. The damage is far-reaching." Madame Ferdinand's tone lowered so that Cecile had to strain to hear her words. "Moreover, I fear poor little Dulcie is not the only girl we are going to lose."

"What do you mean, Janey?" The manager's tone had sharpened.

Cecile flicked a glance across under her lashes in time to note Madame Ferdinand's nod in her direction. A flutter disturbed her pulse, but its message was overborne by Fitzgerald's response.

"Kate? Good God, why? That would be a bitter loss indeed."

"I don't mean Kate, don't be absurd."

Fitzgerald let out a sound in which Cecile thought she detected relief. She only just caught his words. "Ah, you mean the *émigré*? Tretower's little pet?"

A flicker of rage leapt in Cecile's breast. Little pet? But how rude! She did not hear madame's whispered answer and her agitation provoked a protest from Kate.

"Ouch! You pricked me, Cecily!"

She apologised, hastening with her work, her thoughts fastening on the dismissive appellation. She was to understand she was of no account to Monsieur Fitzgerald. Not as compared with Kate. Or, presumably, Dulcie. A bitter loss, he said of Kate. Was not poor Dulcie's end a bitter one?

She caught an admonishing note in madame's voice as she spoke again loud enough to be heard.

"You don't understand, Fitz. That child was like a daughter to me. I groomed her for the stage just as if she had been."

"Don't talk fustian to me, Janey," came the scoffing response. "You plucked a workhouse orphan from your sister's kitchen and turned her extraordinary beauty to account."

"Well, and so? We gave her a better life."

"You took her merely to afford Arthur an ornament to draw the crowds. And it worked, to the detriment of others of greater talent."

At this, madame became angry. "You shall not say so, Fitz. Pray how was it less than an advantage to this other — and I know very well whom you mean — to have a full theatre everywhere we went? To be seen is of first importance."

"Who looked at her when Dulcie was on the stage?" countered Fitzgerald, leaving Cecile in no doubt that Kate was the talent in question. "Besides that, Arthur gave the girl all the best roles. Galling indeed to be obliged to step into them only in this extremity."

Madame Ferdinand let out an exasperated sound. "I cannot talk to you. You are prejudiced, Fitz."

With which, she left him, coming quickly down to join the group just as Kate and Rob came to the end of their running of the lines.

"There, I've done it," said Kate on a note of satisfaction.

"And I am finished sewing you also," Cecile told her, snipping her thread.

"Thank you, Cecily." She wriggled in the costume, adjusting the fit at the bosom. "It feels much more comfortable."

Rob thrust the folio at her. "Take this. Arthur wants me to keep Jasper out of the tavern. Though why the deuce I have to be the wretched boy's nursemaid I really don't know."

He directed a look of annoyance at Janey as he spoke, which she ignored, addressing herself to the actress on a note of anxiety.

"Are you satisfied, Kate? You are not dismayed to be doing these roles for Dulcie?"

Kate's smile was tremulous. "I could wish I had more time to prepare, Janey, but of course I am happy to oblige." She caught her breath on a sob and her eyes filled. "Poor little Dulcie. I miss her, Janey. More than I ever supposed I could."

Madame Ferdinand gave her a hug. "We all do, Kate, we all do."

Instinct sent Cecile's gaze flying back to where the manager stood, his brows drawn together as he watched with narrowed eyes. Kate could not have heard the exchange, could she? No, she was too concentrated on her lines. Did she know he liked her?

The thought flickered in Cecile's head and she balked. Did he like her? Or was it that he admired her acting only? How much did he like her? Enough to rid her of a stage rival?

She watched him surreptitiously as he turned and walked out of the auditorium. In light of her knowledge that he was still very much on George's list, Cecile could not dismiss the conversation. She would have liked to for it made sad hearing. She knew, for Dulcie had told her, of those difficult beginnings and she spoke with affection for the Ferdinands.

"I would do anything in the world for Janey and Arthur, Cecily. I owe them so much. Without them, I would have been nothing but a kitchen skivvy."

No, Dulcie had been inordinately grateful. If only she had not been permitted to be so free with her fellow actors.

For the first time, as she gathered her sewing accoutrements together, Cecile was moved to judge Janey more harshly than she had ever thought it possible to do. She glanced over to where the Ferdinands were now deep in discussion. Lewis and Hilde had disappeared, Kate was moving towards the dressing-rooms and Rob was heading for the stage door with Jasper. Was Madame Ferdinand telling her husband of Fitzgerald's words? It was clear by what she had said to Kate that they had gone home.

The little altercation niggled at the back of Cecile's mind and she wondered if she ought to speak of it to this Madame Fan. Could she seize a chance before this final performance?

The thought she might run into George at the Fanshawe's lodging was both a spur and a deterrent, leaving her in a quandary.

"She won't give him up without a fight, I warn you," Francis told his friend, casting an experienced eye over the smart young lieutenant who accompanied Tretower and was detailed to remove Perkin.

"Precisely why I'm glad I caught you first."

"You may not be when I tell you what happened here on Sunday."

In a few brief sentences, Francis put his friend in possession of the facts. He had been reluctant to leave Tillie alone even though she was recovering well, but Joanie was with her and Hemp was under strict orders not to allow her to venture forth. He met George as he came out of the house on his way to escort his mother home from her morning excursion to the Assembly Rooms. His friend was predictably horrified, but Francis cut him short, reverting to the subject of Perkin.

"I know well you're expecting me to smooth Tillie over, George, but she's not happy. I told her this would happen. She's relying on me to persuade you to treat the boy with leniency."

George exchanged a glance with his junior. "I've already told Sullivan here we'll set him to soldiering. Will that content her?"

"Well, she thought he ought to be set to some trade. He's got used to Hemp, though. He'll likely make a bid for freedom."

The young man stepped up, looking to his senior. "Sir, it occurs to me it might be well for the steward to come along with us, if his lordship don't object."

George snapped his fingers. "An excellent notion, Sullivan."

Francis at once entered a caveat. "I dare say Hemp would be willing, but I don't want Tillie left without her guardian until I return."

"We'll wait for you, Fan, never fear."

"I presume you want the boy because he's a witness?"

"I want him for his protection. I mean to set it about that we've got a witness."

"A lure? A trap?" His friend's face was grim as he nodded and foreboding leapt in Francis's mind. "What's to do?"

"Sullivan found a fellow whose testimony throws all our suppositions into doubt."

When he had heard the details, Francis was inclined to agree. He recommended his friend to go up and confer with his wife — "though you will find her decidedly out of frame, and I won't have her distressed" — while he went to fetch his mother, rather relieved than otherwise to leave Tillie under his friend's protection, and proceeded on his way along the Esplanade.

He had not gone far when he recognised two of the players in a pair of men ambling in his direction. To his surprise, the young fellow Hemp had pointed out in the tavern hailed him.

"Ho, there! Stay a moment, sir!"

"Jasper, you can't accost strangers," came in a hissing admonition from the other, but the boy paid no heed, greeting Francis with a grin as he halted, unable to help wondering if either of these fellows had been responsible for mauling his wife.

"Wanted to ask you where your black fellow Roy is, sir. Haven't seen him for several days."

"He has been occupied. Jasper, is it not?"

Francis eyed him as he answered, taking in the giveaway pallor, the shadows under the eyes and in them a cloudy aspect that bore witness to his early career of dissipation.

A jaunty bow came his way. "Jasper Jefferies, sir. And this here is Rob Collins, my bear leader for the day."

"Jasper, be quiet."

The boy grinned again. "He don't like the job and I can't blame him. Arthur wants me sober, y'see. Pity about Roy, though. I like him. Wish he'd follow us to Bournemouth."

Francis had nodded at Robert Collins, taking due note of the fellow's sulky mien and generally hangdog air. "Unfortunately, I cannot spare my servant to you, Mr Jefferies. He is my wife's steward, you see, and she has need of his services."

Jasper sidled closer, a look of cunning entering his features. "S'pose you wouldn't consider ordering him to give me a chance in the ring with him, would you, sir?"

A short laugh escaped Francis. "Yes, he told me you were anxious for a bout."

"Well, anyone can see he must strip to advantage." The player's mobile features twisted into an expression both wheedling and mischievous. "Roy thinks I'll prove a weakling, but I'm fit as a fiddle despite my excesses, y'know. Have to be when you tread the boards. Takes energy."

"That's true enough," put in the other, unexpectedly entering the lists. "But he'll burn himself out before he gets to my age, the rate he's going."

"Devil a bit," said the other cheerfully, his eyes on Francis. "Will you, sir?"

Francis raised his brows. "What, instruct my servant to oblige you? Certainly not. Hemp is his own man."

Jasper looked crestfallen. "The devil! I made sure you'd step in."

"Then you were mistaken. Nor do I sympathise with your desire to derive entertainment from being knocked about by my servant who has better things to do."

"Is he helping with this enquiry about our Dulcie then?"

The question elicited a buffet on the arm from Rob Collins. "Jasper, will you be quiet? I make you my apologies on his behalf, my lord."

Francis made a swift decision. "No need. In fact, that is precisely what he is doing. He is minding the young lad who witnessed the murder."

He watched the effect of this announcement on the older man. Shock leapt in his eyes. Had he turned a trifle paler? But it was Jasper, blazing with excitement, who took it up.

"Good God, do you mean the lad Roy was seen with? Who fainted because he thinks all black men are devils?"

"He fainted because he thought Hemp was the murderer," said Francis with deliberation.

"What? Why?"

"Because of his height and size and, we think, because the murderer was likely wearing a mask that blacked his face."

Jasper gaped at him, but Francis kept his attention on the other, whose brow had turned thunderous.

"By God, I hope you get him, the dastard! Who was it? Did the boy say?"

"He does not know the man. But his description fits with several my friend Tretower has under his eye."

He watched the change that came over Collins. Shock, followed by fear and then swift fury. His voice became hoarse.

341

"Me, is it? He thinks I did it? I'm one of them?"

Jasper seized his arm. "Steady, Rob. He never said so."

Collins shook him off. "He has no need to say it. I'm of a height with your friend Roy, though I've not his breadth of shoulder. Close enough though, eh, my lord?"

Francis did not speak, only holding the fellow's eyes. He noted Jasper's dawning dismay, but ignored it, waiting for what Collins might say in his own defence.

"It's not so much the insult," came in a low tone of suppressed rage. "It's the downright idiocy. Why would I do it? Does a man kill the thing he loves?"

"Rob, you fool!"

"Yes, I confess it, though I've tried to keep silent. I've a wife and children to think of, and I've fought it hard. But I can't help it. If you'd only known Dulcie…"

To Francis's surprise, it was Jasper who turned on him. "You can't think it was Rob. He wouldn't hurt a hair of Dulcie's head. Everyone outside thinks it was her beauty, but it wasn't that. Not just that in any event. She was a delectable piece, but that wasn't it, sir. Dulcie was a sweetheart. We were all fond, if you want to know, though we all knew she couldn't act. Not that it mattered."

"Of course it didn't matter," snapped Collins. "Nobody cared about her acting and Arthur knew it." He glared at Francis. "Dulcie knew it too. I mean, she knew she had no talent. She admired everyone else's and kept trying to learn. She did as Janey and Arthur told her and it served because she was beautiful and she had charm."

"Unconscious charm," chimed in Jasper. "If she'd known, she wouldn't have been so innocent. She was a decent chit and it's a damned shame she got into trouble."

So that was out in the open, was it? But Jasper had not finished.

"A catastrophe for Arthur too. D'you think Rob would have brought that about? It's his livelihood, sir."

Not a bit surprised to hear what Tillie had already guessed at, Francis nevertheless maintained a cool front.

"Yes, I dare say. I regret I am unable to set your minds at rest, but you may take it that my wife will discover the truth. She has never yet failed." Both men gave him frowning looks at this, but the reminder of Tillie made him impatient to be off so he could get back to her. He gave a perfunctory bow. "If you will forgive me, I am en route to fetch my mother back from the Assembly Rooms. We look forward to tonight's performance."

"Ha! I wish you joy of it," said Collins in a surly fashion. "It won't be the same without Dulcie."

Jasper's lips twisted in a rueful smile. "Not so sure of that, Rob. Kate's a far better actress, sir. Fitz thinks she'll rival Siddons if she gets a chance."

This was too good an opportunity to miss. "Fitz? Do you mean Fitzgerald, the theatre manager?"

"That's him. Thick as thieves with Arthur and Janey. Hilde says they used to act together, all three of them, years ago. Fitz is a judge too. He's seen all sorts."

"Yes, but he need not have despised Dulcie," said Collins on a sour note.

"Balderdash! Fitz was as bemused by her as the rest of mankind. You'd have seen the way he looked at her if you hadn't been so smitten yourself, Rob."

"I wish you'd be quiet, Jasper." The older man turned a slightly anxious gaze on Francis. "Pay no heed to him, sir. He's befuddled with drink half the time. He doesn't notice anything."

"Much you know! If I couldn't observe, I couldn't act, could I?"

"Your arrogance is unbelievable. Just because Arthur thinks you're special, it's gone to your stupid head."

"I'm not listening to you, Rob. You're merely jealous."

Francis left them arguing and slipped away. He had heard sufficient to be keener still to return to the lodgings as swiftly as he might. Tillie would relish these small but revealing details.

Yet on meeting the dowager, his attention forcibly veered. His mother was already on a path towards the lodgings, accompanied by General Godfrey in his wheeled chair, who hailed him with a rallying quip.

"Ha! You're here at last, are you, young Fanshawe, you rascal? Wish you'd take this woman off my hands. Fleeced me, she has, the wretch. Left me without a feather to fly with."

The dowager uttered a snort. "Poppycock! Pay no heed to him, Francis." Then, turning on the general and lowering her voice, she added, "Instead of exercising your wit at my expense, Leo, you will be better employed telling him what you've discovered."

The general dismissed his servant; meanwhile Francis apologised for his tardiness. His mother waved this away.

"I did not wait only because Leo has news of Captain Edgcott."

General Godfrey caught her words as he turned back to look up at Francis, with an unusually grim expression. "Gone to ground. Hasn't been seen since Saturday. Rodber thinks he's popped off to one of the other resorts along the coast. Myself, I reckon he knows Tretower has an eye to him for this murder and don't choose to loiter."

"You may be right. Did you notice if Paglesham has also gone?"

The general's brows shot up. "That young upstart? He's here all right and tight. What d'ye want with him? You can't think he did the deed."

"He is on our list."

"What, that ninny? If he said boo to a goose I'd be astonished. No, no, boy, you have him wrong, I'll be bound."

Francis eyed him with a good deal of interest but his mother forestalled him.

"He may be a ninny to you, Leo, but the fellow admits to a liaison with the dead girl."

The general whistled. "Does he so? How d'ye know it ain't a mere boast?"

"Why should it be? He's a pretty young man, even if he is an impertinent coxcomb, though he fawned enough to me."

"Besides which," put in Francis, "the girl specifically mentioned him for a suitor."

"That may be, but it don't mean he's got gumption enough to carry out such an elaborate ceremonial as this killing. Wouldn't credit the fellow with that much imagination."

Francis could not but agree. "In fact, we don't think he did it, but he may have been complicit in the act."

General Godfrey squinted up at him in a shrewd look. "Think he set Edgcott on to handle the business on his behalf?"

"It's a possibility."

"Well, the feller's vanished, that's all I can tell you, m'boy."

Inviting George to stay and dine with them had been both politic and a move to allow Ottilia more time to think. She was beset with a familiar niggle of having missed something. On

345

this occasion she put it down to the nuisance of being obliged in the main to rely on reported conversations rather than conducting her own questioning of the gentlemen involved. Although Francis was becoming adept at eliciting just the sort of detail to set her mind in a bustle as she sifted facts. Yet, like most men, he lacked that almost innate feminine ability to snap from one position to another in a leap having nothing to do with logic. It could be disconcerting to the male mind, as poor George had discovered with the highly intuitive Cecile.

Nevertheless, with everything taken together there was much for her to ponder. She allowed the conversation to flow around her as she partook rather sparingly of Mrs Horne's excellent fish pie, finding it still hard to swallow despite the softness of the well-seasoned fish and mashed potato. Aware of her husband's narrow glance, she flashed him a smile of reassurance and hoped he would not call attention to her abstraction.

The dowager was engaged in argument with George as to the advisability of attempting to train young Perkin up to soldiering.

"Once a thief, always a thief, my dear Colonel."

"A leopard does not change his spots, you think, ma'am?"

"He might change, but temptation will dog him and the day will come when he cannot resist."

George finished the last of his preferred sirloin and set down his fork. "For my part, I believe the lesson of this murder will prove a sufficient deterrent. Your man Hemp, Ottilia, thinks the boy's fear of retribution from this Truggery is stronger than his fear of the rope. Although I have instructed Sullivan to keep the threat alive if he has any trouble from the boy."

Ottilia caught a flashing glance of concern from Francis and thrust down on the instant rise of indignation. To her relief he took it in her stead.

"A trifle ruthless, George. You'll not win Tillie's approval with such tactics."

George's mouth became set in grim lines as he eyed Ottilia. "I'm sorry if it goes against the grain with you, but if he's to learn discipline —"

"He's a frightened child, George," she interrupted, unable to refrain from breaking out. "Moreover, he's far too valuable to risk losing at this juncture, if you need a more cogent reason than pure fellow feeling."

George reddened and Sybilla intervened. "That is unfair, Ottilia. You can't expect the colonel to fawn over a guttersnipe."

"I don't expect it." She turned her irate gaze on George. "I promised Perkin none would hurt him. I did not agree to let him go so that you might at once return him to a state of terror."

"I've no intention of so doing," returned George with a heat equal to her own. "It's for his own safety, as well you know. And since Fan has already told those players of his value to the investigation, it is not a moment too soon."

Ottilia opened her mouth to retort, but Francis put up a hand. "Enough, Ottilia!"

He spoke with a quiet authority she was obliged to recognise. Swallowing her spleen, she forced a faint smile. "Pardon me, George. I am afraid recent events have revived my sensibilities. I will say no more."

He looked visibly relieved and his tone dropped. "No, it's my fault. You've suffered enough — indeed, far too much. I should have been more circumspect."

Sybilla, with her customary habit of rising to the occasion, reached out a hand for the bell and rang it. "Give the colonel a little more wine, Francis. I requested Mrs Horne to provide us with fruits and cheese to finish. If we are to attend the theatre to see the new play, a light meal is in order, I think."

"Do you go, George?" asked Francis as he replenished his friend's glass.

"Unlikely. A waste of time and I've much to do. However, if I can't catch Rodber beforehand, I might have to follow him there."

"You are trying to find out about this house where our man was seen carrying the girl into a coach?"

"If possible, Fan. The difficulty is we don't know which house it was. Sullivan had no luck with the ostler, and he had no chance to try him again today. But if we can pinpoint the place, we may hope our witness can recognise it."

"Or he may recognise the guilty man perhaps?"

Something shifted in Ottilia's mind. "Not if he was already wearing the mask."

George lowered the glass from which he'd been taking a sip. "But if we know the house, that won't matter. He has to have been lodging there, even if he took the place temporarily, and his actions speak for him."

Ottilia met his glance but her attention was turned inward. "Would he take her to his lodging?"

"Why shouldn't he?" demanded the dowager.

"Precisely because it must incriminate him. This was not a careless murder. It was well planned." She turned to George. "I suspect you may find the place is no lodging house, but a brothel."

Chapter Fifteen

Ottilia found herself under immediate scrutiny from all three pairs of eyes. She was saved by the entrance of Tyler, who removed the remains of the meal at Sybilla's request, loaded up the two hovering maids and instructed them to fetch up the dessert. In the presence of the servants, Francis struck up a spurious discussion with his friend about the weather, which had turned windy with the threat of overnight rain. But the instant platters of fruit and cheese had been set upon the table, the dowager dismissed Tyler and cut the men short.

"Never mind the rain, you two. Ottilia, if it is not just like you to come out with something so outrageous. What in the world made you suppose this dreadful man would take Dulcie to a brothel, of all places?"

Rueful, Ottilia looked from her mother-in-law to George's frown and Francis's quirked eyebrow. "Dear me. I fear I was thinking aloud."

"You don't get out of it that easily," said her spouse, faint amusement visible in his eyes.

"No, and I don't stir from this house until you explain yourself."

Ottilia had to laugh. "Very well, George, though I have not fully thought it through as yet."

"But what made you think of it at all?"

"Your hope the murderer would prove to have lodged in this house. He is far too circumspect. Any landlady must inevitably put two and two together once news of the murder came out. But a bawdy house is another matter. I imagine a man might hire a room with no questions asked. Very likely no one would even trouble to notice whom he brought with him. And he could slip out in the early hours without being seen."

Her husband looked sceptical. "What, carrying an unconscious girl?"

"Why not? If questioned, he had only to assert she was asleep, or drunk. But I should doubt if any would be stirring in such a house. Not the servants certainly."

Sybilla balked at this. "But the clients, Ottilia? Don't these places cater for them at all hours?"

"Not in a town like Weymouth, Mama. In the capital, yes."

Ottilia regarded her spouse with a faint lift of her brows. "Is that a guess, Fan, or do you happen to know?"

He grinned across at her. "It is common knowledge among gentlemen, of course."

She smiled. "I will take your word for it. For my part, I should have supposed any clients still awake would be otherwise engaged."

George was regarding her with his frown still in place. "Be that as it may, let us not forget our murderer had his coach waiting."

"By arrangement, I imagine, George. Remember, he planned it all to the letter. He collected Dulcie before midnight, took her to this house where he drugged her, knowing Truggery and Stowe would be digging up the coffin. He waited until two or thereabouts and then carried her to the coach, in which we must presume he had already secreted his weapon, his candles and a tinder box. And the rest we know."

Silence fell while her auditors digested this. Ottilia could not help her imagination presenting her with the remainder of that night's doings and the thought of poor little hidden Perkin's dismay at the unfolding events could not but obtrude.

"He must have bribed the coachman pretty heavily," Francis observed at length. "The fellow can't have been blind and deaf to the proceedings."

"His own coachman?"

Sybilla's tone was sharp but George cut in before Ottilia could answer.

"Too risky. We cannot find that a coach was hired anywhere locally. I would guess he went further afield. To Dorchester perhaps."

"Or Lyme Regis," said Ottilia, thinking aloud.

"No. I checked while I was there. And before you mention him, there was no sign of Edgcott either, despite his having made himself scarce."

"Yes, that does make it look black for him."

Francis was eyeing her with the look she knew well. "What are your objections to him, Tillie?"

She hid a smile at the acumen with which he read her now. "Your account of him does not lead me to think him capable of quite so elaborate a scheme, notwithstanding what Justice Shellow told you of his customary activities, George."

"Shellow judged against his stooping to murder," the colonel reminded her.

"Yet he sounds a ruthless individual. But a man who goes about things directly, not in the roundabout fashion of this murder."

Francis gave her a keen look. "There is something in that. He would likely have strangled her and thrown her body in the woods, just as he said when he spoke of the candles being an homage to the girl's beauty."

"But they were not intended for that. Nor, as I surmised at the first, to throw suspicion upon the players," Ottilia offered.

"What, then?" Thus the colonel, frowning.

"To present any investigation with a dilemma meant to confuse and to set you, George, hunting for hares."

His brows flew up. "Me? You think the dratted villain was specifically targeting me?"

"Well, he clearly knew you for the highest authority in the neighbourhood. It was likely you would be called in, failing a constable."

"There isn't one."

"Nor a justice of the peace nearer than Dorchester. Which presupposes our murderer knew the town and its environs very well indeed."

The notion set her mind a-roving across new territory as George's frown descended again.

"Edgcott, Charlton, Fitzgerald," he said, counting on his fingers.

"Not Paglesham, then?" put in Sybilla on a note of disappointment.

"She's already discounted him except as a conspirator with Edgcott," Francis pointed out, an edge of eagerness in his voice as his gaze turned on Ottilia, dragging her from her thoughts. "You've just ruled out Edgcott, and I don't for a moment believe Charlton did it."

"Fitzgerald!" George was triumphant. "I said so at the outset, did I not?"

But was it as simple as that? Ottilia was again beset with a tease of being unable to see what she was becoming convinced was staring her in the face.

A knock at the dining parlour door produced Tyler again, looking a trifle harassed as he addressed Sybilla. "I am sorry to disturb you, my lady, but —"

He got no further. A figure ducked under his arm and darted into the room.

George leapt to his feet. "Cecile!"

She flicked him a glance but passed him and ran to Ottilia's side. "Forgive, I beg, madame. I have little time."

Ottilia caught George's chagrined look, but addressed the girl at once. "What is amiss, my dear?"

"A little thing only but tomorrow perhaps I cannot come and I think I must tell you."

Francis had also risen and he pulled out a chair. "Won't you sit down?"

She cast him a brief glance. "*Non, merci.* I stay but a moment."

"Thank you, Tyler, that will be all," said the dowager, signing to Francis to pour wine. "Sit down, *mademoiselle*, and take a glass."

Thus adjured, Cecile plonked into the chair, but waved away the wine. "I need nothing, madame, *merci.*"

Ottilia captured the flailing hand. "Come, Cecile, what is the matter?"

She drew a visible breath and, rather to Ottilia's amusement, turned her eyes on George, still standing by his chair, his gaze fixed upon her. "It is that I hear Madame Ferdinand speaking with Monsieur Fitzgerald."

"Good God!" George came around the table to stand over her. "What is it? We have just this moment past concluded…" He faded out at Cecile's sudden frown.

"You think he it was who killed Dulcie?" She released her fingers from Ottilia's grasp and clutched instead at George's wrist. "It may be so, Georges. He says to madame it is better for Kate that Dulcie is dead." She let go and fluttered the hand. "Not such words, no. I do not tell it well."

Ottilia intervened, distracted now from the path her mind had been following. "Be calm, Cecile. Tell us just what was said, if you can."

She shrugged. "Exactly, I do not remember. Madame says he has prejudice. For Kate, you understand. While Dulcie is alive, he says none will look at Kate upon the stage. Also he is angry that Monsieur Ferdinand gives the good roles to Dulcie and now only he gives them to Kate, when Dulcie is dead." She looked from Ottilia to George and back again. "It is important, no?"

"Extremely valuable, Cecile," Ottilia told her on a note of reassurance. "Was there anything else?"

She seemed to ponder, her eyes seeking George again, who kept silent though his gaze devoured her. "It was of Dulcie," she said at length. "And perhaps he has reason. Madame and Monsieur Ferdinand took her from the kitchen. She was young. This I have known, since Dulcie she told me. But Monsieur Fitzgerald he thinks it was to use Dulcie for profit, not for the sake of Dulcie, you understand. Thus it seems to me he does not care that she is dead and perhaps if that, he also cares too much for Kate and for her sake, he has done this thing."

She cast a pleading look around her auditors, and there was both hesitance and dismay in her voice. "It is possible, no?"

"Very possible, my dear, and we thank you for taking the trouble to come here."

A tiny smile flickered. "I have come to tell you, madame." Her eyes turned on George. "I did think perhaps you may be here."

This frank admission caused the colonel to colour up. His voice became a trifle gruff. "Are you going back to the theatre? May I escort you?"

Ottilia exchanged a questioning glance with Francis, but Sybilla broke out.

"Are you intending to arrest the fellow, Colonel?"

"Not tonight, ma'am." He looked to Ottilia. "We need positive proof, I think, don't you?"

Indeed they did, for uncertainty rankled despite this little reported piece of byplay. But she had to smile at the colonel's new brand of caution.

"I am glad to hear you say so, George. It is all conjecture at this juncture. But Cecile has at least provided us with a potential motive for Fitzgerald — if he is indeed our murderer."

Which, although she did not say it aloud, was not a solution she altogether favoured.

Determined not to make a mull of things a second time, George held his tongue only until he had Cecile on his arm outside the door of the Fanshawes' lodging and was guiding her to the Esplanade.

A glance around was enough to show him there were few persons hardy enough to brave the darkening skies. A couple of liveried men were hastening along the walk and a distant fellow, accompanied by a barking dog, was walking on the beach where the tide was coming in from a choppy sea.

The prospect was uninviting but the opportunity too good to pass up. And it was but a short distance to the theatre. He slowed his pace.

"Are you in a hurry? Will you walk with me a little?"

She glanced up at him. In the uncertain light he could not read her expression. "I think perhaps it will rain, Georges."

Chagrin entered his breast. "That is no answer. Do you wish to walk with me or do you not?"

She tugged her hand from his arm. "*Ma foi*, Georges! This is how you speak? I will go alone!"

He seized her hand. "No, you don't!"

She pulled back, a flare at her eyes. The disturbance in his pulse caused a thump at his chest and anguish gripped him unexpectedly.

"Cecile, don't go! I can't bear this any longer. You are making me crazy and it's not like me at all."

He saw a softening in her eyes and a little smile appeared. "Why is it you are crazy?"

It was a clear invitation but he could not bring himself to say the words. "You know why."

"*Parbleu*! Am I in your head?"

"You are in my heart!"

It was out before he knew what he was saying. She was gazing at him and a stray beam fell upon her face, lighting it up. Or was he imagining it? She lifted her free hand and he felt her fingers on his cheek, a gentle caress. Her voice was husky.

"It is well, Georges. You touch also my heart — *au désespoir*." He went to capture her into his embrace, but she evaded him. "*À bientôt*, Georges. I am late." With which, she darted away before he could stop her, picking up her skirts and running lightly along the Esplanade.

He stood still, watching her until she vanished down the lane that led to the theatre. He could wish he had settled it with her more completely, but at least she had given him hope.

The first drops of rain spattered his face and he started. What was he doing, standing like a stock in the middle of the street? Like a lovelorn fool, forgetful of everything save the impossible creature who was turning his life upside down. Was he indeed crazy, to be jeopardising his untrammelled existence? For the first time, he contemplated what it would mean to burden himself with a wife. And a passionate Frenchwoman at that. His imagination boggled at the shoals ahead. And yet, the alternative he already knew to be unendurable. To let Cecile drift out of his life? The very thought brought on heartache.

With difficulty, he dragged his mind back to duty and remembered he had still to find Rodber. About to curse the murder, he recalled its part in bringing him into close contact with Cecile and duty assumed an importance he had not previously assigned to it. For her sake, this matter must be settled. A new determination sent him hurrying through the drizzle in search of the master of ceremonies.

He ran the fellow to earth in the subscription library, having first tried his lodging, whither the porter at the Assembly Rooms had directed him.

"Ah, Colonel, did you want me? I am taking my chance to read the journals before the play begins."

George hustled him away from the table where two others were also perusing evening papers daily provided by the proprietor, and found a quiet spot by the shelving groaning with volumes of every sort.

"I need your special knowledge of the area, Rodber," he said without preamble.

The fellow regarded him with a keen eye. "Do I take it you are further forward, Colonel? Is an arrest imminent?"

George balked. He had no intention of revealing the extent of the investigation. He ignored the question.

"What I want to know is whether you know of a house of ill repute situated on the edge of town, convenient to the cemetery road."

The fellow's head reared back. "Good heavens, sir! What in the world do you mean?"

"Just what I say. I cannot enlighten you further, as I am sure you must realise."

"Yes, but —"

"Come, come, sir, don't trifle with me, I beg of you. If anyone knows the amenities of this town, it is you. Pray don't attempt to fob me off."

Rodber's cheeks grew ruddy and he became sulky. "Really, Colonel, there is no necessity to take that tone."

"I've no time for niceties, Rodber. The investigation is at a crucial point, if you must know, and your assistance may prove vital."

This was a worthy turn, for the master of ceremonies visibly reverted to his customary pomposity. "Naturally, I am anxious to assist the authorities in every possible way, sir."

"Well, then?"

Rodber harrumphed, cast a glance at the patently uninterested gentlemen reading at the table, and lowered his voice. "I fancy you are referring to Hetty Mason's establishment. A discreet place, sir, known only to a select few."

George lit with triumph and mentally blessed Ottilia's perspicacity. "Patronised by visitors? Gentlemen only? Or do lesser men benefit? Would a permanent resident use it?"

The man looked decidedly disconcerted. "Gracious me, sir, I'm sure I cannot answer you. I am not myself — er —"

George sighed. "Rodber, I am not here to enquire into your personal excesses. Have the goodness to tell me what you know without roundaboutation."

Reddening again, the man sniffed, looking pinched. "Well, really, Colonel. I am not accustomed to be spoken to in this fashion."

"I beg your pardon," George said on a spurious placatory note, "but I would appreciate your cooperation, sir."

Rodber shifted his head in a marked manner. "Very well. So far as I am aware, gentlemen visitors have been known to whisper of Hetty Mason's facilities one to another. I should doubt of lesser men being received there." He cleared his throat. "Those with a fat purse excepted, naturally."

"Her fees are extortionate?"

"High enough to keep the place exclusive perhaps."

"But a resident would be familiar with this Hetty Mason?"

"Whom did you have in mind, Colonel?"

"We will let that pass for the moment, if you please."

The fellow looked dissatisfied, but George did not enlighten him. The matter was far too precarious to be bandied about. He went directly to the point.

"What is the exact direction of this bawdy house, if you please?"

"Francis, wake up!"

The nudging hand, combined with his wife's urgent whisper, drove him out of a misty dream. "What's to do?"

"There is someone in the house."

Francis thrust his eyes open and struggled onto an elbow. "What do you mean, Tillie? The place is packed with people."

The bed curtains were only partially drawn and moonlight filtered in through the window, showing Tillie sitting up in a listening attitude.

"I heard pattering. I thought it was the rain, but it has stopped raining."

Francis yawned. "Likely one of the servants is stirring."

But as he spoke, a grunt and thump sounded from without, followed by unmistakeable footsteps running down the stairs.

"What the devil?"

He was out of the bed and groping for his dressing-gown even as Tillie began to thrust off the bedclothes.

"Stay there! Don't come out until I give the all clear."

She sank back and a second set of thumping steps sounded as he dragged on his dressing-gown and headed at speed for the door, flinging it wide and calling out.

"Who's there?"

There was no immediate response, but the sound of an altercation below brought him to the head of the stairs. Two dim figures were struggling, one enveloped in a concealing garment, the other a dark shape that looked half-naked. Something about the second was familiar.

Francis started down the stairs. "Hemp? Is that you?"

"Seize him, milord!"

It was grunted out. Francis quickened his steps, holding on to the bannister rail. Before he could reach the fray, the quarry wrenched out of Hemp's hold.

Next instant, the front door was dragged open. Francis caught a silhouette of the intruder against the moonlight — a tall cloaked man in a three-cornered hat. Then he was gone, the sound of his boots ringing on the cobbles.

Hemp was out of the door in a flash. Reaching it, Francis stopped in the aperture, watching Hemp's pursuit of the fleeing figure. In the better light afforded by the moon flooding the wide expanse of uninterrupted sea beyond the Esplanade, Francis was able to judge his servant to be naked to the waist and barefoot. Fleet though he was, his quarry outstripped him and darted down an alley. Hemp followed and the chase became lost to sight, though Francis could still hear the steps for some little time.

"What is it, my lord? What has happened?"

Francis became aware of Tyler at his elbow and the landlady hovering in the corridor behind.

"Hemp is chasing an intruder," he said shortly and nodded towards the woman. "Send her back to bed. There's nothing to concern her now."

The footman went to soothe the landlady and hustle her off, what time the dowager's voice could be heard above-stairs.

"For heaven's sake, Ottilia, what are you doing up at this hour? What in the world is all this racket?"

Francis looked up to see both his wife and his mother hovering in the gallery.

"I told you to wait for my word, Tillie."

She paid no heed. "Who was it, Fan?"

"That I don't know."

"What, have we had a burglar?"

"I don't think it was a burglar, Sybilla."

Francis caught the sound of feet slapping against the cobbles and went out into the street. His mother's irritated tones followed him.

"What is he doing? Why doesn't he close the wretched door?"

He heard Tillie murmur a response but his attention was on the entrance to the alley. Presently Hemp came into sight, walking now, and alone. Francis went to meet him as he came up, his breath still heaving. Hemp was wearing only a pair of drawers and Francis held up a hand to stop him.

"Hold hard. The women are within sight."

Hemp nodded and leaned a hand against the wall, still struggling for breath.

"I — lost him — milord."

"So I perceive. Never mind. It was a brave effort, my friend."

Hemp looked up and, his eyes now accustomed in the better light, Francis noted grimness in his face. "He came for the boy, milord."

Shock ripped through Francis and he recalled the silhouetted image he had seen. "Dear Lord, you mean it was the murderer?"

"Masked again. It is just as the boy said. The same who attacked milady."

"Big, cloak, three-cornered hat," Francis recited, a hollow feeling in his chest and his heart out of kilter all over again for his wife's safety, even though the man had not acted against her this time; she had been safe in his arms, thank the Lord. And the boy was equally out of reach. "A good thing we let the colonel have him."

There was time for no more. Tyler came out of the house, clearing his throat. "Begging your pardon, my lord, her ladyship is anxious for the door to be closed."

Francis did not mistake the tenor of this mild request. His mother was no doubt fretting and furious.

"I'll get the women into the parlour, Hemp, so you can make yourself decent and then join us. Tyler, bring wine to the parlour and light the candles again. Then you get back to bed. No need for the lot of us to be up." He was heading for the door as he spoke, which Tyler was holding for him. He paused as a thought occurred. "Ah, you'd best reassure the maids too." With which, he entered the house and ran upstairs where his wife and mother were impatiently awaiting him.

"How in the world did he get in?" said the dowager. While she and Francis discussed possibilities, from cellar windows to climbing drainpipes, Ottilia was concentrated upon identities.

She was seated on the chaise longue, her dressing-gown augmented by a shawl, sipping at the wine in the glass thrust into her hand by her spouse. At first beset by clutching fear for Perkin, this faded upon remembrance of his departure to George's barracks. Thankful she had given in to the colonel's persuasions, her mind began to turn on the intruder himself.

"He panicked," she said aloud.

The discussion in train broke off and Francis turned from Sybilla, who was seated in the chair opposite. Candles had been lit but they were scarcely needed as a pink dawn was beginning to show through the open shutters and Ottilia could see plain the question in her spouse's face where he stood, leaning an elbow on the mantel.

"Because Hemp woke, you mean?"

"To have come at all."

Sybilla clicked her tongue. "I wish you had never kept the boy here, Ottilia."

"But how did he know that?"

She received a keen glance from her spouse. "Why shouldn't he? I spread the word of his being a witness only today."

Ottilia's brain was working swiftly but she paused at this. "You told those two players."

"And they passed it to the rest, no doubt, which means Fitzgerald may readily have heard."

"Yes, for let us not forget there was a performance last night," the dowager put in. "Word likely spread."

"To whom?" Ottilia demanded. "Paglesham and Charlton? Edgcott is absent. No, I doubt it had yet reached public ears."

"Then that serves us well, Tillie, since Fitzgerald is very much to the fore."

Ottilia remained dissatisfied. Her original train of thought returned, but before she could give it voice, the door opened to admit Hemp. He had donned his habitual costume of black breeches and coat. Ottilia fleetingly wondered if he would be persuaded to wear colours in a few months when his period of mourning was up. But his words brought her back to the matter at hand.

"Milady, you will wish to know what happened, I think."

"Very much, Hemp, I thank you."

He gave a small bow, but turned first to Francis. "I took the liberty of inspecting the lower regions of the house, milord, and I believe he came in by way of the kitchen window."

"Good heavens!" Sybilla glanced up at her son. "We never thought of that, Francis. Was the window broken?"

"No, milady. But the latch is bent and may have been forced, though he was careful enough to set it back in place."

Francis intervened. "And then? Did you find him in your room? He woke you?"

"His step on the attic stair woke me, milord. I paid no heed, thinking Tyler may have gone down for a drink and was coming back up."

"Ha! Just as I thought when her ladyship woke me."

"Yes, milord, but it wasn't so. The instant I heard the handle turning on my door, I started up and saw him enter. He must have seen me. Heard me, perhaps, for I think I cried out."

"He took off?"

"On the instant, milord. I leapt from my bed and went after him, but he was wide awake and myself a trifle bleary or I would have got him."

"Don't repine, Hemp. In fact you did get him, as I saw."

Hemp shifted his shoulders. "I erred, milord. I tried to grapple with him. If I had merely held onto his cloak, it would have choked him and stopped him."

"Or he might have divested himself of it and escaped anyway," Ottilia put in, feeling all her steward's regret.

"True enough." Francis was watching her. "Anything else we need to ask?"

Grateful he deferred to her judgement, Ottilia eyed her steward. "I dare not suppose you felt you knew the man, Hemp?"

He gave one of his faint smiles. "I wish I might say so, milady, but no. Apart from realising he was the same who attacked you. I was too occupied in the hope of stopping him to have leisure to sense any such thing."

"I should think he would not, Ottilia," came in irritated accents from the dowager. "How in the world should he know the man in any event?"

"Hemp is acquainted with the players, ma'am."

"But not this theatre manager fellow. Or do you know him?" Sybilla turned to Hemp.

"I have seen him in the tavern, milady, but not to speak to. In general, he and Mr Ferdinand have their heads together. He is not one to fraternise with the lesser players, although of necessity Wat and Aisling, who manage the scenery, must know him better. However, I have not seen them hover about him in the tavern."

Ottilia seized on this. "Have you ever heard either speak about him? Fitzgerald, I mean."

He turned to her, his brows drawn together. "Not in particular, milady. Why?"

She disregarded the question. "Think, if you please, Hemp. Could you tell from anything they may have let fall whether Fitzgerald is a man likely to panic?"

She caught Francis's intent look and Sybilla's raised brows, but kept her attention on Hemp. His frown deepened, but his eyes showed he was considering the matter. Ottilia waited.

"No, milady," he said at last, his brow clearing. "If I take an impression gained from the players in general, I would say he is considered to be a very level-headed sort of man."

Ottilia smiled her satisfaction. "Thank you. That is just what I supposed."

There being nothing further to be done, Francis dismissed Hemp with a word of thanks. He left the room, but poked his head around the door a moment later.

"Milady, all this upset has made me forget something the boy said before I left him with the colonel's lieutenant."

A little fillip leapt in Ottilia's breast. "What was it? I am eager for any morsel at this moment."

"Perkin seems to think the murderer knew both of those gravediggers. He spoke of their trade. He knew it 'of old', he said, and reminded them it was against the law. Also he said he knew the justices at Dorchester."

Digesting this, Ottilia thanked Hemp and he withdrew. She was again struggling with the niggle of remembrance that would not come to the fore. Someone had said something pertinent to her, but what? She found her spouse sceptical of the usefulness of the information as he began to snuff the candles.

"I don't see how that helps. Our man must have known those fellows or how could he hire them to dig the grave?"

"Of old," said Ottilia.

Sybilla, who was already at the door, looked back. "What of it?"

"Perkin said Truggery and Stowe sold bodies to the surgeons at the hospital in Dorchester."

"Very well, and so?"

Ottilia smiled into the relative gloom as the last candle was extinguished. "I don't know, Sybilla. A detail is nagging at me, but I cannot place it."

"Back to bed, my love." Francis was at her side, setting an encouraging arm about her. "We've had enough excitement for one night."

Tired out, Ottilia slept. But she woke suddenly and the missing piece of the puzzle had surfaced. How had she not recognised it before? The conversation with Hilde was days ago. The tiny fact slotted into place and her certainty grew. Only where was the proof?

As Cecile was folding and packing the last of the costumes into the second of the two wicker trunks set in the rear of the stage, she was plagued with a wistful question. Might George speak before she left for Poole? Unlikely, since he had not yet made an arrest. His soldiers, who were to go with them, had already arrived and were lounging about outside, awaiting the cavalcade's departure.

They would wait awhile. No one had told them how difficult it was to round up a set of players the night after a performance, when they must dress, breakfast and pack and were in general accustomed to make a song and dance about their preparations. Cecile had formed the habit of waking early, collecting her belongings together in her portmanteau and, with only a minimal meal since travel invariably made her unwell, slipping away to the theatre to pack up the costumes. She was relieved not to have Dulcie's effects to deal with as Madame Ferdinand had seen to them after the funeral.

She had already packed the costumes not in use in her leisure moments last night, but those strewn about the dressing rooms had to be stowed away. Wat and Aisling were also up early, whistling and chatting as they dismantled scenery and stashed it in the wagon.

Aisling came up. "That one ready, is it, Cecily?"

He nodded towards the other trunk, which she had already fastened and strapped.

"That you may take, yes. This will be but a moment."

"Leave it, Ais," called Wat, passing by on his way to the open dock doors where the wagon waited. "We'd best put them two in last. Hilde is bound to fret as there's something missing and I don't want to go clambering over everything to find it."

Wat being small, it was invariably he who had to work inside the wagon. Moreover, Cecile knew he was right. Despite her careful lists, which Hilde largely ignored, a last minute panic too often occurred.

"I'll get the props then." With which, Aisling went off to fetch the smaller wicker basket into which he had already packed the books, quills, platters and other such articles as the players used on stage. He had just gone out to the wagon when a voice from the auditorium hailed Cecile.

"*Mademoiselle*! I fancy these must be yours."

She turned to see the theatre manager approaching down one of the aisles, burdened with a dark bundle. Her consciousness of George's suspicions of this man threw her pulse out of kilter, but she strove to appear normal as she moved to the front of the stage to meet him.

"*Oui, monsieur?*"

Fitzgerald's dark-featured face wore its customary remote expression, overlaid with faint repulsion. "I found them in the foyer. Somewhat damp, I think you'll find."

He dumped a pile of rumpled black material on the edge of the stage.

"But I have all, *monsieur*, already in the basket."

He waved a hand at it. "Well, it's got nothing to do with me. I checked. Some sort of cloak. There's a hat wrapped up inside it. Oh, and a mask in the hat. It must belong with your costumes."

The words rang in Cecile's mind and she felt as if the blood were draining from her head. A mask! This was the cloak and hat of the murderer. And Fitzgerald brought it to her.

Coursing fear drove her to her knees. She set her hands on the bundle, her head woolly as she struggled to think what to do. She dare not show her realisation. He was standing there, watching her. If she gave so much as a hint of her thoughts, would he dispose of her too?

She felt about the bundle, which was indeed damp, a stale aroma arising from its folds. Beyond wondering why that should be, Cecile came out with the only thing her mind presented to her.

"In the foyer you say?"

Her voice, to her combined surprise and relief, sounded steady enough, impersonal even.

"Stuffed under a chair." Fitzgerald was eyeing her in a way that sent a chill flying through Cecile's veins. "You'd best look at them, hadn't you? I assume you'll know if they are part of the company's effects."

"Yes, I will know."

She was riding on automatic, her mind twisting this way and that as she scrabbled with the bundle, trying to unravel it with fingers suddenly numb and unwieldy.

Why did not he go? For what did he stay, watching her with those paralysing eyes? At any moment, Wat or Aisling would come back in. Or should she run to them now? But she must not. She must remain and keep Fitzgerald here. Get word to George. How? How?

"It is a cloak," she said unnecessarily as she rose with the bulk of material and shook it out. The hat fell out and rolled. The fatal three-cornered hat.

Cecile dropped the cloak and grabbed for the hat. The mask lay on the stage floor. She stared at it, her limbs growing cold.

"I told you," came from Fitzgerald in a tone that filtered through to Cecile as mockery. "Lord knows why it should all be bundled up beneath a chair."

"It is that someone has borrowed it, I think," Cecile dared, casting him a glance as he reached out a hand and picked up the mask.

He twirled it by the strings, his eyes on hers. "For what purpose, I wonder? There has been no masquerade at the Assembly Rooms."

Oh, why did not Wat or Aisling come back in? What could she say now? He knew! He was playing with her.

The thought gave her courage. She picked up the hat and felt it.

"This also it is wet. I cannot put them in the basket." She took up the cloak again and doubled it over her arm, and then held out her hand for the mask. "I will set all aside, monsieur, until they are again dry."

He did not hand it across. "Yes, but it's odd, don't you think? It was raining last night."

"*C'est ça,*" Cecile agreed, forgetting to use English under a stare that she fancied was growing baleful. "It must be that it was used last night."

"Just what I was thinking. But why? And by whom, do you think?"

Cecile managed a shrug, though her breath felt tight in her chest. More to deflect him than anything else, she proffered the obvious. "One of the players, it seems."

"For what purpose?"

Inspiration came. "Perhaps it is Jasper who has taken it. He likes to play tricks, that one. *Sans doute* he has a rendezvous with a — with a…"

"With a prostitute? Or a married woman? That would explain the excessive disguise, you think?"

Parbleu, but why must he torment her so? Was it to test her? Did he know she was in George's confidence? Did he suspect she knew his guilt? Ah, it was enough!

"Give to me the mask, *monsieur*. I must finish my task so the men may put these baskets in the wagon."

Fitzgerald held it out, a smile twisting his lips. "Take it. But if I were you, *mademoiselle*, I should be rid of those items altogether. They stink of sweat and mayhem."

Cecile took the mask with fingers that quivered despite all her effort to appear unconscious. Without doubt he knew just how these clothes had been used. Was it a threat? The mask dangling by its strings from her free hand, she watched him turn and walk up the aisle. She remained where she was, irresolute, as he vanished through the auditorium door.

What to do? Once the manager was safely in his office, she might escape the theatre. And do what? Go in search of George? Or, no. Closer was the lodging of Madame Fan. She must take these things there without delay.

She heard Aisling's heavy step and breathed a little more easily. She was not alone.

"Are you done now, Cecily? Wat and I want to finish and get to the coffee shop for a bite."

The ordinariness of his utterance served to calm her a little. She moved towards the trunks and met him there. "*Oui, mon ami*, it is finished."

His eyes fell on the articles she was holding. "Put them in and I'll strap it for you."

Cecile's heart missed a beat. She could not say the truth. "Ah, these have become wet. They cannot go in."

The big man's brows flew up. "Wet? Dang me! Someone left 'em in the rain, did they?"

"It seems so." She dared say no more. In a bid to deflect him, she smiled. "It is good that you help me to close the trunk. These I will take elsewhere." With which, she clutched the items closer to her and headed for the dock doors. George's soldiers stood idly by, exchanging desultory conversation. Should she accost them? How would she explain? Did they know, these men, all that she knew? No, better she persist in her plan.

She could hear Wat whistling from inside the waiting wagon as she slipped past, making her way to the noisome alley that ran along the back of the theatre and down the side to give access to the general frontage. Cecile hurried up the street, casting a fearful glance back at the theatre, hoping Fitzgerald was by now in his office and therefore unable to look through the foyer windows to see her running away, burdened with the evidence of his misdeeds.

The Esplanade proved to be relatively free of people, though the salty tang was stronger after last night's rain. At the back of Cecile's feverous mind she thought the visitors must be at breakfast, the invariable practice once early morning dips were over. A few stragglers were coming in from the beach and several walkers strolled the grass verge.

Head down, Cecile quickened her step, intent upon her mission. She failed to see an oncoming figure and almost slammed into it.

If a pair of hands had not seized her shoulders, she would have come to grief.

"Hold hard there, Cecily!"

Steadied, she looked up. "Rob!"

The actor released her, a frown leaping to his face as his eyes roved the items she carried. His gaze rose from them to hers and his expression became direful.

"Lord in heaven! What the deuce are you doing with those?"

Cecile drew back, clutching them tight against herself. "They are wet."

His eyes bored into hers. "Where are you taking them?"

Confusion wreathed her brain. What was it to him? Why should he ask?

Her heart lurched as the snaking truth slithered into her head. Not Monsieur Fitzgerald, no. But Rob! Rob was the killer.

She saw his eyes change and knew she had given herself away. Instinct bade her to flee. Terror held her rooted. A hand bit into her arm as he seized her. His voice came, low and guttural.

"Damn you to hell! You don't ruin it for me now."

Chapter Sixteen

At breakfast, Ottilia's appetite had deserted her, so strong was her conviction she had missed the obvious throughout, ignoring the little details that now made sense. She could not be still, rising yet again to tap impatient fingers on the mantel.

A narrow look came her way from Francis, who was keeping watch from the window. "Stop fretting, Tillie. There's nothing more you can do until George gets here."

Her spouse had needed no urging to send Tyler to the barracks first thing this morning with a note to the colonel relating the night's events. Ottilia, acting on her jumping nerves, had despatched Hemp to watch the players' lodging. Nevertheless, her heart misgave her. Had she gauged it right this time?

"So stupid," she muttered. "We almost allowed him to slip from the circle, going round and round with the others."

"You had no real reason to suspect him."

"I had every reason. Aside from Hilde saying he gave up his apprenticeship for the theatre, you spoke of Hemp saying he quacked the company when you related your discussions at Mrs Horniman's and I did not pick it up then. Moreover, his wife and children live in Dorchester." She drummed her fingers and gave out a mewl of frustration. "If you care to say I have been blind, you will not be wrong, Fan."

He crossed the room with swift steps and caught her by the shoulders.

"I won't let you do this. You were not yourself. You are still weak in body and it's hardly surprising if it affected your mind."

"Oh, a poor excuse."

But she sighed and sank against him, taking the balm of his affection as of right as he held her close, stroking her back.

A thunderous knocking on the front door made her pull away. "George!"

Releasing her, Francis went to the door and flung it open, walking out to lean over the bannister. Ottilia, her pulse rippling, remained where she was, her mind flying over the pieces of the jigsaw she meant to present to George to convince him of the truth. Perhaps she was not so very much to blame after all, if she felt so great a need to turn him to her mind. Where it was so clear now, it had escaped them all these last days.

"George, come up at once!"

An indistinct response and voices in the hall below followed her husband's command, but footsteps thumping up the stairs signalled the colonel's presence. Francis could be heard ushering him along the gallery and Ottilia braced. The first sight of his face showed her a look both grim and determined. She spoke before he was well in the room.

"George, I'm so sorry, but we had it all wrong. It is not Fitzgerald."

He gave a curt nod as he stepped up and his tone matched it. "I know. Sullivan discovered our man's identity at the bawdy house last night. Robert Collins is a regular there."

Ottilia struck her hands together. "Why didn't I think of that? He is in an unsatisfactory marriage, to say the least."

"We didn't know about any bawdy house until yesterday, Tillie," her spouse objected. "You need not berate yourself for that."

Ottilia paid no heed, her eyes on the colonel. "But you made no arrest last night, for the wretch came here as Fan told you, looking for the boy. Is there more, George?"

His lips twisted in a quick smile and his grimness relaxed briefly. "Acute of you, Ottilia. It wasn't enough on its own. Hetty Mason knew nothing more than that he took a room that night, and she could not swear to the date either, since he had done so often."

"You mean he was in the habit of taking women there?"

"It would seem so."

"Then have you come because of my note?" Francis cut in.

"That and another I received this morning from Justice Shellow. Collins's name came up when he was seeking help about the resurrection men from Keymer, the surgeon who runs the hospital at Dorchester."

"I knew it! Oh, I should have seen it before," Ottilia said, agonised. "That is where he learned doctoring, before he took up acting. He gave up his apprenticeship."

Triumph entered George's features. "He did not give it up. He was expelled for having dealings with gravediggers."

"Good God, then he did know them," Francis exclaimed. "I dare say he knows that ghastly tavern as well as Jasper too."

"The Old Fiddler? Yes, it is known as an underworld haunt," said George.

"Do you mean to arrest him then?" Francis was crossing to the window. "Have you got your fellows outside?"

"Sullivan is waiting for me downstairs in the hall. But Puckeridge and two of our fellows are already at the theatre, ready to go with the company to Poole."

"Yes, but they're going nowhere today, I presume?"

"I doubt it, though I'm expecting trouble from Ferdinand. They'll none of them believe it."

376

Ottilia sighed. "One can scarcely blame them, for —"

She was interrupted. Francis gave a sudden shout, leaning into the window embrasure.

"What the devil's afoot out there?"

Ottilia looked across and George moved in that direction as her spouse turned his head to glance round.

"It's Hemp!"

Alarm ran through Ottilia. "Then Rob is here!"

Francis had turned back to the window. "Yes, but what the deuce should take Hemp to go careering off down the beach?" Then he swore. "Hell and the devil, he's after Collins! George, look! Isn't that Collins? Who's he got with him?"

Watching in bewilderment and question, Ottilia saw the colonel peer into the window. He cursed and straightened, the colour draining from his face.

"He's got Cecile!" He turned on the words, leaping for the doorway and crashing through, shouting for his lieutenant. "Sullivan, open the damned door!"

Ottilia, her heart in her mouth, made to follow and found herself stopped by her husband, who seized her before she could reach the door, speaking over the top of the cacophony of shouting and footsteps belting down the stairs.

"No, you don't, Tillie! You'll only be in the way and you haven't the strength. Wait here!" With which, he shot through the door, adding to the thunder of running footsteps already on the cobbles outside. Ottilia went out into the gallery and came face to face with her mother-in-law, standing open-mouthed above the stairs. Sybilla had retired after breakfast to try and catch up on her sleep.

"Has the whole place gone mad, Ottilia? What in the world is going on? Last night wasn't enough of a disturbance? One might as well be living in Bedlam!"

Ottilia wasted no words on refutation. "Robert Collins has captured Cecile."

Sybilla stared. "What? How?"

"That I don't know."

She gave a brief account of what she understood as she went back into the parlour and headed for the window, the dowager on her heels. She could see two flying figures in scarlet coursing down the beach, her spouse in hot pursuit, but Hemp and their quarry were now too distant to be fully made out.

Sybilla raised a hand to shade her eyes from the sun as she too peered through the window. "Heavens above! Well, if nothing else, they are attracting a crowd of spectators."

Withdrawing her gaze to the nearer prospect, Ottilia saw that a number of interested persons had paused in the business of their day to watch. Extraordinary how readily the place began to fill the moment something unusual occurred.

Her gaze swept the immediate area of the Esplanade and beyond and caught on an oddity. A long black shadow lay on the grassy bank. It fluttered in the wind and something rolled away from it, abruptly taking form in Ottilia's sight. A series of connections clicked into place.

"She found his disguise. That's why he seized her."

Ignoring Sybilla's startled question, Ottilia hastened towards the door. If she was right, she must secure the discarded items before some passing wayfarer took advantage.

George ran, his gaze fixed on the tell-tale flurry of petticoats flying away from him, tight and pale against the dark of the villain who had his heart's desire clamped under a vicious arm. Cecile looked to be half-dragged, half-carried, a burden now when Collins must know he was pursued. No sound of screams came back upon the wind. Had he a hand about her mouth, stifling her cries?

Hemp was closing on the pair. But Collins seemed now to be splashing into the edging waves. Did he mean to drown her? A streak of raging protest tore through the fire of effort in George's chest and he willed more speed to his legs.

Sullivan, younger and fitter, was ahead. George yelled at him to hurry, his voice hoarse and breathless.

The scene ahead appeared, in his disordered state, to be distant. As if he saw the figures from afar, although common sense dictated he was in fact getting nearer by the second.

Hemp was almost upon them. Collins threw his burden from him and set off with renewed speed. But George had eyes only for the small figure that flailed in his wake, and then fell, a bedraggled little heap upon the wet sand.

An eon passed before he reached her, his mind jolting back to reality as he spared one glance for the chase ahead. Sullivan had not broken stride, streaking after Hemp, who was again closing on Collins. Francis, going well, shot past. Three of them. Enough to subdue the fellow. The fleeting thought was gone as, for the first time in his life, George abandoned duty for the dictates of his heart. He dropped to his knee beside the fallen girl.

"Cecile!"

She was face down but not completely flat to the wet sand, her hands concealed beneath her. He hoped she might have saved herself from being badly hurt. He could hear her breathing, more laboured than his own as he began already to recover. Lifting her bodily, he turned her, catching her close, his gaze roving the beloved features for damage. She took in gasping breaths, her eyes closed. He brushed sand from her pallid face.

"Cecile, my heart's darling, look at me!"

Her eyes fluttered open. She brought up a wavering hand and clutched feebly at his coat. "Georges … *tu viens*."

He took her fingers and brought them to his lips. "Are you all right? Did he hurt you?"

Her lids had sunk again but they lifted at this, anxiety leaping to her eyes. Her fingers grasped his tighter. "Georges, it is he! Rob he is the killer. I know it, for —"

"*Du calme, ma petite*," he murmured, switching to French almost as of instinct. "It is known now. He has been found out."

She peered up at him, frowningly intense. "Is it so? I thought it was Monsieur Fitzgerald, for he it was who gave me the cloak and the hat and the mask. I was bringing them to Madame Fan and then I met Rob…"

She faded out, her gaze fixing on his, as if she saw there the overwhelming emotion in his breast.

"Thank God we saw you! Oh, my love, I've never been so afraid!"

George leaned down, placing his lips to hers. The contact was tender, the response warm. Elation soared within him. She was his.

The soldier in him awoke and he became brisk. "Come, let us get you up."

He rose with difficulty, bringing her with him and setting her on her feet, but holding her firmly withal. "Can you stand?"

A tiny laugh escaped her. "But, yes, Georges. Do you think it is a silly, fainting fool that I am?"

She was smiling up at him and George lost his head, catching her into a comprehensive embrace and squeezing her so tightly that she protested.

"Do you wish to break me?"

He slackened his hold. "No, I wish to cherish you, *ma cherie*. All of my life. Will you come to me?"

She pushed away, looking up into his face with an odd expression he could not interpret. "Does she have a name, this *mademoiselle* you wish to cherish?"

He drew an unsteady breath. "She will have my name, if she will take it."

A smile quivered on her lips. "*Eh bien, monsieur le colonel*, I believe she will take it."

"Sir, we have him!"

The shout came from a little way away. George returned to the real world with a bang. He kept a protective arm about Cecile as he looked across.

Collins was down, Hemp atop him, holding him there while Francis stood by, resting his hands on his knees as he recovered his breath. Sullivan had run halfway back towards his senior, negotiating a converging gathering of onlookers. George raised his voice.

"Good work, Sullivan. Bring him to the theatre and you can hand him over to our men."

He saw his lieutenant make off back towards the fallen man and at once his attention was drawn back to Cecile, who was shivering.

"You're cold."

"I am wet, Georges."

"Come, let us get you back to warmth and safety."

She looked up at him, a gratifying affection in her eyes. "Safe I am already, *mon cher colonel*. It is that I have my very own guard now, no?"

Happiness threatened to choke him. "It is so, *ma petite émigré*." His hold about her tightened. "My very own French captive."

The young player Jasper, to Ottilia's surprise, seemed the most upset.

"Not Rob. It can't be Rob. He wouldn't. I know he wouldn't. He cared more for Dulcie than any of us."

"There is no doubt, I'm afraid. He damned himself." George, who had broken the news, pointed to the cloak and its accoutrements Ottilia had laid over the front of the box nearest the stage. "Cecile was carrying those when she met him. Collins must have realised she meant to give them up to me and he lost his head."

All eyes turned to Cecile, seated in the pit and wrapped in a makeshift swathe of material produced from somewhere by Hilde Larkin, who had a plump arm around the shivering girl.

The rest of the company members were grouped about the empty stage, where light sprayed onto the scene through the dock doors and filtered down from high windows in the flies. From Ottilia's vantage point by the box, they had as well have been a tableau in a scene from one of their plays. The Grand Ferdinando looked broken, his flamboyance quenched under the blow. His helpmeet stood with him, one hand absently stroking down his arm, her features drawn and white. Near them Kate Drummond had sunk to the floor, hiding her face in her hands. Lewis Payne sat on the edge of the stage, an arm resting on his raised knee, his chin on his closed fist. The stagehands, small and large, were centre stage, dazed and staring at the colonel's scarlet-coated figure. Only Jasper, belligerent and protesting, provided the motion of the unfolding tragedy.

"What does that prove? What have those things to do with anything?"

"Collins wore them that night, and was again wearing them when he tried to strangle Lady Francis —" That this was news to the company was patent by the gasps and horrified glances towards Ottilia. "He wore them last night and they became damp in the rain. He broke into the Fanshawe's lodging to try to get at the boy who can bear witness against him. "

Lewis looked up. "The one Roy found?"

"Precisely. His description put several men in the picture, but subsequent enquiries have shown conclusively that Collins is our man."

This produced a sudden silence. No one asked for details. Only Jasper stuck to his guns.

"But, why? He said it himself. Why would he kill a girl he loves?"

George shook his head and, rather to Ottilia's dismay, turned to her. "Perhaps Lady Francis may be able to enlighten you."

She cast an agonised glance at her husband, standing close by. He gave her an encouraging smile. She sighed and moved a little into the light to face the despairing stares.

"It is only surmise, I warn you."

"Collins is not talking," George put in. "He refuses to say a word, either in his defence or to explain his actions."

"Then he's innocent!"

Ottilia felt obliged to quash the young man's eager utterance. "Sadly, he cannot be innocent, although he very nearly fooled us all into accusing someone else."

"Myself, for instance?" Fitzgerald walked out of the shadows in the background of the pit, moving to look up to where Ottilia stood. "Though why I should be supposed to cherish ill designs against the beautiful Dulcibella I have yet to understand."

Ottilia faced his mocking stare. "You were indeed under suspicion, sir. We had reason to include you."

"Fitz?" Mr Ferdinand seemed to come alive. "I told the colonel it could not be Fitz."

"And I'm telling you all it couldn't have been Rob," insisted Jasper, pushing in again to confront Ottilia.

She eyed the handsome young man's violent gaze, suspecting he was suffering from shock at his colleague's perfidy. Likely he had not before had reason to understand how duplicitous a man could be.

"I think, you know, he was indeed motivated by his feelings for Dulcie," she said gently. "That, and his fear of his wife."

Jasper blew out a scornful breath. "He wasn't afraid of Trix."

"Yes, he was," came from Lewis suddenly. He jumped up and came to join the coterie about Ottilia. "Trix could break Rob if she chose." He threw up a hand as Jasper opened his mouth to retort. "Not with her pots and pans, though she wasn't above using them if he crossed her." He looked at Ottilia. "Trix's father is a merchant. He's been keeping his son-in-law solvent for years. Trixie held the threat over Rob she'd put a stop to it. He'd get nothing when the old man died either."

"Then he could live off his pay, like the rest of us."

Lewis ignored this, his eyes on Ottilia. "But it doesn't explain why he would murder Dulcie all the same."

She drew a resigned breath. "Men's true minds are hard to fathom, do you not think? We are apt to superimpose our own values upon another. You are all players. You must have encountered roles whose surface personality proved different to the individual beneath."

There was a shift, as of interest beginning to overlay the effects of shock. Lewis cocked his head as if in thought; the Ferdinands exchanged a glance; even Jasper's tight shoulders dropped a fraction, and Kate uncovered her face and looked up.

"Yes. Yes, it's true."

"But I know Rob through and through. We are all too close to be fooled so."

Ottilia reached out a hand towards the boy, moved by the desperation in his voice. "You are trying to picture an out and out villain in your friend, Jasper, but it is not so. Rob is as much a normal man as any of you, but driven, by strong emotion, to desperate measures."

"A normal man does not kill a woman he loves," Jasper cried.

Kate was up, moving to clasp his arm. "What of Othello, Jasper? Lady Fan is right."

"But Othello kills Desdemona out of jealousy, not love."

"Just so." Ottilia glanced at the others and saw dawning realisation in Jane Ferdinand's face.

"Was it this fellow Paglesham then?" She left her husband and came across to join the little group. "Was he responsible for her condition?"

"As far as we have been able to ascertain," Ottilia said, "he was the only man who succeeded with her."

A groan escaped Jasper. "I thought you meant Rob had done it."

"Oh, no, I don't think so. Moreover, Dulcie believed she was going to a happier destiny that night. And if it comforts you, I think she went to her death believing it. She knew nothing of what happened to her, and I am almost certain she thought Rob was her Perry throughout."

At this, another frisson of shock rippled through the players. Kate's gaze showed distress as she stared at Ottilia.

"You mean he acted the part? He meant to deceive her, deliberately?"

"He wore a mask and I have little doubt he cultivated the manner and voice of his rival. He is much of Paglesham's height and build, and it may even have been in his mind to ensure suspicion fell upon Paglesham."

Jasper was yet unconvinced. "Why shouldn't it have been Paglesham then? He had more reason than Rob, if he'd made Dulcie pregnant."

"Oh, be quiet, Jasper!" Jane Ferdinand was abruptly angry. "You know nothing of the world if you think Peregrine Paglesham would suppose he must needs kill a girl like Dulcie to be rid of the business. He had only to pay her off. Which he would have done had poor little Dulcie confided in me. I would have made sure he faced up to his responsibilities."

"She would have too," put in Lewis, looking at Ottilia. "But it's puzzling nevertheless, ma'am. If, as Janey says, this Paglesham would never marry Dulcie, how could Rob persuade her he was going to?"

Ottilia sighed. "We cannot know just what he said. Or more likely wrote in a billet doux, purporting to come from her Perry. What is certain is that Perry himself had no notion of whatever promises Rob made on his behalf. I should imagine Rob played on Dulcie's fond hopes of becoming a lady."

"But she would not have confided in Rob," Kate objected.

"No, she said as much to you. But you are a close company, as Jasper says. I dare say there are few real secrets among you."

A dry laugh came from Lewis. "True enough. Though it seems some secrets were well enough kept." He glanced at Cecile, who flushed and turned away.

George at once cut in, his tone sharp. "That will do, Mr Payne. Cecile's honour in keeping her friend's confidence is to be commended, not condemned."

Lewis threw his hands palm up, his brows rising. "No offence intended, Colonel." He turned back to Ottilia. "You're saying Rob killed Dulcie because she was ruined?"

"No, rather because he could not endure the knowledge she had been with another man. It may be he cherished a romantic notion of Dulcie's innate purity."

At this, Cecile intervened, rising and coming to the edge of the stage. "But how can he know? Dulcie told no one of the child."

"She told you," Hilde said, coming to join her. "Rob might well have been listening. Always thought him shifty. It wouldn't surprise me if he looked through keyholes or hid behind the bed curtains."

A scattering of mutters greeted this.

"It's true he always knew everything."

"He could be sly."

"And sarcastic."

"Morose, that was Rob."

Jasper said nothing, fairly glaring at his colleagues. He was too young to understand they needed to distance themselves somehow from a man who had, to all intents and purposes, betrayed them. Each had been dealt a blow, even if the young man was the only one to make his public. He held to his denial.

"It's not good enough. This isn't Shakespeare. This is real. This is life. It doesn't happen in life."

Ottilia sighed. "I fear it happens all too often, Jasper. Such deeds are nearly always brought home to those closest to the victim."

Kate shuddered. "Yes, because they have most reason to harm. I can believe Rob's passion for Dulcie overcame him."

"It was not passion alone, I think." Ottilia turned back to Jasper. "In addition, I imagine there was the powerful fear his wife would believe he had seduced Dulcie and got a child upon her. I suspect she knew how he felt about the girl, for she was altogether callous when questioned."

It was plain Jasper was shaken by this, but he was not yet ready to accept it. "Why go to such trouble? Why make such a production out of it, with the burning candles and the coffin? That's not like Rob at all."

"Oh, yes, it is." The contradiction came from the impresario, of all people. Throwing back his leonine head, he surged forward. "It's Rob all over, only you're too befuddled half the time to see beyond the end of your nose, you plaguey brat."

His helpmeet threw up a hand. "Don't roar at him now, Arthur. But it's true, Jasper. Rob was always full of imaginative ideas for the staging of our plays."

"Most of them far too expensive to be considered," put in her spouse on a sour note. "Not to say too elaborate for a touring company. We'd need three wagons to accommodate his sketched out scenery, not one."

Argument and discussion broke out, urgent, perhaps necessary for minds still struggling to come to terms with what was, Ottilia surmised, disaster for the company of the Grand Ferdinando. To lose one player was bad enough. To lose two must spell the end.

She said as much to Francis, shifting out of the heated fray to re-join him. She had not thought George heard until he spoke.

"You underestimate Ferdinand, Ottilia. From what I know of him, he will bluster and roar, but he will find a way."

He received an odd look from Francis, accompanied by that endearing quirked eyebrow. "Even though he is also going to lose the convenience of his little French seamstress?"

Ottilia saw George's colour deepen even in the uncertain light in their shadowed portion of the stage. "Is it settled then, dear George? Have you taken the plunge?"

He cleared his throat. "It — er — rather fell out that way, yes."

"I am so glad." She was moved to close in and, setting her hands to his shoulders, kiss his cheek. "She is a delight, George, and I wish you very happy."

A twisted smile came. "I am more like to be driven utterly demented, but let that pass."

Ottilia received a wry look from her spouse. "It goes with the territory, my friend, but you will find the compensations are worth it."

She laughed and tucked her hand in his. "Well, at least Cecile's felicity is certain, if I go by mine."

Francis had left his mother holding court in the Assembly Rooms, and seized the chance to take his wife for an evening stroll along the Esplanade. Ottilia was very willing, feeling all the natural mix of exhaustion and deflation that accompanied the end of a period of high drama. A light breeze accompanied the warmth of the dipping sun and it was balm to be alone with her spouse.

"Sybilla does not mind you leaving her?"

"She has the general to protect her. Besides, she is thoroughly enjoying herself relating all the circumstances of the murder and your discoveries."

"Our discoveries. This has been a joint endeavour, my dear one, and your part has been especially vital. You were the first to think of jealousy as a motive, whereas I dismissed it."

"That? A mere stray notion."

"And you tackled the men on my behalf."

He threw her a rueful look. "I could hardly do less. It was after all my blame that you were saddled with this affair."

She tucked her hand into his arm. "Yes and I am glad of it. It was just what I needed to blow away my crotchets." She could not resist a teasing look. "How is it you have come to know me so well so quickly? I thought we were to spend a lifetime discovering one another."

"When you are so transparent?"

"Fiend! How dare you? Have I not one shred of mystery left?"

"None whatsoever." He lifted her fingers to his lips and kissed them before setting them back on his arm. "I have besides quite enough mystery to contend with in these murderous adventures of yours."

Ottilia fairly sputtered. "I don't know how you have the gall to say so when this was all your doing."

He gave her a mocking grin. "You rise so easily to the fly, my darling, I cannot resist."

She was betrayed into laughter. "Abominable creature!"

"But useful withal. You have just this moment past said so."

"Oh, stop, you wretch! Is this designed to tease me out of the dismals? I assure you I am not falling back into the doldrums."

"Are you sure? You are not feeling flat?"

The underlying note of anxiety could not but touch her. She pressed his arm and smiled. "A little perhaps, after so much excitement. By the by, did you remark Hemp's smug satisfaction? He insisted it was Rob all along."

"He did indeed. He was certainly delighted to be in at the kill. I dare say he is entitled to feel pleased with himself, since he proved a useful ally."

"Yes, and he found Perkin. We could scarcely have succeeded without that piece of good fortune."

"Well, you may count me heartily glad that villain is locked up after what he did to you," Francis said, setting an arm about her and giving her a hug. "For my part, I am thanking heaven it is all over."

Ottilia threw a mischievous look at him. "Ah, but we still have George on our hands, don't forget. With Cecile gone, he is bound to fret."

Francis cast up his eyes. "Do you tell me we are to be driven to distraction by my lovelorn fool of a friend?"

"Well, of course we are. Poor George is so severely smitten and he —"

"He is, isn't he? I should never have believed he could fall so hard and so fast."

"And for so wayward a creature. I fear he is in for a rough ride."

"Do him good. He's been far too complacent for years. I hope she may lead him a merry dance and I shall tell him so if he comes haunting our doorstep."

Ottilia could not help laughing, but she chided nevertheless. "How unkind, Fan. But I think she is just as passionately in love with him, you know."

"So she may be, but I should doubt of his succeeding in prising her away from the Grand Ferdinando's company for some little time."

Distracted, Ottilia's thoughts turned to the players as her spouse tucked her hand back in his arm and drew her onward. "George was right about the impresario. An ingenious solution to persuade Fitzgerald to take the place of Robert Collins. Apparently he trod the boards for years before taking over this theatre."

"I gather it is only until Ferdinand can hire another fellow. There must be scores of players in need of employment."

"Yes, and Jane Ferdinand said they must find another actress too, although she is convinced there is small hope of a true replacement for Dulcibella Ash." A little sigh escaped her. "My one regret in this business is that I was not privileged to see her. Or no, perhaps it is better so."

"Undoubtedly. You would have become far too personally involved and found some way in which you were to blame."

Indignant, Ottilia withdrew her hand from his arm and halted in the middle of the Esplanade. "I have never done so without cause, Fan."

He faced her, and his look was tender. "You have a plaguey conscience, my dear one, and it is the bane of my life." He dropped a swift kiss on her lips. "But I would not have you any other way and you know it."

She heaved a resigned sigh and, disregarding any prying eyes there might be in the vicinity, set her hand to his chest and leaned into his strength.

"You are my rock, my dearest Fan. I hope I may never plague you into deserting me."

He set his arms about her and held her close. "Never in this world." He kissed her again and hesitated. "Are you tired? Do you wish to turn back?"

Ottilia looked along the lengthy distance they had already walked, but the peace of the evening was too enticing. "Let us go on a little further." She tucked her hand back in his arm and walked slowly on.

"This has been a particularly sad event, but for George's good fortune."

Francis murmured agreement, but the tease was back in his voice.

"Though I cannot help wondering what horrid debacle may next fall into your lap, my inquisitive Lady Fan."

A NOTE TO THE READER

Dear Reader

The setting for *The Candlelit Coffin* provided scope for my story in several ways. The Duke of Gloucester, George III's brother, had a house there, and when the king came to recuperate from an illness in the sea air, Weymouth took a leap in popularity and an already thriving resort became suddenly fashionable.

Grouped about the front where the gentry congregated were the Assembly Rooms (presided over by the real Mr Rodber from 1784 right up to 1815) where the gentry could enjoy balls, whist and a general saunter to chat with friends and acquaintances of a morning; a circulating library with a reading room and a supply of daily journals; and, crucially, a theatre.

The Theatre Royal, built in 1771, was "elegantly fitted up, and the performances are very respectable. The boxes are sufficiently large to accommodate 400 spectators." Touring companies came for a week or two, performing up to 3 times a week with their repertoire of plays. A perfect venue for The Company of the Grand Ferdinando.

The Assembly Rooms, built in 1785 were "Lofty, light and spacious; and very handsomely decorated, as well as delightfully situated", whereas St Mary's Church, despised by Perkin for its central location and patronage by the gentry was a "low, uninteresting structure" despite boasting three aisles.

Bathing was for health rather than pleasure. Bathing machines did not yet abound and informality prevailed with men bathing nude and woman wearing a loose but voluminous garment described as a chemise sack. The women, "rise early, put on our bathing dresses, with a loose wrapper and shawl over, slip our feet into warm slippers, and with a bonnet on our heads our toilet was done. The servant girl with a bundle containing our linen and petticoats, with sheets and towels followed us to the shore." One or two are hurrying to the shore when Colonel Tretower knocks on the theatrical lodging house for his early morning raid.

Early risers could also benefit from the best of the night's catch, haggling with the fishwives who sold their wares directly off the boat brought in by the fishermen. Fish might be scarce, or of poor quality, or simply badly cooked like the fish stew Francis rejects with loathing.

Playing perhaps the largest passive role in our story, we have the newly built Esplanade, "about a half mile long and 30 feet broad, beautifully bordered with turf, and a grass slope of nearly 8 feet which leads to the sands." Our characters either saunter gently like Ottilia, or bustle out of the wind like the dowager and General Godfrey.

Outside the fashionable quarter the town as a whole in 1791 was "a little, narrow, dirty place, ill-paved and irregularly built..." Licence for me to invent the conveniences I needed like Mrs Horniman's coffee house, along with The Black Dog and The Old Fiddler.

All in all, Weymouth proved to be a thoroughly useful setting for my temporarily downhearted couple, Francis and Ottilia, to recuperate and revive the charm and magic of their marital and sleuthing partnership.

If you would consider leaving a review, it would be much appreciated and very helpful. Do feel free to contact me on **elizabeth@elizabethbailey.co.uk** or find me on **Facebook**, **Twitter**, **Goodreads** or my website **www.elizabethbailey.co.uk**.

Elizabeth Bailey

Sapere Books is an exciting new publisher of brilliant fiction and popular history.

To find out more about our latest releases and our monthly bargain books visit our website: **saperebooks.com**

Made in the USA
Coppell, TX
29 April 2020